The Judge

Book One of the Coranite Chronicles

Egan Yip

This book is dedicated first and foremost to the One for whom this book was written. Then to my dad and mom for their great support over the years with their patience and love. To my sister, who has helped out along the way. And lastly, to all the LCBC Youth, for their encouragement.

-C o n t e n t s-

CHAPTER 1
Delivery

His back against the wall, Darek sat down near the thriving marketplace and placed his satchel by his side. The wait was getting on his nerves. He watched as the crowd moved about. Biting his lip, he glanced at the faces of the people, searching for a certain someone.

Then he found him. An old man came walking down the busy street. Their eyes met.

The old man was grim and solemn, not a hint of anything pleasant in his expression. He stood near Darek and said, "You're the delivery boy?"

"That's right," said Darek, looking up at him. "And you're late."

The man nodded but said nothing in reply.

"What's the pay for the job?" Darek said. "That's all I need to know."

"Five thousand credits."

Darek jumped to his feet and exclaimed, "Five thousand?" His loud, disappointed voice startled the people around them. "Are you kidding me? I thought this was an off-world job! Some of the local jobs are worth just as much!"

"It *is* an off-world job," said the old man, his voice cracking. "But don't you worry. That's just the advance. I'm not the client. I'm what you'd call a middleman. When you deliver the package to the real client, you'll receive ten times the amount." The man held up a thick envelope and waved it in front of Darek.

Darek hesitated, trying to hide his desperation with a poker face. He needed the money, but such a low advance was suspicious. Too suspicious.

"Take it or leave it," the man said, tapping his foot impatiently, "I already have others lined up for this job."

Gritting his teeth, Darek snatched the package from the old man. "I-I'll do it."

"A wise choice." The old man revealed a fleeting smile and handed Darek a piece of paper. "Here are the instructions for the delivery. I will deposit the credits in your account by the end of the day." Then the old man walked away without so much as a goodbye.

As he watched the old man disappear into the crowd, Darek heaved a heavy, heartfelt sigh. He wondered how wise of a choice it really was. Darek had worked in the delivery service for years and knew the risks that came with it. No one cared about delivery boys. Off-world jobs were often dangerous—sometimes even suicidal. Receiving high pay in any other job would be considered a blessing. But for a delivery boy…it usually meant death. If you survive, you bask in glory and riches. If you don't…they'll always find someone else.

Darek stuffed the package in his satchel and went back to the Albiore City Delivery Agency, which was only a block away from the market. He stopped to look at his reflection in the front window. He looked like a wreck. He straightened his ragged black jacket, dusted off his ripped jeans, fixed the shoulder strap of his bag and roughly combed his shaggy brown hair with his fingers. When everything looked as good as it could, he smiled at his own reflection. Then he turned bright red as he looked through the window and saw people snickering at him.

He entered the agency through the sliding glass doors.

"Darek," said the female receptionist at the front desk, "what are you doing here? I thought you went home."

Walking past her, Darek said, "Just went to speak with a client."

"Oh, Darek." The receptionist frowned. "So you took *that* job? Leave that job up to the veterans. If you wait a few more days, I'm sure we could get you something more suitable."

"Thanks for the concern." Darek stepped into a closing elevator. "But I don't think I can wait a few more days."

Darek got out on the fourth floor. He walked down the hall and headed straight for room 406. The door was already open. Darek peered inside.

A man sat at his desk, hammering away at the keys of his computer. The man was thin and pale, his blond hair combed down with a greasy shine. He kept the blinds shut, leaving just an ounce of sunlight through the cracks. As he typed, he kept one hand on the keyboard at all times. Every so often his other hand would venture off, seizing a piece of pie for his pointy lips. The trash bin by his side was overflowing with crumpled pastry boxes.

Even though Darek was at the door, the man ignored him, continuing to work. In an attempt to get his attention, Darek rapped on the door. The man didn't even blink; he intensified his typing until it sounded like a sudden downpour. When he finished the last word on the page, he placed the final period with a slam of the finger and then looked up.

"Darek Wayker," the man said, as he adjusted his glasses. "Did you take the job?"

"That's a stupid question," said Darek. "Of course. Why else would I be here?"

"Heh, all right. Then I'll take it off the listings," said the thin man, chuckling. After he stared at the computer screen for a moment, he burst out laughing. "Man, you took it! You really took it!" He laughed so hard that tears jetted from his eyes. "I can't believe it! You actually took it! The day has finally come!"

Feeling somewhat uncomfortable, Darek shot him a look of disapproval. "If you don't need me for anything else, I'll be going."

"Wait, wait." The man calmed down, wiping away the tears. "Darek, we've worked together for a while. Do you mind if I'll be honest for just a second?"

Darek crossed his arms. "I think I'm going to regret this, but I'm listening."

"I hate your guts, Darek. I really do," the man said. "You've caused me so much trouble. You have no idea how long I've waited for this day. You've finally chosen a really bad job, Darek. *Really* bad. Quite a few boys haven't returned from this one."

"I bet you're happy," Darek said, his eyes narrowing.

The man nodded with a wry grin. "I am. But let me just give you a word of advice—full of truth and clarity. Don't do it. The job is *not* worth it. As much as I hate you, I'd be downright heartless not to warn you. Fail this one, Darek. Fail it and never return."

Darek walked to the Guridoh, the only tavern by the agency. Since it was so close to the delivery agency, many delivery boys would frequent it for meals and socializing. He sat at a table with a few of his friends, including his best friend, Jenson, whom he had worked with several times on occasion.

Jenson was chubby, had curly brown hair, and always wore a pair of black goggles atop his head. Though only seventeen, just two years older than Darek, he was highly respected by all the delivery boys. He held the record for the most jobs completed with a perfect success rate. He was also a genius. Jenson would take international placement tests for fun and, though he'd get perfect scores, he'd never submit them for review. He was a strange person for sure. Darek knew that once Jenson was out of this dump, he'd be able to land a high-ranking government job easily. But he never seemed like that kind of a guy.

Jenson inched his chair up to Darek's, poured him a glass of sweet punch and asked, "So, how'd it go?"

Darek banged his head against the table in despair, surprising everybody. Darek lifted his head slightly to speak, his forehead now swelling bright red. "Well, I did it. I took the job—the only job that was available." His head fell back down. He muttered, "It's all because I failed the last few jobs. Talk about bad luck. And if I fail this one…" Darek sighed.

Even if he didn't finish the sentence, Jenson knew what Darek had on his mind. All delivery boys had reputation points. Success helped them garner more points, and if they had more reputation points, they would get higher priority when it came to picking jobs. But if they failed jobs, they would lose points. If they had no more points left…it'd be the end. Darek would be thrown out—all ties severed—and he'd have nowhere to turn to.

"Now come on, it can't be *that* bad," said Jenson, trying to cheer him up.

"Yes, it is *that* bad. This job probably won't be easy. A guaranteed one-way ticket to…"

Darek couldn't draw up the breath to finish what he was saying. His head facedown against the table, he just stared at the wood surface and sighed again. Jenson watched Darek mope for a long time. It hurt to see his friend so hopeless and sad. The pain was unbearable. He needed to help him, somehow, someway. There was only one idea he had in mind, one that was a big risk. But if it could save Darek from his troubles, it would be a risk well worth it.

"Say, I've got an idea!" said Jenson. "How about we trade jobs? I've got a local delivery to make and it pays well. As long as I'm successful, they'll never find out we swapped. I'll let you log it under your name. That way you get both rep and credits."

Darek said uneasily, "I don't know. If you mess up, we'll both be kicked out."

Jenson grinned. "You think I'm going to mess this up? Who do you think you're talking to? I'm Jenson the Great! I've never screwed up *any* job in my entire life!"

"Your entire life, huh?" Darek thought about it. It wasn't a hard decision. Jenson *was* the best in the business. He straightened up, handed Jenson the package and gave him a great big smile. "Well then—Jenson the Great—I'm forever in your debt. If there's anyone in the universe who can handle this job, it's most definitely you."

Jenson examined the small envelope. It felt pretty light. "What do you think is inside?"

"Don't know, don't care."

Darek took a sip of the refreshing punch. It was called Heaven's Punch, a specialty of the Guridoh; though, with its thickness, you'd think it was a smoothie. It was so rich, so sweet and creamy that a single cup would make you spoil your appetite—which was perfect for those who couldn't spare the credits for a meal.

Jenson read the directions and found it interesting. "Deliver to a man named Liam on planet XR36-B." He looked at Darek. "What kind of crazy job did you pick up? No one ever uses a planet ID."

Darek shrugged, scratching his chin. "Maybe the client thought it'd make things easier."

"Planet names are always enough." Curious to find out the name of the planet, Jenson flipped open his pocket computer and accessed the planetary database. He thumbed through it and said, "What the— a nameless planet…outside Federation space! No wonder everyone's been avoiding this one. Hitching transports won't even get you within a hundred parsecs."

"Look, it was literally the only job they had open," said Darek. "I would've waited for another job, but the barkeep is serious about kicking me out if I don't pay the rent on my shack. But that doesn't matter anymore because *you* have a way to get there, right?"

Jenson tried to keep a straight face but soon smiled. "As a matter of fact, I do. I'll show you something cool later. It's something *amazing*…that's all I'll say…" Jenson paused. "Speaking of which, I just remembered something. That old man—I forget his name— stopped by. He said something about an early shipment."

"*What?*" Darek's face lit up, bright as a summer's day. It was as though all of his worries vanished for an instant. Even if Jenson didn't mention the name, Darek knew whom he was talking about. "Rodrey stopped by? And the shipment came in early?"

Without waiting for a reply, Darek bolted for the door. Then he ran through the bustling city streets, tripping several times along the way as he bumped into pedestrians. Though he knew the way to

Rodrey's shop by heart, he still glanced across the street signs, afraid his bubbling excitement would cause him to miss his destination.

His dash soon came to a screeching halt as he reached a suspiciously empty part of the road. Everyone seemed to be avoiding that one area for some reason. He thought he heard a murmur coming from the alleyway and decided to take a little peek. Some people were in the alley. It was the city police. They were wandering about, interrogating some men. Darek's attention was drawn to the posters they had plastered all over the wall. It was an unsightly picture of Darek in the middle of a meal, belching, with food bits strewn around his lips.

Darek wondered why they were looking for him. He also wondered how they managed to take that photo. He observed them for a while, trying to catch even the tiniest bit of the information from the movement of their lips. The honking and rumbling of the cars made it impossible to hear anything. Darek tiptoed closer, his hand cupped around his ear.

While focusing on their conversation, he felt a hand rest upon his shoulder. A shiver ran down his spine. The sudden fright made him want to scream. Another hand came from behind and covered his mouth. Next thing he knew, he was dragged into a building. Darek wrestled to break free, but then he stopped struggling when he realized where he was. It was Rodrey's shop. He turned and saw Rodrey—the bald, portly shopkeeper.

"What'd you do this time?" Rodrey crossed his arms, looking rather stern.

Darek smirked. "No idea."

Rodrey shut the blinds to block out prying eyes. "Looks pretty serious. Just this morning, I've seen several new patrols." He opened a slight crack in the blinds and peered out. "You'd better lay low for a while. Who knows what they're up to?" Rodrey looked back to find Darek already taking a seat by the counter. "But I guess you could care less about that, huh?"

Darek fidgeted, watching as Rodrey crossed the room. He couldn't wait to see what Rodrey had in store for him today. This was a tradition between the two of them. Every week Rodrey's shop would receive new shipments, and Darek would get a chance to see some cool stuff. His shop sold all kind of things a delivery boy could use, including the latest hi-tech gadgets and weapons.

Rodrey rummaged through the box on the counter. Then, when he found what he was looking for, he placed it on the counter and grinned. "Ah, here's something that'll interest you."

Darek gaped. It was pair of daggers. Delivery boys were no assassins, but self-defense was always necessary. Local jobs never held much excitement. Off-world jobs on the other hand were trouble. When traveling to other planets, he would often have to deal with guards, soldiers and even thugs. He wasn't a fighter. Running away was always the best course of action. But having a weapon on hand would make pursuers think twice about charging at him.

"Check it out." Rodrey pushed the daggers closer to Darek. "Aren't they nice?"

"Is it okay if I touch it?" Though eager to hold them, Darek didn't want to get them dirty.

"Sure!" Rodrey said, smiling.

Darek held a dagger in his hand. He warmed up to it, slowly tightening his grip around the hilt. His eyes were mesmerized by the splendor of the blade. It was ivory in color and gave off a chilling glow. Running his fingers across the blade, he marveled at the smooth surface.

"So...beautiful," Darek uttered, as if he were in a trance.

Rodrey rubbed his chin as he also marveled at the handiwork. "A great bargain too. I know you're a sucker for this kind of stuff, so I got them as soon as I laid eyes on them."

Darek blinked in confusion. While he did ask Rodrey to look for something good, there was no way he'd be able to afford this. The quality of the craftsmanship was amazing. He took one last look at the pair and then reluctantly placed it on the counter.

Rodrey didn't take it back. "What? Not good enough for you?"

"No, it's not that," said Darek. "It's just that—I don't know. It looks expensive."

"You're darn right about that. Cost me well over three hundred thousand."

"Three hundred thousand!" Darek was awestruck. He grabbed the credit card out of his bag. The credit card looked like a solid black card. But when he pushed a thin button on it, it revealed a small screen. The screen showed him his current balance. He had less than two thousand credits left. "At this rate, I'll never be able to buy it."

Rodrey laughed. "Now don't be so sure."

Darek raised a brow, his interest piqued. "What do you mean?"

"How about you keep them and pay me back gradually?" Rodrey rested his arms on the counter. "No interest, of course."

Darek pinched himself in the cheek to make sure he wasn't dreaming. "Are you sure?"

Rodrey nodded. "You've been a good customer. Think of it as special service."

Darek didn't hold back his feelings. He jumped for joy and gave Rodrey a big hug, squeezing him until he let out a gasp for air.

"Thanks! Thanks a lot! I'll take good care of them!" Darek grabbed the blades and tucked them away into his bag. He couldn't wait to show them off to Jenson. "Thanks again!" He shot out the store, eager to head back to the Guridoh.

As soon as he stepped onto the sidewalk, he heard a voice say, "Figured you'd be here."

Darek spun around. Officer Bellum was standing in front of Rodrey's shop. Even with his head down, it was easy to recognize him. Bellum was the hairiest police officer in town. He never shaved and never cut his hair. When he walked, his head was like a bobbling hairball.

Bellum was a respected officer in spite of his untidy appearance. He took it upon himself to watch over the orphans that wandered the streets, even during his off-hours. He believed that guiding these young men and women during their bleakest hours would help them grow up to be fine citizens.

"Oh...you know," said Darek. "I was just heading to the—um—thing called home." Darek rolled his eyes, trying a little too hard to act innocent. He discreetly groped the sides of his bag to make sure the daggers weren't showing. It wasn't illegal to carry weapons; however, Darek was sure Bellum would confiscate them if he found out about them.

"Well," said Bellum, "now you're going to the thing called the police department."

"I didn't do anything wrong!" Darek protested.

"I didn't say you did. A Federation law was passed a few days ago that requires everyone, including orphaned children, to be registered for the census. You *have* to go."

"What? Since when did *they* ever care about orphans?" Darek hesitated and then finally said, "Okay, but if this ends up taking a while, you have to treat me to something good! My time is pretty important, you know."

"We'll see." Bellum slapped Darek on the back to get him moving.

The process of registration took Darek a few hours, much longer than he had hoped. He had to wait in line for two hours before he could even begin. And the process itself had been pure tedium from the start. First, they had to get as many prints and scans of his body as they possibly could, and then he had to fill out mountains of paperwork detailing every second of his waking life—or at least it seemed like it to him. It was a nightmare beyond nightmares. After he was done, he was never happier to be alive.

Darek gleefully jumped out the front door of the station with his lips in a perfect smile.

"Yes, yes! We're finally done! IT'S FINALLY OVER!"

Bellum patted him on the shoulder. "See, that wasn't so bad."

"You're insane." Darek stretched his arms and legs as much as he could. "Those were some of the worst hours of my life. You have no idea how dire the situation was. It was so boring!" Darek put his arm over Bellum's shoulder. "That said, since you've put me through hell, you might as well offer me a little something for my trouble. I can't let you off that easily."

Bellum chuckled. "How about a nice cold drink at the Guridoh?"

"A nice cold drink?" Darek's stomach growled ferociously in protest. *"That's it?"*

"All right, all right," Bellum agreed, scratching his head. "I'll treat you to dinner. Just don't get too used to it. A man's got to make his own keep."

CHAPTER 2
Nostalgia

As the morning sun climbed up the smoggy sky, it baked a shoddy shack with its rays. Standing shakily on the roof of Guridoh Tavern, the shack was Darek's home. It was thrown together with broken planks of wood, rusted nails and barely-intact shingles. But no matter how crummy it was, Darek didn't complain. Instead, he embraced its finer points.

For one thing the place was large enough to fit everything he needed: his toiletries, a soft blanket and some clothes. There were a few other things inside. A faded photo of his childhood friends—Slade, Rex and Elize—was pinned on the wall. Catalogs from Rodrey's shop were sprawled on his blanket. A small watch, which he used as an alarm clock, hung over his pillow. Aside from the daggers he had recently acquired, Darek didn't have anything of much value.

The thing he loved most about this place was that he could catch the sunrise every morning. Darek continued with his daily tradition and sat on the edge of the roof to get a good view of the city. The Guridoh was not large enough to compete with towers and skyscrapers for supremacy in height—far from it. Luckily, the tall buildings were positioned in such a way that it opened a pathway for the sun to shine through. With the sunrise before him, he began to reminisce his days at the orphanage.

Back then, he was much more carefree. He didn't have to worry about anything. The orphanage may have been small and poor, and it may have been isolated from the rest of the galaxy, but that didn't matter. Everything he needed was there—even the best of friends. Every day there was filled with laughter and joy, and he longed to regain those feelings. Even with new friends it was never the same. No matter where he went, he could never find another place he could truly call home. Even though he tried to find happiness in this town, there was still something lacking.

As Darek gazed at the beauty of the sunrise, he wondered what everyone else from the orphanage was doing now. Slade was always a loner. Being the oldest of the bunch, he assumed the position of leader whenever they did tasks and chores. Darek imagined Slade to be a mercenary. Elize was always the kind and gentle one. Whenever someone was hurt, Elize would be the first to go and get help. Darek had encouraged her to be a nurse or even a doctor. And Rex…well, Rex was always a crybaby. Darek remembered all the times he had to help Rex out whenever he was in trouble. Darek couldn't imagine what Rex would be doing.

"Enjoying the sun?" asked Jenson. He had walked up to the roof and Darek, consumed in his preoccupation, had never noticed. "I was looking for you yesterday. Didn't I say I was going to show you something? Where'd you go?"

"Yeah, sorry about that," Darek said. "There was some strange stuff about a census. We had to take photos, fingerprints, retinal scans and everything. First time it ever happened. And boy was it boring."

Jenson laughed. "I've heard about that and I've been avoiding it." Jenson gestured to his bag. "Anyway, let me show you my latest and most spectacular invention!"

Darek searched his satchel. "Ah! I've been meaning to show you something also." Darek revealed his newest pair of daggers, twirling the hilt around his fingers. "Got it at Rodrey's. Isn't it awesome?"

Jenson looked worried. "If Bellum catches you with that—"

"Relax." Darek cut him off and looked at him with disapproval. "You worry too much. He'll never find out. Besides, what'll he do? Call the cops on me? You know how he is."

Jenson shrugged. "I guess you're right. Anyway—as I was saying—let me show you something amazing." Jenson opened the bag he had been carrying. "I've been a bit jumpy ever since I made this." He took out a fairly small device that could be strapped on his wrist.

"Wow, amazing!" Darek said. "What is it? A wristwatch on steroids?"

"No," snapped Jenson. "It's a personal ITD!" Jenson couldn't contain his excitement and squealed, "Amazing, right?"

Darek fiddled with the buttons. "ITD? Isn't that some kind of disease?"

"What? No! It's an Intergalactic Teleportation Device. This thing can teleport you *anywhere* in the galaxy. Although, it does eat up batteries like a rodent on peanut butter, so I wouldn't call it a free ride. You'll have to recharge the batteries after every use."

"A teleportation device? Did you make this yourself?" Darek was skeptical. It sounded too farfetched. "And why does it look like a giant watch?" Darek strapped it on his wrist and moved his arm around. "Couldn't you have made it cooler looking?"

Jenson dug around his bag, pulling out a number of nuts, bolts, circuit boards and wires. "Hey, it's not like I have access to the finest materials known to man. I scrounged up all the parts I needed from the hardware shop across the street."

Darek shook his head in disbelief. "You expect me to believe this? It's large for a watch…but for something as powerful and impressive as a teleportation device, it looks way too small. How'd you even come up with this?"

"Okay, you got me. I wouldn't exactly call it a *new* invention. I downloaded the basic schematics from the X-Net. But of course I had to change everything to match the parts I could get. The homemade aspect and the portable size of it would be my part of the invention. A homemade ITD has never been done before!" Jenson took the device from Darek's wrist and, with a screwdriver, tampered with the inside, making several adjustments to ensure working order. "It wasn't easy. It took me a few months to save up enough money to buy all the parts. Not to mention, it also took a few months before I could get it to activate."

Darek continued to shake his head.

"What? You still don't believe me?" said Jenson.

"You still expect me to believe you?"

"What you need is a demonstration," Jenson said with a smile. He jammed a small blue vial into the back of the device and locked it in with a click. The red and green lights on the top screen blinked weakly before staying solid. The ITD emitted a soft buzzing sound.

Seeing that it was working properly, Jenson tied it on his wrist. "Oh and this is the fun part." Jenson brought out two long boards, which had been protruding from his bag. They were simple wooden boards, but had small straps for the feet. "Follow my lead." Jenson took one of the boards and locked the buckles on his feet; Darek did the same with the other board.

Darek stared at the board and said, "Explain to me why we're wearing boards on top of a roof? No wheels, no engine. What is this, a snowboard?"

Jenson ignored his question and eagerly flipped the switch on the ITD. A murky green beam of light shot forth from the ground beneath their feet and extended deep into the grimy sky, past the highest clouds and billows of smoke. The light surrounded them and raised them up off the ground. As the two of them levitated for a moment, they both stared at each other, speechless and dumbfounded.

Jenson began laughing hysterically. "It works! My first test run and it's going to work!"

Darek glanced around in fright and gasped, "You've *never* tested it before?"

In a blurry flash, they were sucked into space headfirst. The afterimages of their bodies were seemingly stretched like thin rubber while being carried off into the sky by the green streak of light. The stream of light curved and twisted into the form of a spiraling tunnel. Darek kept his eyes shut, afraid to see what was happening. What if they were actually in space? It'd be terrifying to be in space without a spaceship! Without the courage to open his eyes, Darek fanned out his arms and legs, letting his body float about.

Jenson jerked him by the arm. "Hey, concentrate! You're drifting to the side!" Jenson pulled Darek toward the middle of the tunnel.

Slowly, reluctantly, Darek opened his eyes, one after the other. He looked around and was shocked to see them drifting about in this strange tunnel. "This is insane!" The tunnel was swirling green all around, but it was somewhat translucent; he could see the passing stars and planets on the outside.

Jenson laughed at Darek's tense face. "Don't worry and have fun! I was just kidding about the first test run." Jenson crouched over and put one hand on the board. He then started to spin around. As the board shifted left and right, he drifted left and right. He had complete control over his weightless movement in the tunnel. "Come on, try taking control! This is awesome!"

Darek breathed deep. He bent his knees and leaned down on the board. He got into a crouched position and could feel a force flowing under his feet like the rushing of a river; the mysterious flow pushed him forward, and Darek felt like he was surfing across the galaxy. He began to wobble, so he tried to shift his weight to maintain his balance.

"Now you're getting it." Jenson cheered him on.

Darek moved left and right, up and down. And soon enough, he was doing flips, spins and all sorts of tricks. "I think I've got this. This is easy!" He clasped his hands on the back of his head and closed his eyes, enjoying the freedom of floating effortlessly.

However, due to his carelessness, Darek started to drift away to the boundaries of the tunnel.

"Don't get too close to the outside!" Jenson warned him.

"What's the big problem? I'm not that close." But the closer he got to the edge of the tunnel, the less control he had. When he tried to return to the center of the tunnel, he was no longer able to move the board. He flailed his arms, but nothing he did helped.

Jenson surfed to Darek's aid right away. "Take my hand!" Jenson stretched out his hand.

Darek used all of his might to reach Jenson. The moment their hands interlocked, Jenson reeled him into the inner part of the tunnel.

"That's the second time!" Jenson said, exhausted. "Do *not* do that again!"

"Sorry, I got carried away."

"That's okay," said Jenson. "I was just afraid you'd be sucked into outer space where you'd be devoid of a living, breathable atmosphere and die a relatively quick, but painful death, subject to freezing temperatures, radiation exposure, bullet-like projectiles and an inescapable vacuum—which would also cause your insides to swell and boil."

"There's no need to explain," said Darek, sounding appalled at the thought of it.

"Where's the fun in that?"

The ITD started beeping.

Jenson said, "Oh, time's up. Try landing feet first or else it'll hurt. Point your feet at the direction we're headed."

The beam of light fell from the sky and touched the ground. Darek and Jenson followed through the light and landed smoothly onto the outskirts of an industrial city.

They stood there in silence for a moment before Jenson said, "Well? What do you think?"

"It was fun." Darek couldn't quite find the words to express how he felt. "It was exciting…a little scary, but exciting."

"I'm not talking about your experience," said Jenson. "Think of how it can help us with deliveries! We can go to any planet we want, anytime we want and it's extremely fast too. No more sneaking into freighters or paying for cheap roundtrip passes on the ferry. With this device, we can handle all the long distance deliveries! We'll practically have a monopoly on it. And ITDs aren't even mainstream. Once I market this baby, I'll be rich!"

"That's great and all, but where are we now?" Darek looked over the surroundings. There was a city nearby and forests all around.

Jenson checked the screen of the ITD. "If everything went well, this should be a planet called Whardhime."

"Whardhime..." Darek paused as if he were contemplating. "No wonder..."

"You know of it?" asked Jenson.

Darek shook his head. "No...not really. I remember hearing them talk about this place on the news. A planet with high poverty."

"It wasn't always that way. There was a civil war a while back and it devastated the economy and depleted their resources. After the war, the Federation thought it'd step in and offer aid so that the population could rebuild the infrastructure. Their plan failed. So the Federation decided to provide transports for the people to emigrate off this planet. No one really lives here anymore. There are a few small towns and cities. But that's it."

"I'm impressed." Darek smiled. "I thought you only knew everything about our planet."

"I always research where I'm going. There are precautions to take wherever you go."

Jenson started walking towards the city.

"Where are you going?" asked Darek.

"Ah, I have a job here," Jenson said. "It'll be quick. You can walk around. Just make sure to meet me back here in a few hours. Don't stray too far. I've been told some intergalactic criminals may be lurking around since the Federation rarely patrols this part of space."

Darek watched Jenson enter the city gates. When Jenson was no longer in his sights, he followed the dirt roads. The roads stretched far past a small forest and into an old, rundown town. The aged buildings cast their decrepit shadows over the scraped, untidy paths of dirt. Weeds were everywhere, taunting a lonely gardener with their resilience. In this ghastly town, there was no banter of children or strolling of tamed dogs. It was a town inhabited by only the elderly. The townsfolk shuffled along the sidewalks, and with their kind eyes, they looked at one other and smiled.

Darek had lied to Jenson. He knew of this place. In fact, he had lived here most of his life. "Marwood hasn't changed much at all," commented Darek as he took a stroll around the block. "Same old stores...same old houses..."

He wandered to the front door of a red brick house. The windows and doors were boarded up. Darek tried to take a peek through a crack in one of the broken windows, but it was too dark to see anything. A cobblestone path led the way to an open backyard where the grass had grown too tall for children to run around freely. Though he saw nobody in that playground, the subtle echo of laughing children rang in his ears. With glazed eyes, he watched as a pair of butterflies rested at the top of a metal slide. With his imagination, Darek started to see his old friends—Elize, Slade, and Rex—playing tag around the field.

Darek never thought he would return to Marwood so soon. It had only been three years since he had departed from this town. He had always believed he would only return here when he was close to death. It'd make a fine grave.

While Darek was silently reminiscing, he was knocked off his feet. A man had run into him from behind. The man glanced at Darek and left without a single word. Darek didn't really get a good look at him. But for the split second that their eyes met, Darek felt uncomfortable: he saw an undeniable fear etched on that man's face.

"Kid, you all right?" A police officer saw the whole incident over the chain link fence. He rushed to Darek's side to help him up. "Just goes to show you, you shouldn't space out. It's dangerous. Sometimes we get people with a screw loose, if you know what I mean."

"Yeah, I know. I was just—" Darek broke off when he saw someone crossing the road. A girl had appeared out of nowhere. She smiled gently at Darek. It was Elize. Darek was sure of it. A mysterious, hazy fog formed around her feet. A sudden gust of wind blew across the street, causing the fog to rise up and cover her from his sight. Darek shouted out, "Elize!" She didn't respond. He leapt over the fence. But when the fog dissipated, she was gone.

"What's wrong, kid?" The police officer followed him. "You seem a bit high-strung."

"Did you see a girl standing here?" Darek pointed to the road. "She was standing right here." Darek scratched his head, puzzled by her sudden appearance and disappearance.

"Can't say that I have," the officer replied.

"Then do you know of any girls that live around here? Have you seen any teenage girls around here lately?" Darek pressed hard for answers.

"Son," said the police officer, "after the orphanage closed, I haven't seen a single girl around these parts for years. Now if you are looking for a girlfriend, I must say, this is an odd spot to begin your search. The only 'girls' here would start around the age of fifty-five." The officer paused. "You do seem like a fine young man though. If you're interested, I have some relatives who live in the city over and they have a daughter—"

"No," Darek interrupted him, "that's quite alright." Then he turned to leave. "If you'll excuse me, I'm in a bit of a hurry."

Running from street to street, Darek searched for any sign of Elize. *It's not an illusion!* Darek thought. *The only image of her in my head doesn't resemble what I just saw. She looks different, yet I know it's her! Is it her ghost? Is she trying to tell me something?*

Darek struggled to make sense of what was going on, but no answers would dare come. However, in his heart, a strange feeling began to take shape. It was as if he could suddenly sense her presence nearby. In the corner of his eye, he caught a glimpse of a shadow flitting across the rooftops. The shadow was moving toward the far end of town.

Elize stooped over, examining the dirt. After a quick study, she immediately concluded that the trail was fresh. She looked up and, by visualizing the tracks, determined that the trail ended at a house just a block away. She approached the door of the building and pressed her ear against it, listening for any sound. Elize heard a panicky breath through the wood. The target was here, and better yet, he was standing right behind the door.

Her hand shaped in the likeness of a gun, Elize touched the tip of her index finger against the door. Then she drew circles with her finger, wandering about until she could find the perfect spot. Her finger stopped just a foot above the center of the door.

"Gotcha," she whispered. Her fingernail hardened like steel and extended forth, piercing through the door. The sound of breathing was silenced.

"Target eliminated," Elize whispered, "I'll dispose of the evidence now."

"Elize!" Darek finally caught up to her and gasped, "Elize, it *is* you!"

Elize turned back to see Darek coming down the road in a hurry. She took one powerful leap and landed on the roof of the building. "I've been…compromised."

A voice came into her head. *How could you be so careless? Silence him or else we risk being discovered.*

"No, it's the one we've been waiting for." Sullen, she stared at him for just a moment. Then, as another thick fog swept across, she disappeared into the sky.

"She's gone...again," said Darek. "But what was she doing here?" Darek walked up to the door where he last saw her standing and looked around for any clues as to what was going on. He analyzed the ground, then the surrounding environment, and lastly, he examined the door. That was when he noticed it. A tiny, misplaced hole near the middle of the door. But there was more. Out of the hole leaked a dark liquid.

His eyes wide, Darek whispered under his breath, "Blood..."

CHAPTER 3
The Judge

A sleek ship sailed its way through the deepest reaches of space. Its shape was sharp like the head of an arrow as it pierced its way across a nebula, its sights firmly locked onto the small planet of Quurtha. This slender spacecraft was the *Vagrant*, a *Recon*-class Federation starship. Though it was routinely assigned to patrol the border of Federation space, it was now entering the orbit of Quurtha in order to resupply.

When the ship reached the orbiting space station, it slowly eased its approach, preparing to dock. Shaped like a diamond and having the color of an aquamarine, the station was like a celestial jewel. Embedded at the corners of the station were black pincer-like thrusters, which were only used to move the station in case of emergencies.

On board the *Vagrant*, Lieutenant Rex Galvin was lying in his quarters, resting comfortably on the couch. It was his fifteenth birthday and his idea of celebration consisted of a good long rest. He did think of other ways to enjoy his day off, but this was the least complex and most satisfying. Besides, there were no recreational facilities that he could visit because Quurtha was a military base.

The computer beeped. "Lieutenant," the computer said, "I'm sorry to disturb you on your day of rest, but Commander Blazon wishes to meet with you."

Rex groaned as he got off the couch. Taking his time, he tried to wake himself up by rubbing the tense muscles in his face. A slight yawn broke free as he stretched. "Tell him I'll be there within the hour."

"Affirmative, I will relay your message," said the computer.

Rex massaged his eyes as he stepped into the shower. The showers on board the *Vagrant* were typical of Federation ships. In order to conserve water for drinking, a cheap synthetic liquid called Vapex was used for showers. Vapex was useful because it was recyclable. Ten gallons of Vapex were allotted to every shower. Soldiers could take showers for as long as they wanted because there was no fear of wasting the liquid. The small tubular shower room was riddled with holes where the Vapex would come out in short bursts. For convenience, soap was also dispensed on command with the Vapex. The shower was designed with comfort in mind, so all of the settings, such as temperature and strength of the burst, were customizable.

Rex didn't like Vapex showers much. It just wasn't the same as the real thing. The synthetic liquid was stickier than water and was accompanied by an odd odor. Rex hopped into the shower for only a few minutes before running out, eager to dry himself.

Standing in front of the bathroom mirror, he took a slick razor and shaved off any extra hairs along his cheek. His hands rubbed the skin beneath his chin, feeling for any hairs he may have missed. While he took a good look in the mirror, he realized how much he had changed in three years. He was no longer a scrawny, useless runt. He was becoming a man. The rapid transformation startled him.

Rex had just turned twelve the day he had walked into the Navy recruitment office. At that time they had said he was a year too young to begin the physical training, so they had placed him in a training program for enlisting children. During his days at the military academy, he had often wondered if he would be able to handle the intense training that would follow. But no matter how hard things were, one thing always pushed him forward: being weak and regretting it. He would never allow himself to be weak again…to be helpless again…*never*. Things were different now.

Without wasting anymore time, Rex blew dry his red crew-cut hair, put on his glasses, donned his green uniform and left his quarters.

Rex walked by the side of the hallway nervously, twiddling his thumbs as he went. Whenever his fellow officers passed by, he straightened, gently smiled and waved a greeting. But when they were gone, he went back to his nervous state. Rex tried to calm himself down by looking out the windows that lined the corridor.

Throughout his years of service it was not often that his commander, Dionus Blazon, would call him down to his office. Even seeing the commander face-to-face was a rare occurrence. While he had always seen him during large ceremonies and public appearances, it was quite a different thing to see him in person.

The thing that disturbed Rex the most was the commander's young age. The commander was only twenty-nine years old and yet he was highly honored. It was hard for Rex to respect such a young commander. He doubted Dionus's motives, ambition and qualifications.

Regardless of his doubts, Dionus had already proved himself worthy in the eyes of the Federation. He was a brilliant tactician. With a single battleship, he had cleared the Hapnos system of the infamous pirate crew, the Soulless Marauders. From that one incident alone, Dionus had become a household name across the galaxy.

Still, Rex always had an uneasy feeling about him. Dionus had been making radical changes to the Federation. As a matter of fact, it was because of Dionus that young recruits were allowed officer ranks in the first place. Was it something to be thankful for, or would be it a great mistake in the end? Rex wasn't sure.

Rex's mind wandered back to the outside of the window where he found peace. The serenity of outer space was what made him join the fleet in the first place. All the thoughts of the difficult operations and monotonous writing of reports seemed to fade away every time he observed the pristine beauty of the galaxy. He had a deep and inexplicable love of the freedom of outer space.

When he reached Dionus's office, Rex firmly pushed the button by the door.

"Come on in." A small screen on the side of the door flashed on and depicted Dionus's friendly young visage. His long golden blond hair was slicked back with gel. His uniform was neatly ironed to perfection without a single speck of lint to tarnish its appearance. His body was lean and strong, showing no signs of negligence to its fitness.

Dionus grinned. "Galvin, I've been expecting you."

Rex laid his hand flat on a thin panel that was on the center of the door. A faint red flash was emitted from the panel and it scanned up and down, from the tips of his fingers to the lower edge of his palm. After it recognized the unique pattern of his hand, the metal door slid open.

Dionus was standing there to greet him. "Please have a seat." He amiably led Rex to the closest chair by the desk.

"Care for a drink?" Dionus cracked open the fridge and pulled out a few cans of Neetros, an energy drink popular among Federation soldiers.

"No thanks." Rex declined the drink politely. He hated Neetros. It always left a gross, lingering aftertaste in his mouth. For some unknown reason, the aftertaste always brought to mind bug guts—not that he knew what bug guts tasted like.

Dionus smiled. "Just take it. That's an order. Think of it as a…birthday present."

Rex glanced at the can and felt his stomach cringe. "Yes…sir. Thank you, sir."

He lifted the can and stared apprehensively at it before taking a few sips. The viscous, foamy drink oozed into the back of his throat. He could feel globs of Neetros roll down his esophagus and land on the pit of his stomach. Muscle spasms coursed their way through his body as the thick fluids flowed into his bloodstream. Rex felt like he had lost control of his body. His legs began kicking the desk ahead, and occasionally, his shoulder would pop up.

"Now about the situation at hand." Dionus sunk into his chair, amused by Rex's reaction to the drink. "Were you notified about the Judges?"

"Notified about the Judges?" Rex repeated. "You mean the *story* of the Judges? Are you talking about those fairy tales? I've heard of them. The Judges are supposedly monsters in human form. They live in the world of the shadows, stalking and executing people who commit crimes." He laughed and said, "They really are quite ridiculous stories, aren't they? I mean, it's been told for hundreds of years, and yet no one can prove they exist."

"Ridiculous?" said Dionus. "Teleportation was long thought to be impossible by the miracle of science. It was believed to be a territory that only masters of anti-law could enter. The notion that we could teleport ships across long distances was 'ridiculous' but now we are more than capable of it! Is it not possible that there was a truth in all of the lies? If someone did see a Judge and told everyone about it, he'd get ridiculed regardless. Then don't you agree that even if it were true, no one can truly prove or disprove such a wild claim?"

Rex scratched his head. "I don't quite understand where you're going with this."

"Sounds to me like you're still skeptical." Dionus leaned forward. "But not to worry. We've already got the evidence we need to prove they exist."

Rex said nothing for a moment and then cleared his throat. "Is this a joke, sir?"

"No joke." Dionus's expression was as serious as can be. He reached inside a drawer, pulled out several folders and laid them on the desk. "Take a look at this."

"What's this?" Rex slowly picked up a report and flipped through the pages, knowing that within these pages he would have to read something he'd dread. "This can't be real," said Rex. "The incident at the MTRI colony was done by one person? Impossible."

"And that's just the beginning," said Dionus. "As you well know, the MTRI is one of the largest mining corporations. All their colonies are secured with a small but strong militia. The soldiers they employ are about as well trained as any Federation soldier, and in regards to weapons, they've got quite an arsenal."

Rex placed the folder on the desk. "I don't understand. This is just pure speculation, isn't it? I mean, how do we even know it's a Judge? There are hundreds of skilled assassins capable of this feat. They could be from any organization. Maybe it's a hired from the Assassin's Guild."

Dionus cleared his throat before continuing. "Well, it is true we don't know exactly who they are, where they come from or what they call themselves. We have merely dubbed them Judges based on the stories of old. But what we do know, based on the reports, is that the perimeter was not breached, many of the soldiers were killed without firing a single shot and there was no evidence of anyone leaving the premises. In other words, they came from within and escaped without using conventional methods. Even if these are not Judges, they are still a threat that needs to be neutralized."

Rex took a few more chugs of Neetros and eased more into the ideas that Dionus was discussing. "Okay, let's assume it is a Judge. Why would he attack a mining facility? As far as I understand, there's no reason to do so unless he was in dire need of their resources."

"It seems you still aren't catching on." Dionus smiled. "Our investigation has found several survivors near the remains of the facility. These survivors are native to the planet. Apparently, they were enslaved by the MTRI and were forced to endure hard labor."

"So you're telling me that the motivation for this attack is—"

"Justice," Dionus said. "And as proof of this, the natives were allowed return to their homes unharmed. If we were dealing with thieves, the facility would be missing something—resources or equipment, but it is untouched. If we were dealing with any assassin or even a crazed psychopathic killer, there is no reason for them to let potential witnesses live."

Dionus got up from his chair and paced back and forth near the window. "This is what I believe: we are dealing with vigilantes—and of the worst kind I might add. They are deadly, idealistic assassins with no regard to the laws we have established. Only God knows how long they've been operating. For all we know, they may have done this for several hundred years. Worse yet, they continue to do so right under our noses and we are helpless about it. If word gets out, we may have a crisis on our hands. People will doubt our competence as a military force."

The light on the intercom buzzed and flashed red. It was an emergency call.

"Excuse me," Dionus said to Rex, as he activated the intercom.

Dionus sat back down. "This is Commander Blazon speaking."

"Commander, there's a news broadcast that I think you should see," said the male voice over the intercom. "May I relay it to your monitor?"

"Very well," replied Dionus. "You may do so."

The entire sidewall flickered on, revealing images of a local news reporter reading a report. "This just in—workers at the largest penitentiary on Yulguren have reported that all the prisoners on death row are now confirmed dead. The murderer is still unidentified. From the current details of the investigation, it is now known that the use of a weapon is apparent. As of now, there is no word from officials as to whether this incident is related to the mysterious MTRI colony attack of last week—"

Dionus turned off the monitor with a remote. "Talk about bad timing. It won't be long before the wolves of the media will breathe down our necks for answers." He turned to Rex. "I called you here because I believe you are the best man for the job. You have earned my trust over the past year with your excellent performance. Galvin, I want you to deal with this. The culprit must stand trial for his crimes."

Rex stood at attention. "I'll get on it right away. Do we have any leads?"

"I'm glad you asked." Dionus searched his jacket pockets and threw down a few photos. "Just yesterday, there was a report from the local authorities on Whardhime. The victim was a man known as Greg Whelster. Ever heard of him?"

Rex held the photos in his hand and observed them closely. "He's on the galaxy's most-wanted list, is he not?"

"Yes," Dionus said, nodding, "which makes this case so suspicious. His heart was pierced through a door. Murder weapon unknown." He then pulled out two more photos and showed them to Rex. "But that's okay, because we already know who the murderer is."

Staring at the photos, Rex uttered, "It *can't* be..."

"I'm sorry," Dionus said, "did you say something?"

His eyes wide open, Rex asked, "Th-this is the murderer?"

"Yes, he was last seen on Whardhime. After analyzing the scene of the crime, we found footprints and fingerprints that shows this man was there at that exact spot." Dionus pressed a button on a control panel on top of his desk. The large screen on sidewall turned on again. "Here, let me show you the data we've gathered. His name is—"

"Darek Wayker," said Rex. "I know him."

"You know him?"

"Yes. Before I joined the military academy, I lived at an orphanage with him and several others. When we were young, we used to play together, so I know him very well."

"Ah, so he's a friend?"

Rex shook his head. "He *was* a friend. After we left the orphanage, we went our separate ways. I no longer have any affiliation with someone who could be considered a criminal."

Dionus studied him. "Then can I trust you with this mission, or will this be too hard for you to deal with?"

"I'll get on it right away, sir," is what Rex said, but his voice quivered slightly.

"Good," said Dionus with a sly grin. "I'll have the details of your mission ready by tomorrow. See you then."

Rex left the room. As he went back through the narrow corridor, he stopped and looked out the window. A few small meteoroids drifted about, rolling their way toward the planet. The beauty of these rocks in space mesmerized him and he slowly raised his hand, reaching for them. As he pressed his hand against the window, he realized he would never be able to catch them. He would never be able to save them from burning away in the atmosphere. And so he turned away and continued to walk—down the empty and lonely hallway, he walked.

CHAPTER 4
Hunt

T hunder roared and lightning split the sky across Albiore City. Numerous raindrops drenched the streets with deep puddles and washed away the smog from the unceasing factories. The cleansing rain was so thick that it was nearly impossible for pedestrians to see farther than three feet ahead. While people sat in their homes, sipping their morning coffee and tea, they listened gloomily to the pitter-patter of the dismal rainfall hammering at their rooftops. Since the sky was blocked out by the clouds, the sun did not rise that day.

As Darek stayed in bed, the mind-numbing racket from the rain annoyed him to no end. He wrapped the pillow around his head to drown out the noise, but it didn't help much. After much twisting and stirring, he sat up in his bed, lethargic.

The roof was flooded with rain and the water crept its way into his crummy shack, but Darek didn't care—or rather, he was used to it. It was a normal occurrence. Sighing from his feelings of dreariness, he forced himself to get dressed. He grabbed an old umbrella, wore his usual and only pair of jacket and shorts, and climbed down the side ladder.

It was an ordinary rainy day. The streets were less crowded, but he was sure that the agency would still get a sharp boost in business. The request for local deliveries always skyrocketed when it rained. These jobs in the rain were always terrible. The agency would get ridiculous requests like grocery deliveries or fast food deliveries— mostly low paying and time consuming. The agency prided itself in reliability and low cost. The agency never turned down any job. Their reputation was at stake and the only ones who suffered were the delivery boys.

Darek recalled the worst local job he ever had in the rain: he had to look for a runaway cat. Its owner had been worried sick about it. It wasn't really a delivery, but they make you do all kinds of stupid stuff. Darek shuddered just thinking about it. He remembered running up and down through the entire city, kicking open foul-smelling trashcans and climbing up trees. All that grueling work had been done in a raging storm. In the end he never found the cat and never got paid for the job. The cat had gone back home by itself.

His flimsy umbrella collapsed and broke apart after getting worn-out from the heavy downpour. After tossing it in the trash, Darek moved to the sidewalk, cautiously staying under the awning of shops to enjoy their small cover. He ignored the sharp glances of people through the shop windows.

When he reached the agency, he saw some police officers by the entrance. They chatted among themselves, cramming bagels and donuts down their throats in a rush. One of them, his mouth open, saw Darek and started jumping up and down, pointing frantically at him. All of a sudden, whistles blared and police started appearing all over the place, exiting the cars and shops nearby.

What is it this time? Darek stood there, his hands raised.

The officers drew their pistols and surrounded Darek. They gripped their guns with their fingers almost itching to pull the trigger. They screamed hoarsely, "GET DOWN! GET DOWN! DOWN ON THE FLOOR, NOW!"

"Don't shoot! I'm unarmed!" he exclaimed.

Darek knelt down, his hands interlocked behind his head, but they still kept the barrel of their pistols locked on him. Even though he didn't resist, they handcuffed him and shoved him to the ground, roughly pinning him against the wet pavement. Then they patted him down and searched his belongings.

When an officer discovered the daggers, he cried in a panic, "He has a weapon!"

Officer Bellum was there among them. He looked down at Darek in contempt. "I'll take the weapon," he told the officer. As Bellum held the daggers in his hand, he lowered his face. "Darek, I would've never guessed." He brought Darek up to his feet and forcefully pushed him toward the police car. "Come on, let's go."

"Wait, what did I do?" Darek asked. "What's going on?"

"Don't play dumb," snapped Bellum, pushing him forward.

"No, really—I have no idea what's happening." Darek's face was flushed from the harsh treatment and scornful looks. "Is this because of the daggers? I didn't steal them! Rodrey gave them to me. Ask him! He'll tell you everything."

Bellum took a quick glance around and then whispered into Darek's ear, "You really don't know what's going on?"

Darek shook his head.

Bellum said, "You're a good kid. How long have we known each other?"

"I came to live here about three years ago."

"Three years…Time sure goes by fast." Bellum glanced warily at the nearest officers. "Listen," Bellum said quickly, "I want you to run as fast as you can into that alley straight ahead. Take cover where you can and stay out of sight. Understand? I'm going to investigate this myself, but until then, I want you to be safe."

"I can't run away that easily—they'll shoot."

Bellum unlocked the handcuffs, slipped the daggers into Darek's pouch and said, "Just trust me and go!"

Darek tossed the handcuffs to the concrete floor and took the opportunity to escape. Still wondering why they were eager to catch him in the first place, he dashed toward the alleyway to make his getaway.

All the officers were caught off guard. "He's headed for the alley!" they yelled. They drew their guns again and, without a second thought, opened fire; but they were only aiming to cripple Darek. Bellum ran behind Darek, intercepting the gunfire. Several bullets punctured Bellum's leg, but he stood firm, refusing to fall.

Darek rushed into the bustling throng that filled the marketplace. The marketplace was packed with food vendors and various stalls. He squeezed himself through, pushing aside everyone in his way. With great perseverance, he managed to make it through the crowd without any police behind him. But what was he going to do? His first and foremost thought was to head back to the Guridoh Tavern. Even though the cops were sure to investigate it, he was fresh out of ideas. All he could hope for was some advice from his friends. Maybe they would know of a place for him to hide.

Soaked to the bone like a wet dog, he pushed open the door of the tavern to find Locke, the bouncer, standing at the entrance. "Hey Locke, can you move over? I'm kind of in a hurry here." Darek tried to walk past Locke, but Locke pushed him back.

"Where do you think you're going?" Locke stared him down.

"Inside, of course." Darek tried to walk past him again, but Locke clamped down on his shoulder, making him squeal in agony. Then Locke picked him up with both hands and tossed him into the streets. Darek felt the hard asphalt scrape away some flesh. There was a little blood, but it was washed clean by the rain.

Because people were so interested in the sudden burst of violence, a small crowd started to form outside the tavern. Intrigued citizens stopped to watch Darek pick himself up.

"What's the big idea?" Darek rubbed the throbbing pain in his arm.

"Scram." Locke crossed his arms. "You're making it hard on the customers."

At that moment, Jenson walked out of the tavern; he paid no attention to Darek and pushed his way through the crowd as though in a hurry.

"Jenson," Darek said, "can you believe it? This guy won't let me through." But Jenson ignored him and kept walking. "Hey." Darek touched Jenson on the shoulder but Jenson brushed his hand off.

"Excuse me," Jenson said coldly, "I'd appreciate it if you'd just let me be."

"What are you ignoring me for?" Darek grabbed him by the collar of his shirt and shook him. "It's me, Darek! What's wrong with you?"

Jenson shoved him away and said, "Just get out of my sight."

"Wha-what?" Darek watched Jenson head down the road. "Is this a sick joke?" He looked back to the entrance of the Guridoh to find curious eyes peering through the windows. He turned to the crowd and asked them, "Did I miss something? Why is everyone treating me like a criminal?" The crowd backed away from Darek and scattered.

A broadcast over the large television monitor on a nearby building caught his eye. At first he thought nothing of it, but then he recognized a person on the screen. "Is that a picture of me?" Dumbfounded by his appearance on national television, Darek went closer to listen to the news.

He heard the news anchor say, "And here again we have a photo of the current suspect. The suspect is charged with a series of murders and destruction of property. If anyone has any information regarding this case please contact your local authorities. Do not—I repeat—do not attempt to engage the suspect as he is believed to be armed and dangerous."

Darek gawked at the screen. "Murder? Me? When did this happen? I'd never—" He was interrupted by a group of police officers that managed to catch up to him.

"There he is! Don't let him get away!"

Darek ran away. As he searched for crowded places to get lost in, he thought about his next destination. Bellum was injured and Jenson had ignored him. There was only one hope left. Using his extensive knowledge of the city streets, he took a series of shortcuts through buildings, across fountains and under roads. He stayed hidden and unnoticed, only moving about when he knew it was safe. At last, he found himself standing in front of Rodrey's shop.

As he looked at the shop, Darek's heart felt burdened. It was possible Rodrey would act the same way Jenson did. Thinking back on it, while he was angry at Jenson's reaction, he couldn't blame him either. He'd only end up dragging Jenson down for no reason and there was nothing that Jenson could do to help him.

He turned away from the door of the shop. There was nothing Rodrey could do for him. And after what had happened to Bellum, Darek wouldn't forgive himself if someone else got hurt because of his problems.

"Darek!" Rodrey opened the door of his shop and shouted, "Get in here!"

Darek couldn't help but smile. Maybe there was nothing Rodrey could do, but that didn't change the fact that there was still someone who cared. How could he refuse? He wasted no time and snuck into the shop. Rodrey locked the door and sealed the blinds shut.

He gave Darek a great big hug. "Darek, you're okay!" Darek felt embarrassed to be hugged in such a manner but let it slide, seeing as Rodrey was so happy to see him. Rodrey handed him a dry towel. "Here, dry up. I heard the news. I've been worried ever since."

"So…you're not mad?" Darek asked, drying his hair and face in a rush.

Rodrey laughed. "Mad? You think I'd believe the government? I wouldn't trust those selfish little gimps for a second." He paused. "Anyway, we've got to get you out of here. This place isn't safe."

"But where can I go?" Darek wondered out loud, placing the towel on the counter. "It's almost like there're people watching every corner of every street." In anguish, he said, "Maybe I should just…surrender myself. There's no way I can escape."

Rodrey looked at him and shook his head, disappointed. "I didn't think you were the type to give up so easily. It would've never crossed my mind."

Embarrassed, Darek blushed and said, "Apparently, you don't know me that well."

Rodrey gave him a pat on the back. "Maybe not. But I know myself. And I went through almost the exact same thing you're going through…except the—um—the murderer part. I was a delivery boy too, you know!"

"You were?" Darek sounded surprised.

"Yup," said Rodrey, nodding. "I've lived in Albiore all my life! And I know how hard it is. Everyone treats you like dirt. Meals are hard to come by. It's like no one really cares about you, and some people even hate you! But if there's something I've learned over the years, it's this: even if everyone hates you and turns their back on you, it doesn't mean it's deserved! Just because people treat you like dirt, doesn't mean you are dirt! And just because people treat you like a criminal, doesn't mean you are a criminal! Don't let them get you down! If you give up here, we'll never know what you might accomplish one day! You might do something incredibly amazing and you might not. But whatever it is you do, that's something I'd like to see."

Darek grinned at Rodrey's encouraging speech. "Thanks. That's just what I needed."

Sirens wailed outside. Darek heard the screeches of cars parking outside. Rodney gestured for Darek to be silent and to follow him into the backroom. Once inside, he shut the door behind them and locked it.

Rodney whispered, "We'll be safe in here."

"Open up!" The front door shook about violently. Gunshots blew off the locks of the door. With an explosive kick, the door flung wide open, allowing a squad of police to pour into the facility. They quickly scanned the corners left and right, searching for any hostile activity.

"There's nothing here. Check the backroom." One of the officers tried to open the door. "It won't budge. They must've locked themselves inside." Once again, with a few bullets, they shot off the doorknob and tried to kick open the door, but it wouldn't budge. It was much more secure than the front door.

"I don't care what it takes," said the sergeant. "Break it down!"

The officers shot off the hinges of the door and aimed along the side of the door, hoping to knock off a few more of the locks. A group of policemen repeatedly slammed into the door with their shoulders. After much banging, it tumbled over. As the dust cleared from the collapse of the door, they kept careful watch of the backroom. They rushed in, hoping to catch the trapped criminals, but after a brief inspection, they found no one.

"You smell that?" Darek asked with his fingers clamping his nostrils shut.

Rodrey replied with a wide grin, "Yeah...the sweet smell of freedom."

"The smell has gotten to your brain," said Darek, as he sloshed through the grimy sewer waste. "My lungs! I seriously want to puke! It's a good thing you had that escape route. Why'd you have something like that anyway?" He swung around to find Rodrey catching his breath.

Rodrey said breathlessly, "Sometimes I stumble upon some odd rarity, and when that happens, you never know who'll come knocking on your door. Better safe than sorry."

"Sorry about your shop," Darek said. "It's all my fault."

"Don't worry about it. All that matters is you're safe and sound."

"Thanks...I...I can't take this anymore..." Darek leaned on the wall of the sewer, clapping his hand over his mouth to refrain from vomiting. "Let's get out of here. Please."

Rodrey laughed. "All right, I think we're far enough. I thought you'd already be used to the smell by now. Don't you sometimes take the sewers on your deliveries?"

Darek frowned. "I don't think you can get used to this horribleness."

Darek and Rodrey climbed out of a manhole in the remote part of the city. Darek spun around and flapped his arms wildly, airing out the rotten stench that clung to his skin. Rodrey neatly covered back the manhole.

"Where are we? I don't recognize this road." Darek tried to read the street sign, but the wet mud splattered over the rusted letters made it impossible.

"This is the Old Town," Rodrey explained. "Few people live here. Even though it's connected to the city, it's relatively independent. People from the city usually don't come to this side. There's really nothing of interest." He pointed down the road. "There's a checkpoint this way. If you can sneak past the guards, you'll make it out easily."

Darek asked, "Are you coming with me?"

"I'm going to back to the city. While you're busy escaping, I'll lead them away. Better to give them the early slip."

"Will I ever…" Darek's voice trembled. "Will I ever see you again?"

"Of course," chuckled Rodrey, "I still need payment for those daggers. I'm not letting you off the hook." With those final words, he waved goodbye and left him.

The Old Town—as it was called—was like a ghost town. It was the part of the city that had been forgotten when the major industries boomed and the factories took over. At the time of the industrial revolution, the mayor had decided it would be too expensive to demolish the town and rebuild over the land, so they had built the modern city apart from it instead. It remained as timeless as when it was first abandoned. The streets were empty. The windows were cracked. The signs were faded.

Darek whistled a nostalgic tune from his orphanage days as he walked to the checkpoint. He tried to erase every inch of doubt from his mind. But for every glimmer of hope that pervaded his thoughts, he could feel a flood of doubts invade and suppress it. He became engrossed in his thoughts, dwelling on the happy memories of the past and melancholic situation of the present.

Did his life matter? Though he hated this question, it kept popping up in his mind. He was a mere delivery boy, one of many. It was a life-risking job that the world saw as a cheap convenience. Even if they were to lock him up, life would go on without him. But there was more to life than that. All he ever wanted was to break free from everything, to find his purpose and his place in the universe, as small as it might be. He always believed that everything had a purpose. But those ideals were fading quickly.

His preoccupation was cut short by the sight of a lone person at the far end of the road. Could it be a nearby resident taking a stroll around the block, or could it be a cop making a quick sweep of the area? Regardless, there was a possibility of getting recognized.

Darek considered running away, but that would probably draw too much attention. Darek flipped up the collar of his jacket, trying to use it as cover. He figured the best way would be to play it cool. No one would think twice about his identity if he didn't show too much of his face.

The two of them continued to walk straight along this narrow road. Step by step, Darek paid no attention to the stranger. He kept his eyes on his side of the road. When he hit the point where they were only an arm's length from each other, he could feel every fiber in his body tensing up. As the gap between them narrowed, his heart beat ever more rapidly. A shudder ran down his back when the person's shoulder brushed up against his.

Darek held his breath. Why didn't the man step out of the way? The suspense was eating at him. It was almost as if time was standing still. Then, when he finally passed the man, nothing happened. Realizing he was safe, he took a deep breath to calm his nerves.

"Excuse me." The man spun around and tapped Darek on the shoulder, startling him.

In an attempt to scare off the man, Darek snapped, "Don't bother me!"

"I'm lost." The man pulled out a map. "You see, I want to get to over here, but I'm not even sure where I am right now."

"No time." Darek tried to walk away but the man held him at the shoulder.

"Now don't be so cold," said the man. "I'm also in a hurry and would really appreciate the help. Just show me where we are and I'll be on my way."

"Leave me alone!"

"What's the big deal? Just show me on the map. I'll even pay you for your trouble. If you're in such a hurry, I'll compensate you for your time."

Darek gave in to his temper. Curling his lip, he faced the man and shouted, "WHY WON'T YOU LEAVE ME ALONE—"

"Hey," said the man in a surprised tone, "you're Darek, aren't you?"

Darek got a look at a familiar face. "Rex?" Darek was shocked to see him. "What are you doing here? Don't tell me you came to see me. You didn't even tell me you were coming!"

Rex laughed. "I didn't even know you were here! I came here because of my job. Wow...I never thought I'd see you again." Rex paused. "How about we get a cup of coffee?"

Darek shook his head. "Not right now. Maybe some other time?"

"Another time?" Rex said defiantly. "I haven't seen you in three years! Surely we can just chat for a few minutes."

Darek thought about it. He knew he shouldn't stay any longer, but he couldn't help but feel a little guilty. Rex was right. It *has* been a long time. Darek said, "I guess a few minutes wouldn't hurt—for old time's sake."

Rex looked pleased. "There's a café nearby. It'll be a good place to catch up on things."

They found the café a few blocks away. The sign of the store dangled from a nail above. The awning overhead was tattered and ruined. Inside the shop, a young lady sat at the counter, reading a book. Her uncombed, disheveled hair and the thick bags under her eyes made Darek wonder how long she had been sitting there with that book. He couldn't help but stare at her, but even so, she ignored him and continued reading, chewing her nails in silence.

The two of them walked through the empty café. They briefly examined each table before finding the perfect place to sit. Though it looked like no one had entered the shop for several days, the tables had gooey stains, old half-filled cups, and some nibbled off food particles. None of the tables were clean, so they chose the cleanest table of them all, down in the far right corner.

"I'll get a napkin," said Rex. He walked up to the counter and seeing that he could not find any napkins, asked the lady, "May I please have some napkins?"

"Sure, go ahead," she replied, not even looking up.

"Where are they?"

"Don't know. Help yourself."

A little annoyed, Rex cleared his throat. "So are you telling me you don't have any napkins?" She said nothing in reply.

Darek tapped Rex on the shoulder. "We're both in a hurry so just forget about it."

"What about a drink? Don't you want to get something to drink?" Rex asked him.

"No." Darek motioned for him to just take a seat. He analyzed the lady's stoic expression. "I don't really want to…disturb her."

"Yes," said Rex, as he pulled up a chair, "you're right. Let's just take a seat and relax."

"So what are you doing here?" Darek asked, sitting down at the table.

"Listen closely." Rex's tone suddenly became more serious. "The truth is that I'm working as a Federation officer."

Shocked, Darek said, "Federation officer? Wow, you really hit it big. Congratulations!"

"Don't you understand? I've been ordered to arrest you!"

Darek examined him for a moment. "You don't *really* believe I'm a criminal, right?"

Rex pursed his lips. "Not to be insulting, but I'm sure you're as harmless as a mouse."

"Thanks," said Darek, feeling slightly offended. "And why are you telling me this?"

"Because you're in trouble. All the exits are blocked and hundreds of Federation soldiers have been sent to scour the city. Barring miracles, it'll be impossible for you to escape."

"Why would the Federation go through so much trouble?"

"They want to apprehend you at all costs. But I've got a plan. Everything will work out."

"Rex," said Darek, smiling, "I'm surprised. You've really changed. Never thought I'd have to depend on you, but I'm thankful you're here."

"Don't mention it." Rex leaned back on his seat. "It's destiny after all. Think about it. Out of all the Federation officers, I'm the one who was chosen to lead this operation to catch you. And while I'm lost in this city, I'm the one who manages to find you all alone where we can talk in private. This must be destiny. I'm sure of it."

"What do you have in mind?"

Rex leaned forward, avoiding contact with the sticky table. "The plan itself is simple. I'll take you back to the spaceport. I have my own personal ship there." He pulled out some handcuffs. "If you wear these, it'll be no problem. No one will think otherwise."

Darek eyed the handcuffs. Already, he had felt the cold metal against his wrists and had no intentions of willingly doing so again. "I don't know about this."

"It's the only way," Rex assured him. "You have to understand, these chains will only be temporary. Once we're on the ship, I'll remove it. Then I'll take you someplace safe."

"Okay," said Darek. He looked Rex in the eye and could see his sincerity. "I understand. What kind of friend would I be if I didn't trust you?"

The cylindrical spaceport was a famous landmark of Albiore City. It was a locale that was hard to miss; it could even be seen from the outskirts of town. Most of the city was built out of bricks and mortar, but the spaceport was fully constructed of steel and reinforced with pliable Alutanium. The port was a gift of the Federation in order to begin interplanetary trade with their developing planet. The glaring reflection of the metal showed the path to the port in the daylight, and bright beacons on the roof led the way at night.

While the port was as busy as ever, it was no longer the civilian transports that went to and fro. Armed soldiers had secured the area and restricted access from civilians; only military ships were allowed to dock. Merchants were unable to land and all flights off the planet were postponed indefinitely. Hundreds of outraged citizens lined up outside the door complaining to the guards about their rights, but the guards responded by pushing them back, threatening to use force if they did not calm down.

The guards recognized Rex and saluted him. When a guard saw Darek behind him, he said to Rex with a smile, "Good work, Lieutenant. Your ship is ready and waiting. I heard the local police force had some trouble catching him this morning, but I guess it's a simple job for someone like you."

"No," Rex replied. "I was just lucky."

One of the guards laughed. "Share some of that luck with us too!"

They opened the doors to the spaceport and urgently pushed Rex and Darek inside. Then they slammed the doors behind them and braced themselves as the crowd desperately tried to rush in. Once inside the lobby, Darek kept his head down to avoid eye contact with the soldiers that they passed by. He felt intimidated by the glares and angry stares. But when they walked into the circle of gates, he lifted his head up to get a view of the area.

The circle of gates was the heart of the spaceport. It was simply a large circular corridor with many numbered doors that line the walls. Each door led to armored compartments on different floors where they housed the spaceships. The walls stretched up hundreds of feet high, which was tall enough for most of the transports that docked there. The sky could be seen through the glass ceiling above them, but because the hallway was so wide and tall, the light that came from those windows was not enough to brighten the place. Small light bulbs were placed along the walls so that people could at least have an idea of where they walked.

The two of them took Gate 46 to where Rex's private shuttle was located. The shuttle looked much better than Darek had anticipated. He had been riding in rusty, broken-down transports for the past three years and never expected to ever ride in something that looked remotely new. Stylish streaks of green paint wrapped around the hull. Along the top of the frame were small stubs of retractable wings on the side and a sail-fin at the zenith. The overall shape was a bit like the head of a snake, the front narrowed in slightly while the back was wider and rounded out. It appeared small and compact on the outside, but the inside felt much more spacious, leaving plenty of legroom and walking space. The ship had four seats: one for the pilot, one for the copilot and two backseats for passengers.

Everything is going smoothly, maybe a little too smoothly, thought Darek as he sat in the backseat, admiring the aesthetics of the interior. Easing into the chair, he felt the soft cushion mold to fit the contour of his body.

"This is a nice ride," Darek blurted out to break the prolonged silence. "Must be nice to cruise around space with something like this."

Rex collapsed into the pilot's chair and began initiating the startup sequence. "It is nice. But I don't use it much. It's only useful for missions such as this one."

Darek wondered if Rex had forgotten about the handcuffs. He looked at the back of Rex's chair and saw that he was busy operating the ship. Darek rattled the chains to catch Rex's attention. Rex paid no mind; he continued to focus on the controls.

Then Darek said, "Hey, Rex." He didn't want to be distracting, but still, he couldn't wait to have his hands free. "Do you mind taking these off?"

Rex glanced back. "Sorry about that. But the ride isn't too long. I'll take it off later."

"How cruel." A female voice came from behind. "Giving him hope at a time like this?"

The sudden appearance of the young woman startled Darek. Her presence made the air in the ship feel suddenly heavier. Her straight black hair was cut short except for the front where it hung and veiled over the right side of her face. Her exposed left eye left a chilling impression that made Darek sweat, even in the cool air-conditioned interior.

From the uniform that she had donned, Darek could tell she was also a Federation soldier. Darek immediately took notice of the long, sheathed sword on her belt. It was unusual to see a Federation soldier carrying a sword in this day and age.

"Layne, what are you doing here?" Rex asked. He stood up and confronted her. "This is my ship. You have no right to be here without my permission."

"Dionus sent me to assist you. He thought you might need some help." She smiled. "Do you have any more problems that you would like to address?"

Rex glared at her and then returned back to the pilot's seat without another word from his lips. If Dionus had sent her, there was nothing he could do or say that would get her to leave. Dionus was, after all, their commanding officer.

She rested her arm at the head of his chair. "But I must wonder…would you have released him earlier if you hadn't sensed my presence?"

Rex ignored her and took the ship out of the spaceport. He was slightly disappointed that things didn't quite go as he expected.

"Sedate the prisoner," he ordered her. "It'll make things easier on all of us."

CHAPTER 5
Sentenced

"It's time," grunted the burly, yet remarkably handsome jailer. The jailer's complexion was smooth and glowing, his facial features chiseled to perfection, perhaps through extensive surgery. His appearance was a direct contrast to the horrible dungeon he watched over. He pounded his fist against the wall, the dull sound echoing. "Wake up, runt!"

Darek was roused from his artificially induced slumber. He opened his eyes, blinking. "Where am I?" Darek found himself lying on the concrete floor of a filthy jail. Trapped within these impenetrable stonewalls, Darek couldn't tell whether it was morning or night, for there were no windows. However, the prison was stunningly bright because of the radiant fluorescent tubes on the ceiling. The brilliant lights were perhaps a method of subtle torture by keeping prisoners awake for hours on end.

Darek's thoughts were a mess. *What did I do to deserve this? Can I wake up from this nightmare? Is there any hope left for me?* All he had were questions that could not be answered. He curled up, wishing he wasn't there—wishing it was just a bad dream.

"Hurry up!" The jailer grew evermore impatient and smashed his fist against the walls harder, such that it displaced several concrete blocks. "You're wasting my time." His right eye twitched unnervingly as he observed Darek's sluggish behavior. Then he muttered scornfully under his breath, "You aren't the only one getting executed today." Sweat dripped off the jailer's arms as he fumbled for the keys along his muscular waist. He unlocked the cell, entered and stood over Darek. Darek closed his eyes and uttered a few simple prayers. The jailer picked Darek up by the back of his shirt, dragged him across the cell and handed him off to the Federation soldiers who were waiting by the door. "He's all yours."

Two tall soldiers grabbed Darek by the arms and carried him down the corridor. Darek panted as he was taken through the dreadful passageways of the dungeon. Screams and pleas for help resounded vividly up and down the halls. Innocent, weak hands reached out from their cells hoping to touch the shadow of Darek, while nefarious inmates, disgusted by the sight of him, spit at his feet.

Darek looked up at the clock above the doors of the courtroom as they hauled him through. As a cruel joke, the words on the clock read: **Your Time is Up.** At the entrance of the chamber, the soldiers tied his hands and feet with Slythian shackles, which were crafted from the hard scales of the serpents of Lornhark. Darek struggled against the shackles but the more he struggled, the more the grip tightened around his arms and legs.

They brought him to the round platform in the center of the room; it stretched over a deep, endless abyss. Overhead, the ceiling split evenly in two and retracted away into the walls, revealing an enormous stadium above with an audience numbering in the thousands. The soldiers placed him on the platform; it was raised into the center stage of the stadium. The flocks of people were quiet until the moment they saw Darek. Once they laid eyes on him, they began to shriek and shrill. The crowd sneered, showing contempt for the one on trial.

His eyes wide, Darek fearfully watched the multitude shout and scream. Though he could not make out any of their words, he could feel their enmity against him. Their piercing tongues spewed bloodthirsty hatred that crushed his heart by the agony of humiliation. Sheepish, he hung his head and did not want to meet their derisive scowls.

The soldiers pushed him to the edge of the platform. The judge's podium was located on a smaller platform that appeared in front of Darek. A dozen soldiers stood on a ledge that stretched along the inner wall of the stadium; they had their guns pointed at Darek to deter him from any escape attempts. Darek flinched as spotlights shone brightly over him.

Dionus proceeded to enter the room and sat at the podium as the judge of this trial. Darek was surprised to see that he had on a suit of armor like the knights from the age prior to the millennium, before the great space age. Despite his archaic appearance, he carried himself very professionally, and he emanated an air of strict authority. With his gavel, he struck the podium thrice. All the chaotic commotion faded into a dead silence.

"Court is now in session!" A gruff voice bellowed throughout the chamber.

"Now let's see here…" Dionus casually perused through a thick stack of papers that was before him. "It says here you are charged with the mass slaughter of nearly…" He rubbed his eyes and looked again at the paper. "Fifty billion people? Sounds like a case of genocide."

"What?" Darek was astonished by the outrageous claim. "I don't know anything about that!" He pondered in his head about how such a thing could even be done. It was inconceivable.

The judge continued, "However, to tell you the truth, it is a mere estimation and may not even hold a candle to reality. Who knows how many have died at the hands of you and your accomplices over the past two thousand years?" Dionus continued to flip through the papers. "Let's see…there's also trespassing on private grounds, assaulting officers, evading arrest…"

"I've never hurt anyone!" Darek shouted. "I must have been framed!"

"A convenient excuse."

"I'm telling you—you've got the wrong guy!" Darek tried to run up to the podium but since his feet were tied together, he stumbled and fell flat on the ground.

"Well, I suppose that is possible." The judge rubbed his chin thoughtfully while he analyzed the case. "But that would take far too long to figure out. So let's continue, shall we?" Dionus stood up and pointed toward Darek. "How does the jury find the defendant?"

"GUILTY! GUILTY! GUILTY!" The assembly chanted in a deafening uproar.

When he heard this, Darek slumped to on the ground in despair, realizing his fate was sealed. *This is so unfair!* He thought solemnly, *Why are they doing this to me?*

Dionus grinned. "And what shall be his sentence?"

Everyone shouted, "DEATH! DEATH! GIVE HIM DEATH!"

"Then it shall be as you have said: his sentence is death!" Dionus picked up his sword and scabbard and drew forth his blade. Though it was not in the presence of light, his long sword still shined. The blade, almost white as snow, glistened as yellow dust trickled off the edges. All the soldiers averted their eyes away, for the sight of the blade nearly blinded them. As the judge swung the sword in the air, demonstrating its grace and beauty, the assembly quieted down and was awestruck by the spectacle. "I hereby declare the defendant guilty. I shall carry out execution with swift and *blind* justice." Dionus lunged over the podium and landed before Darek.

"This can't be…" Darek kept his face down. He was too afraid to see his executioner standing before him. Though he feared the afterlife, he wished for a quick and painless death.

Dionus slowly raised his sword. "This is the beginning of the end…"

Before he could bring the blade down, an abrupt wind formed around them, almost knocking Dionus off his feet. A strange orb of swirling blue light suddenly appeared between them. Dionus warily stepped back. The orb—which was originally the size of a tiny speck—grew steadily and created a massive vacuum, sucking in all sorts of things from sheets of paper to cloth hats. The weird phenomenon flattened out in the likeness of a door. Dionus watched the door carefully. There was nothing on the other side of the open door, only darkness. Then three people emerged from the darkness.

The first to step out was a slim man with a red cape across his shoulder. He appeared to be much older than the others with him. His facial features were very distinguished, especially with his sunken cheeks and pale complexion. The stringy, long white hair on his head was dry and withered. Next was a slender and vibrant young woman. Her wavy brunette hair bobbed as she took strides. She wore black loose-fitting garments with sleeves so long that they nearly touched her knees. The last to come out was a young man with short brown hair. He wore a sleeveless black t-shirt that accentuated his brawny body. The door closed behind them.

Darek recognized the younger ones immediately as his childhood friends.

"Elize…Slade…" he gasped.

"Stop this trial," said Slade. "He's innocent. We are the ones you want." Slade raised his hands in surrender. "Let him go. We'll take his place."

Looking ecstatic, Dionus exclaimed, "So you've come at last! I've been expecting you—the infamous Judges of Verras." Dionus motioned for the soldiers to stay on guard. "I'll consider it if only you'd tell me, fair Judge, of your purpose. For what reason do the Judges exist?"

Slade hesitated. Unsure of Dionus's intentions, he exchanged glances with the other Judges and then said matter-of-factly, "We, as Judges, must vanquish the evil in the galaxy. It is the only way to maintain peace and give hope to the innocent. That is our purpose."

"A commendable purpose." Dionus clapped mockingly. "But for however long the Judges have existed, evil still lives! That's the truth of the matter, isn't it? No matter how much judgment you pass, no matter how many people you kill…there will always be evil. If you had succeeded, there would be no need for police or military power. Don't you see? What you're doing is useless. Evil will always exist. You cannot vanquish it."

"This is a waste of time. Let's go," said Elize, as she quickly snatched Darek and pulled him away from Dionus. She turned to the older man beside her and said to him, "Lyonil, open up the portal so we can get out of here! We'll have to take Darek with us."

Without saying a word, Lyonil placed his hand on the door. But the door did not open. Instead, the door shrank in an instant and vanished from their sight.

Slade grabbed Lyonil by the collar. "Are you crazy? What are you doing? She told you to open it! You've trapped us here! Now we have to—"

"Trapped us? That's right." Lyonil grinned maliciously and pushed Slade back. "I told you this was a trap, but you didn't listen. Don't say I didn't warn you."

"You—it was *you* all along…" Slade looked at him with suspicion. "I knew it was strange that we were discovered. You set us up!" Glaring at him, Slade confronted Lyonil and pushed him to the ground. "How could you betray the order?"

"There's no need for such hostility." Dionus bowed to appease them. Lyonil scrambled to his feet and stood by Dionus's side where he felt much safer. Dionus continued, "You see, I asked Lyonil to bring you here, but with good reason. It's no big deal. I just have a proposal to make."

"What kind of proposal?" Elize asked.

"It's quite simple. Right now, as it stands, the Judges are nothing more than vigilantes. We could both benefit if we work together."

"And if we don't agree to work with scum such as yourself?"

"I think you'll find the alternative quite unpleasant." Dionus snapped his fingers.

Hundreds of soldiers marched into the court with their rifles armed and ready to fire. They entered from all of the entrances and surrounded the central platform where Darek and his friends were located.

"Those who are not for me are against me." Dionus raised his hand and motioned for the soldiers to hold their fire. "What is your answer?"

While Darek was still tied down, he asked Slade and Elize, "What's the plan?"

Slade said to Darek, "We'll distract them. Take this chance to run." Slade exchanged glances with Elize. Elize lifted her hands; the end of her long sleeves fell down to her shoulders. She stretched out her fingers and her claw-like fingernails extended several inches.

"Wait, you forgot to free me! I can't run away like this." Darek called out to them, but they were so focused on the soldiers around them that they did not hear a word he said.

"The Judges are turning hostile. Open fire!" The soldiers let loose their guns, showering the central platform with a massive hail of bullets.

It was then that Elize's nails seemed to come alive; they rapidly grew nearly seven feet long, twisting and slithering on the floor like snakes. As the bullets drew near to them, her nails lashed out like whips. Every bullet aimed at the central platform was repelled back; not a single bullet could get through. Shocked at how the bullets ricocheted in midair, the soldiers ducked for cover.

Elize leapt across the room. With a few large swipes of her giant claws, their rifles were shredded apart. The soldiers hoped that their armor-plated uniforms would defend against her onslaught, but she tore right through their armor and into their skin.

As Slade watched Elize engage the enemy, his right hand began convulsing; the veins in his forearm became increasingly visible. Small globs of liquid metal leaked out from the skin of his palm. The liquid metal merged together as a thick coating from the tips of his fingers all the way to his elbow. It solidified into a large, flexible gauntlet. Baring his metallic fist, he valiantly charged into a group of soldiers, pummeling them out of his way.

Darek, his hands and feet still tied up, squirmed along the ground. There were stairs that connected the elevated platform to an exit. He tried to worm his way down, but a few soldiers came out of that door and curiously watched Darek as he attempted to pass them.

"Hey look, the criminal is trying to get away," they said, blocking his path.

Darek inched faster, attempting to squeeze between their legs, but they grabbed him with ease and held him at gunpoint. The soldier shouted, "We have your friend! Cease your attack!"

When Elize and Slade heard Darek was captured, they stuck their hands up in surrender. The lights in the room flickered on and off several times before they went out completely. The blackout was momentary. Within seconds, the lights came back on. But Darek was gone. The soldiers, who had been holding onto Darek a moment ago, looked dumbfounded.

Elize stood close to Slade and whispered, "You think they took him somewhere?"

Slade whispered back, "No, it doesn't look like it."

Dionus told his soldiers, "Make sure every exit is sealed. The prisoner must not escape."

The captain nodded. "Yes, sir. We'll get on it right away." He then told his soldiers, "Alpha team, follow me. The rest will stay here and protect the Commander."

As the soldiers marched out, Slade saw this as an opportunity to make an escape. After he made sure no one was watching him, he sprinted to the exit. When he reached the closed door he smashed it open with his fist. But there—waiting for him as the door flung wide open—was Dionus. Slade couldn't believe his eyes. Thinking it was an illusion, he looked back to the place where Dionus was just standing a second ago and did not see him there. Dionus was truly standing right in front him; the man had moved nearly twenty feet in the blink of an eye.

Confused, Slade gasped, "What's this? Anti-law? Spirit displacement?" Slade tightened the grip on his right fist. The metal alloy around his entire arm glowed dark red. He thrust knuckles forward. Slade hit nothing but air, missing the tip of Dionus's nose by less than an inch. Slade tried again and again to punch Dionus. However, one after another, his punches kept missing by just an inch.

"Surrender, Slade," Lyonil advised him. "There's no need to resist. Dionus is not our enemy. We can work together with him."

"You traitor," snapped Slade. "Maybe he's not your enemy, but he's still mine!" Slade threw one more straight punch with all his might. But Dionus sidestepped the attack and cut Slade's legs with his sword. Feeling the sharp pain, Slade reluctantly kneeled down, his thighs bleeding profusely.

"Slade!" shouted Elize, sounding concerned.

Elize aimed her fingernails at Dionus. In an instant they stretched toward him, piercing through the air like javelins with astonishing speed. Dionus dodged her talons and used a rapid succession of slashes to shred her overgrown nails apart. He closed in on her and held the tip of his sword against her throat.

"Get away from her!" Frustrated and furious, Slade struggled to stand, but his bloody legs would not carry him.

"THAT'S ENOUGH, DIONUS!" An alarming shout roared through the chamber.

The upper ceiling of the auditorium crumbled apart and three men fell from above. These men floated down hundreds of feet to land safely upon the central platform.

"Stop this foolishness now!" said the man in the middle, who was robed in red and white garments. The garments covered his head such that his face could not be clearly seen. He wore a mantle over his body that was elaborate and ornamental, studded with gold buttons.

His eyes wide open, Slade said, "At last! Heroes!"

"Heroes? How troublesome," Dionus muttered, as he sheathed his blade and stepped away from Elize. He asked the intruders, "You there—are you truly from the Legion of Heroes? To what do I owe this honor that the Heroes of old should come to see me?"

"Dull your wicked tongue and bow in reverence," the man on the left proclaimed to Dionus, "for the one who stands before you is none other than Xavius!"

Dionus said, "The Archlord Xavius? This is the greatest honor I could possibly receive."

Xavius unraveled the garments around his face. His red hair was like a mighty flame. His light blue eyes, cold as ice, were fixed upon Dionus. He said, "Dionus, I have not come to see you, but to question your actions. First, you must understand that I did not come to impose on your rules and regulations. However, since the dawn of time we—the Legion of Heroes—have had an alliance with them—the Order of Judges. We feel it is only fair to come to their aid as a neutral arbiter.

"For you see, I have received word that you personally produced false evidence against the defendant on trial." Indignant, Xavius yelled out, appealing to the crowd, "Unfair judgment is a crime in the eyes of our law as well as yours! The one known as Darek *must* be released from all charges!"

"I will see to it personally. You need not worry." Dionus smiled and bowed.

Xavius motioned toward Slade. "Since the Judges came to help the defendant who was framed, they must not be held accountable for the damages they have caused in self-defense."

"Of course, I would never think of it." Dionus bowed his head again.

"Xavius!" Slade limped to the Archlord and stumbled as he grabbed the edge of his robe. "Execute Lyonil! He's the one who did this…"

Xavius shook his head. "That is an internal matter for the Judges to deal with. I cannot interfere. Also, the Legion of Heroes only exists to protect good—not to slay evil. Executions are for you, as a Judge, to carry out." He bowed his head toward Slade. "Now that we are done, I must take my leave."

The three Heroes raised their hands. Blue energy sparks rose from the ground and lit the area around them in a radiant glow. They muttered a few words, causing a tornado to rise up from the platform. The Heroes were sucked up instantly into the sky by the powerful whirlwind.

Darek was rudely awoken by a knock to the head. While regaining consciousness, he examined his surroundings and found himself, strangely enough, inside a tight air duct. For every second that passed he felt a heavy tug pull him along. Someone or something was dragging through the ductwork.

Darek screamed, "Hey, let me go! I'm innocent!" He resisted being pulled and struggled to break free, kicking his legs in frustration.

"Stop that. Someone might hear you."

"Jenson! You came!" Surprised to hear the voice of his best friend, Darek calmed down and said, "What are you doing here? I thought you didn't want anything to do with me."

"Did you really think I wouldn't try to help you out?" Without waiting for a response, Jenson warned softly, "By the way, speak in a whisper." He continued to pull Darek along with a rope. "We're not safe just yet."

"Sorry about that." Darek whispered, "So how did you get me out of there?"

"You really want to know?" said Jenson. "It's quite simple. I just had to get past all of their security systems and security guards without being noticed. Then I had to sneak inside their ventilation system and wait for the right time to save you."

Darek laughed. "I bet you're the only one who'd think that's simple."

"Well, that was the simple part. There was nothing I could've done if there wasn't so much chaos in the court." Jenson stopped and cupped his hand over his ear. "Hush."

"What? Do you hear something?" Darek asked.

"What part of hush don't you understand?" snapped Jenson.

Darek heard a loud voice shout, "There are sounds coming from the vents! Check it out!"

"They're onto us," said Jenson. "I'm going to try to rush out of here as fast as I can. Hang on tight! This is going to be pretty rough!"

Jenson crawled like a madman, scrambling through the convoluted, intertwining network of pipes and ducts. Giant rats, each one nearly half the size of a grown man, scurried their fattened selves along, occasionally blocking Jenson's path. However, several loud noises behind him impelled him to get over his disgust and push onward. In his attempt to shoo them away, Jenson slapped the rats around, but not without being gnawed at. Darek lifted his head and saw the soldiers clumsily climb into the ductwork with their guns by their side.

"They're gaining on us," said Darek. "Can't you go any faster?"

"I'm moving as fast as I can!" Jenson replied.

"Halt! Stay where you are or we'll open fire." The soldier right behind them fell into a prone position and aimed his gun at Darek. "This is your last warning."

"Geez, you're so slow, Jenson," Darek grumbled. "What's holding you back? They're going to kill us and here you are pacing yourself!"

Jenson spat, "You're the one holding me back! Do you have any idea how heavy you are? Besides, you were the one blabbering with that big mouth of yours and got us caught in the first place. You know what? I'm not risking my life for this." Jenson shouted to the men behind them, "Don't shoot! We surrender!"

The soldiers slung their rifles across their side and began crawling toward the boys.

"What are you doing? Don't surrender," Darek said. "They're still going to kill us! The only difference is when!"

"Yeah, you're right." Jenson kicked the bottom of the duct as hard as he could.

"Wha-what are you doing now?" Darek turned his head around as far back as he could to see what Jenson was up to. "You're not serious?"

Jenson kicked the bottom of the duct six times with all his might and the bottom gave way, opening up a small hole. "Stop fretting, I've got this all planned out."

"We're going *down*? You're crazy! At least untie me— AAAAAAAAAAH!"

Darek couldn't tell much of what was going on. His body felt weightless as they fell and he could see the light fading behind them as they went deeper and deeper. The blind ride was extremely rough. Since he was still restrained, he was slammed against the walls, giving him a big headache. After five long minutes of sliding, falling, and smashing around, they finally fell through a chute and landed awkwardly on top of each other on the tiled floor.

Darek looked around. They had fallen into the maintenance closet—a small room filled with robots of all shapes and sizes that kept the facility in good shape.

Jenson, still dizzy from the ride, hopped up to his feet. In a hurry, he plugged a cable from his handheld pc into the sidewall panel; fingers rapidly buzzing across the keyboard, he typed in all sorts of codes to hack into the system. Darek heard the loud banging above them, expecting the soldiers to fall out of the chute at any moment.

"Stop wasting time! We've got to get out of here!" His limbs shackled, Darek wriggled around helplessly.

Jenson said nothing and stared at the screen.

Darek asked, "What's wrong?"

He shrugged. "You can't be too sure with these things."

"Well, hurry it up!" Darek froze. He could hear their approach getting ever closer. He wanted to run, but with his arms and legs bound, all he could do was squirm.

When the soldiers reached the exit, it looked as though they had slammed up against an invisible wall. The soldiers were right there in front of them, and it looked like they could just step out of the chute. However, all they did was pound their fists wildly in the air. They opened their mouths wide to shout and scream, but no voices came out.

"Looks like the force-field is working properly," Jenson said. "I had to disable it earlier to get in. Don't worry. It's also soundproof." Jenson hurried to a stash of his belongings hidden inside the remains of an old, broken robot in the corner and took out a few things. He slipped a protective covering over Darek's skin where he was bound. Then Jenson poured an acidic solution on the Slythian shackles, corroding them into a black sludge.

Finally free from his bonds, Darek jumped to his feet, grabbed Jenson by the shoulders and shook him back and forth; his head bounced like a bobblehead. "What's wrong with you? You should've told me your plan! You had me all worried for nothing!"

Jenson shrugged in reply, smirking.

Darek sat down on the floor, looking exhausted. "All this excitement is wearing me out."

"Don't take it easy just yet." Jenson reached for the ITD in his pocket and handed it to Darek. "We're not safe until you get off this station. Take my ITD."

Darek pushed it away, shaking his head. "I can't accept this."

Jenson grabbed Darek's hand, pried open his fingers and smacked the ITD in his palm.

He said, "Just take it. Think of it as a farewell present. I can always make another one. It'll just take another year of savings."

"A farewell present?" Darek chewed his lip as some emotions riled up within him. "I'm not going anywhere. I'll just hide out somewhere in Albiore."

"Darek!" Now it was Jenson's turn to grab him and shake some sense into him. "Listen to me. It's the Federation we're dealing with! If you go back to Albiore, they *will* find you. No…if you stay anywhere in Federation space, they'll find you! You saw what they were going to do—they were going to kill you!" Releasing Darek, Jenson said reasonably, "You have to get out of here!"

Darek fell silent and closed his eyes. After thinking about it, he opened his eyes and looked straight at Jenson. "You're right. Even if I don't mind endangering myself, I don't want anyone else dragged into this." He clenched his hand around the ITD. "Fine—I'll go."

"Good." Beaming, Jenson looked satisfied. "We don't have much time. Let me quickly explain all I can about the ITD and how to use it." He strapped the ITD on Darek's wrist and flipped open the top cover to reveal several buttons. "Pay attention. On the top is your destination. You can either put in the planet name or code." Jenson pointed to the various buttons. "This starts the teleportation and the other cancels it. One thing you must know about teleporting is that it does not send you straight to the destination, but rather it follows a certain path. You'll be sent to the nearest planet along the path, and then when you arrive at that planet, it'll send you to the next planet. It'll keep going like this. Understand?"

Darek scratched his head quizzically. "No."

Jenson said, continuing, "Each planet is basically what we'd call a hop point. You hop from one planet to next. The line of planets will form a path to the destination. This ensures that you reach the destination safely. Because of this simple system, you won't end up in some random nebula. I won't say that it's absolutely safe, but your chances of survival are high."

"Chances?" Darek was appalled at the thought of it. "It doesn't always work?"

Jenson cleared his throat and tapped his fingers against the wall to hide his nervousness, though it seemed to have the opposite effect. "Er—well, you know, it's almost guaranteed to work...most of the time. There are some factors that may change the result. Like, for instance, if the device goes haywire, you may never escape the tunnel, or if your final destination is no longer around, you may land in space. But other than that...it *should* be pretty safe."

Darek gulped. "That doesn't sound very reassuring..."

"It's your only hope, so just utter a prayer before you use it." Jenson opened the door of the room. "That's all you need to know. It's time for you to get out of here. Don't worry about anything and go. Make a left here and look for a window on the right side. Jump out. From there, you can use the ITD. I don't know if the ITD works indoors and now's not a good time to test it." Jenson passed a sealed envelope to Darek. "This could also be useful."

"What is it?"

"The package for the job we swapped. I was going to do it myself but I figured we could knock the lights out of two birds with one stone. Since the destination is out of Federation space, it'll be a good hideout. And after you get paid, you'll have some credits to use. You'll need the money."

Darek nodded. "Thanks. I'll try to contact you when I can."

"Don't take any risks. If you really have to contact me, use the most indirect way possible. Oh, and I almost forgot." Then Jenson walked over to a box on the floor and opened it up. Inside the box was an assortment of things that he had hidden there. He took out a wooden board and gave it to Darek. "Here, you'll need this for the trip." Jenson also pulled out Darek's daggers. "It could be dangerous. You might need these too. I found them...lying around."

Darek looked at the things Jenson gave him and grinned. "Great job. You've gone above and beyond again, my friend."

Even though Darek smiled, Jenson could see a tear in his eyes— a tear of worry. He patted him on the back. "I'm sure it won't be long before everything sorts itself out. I don't know what the future holds, but be strong. Space…is really cold. And I don't mean that in a literal sense. It's corny, I know, but it's the truth. Out there, where you don't know anyone, you'll be all alone. No one will help you. No one will care about you. But don't doubt. Don't worry. I want you to promise me…"

"What?" Darek cocked his head.

Jenson continued, "Promise me no matter what happens, you won't give up hope. I know it'll be hard, but never give up. When you sit under the starry sky…wherever you are…remember. We'll see each other again—as long as you stay alive."

"I-I promise." There was uncertainty in Darek's voice. When he was in jail just moments ago he already had abandoned the concept of hope. Giving up was so easy and tempting. How much harder will it be to persevere when there are no friends around to support him?

Jenson said, "All right then! Have a safe trip and good luck."

Darek took a deep breath and then recklessly jumped out the door. He ran as fast as he could, hoping no one would notice. Before he even had time to catch another breath, gunshots blasted all around him. One bullet barely managed to nick him in the knee. It was a light flesh wound, but even so, it was his first time getting shot; he was shocked and collapsed.

The soldiers' surprise attack even caught Jenson off-guard. He never expected them to storm the hall so quickly. He tried to stall them by turning their own security systems against them. The rest of the fired bullets bounced off a newly activated force field. Smoggy exhaust poured out of the vents, smothering the soldiers.

Fully aware that staying in the middle of the floor would be dangerous, Darek gritted his teeth and ignored the pain. Taking the opportunity given by Jenson, Darek crawled along the ground and pulled himself over the small window.

Splash! He fell ten feet down into a deep fountain of water. Darek stood up, completely drenched. *I made it*, he thought. *Now I just have to…*

Soldiers surrounded the fountain and locked their sights on Darek. "There he is! Don't let him escape! Restrain him! Even if he is marked for death, a public execution is preferred."

Darek sighed. "I never get a break, do I?" He flicked open the cover for the ITD and pressed the start button. He mockingly waved goodbye to the soldiers as the stream of light came over him; within moments he vanished from their sight, freely soaring high into space.

CHAPTER 6
The Encounter

A stream of brilliant light tore through the blackness of space. The bridge of the *Avenger 076*, a mercenary spacecraft, watched in curiosity as the light fell onto a nearby planet.

"Can you identify it?" asked Captain Bayrum, stifling a yawn.

Captain Jim Bayrum slouched into his chair. No longer as young as he once was, the mercenary found it difficult to stay sharp after going thirty-six hours without sleep. He wearily glanced at the cup of coffee by the armrest. The coffee wasn't doing its job. His heavy eyelids struggled to stay over his throbbing red eyes.

Ever since it had been discovered that the Judges did indeed exist, rich rewards were being offered left and right for the capture or killing of Judges. The bounties offered by the Federation were next to nothing compared to the riches being offered by the heads of the underworld. This hapless crew of money-hungry mercenaries happened to be one of many who had entered this great race to be the first to find the notorious Judges and their elusive hideout.

A young crewman responded to the captain, "Sensors detect abnormally high energy readings. It's a teleportation stream."

"Oh?" The captain's interest was piqued. "Any kind of identification signature?"

The crewman shook his head and replied, "Nothing at all."

"Nothing?" The captain's eyes grew wide as he jumped out of his chair and clenched his fist. "Great, this could be it—our first big lead! Trace its origin now!"

The crewman tried to follow the captain's orders. But as soon as he began checking the computer, his expression changed to bewilderment. "The trail…disappeared. The particles dispersed almost immediately."

A grin managed to sneak upon Bayrum's face. "Interesting. Very interesting." Bayrum slumped back into his chair and let out a sigh. "Right now it could be anything. I want to thoroughly investigate this. Pinpoint the destination of the light. Oh, and tell Sorren to get up here."

"No need." Sorren entered the bridge. "I came as soon as I saw the light."

Fear struck deep in the hearts of the crew as Sorren walked into the bridge. His dark gray robe, tied with a cloth belt at the waist, draped to the floor, swaying side to side as he walked forward. A large hood covered his face, making it hard to see what his visage.

"I want you to check it out," said Jim. "Hopefully, we'll have our first target." Bayrum rubbed his chin a bit. "Do you mind handling this on your own? I don't have crew to spare. I'll need all my men to investigate the possible origin of the stream."

"I work better alone anyway," said Sorren.

"I'm glad that won't be a problem." Bayrum looked Sorren in the eye. "Our scans of the surface aren't showing much aside from ruins. The planet may very well be deserted. Just do a brief search of the area. We'll be back in a week to pick you up. Is that enough time?"

Sorren headed for the elevator. "I'll see what I can do." After Sorren had left the room, the tense atmosphere that filled the bridge was lifted, and all of the crewmembers heaved a collective sigh, relieved that he was gone.

One of the crewmen said to Captain Bayrum, "I don't see why you had to go and hire an assassin like him."

Captain Bayrum laughed heartily. "I've worked with him several times in the past. He has never let me down. He might seem unpleasant at first, but he's really not that bad once you get to know him."

Sorren stood motionless in the descending elevator. The elevator doors were crystal clear, allowing him to look through each and every floor as he went. Each floor of the ship was long and fairly wide but there were only seven floors in total from top to bottom.

Originally a small cargo ship, the *Avenger 076* had been refitted for general mercenary use. The overall structure of the ship was simple in design, shaped almost like a rectangular solid. Some of the cargo space inside had been sacrificed to make room for more living space to house a larger crew. For combat situations, the entire hull was reinforced from the inside out and the exterior had multiple camouflaged turrets. Most of the ship was lightly armored to maximize agility. The seemingly defenseless appearance allowed it to be seen as an average cargo ship. Heavier plates of armor were secured around the bridge and the engine room, which the crew had considered to be the most vital components.

The elevator came to a halt and the elevator door opened. Sorren walked into the docking bay, which was bustling with activity. The bay was only able to accommodate a handful of space fighters and shuttles.

The space fighters they had on board were Fuzers, which were typical among mercenary circles. They were easily identifiable by its butterfly-like design. The fragile spherical cockpit was nestled safely between two thick boomerang-shaped wings.

Despite the craft's odd-looking design, the main reason for their popularity was because Fuzers were perfect for the growing needs of a mercenary. Buying a Fuzer was affordable and easy. Though their starting performance was poor, mercenaries could constantly refit the ships with upgrades as they worked their way up. More importantly, mercenaries could modify Fuzers to deal with specific scenarios. However, it was practically only used by mercenaries because, in the long run, it proved to be far too time consuming for anyone else to consistently upgrade the ship to acceptable levels of performance.

They only had four Fuzers in the bay. Though the ships were few, the ardent mechanics worked feverishly to ensure that each and every ship was in perfect condition. As veteran mercenaries they knew all too well that scouring the unexplored regions of space could lead to unforeseen and dangerous circumstances. They had to be ready for anything: pirates, fugitives, rebels, terrorists, zealots, and maybe even…space monsters.

However, what they feared most in this forsaken region were the violent Anarchists. The Anarchists were a fearsome group of extremists. For some unknown reason, they had access to technologies far more advanced than anything in the Federation. Against any other foe, the mercenaries might be able to escape; however, to escape a fight from the Anarchists would be near impossible.

Sorren proceeded past the diligent workers and headed for his shuttle. He had left his shuttle at the very end of the docking bay, as close to the exit as possible. This was because Sorren wasn't really cut out to be a pilot, and he knew that very well. If he were to steer his shuttle around the docking bay, it was quite possible for him to snap a wing off a Fuzer or even knock a few helpless mechanics into space.

An uneasy feeling settled in his stomach as he sat in the pilot's seat and buckled himself in. Sorren glanced over to his left side and found his sword propped up against the wall.

The sword was his life. It was not a special sword by any means. In fact, he had just recently purchased it from a thrift shop. It didn't matter what kind of sword it was; he just needed one by his side. It was his security blanket and he wouldn't go anywhere without it.

His fears subsided and he took the shuttle into space. From the cockpit he could see a glimpse of the planet ahead. He was about to switch on the autopilot, but hesitated when he noticed a strange object shooting through space. He had a bad feeling about it.

Sorren initiated a comlink with the *Avenger 076*. "Command, are your sensors picking up anything? I think I see something—but it's not showing up on radar." Wary, Sorren eased up on the throttle and waited for a response from the captain.

"Our friend seems concerned," Captain Bayrum said to his crew. "Does anyone have an answer for him?"

"Sorry," one of his crewmen replied, "I don't understand it myself. Whatever it is, it's not showing up on our radars either. Should I bring up a visual?"

"Please do."

A room-enveloping hologram was projected from the floor of the bridge and the entire bridge became like space itself. The mysterious object in question was revealed in the center of the room, near Captain Bayrum's chair. It appeared to be a black, egg-shaped object, no greater than six yards in length. Its exterior was of a finely polished crystalline coating. On the front it had the basic design of the human eye etched in, and on the back was the engraving of a mouth.

Everyone on the bridge gawked at the object.

Captain Bayrum got up from his chair and broke the silence. "What is that *thing*?"

"It doesn't look organic. Could be an artifact from the lost civilization of Erdaska," said a mercenary uncertainly. "I've never seen anything like it in my life before."

"Sir." A crewman stood up with a look of surprise. "We're picking up a signal coming from the object."

"A signal? Decode it immediately," ordered the Captain.

"I can't!" He hammered away at the computer, panicking. "That was the first thing I tried, but now it's hacking into—"

The ship trembled. All the monitors of the bridge began flickering on and off. The displays, instead of performing their intending functions, now showed the face of a woman. A large glossy visor was over her eyes and a strange black chain was attached to her neck. The woman appeared to be cramped inside a dark cockpit.

"You cannot land on this planet." A woman's voice came from the speakers and it was believed to correspond to the woman on the screen, however, her lips did not move as she spoke. "Have your shuttle return to your ship."

Bayrum was a little shaken at how eerie the whole encounter was. He regained his composure and said, "You have no authority over us."

"Authority and law do not matter," the woman said. "You cannot land here."

Captain Bayrum paused and tried to think of the best way to approach this. "Is there any kind of deal we can strike? I'm sure we can work something out."

"No," said the woman. "Leave immediately…or face death. You have no options."

"Are you threatening us?" snapped Bayrum. "We are citizens of the Federation! I suggest you leave us alone, unless you want to be in trouble with the Federation fleet."

"The Federation? My apologies, then." In an instant the woman's face disappeared from all of the display screens, and the screens returned back to normal.

Captain Bayrum fell back into his chair. He wiped off the sweat from his brow and took a few deep breaths. "Now that wasn't so bad. I thought for a moment there—"

A violent tremor ran across the entire ship. Sparks of electricity began bursting through all of the electrical systems. All the computers and lights shut off completely.

"A virus has terminated existing systems," said the voice of the computer. "Emergency systems are now online and functional." Red lights dimly lit up the bridge and the crew tried their best to remain calm in their state of fear.

The emergency communications was activated. "This is Sorren speaking. The black object is now pursuing me. Requesting back-up or further orders."

"Keep going," Bayrum said, "we're coming to help." Captain Bayrum then told the rest of his crew on the bridge, "Get those systems back online!" Everyone nodded in response and immediately began working on repairs.

The captain ran to the elevator. Since the power was down and the elevator door wouldn't work, he kicked open the side hatch and slid down a long ladder that went all the way to the docking bay.

Dashing into the docking bay, Bayrum shouted, "Let's go, let's go!" He hollered as he ran toward his own Fuzer. "Let's get these ships out of here now!"

The pilots answered the call of their captain. Captain Bayrum and three of his best pilots hopped into their ships, put on their helmets and locked themselves inside their cockpits. The Fuzers scrambled out of the docking bay like birds taking flight and they rocketed into space one after the other.

The space fighters slowly moved into a triangular formation and set their sights on Sorren's location. With the full acceleration of their boosters, they managed to catch up to Sorren quite easily.

"Sorren," said Captain Bayrum through the comlink, "we'll cover you. Don't look back. Just head for the planet."

Sorren tried his best to ignore the strange spacecraft that hovered around him. An unnerving feeling crept over him. Sensing the danger, Sorren tried to squeeze as much power out of the engine as he could. It was risky to enter the atmosphere at full speed, but it was a risk he had to take. There was no telling what that black ship was capable of.

The Fuzers opened fire, blasting the mysterious craft with high-intensity lasers. Every shot was smoothly reflected off the surface of the black ship. The black ship continued on, unscathed. However, the ship seemed annoyed by the Fuzers' attempts to injure it and, all of a sudden, began maneuvering sporadically, as though it had lost control of its thrusters.

"Lasers have no effect," said one of the pilots, "Time to try out the missiles." He moved his Fuzer ahead and, with his excellent piloting skills, managed to keep up with the black ship despite its odd maneuvering.

"Watch it," warned Bayrum, "don't get too close!"

The black ship reversed its momentum, suddenly accelerating in the opposite direction. The mercenary didn't see it coming. It was too late for the Fuzer to evade. As the black ship rammed into the Fuzer, the pilot screamed. In the blink of an eye, the Fuzer was shattered into space dust.

"Did you see that? It just ripped right through!" shouted a pilot, sounding deathly terrified.

"Don't bother thinking about it," Bayrum said. "Just blow it apart!"

"Roger that," the pilots answered.

The remaining three Fuzers hastily surrounded the black ship and launched a round of their missiles, hoping to end the conflict in one blow. When the missiles got closer to the strange craft, the missiles began to decelerate as if time was slowing down; each and every missile that was fired came to a steady halt. It was then that a giant red net of energy could be seen floating around the black ship, ensnaring the missiles in its sticky web.

"What is that?" asked a bewildered pilot.

The net of energy grew in intensity. All the missiles exploded in unison, unleashing a massive, amplified shockwave that caught all three Fuzers off-guard and enveloped them in a breath of fire.

"AAAAAAAARGH! I-I CAN'T SEE!"

"IT'S COMING BACK! WATCH OUT!"

"TOO LATE! I CAN'T GET OUT OF THE WAY! I'M—"

CHAPTER 7
Desert Nights

The noonday sun took its place proudly at the top of the sky, heating up the desert with its brilliant rays. It was a rather plain desert. Monstrous dunes stretched across the land. Life was scarce, consisting mainly of little critters that scuttled back and forth, shuffling into the shade of whatever they could find. But amidst this ordinary desert, which seemed relatively uninhabited, there was a lone person who made his way across the endless inferno. And his name was Darek.

All he did was groan as the sweat of his skin sizzled off. He had never been in a desert before. But he hoped that this first experience was his last. The desert was far too inhospitable for his tastes. *This is torture.* If he was going to die anyway, a painless and quick public execution sounded more appealing. Displeased with his own grim thoughts, he slapped himself in the face. *No, no, no. I must stay optimistic. I must be as cheery as can be. This boiling heat feels great! It's so great to be alive!*

After traveling for a while he finally came across a small boulder. It was the only boulder in the middle of the desert and struck his mind as peculiar. But things like its life's history or how it got there was none of his concern. Darek took the pleasure of resting under its shade. But what was he going to do now? There was nothing to quench his growing thirst. It wouldn't be long before he'd succumb to dehydration.

With no end to the heat and no place to go, Darek lay there, thinking something good might happen if he simply waited. As he closed his eyes, several possible scenarios crossed through his mind. Maybe, if he were lucky, someone would walk over, see him lying there and take him to a nearby village where he could eat and drink his fill. But that was a bit of a stretch, even for wishful thinking. It would be more probable for a rainstorm to conveniently pass over with its deliciously cool droplets—except there was not a single cloud in the sky.

Darek opened his eyes and sighed. He hissed out plenty of unpleasant curses at the ITD. Why was there no function on the darn thing to steer clear of death traps? Going to a remote planet to hide was, in theory, a good idea. However, why—out of all the millions of possible places on this huge planet—did he land in the middle of a desert? On the worst day of his life, this was the worst place to be.

Darek sat up and checked the ITD. He was not going to stand for this. There had to be somewhere else he could go—anywhere but here. The ITD's screen came up blank. He impatiently pushed a few buttons and tapped the screen, hoping it was merely turned off or that it had a standby function. There was no response. It was out of power.

"This sucks," he muttered, falling back into the sand. "This *really* sucks."

He was stuck on this planet. All he had was an ITD that didn't work, a pair of daggers and a wooden board. The wooden board was useless now, so he tossed it aside. There was no food or water. And this little slice of shade wasn't going to save him from sweltering under the sun. Death seemed ever so close now.

But if he gave up so easily, he knew his friends would never forgive him. Darek sat up and scanned the vast desert as far as his eyes could see. He took off his thin ragged jacket and put it over his head in an attempt to avoid a heat stroke. Since there was nothing for him in that place, staying there wouldn't help him at all.

Darek began on a long trek across the desert. He would look up at the sky from time to time, searching for rain clouds. But every time he looked, there was nothing except for the clear bluish-green sky. He constantly grumbled. His muddy sneakers were now filled to the brim with sand that painfully rubbed between his toes. An occasional strong gust of wind blew coarse sand into his eyes and teeth. The blazing heat radiated all around. His view of the land was distorted and warped, making him feel very dizzy as he walked around in circles.

Darek walked on for half an hour. Even though it had only been a short time since he began his walk, his parched mouth desperately craved water. Darek thought his tonsil was going to dry up and crack apart. Filled with so much frustration at his dire situation, he yelled to the sky, "Even a little droplet will do, just give me anything! Please!"

No droplet fell from the sky. But, seemingly as if his request had been granted in an unexpected way, he stumbled across a small field of cacti. He had seen pictures of cacti in television shows and magazines, but this was the first time he saw them in person.

But there was something strange about these cacti, like a possible mutation of some sort. Each cactus was round, plump and extremely large, like giant green spheres. Darek estimated them to be more than ten feet in height since they were nearly double his size. Despite their staggering size, the brown prickly needles that protruded from the surface were tiny, like fine hairs, almost giving the impression of a cactus having fur.

Darek's imagination ran wild with the ideas of a massive reservoir of water that lay untapped under the surface of the cactus. He was so eager for a drink that, no matter how unwise and painful it might be, he was compelled to chomp down into it for that refreshing thirst quencher. Fortunately for him, the risk for that one life-threatening bite of water was unnecessary because he had his daggers to work with as a tool.

He glanced across the field of cacti and found one suitable to his liking; it was the biggest of them all and appeared most ripe. Of course, Darek had no knowledge of how to determine the ripeness of a strange, alien cactus, but it appeared best because of its darker green color.

He casually walked toward it. With every step he took, the ground shifted slightly—something he found very odd. Even more surprising was that the cactus had a reaction to his advance. As he neared it, the cactus started getting bigger and bigger. It wobbled and swayed like a pendulum. Darek had a bad feeling about it. Crouching down, he brushed away the sand at his feet and found a large network of fat squishy roots that fanned out far from the cactus.

With his finger, Darek poked the moist root and every time he did so, the cactus responded by ballooning. It swelled up so much that it looked like the plant would burst at any moment. Darek gawked at the sight. Whatever was happening, it looked dangerous. Fearing for his life, he ran away, trying to put as much distance as he could between him and the cactus. But in doing so, he stomped carelessly over the underground network of roots. The giant cactus was now over fifteen feet tall, stretched and expanded beyond recognition like a bubble about to pop.

All at once, thousands of tiny needles burst out of the surface of the skin. It literally created a massive barrage of needles, like shrapnel, that flew in all directions. Darek cried when hundreds of these tiny needles penetrated the back of his body from head to heel. He fell facedown in the sand, helpless. First there was pain—then the pain faded and his vision went blurry. He pushed against the ground, trying to get up, but there was no strength left in his arms. Darek collapsed, slowly drifting out of consciousness.

A gust of bone-chilling air found its way inside the cave. Darek woke up, agitated by the frigid temperatures. He rubbed his arms frantically to stay warm. While observing his new surroundings, he shivered uncontrollably, his teeth chattering.

The last thing he remembered was being in a field of cacti; at that time, he was nowhere near any kind of shelter. Also, when he had passed out, the sun was still shining, but now the sun was long gone. Only by a sliver of moonlight was he able to see anything in that dark cave. How long had he been asleep?

The cave was shallow and narrow. Darek could just barely make out where the end of the cave was and it was only a few yards from where he was sitting. The cave was large enough, however, that he could stand up straight and not hit his head against the ceiling.

His only clue as to how he got there was the crusty remains of a fire. Someone must have carried him inside. There weren't any other manmade items around, but the embers still gave their soft orangey glow, leading him to believe that the fire was snuffed out not too long ago. Even the scent of the smoke still lingered in his nostrils.

From the corner of his eye, he noticed several small logs along the ground that he could use as firewood. Since nobody was around, and Darek had no idea when or if anybody would ever return, Darek decided to start up the fire again.

Now Darek was no expert on making fires. During his days at the orphanage, Miss Kurt would give certain duties to the four of them, but since Slade was the oldest he was the one in charge of making the fires. Darek had never done it before, but there was a first time for everything.

Darek took the logs and placed them neatly on top of the charcoal. He ran into his first problem when he realized he didn't have any matches or a lighter. Taking several sticks, he scraped them together, thinking he could start up a spark. To his dismay, Darek did this for about ten minutes without any results. Darek stopped when he heard a loud shuffling noise.

Darek swallowed. "Is someone out there?" The wind howled at the entrance. Darek took a few steps back. "Hello? Is anyone there?" Darek watched the entrance closely.

The sound of soft footsteps gently prodded Darek's ears. Was it his imagination? He was did not see anyone coming inside, yet the footsteps could still be heard.

Darek continued to watch, waiting patiently for something to happen—and something did happen, but not what he expected. Darek gasped and gagged. He felt like he was being choked. Struggling, he could feel his entire body being lifted off the ground. He was not able to see anyone or anything around at all. Darek dropped the sticks in his hand, reached for his dagger and swung it wildly, trying to break free from the mysterious grasp on his neck. A howl, full of pain, resounded throughout the cave as Darek fell to the ground.

Darek scrambled to his feet. The sound of bodiless footsteps began once again, inching closer to him. Darek threw a dagger ahead. He watched in horror as the daggers were deflected in midair. *What is this? A ghost?* Huddled against the back of the cave, Darek stared at the cave entrance. His heart skipped beats when he heard and even felt the warm breath of his invisible assailant.

Darek buried his face in his arms, too terrified to look up. "What do you want? Go away! Leave me alone!"

A loud snarl cut him to his heart. Despair gushed in his mind. This was not the sound of a human. Before he could let out a scream, he heard the voice of a young woman.

"Sorry I'm late!"

A woman entered the cave and, with a bucket, tossed wet sand along the back of the invisible creature in order to reveal its hideous form. With only its back visible, Darek could tell that it was quite large, much bigger than he was. He couldn't really make out its shape. It looked to him like a hornless bull with a huge head.

She kicked the beast aside and walked up to Darek, saying, "I'll deal with this."

The girl, who was not much older than Darek, had long dark blue hair. Her attire consisted of loose fitting garments that bore a lion's insignia on her back. She had a strong demeanor and stared down at Darek with a condescending smirk. Her eyes gleamed from the moonlight, revealing sharp, catlike pupils. She turned around and faced the monster.

The hungry beast charged toward her head first, but she easily sidestepped its momentum. The monster spun right around and rushed at her again, but this time she slipped away, just barely dodging its head. Poised for her counterattack, she landed a swift and sharp chop at the back of its neck.

Knees buckling, the beast froze in place. Her opponent now stunned and defenseless, the young woman pulled her fist back. With one explosive punch, she sent the beast flying into the wall. A large crack formed along the wall of the cave where the beast was felled. The strange creature did not appear so terrifying anymore as it lay there unconscious.

Darek watched as the woman stood over the beast. She fumbled around with her hands until she got hold of the slightly visible head of the monster.

"What do you think you're doing?" Darek almost felt sick to his stomach and winced as she let out a loud crack from the beast's neck. At first he was still quivering from the incident but now he was just disturbed by what she had done. "You didn't have to kill it, did you?"

The young woman raised her brow. "Did you bump your head or something? This thing tried to eat you! I'm just returning the favor."

"Of course it's going to try to eat me. The creature was hungry."

"Well," she said with a grin, "I'm hungry too. Now be a good boy and hand me your knives. I want to clean up the meat."

"You're not serious are you?" The thought of eating some weird monster made him want to puke.

"Oh, I'm quite serious." The woman set some kindling upon the logs. Within a few seconds of igniting a spark with flint, she was able to get a small fire going. A few more steady puffs of air and the flame started to look like a strong fire. "What's your name, kid?"

"I'd appreciate it if you stop calling me kid. You don't look much older. The name's Darek...Darek Wayker."

"Oh," she said, sounding uninterested. "Not much older, huh? How old are you?"

"Fifteen," Darek replied.

"Well, I'm twenty," said the girl, "and that's enough for me to keep calling you kid."

Darek had a look of disdain at her comment. He was quite bitter at her attitude.

"Lighten up," she said, laughing, "I'm only kidding." She set up a rough construction of moist sticks to hold up the meat along the flames. "I'm Azura. Nice to meet you." She grabbed one of Darek's daggers that he had thrown before and started to slice off some of the meat.

"Don't do that!" Darek protested, snatching his dagger away from her. "I don't remember giving you permission to use it."

Azura shrugged. "Fine, have it your way." She picked up a lump of meat and simply chomped down on it, tearing off the bits of meat with her teeth. After a few chews, she spit out a wad of hair. She licked her lips saying, "Not bad. Not bad at all." She glanced at Darek. "I was pretty surprised to find someone in this desert. What were you doing out there?"

He glanced at her with a careful eye, thinking of how to reply. "Just waiting for my friends," he lied. He didn't lie for the sake of lying, but on an unknown primitive planet, it was taboo to speak of other worlds. There was no telling what might happen.

"Friends? There's no one around for miles!" Azura let out a hearty belch and tossed aside the meatless bone.

"I got a little lost." Darek averted his eyes as he changed the subject. "And what are you doing here?"

"Isn't it obvious?" Azura brushed the sand off the meat as she took another bite. "I'm eating." Within a few minutes of voraciously snacking upon the invisible meat, she began explaining. "You see, it's hard to find a decent meal around here—too many poisonous little creatures. The larger monsters also seem to avoid me. So when I found you unconscious, I thought of a great idea. Since you looked so defenseless, you'd work great as bait!" She smiled to herself, looking pleased that the idea had worked so well.

Darek gaped at her, awestruck. "You used me as bait? What kind of person would use a defenseless person as bait for a monster?"

She ignored him and kept on eating. Darek sat there silently, examining her like some kind of weird animal. Her appetite was unfathomable to Darek, for she was able to eat the whole body of the monster, eyeballs and brains included, and still clamored for more. The sight of it totally grossed him out but he held back all urges to retch. After she finished eating, she got up and walked toward the exit of the cave.

"I'm full enough," she said. "Ready to go?"

"Go where?" asked Darek. "There's nothing out there."

"Are you from this planet?"

"Of course. Where else would I…" His voice stopped as soon as he realized what she was asking. That question was not something a native would ask. They would usually ask about where he was from, but not if he was from another planet. Sensing no hostility from her, he gave in and revealed the truth. "No. I just got here. I kind of came here on accident."

"Ah, so that explains it."

"Explains what?"

Azura looked him straight in the eye. "This is no place for travelers," she warned, her face darkening. "You should leave immediately." She left the cave.

Darek followed after her. "What do you mean?"

She tried her best to explain in a calm voice. "I was sent by the Legion of Heroes to investigate this planet because of mysterious reports. As you probably know, this area of space is far from Federation territory. There was a recent spark of activity in this sector. It was odd for activity in a remote area. Upon exploring we found remains of an advanced civilization.

"We thought this civilization had reached an age of space exploration. But I've been investigating for several days and have found nothing—well, nothing but monsters that is."

"Monsters? You mean like that weird invisible thing?" Darek turned pale.

She nodded. "Yes, the existence of monsters is rare. Their existence and birth are shrouded in mystery, but since they are few, it was never a problem. But that is different here. I cannot even begin to grasp the magnitude of the infestation."

"Then help me get off this planet," Darek demanded.

"Why? Can't you just leave the way you came?"

"Well...no." Darek scratched his head. "You see, my teleport is out of power and my friends won't be coming after me, so—"

"Can't help you," Azura interrupted. "I'm sorry."

"Why not?" Darek was frustrated and a little scared. The thought of staying on a planet full of dangerous monsters, like the one she had just eaten, was not his idea of an escape. He'd much rather be hiding from people, who want him for crimes, rather than be hiding from monsters that want him for a snack. "You must have some way out. A ship! A teleport! I'll take anything!"

"Well, to tell you the truth," there was sadness in her voice as she spoke, "I came here with a partner. He was proficient in anti-law and knew the power of teleportation. But when we landed...let's just say, we landed in a bad spot. I barely escaped, but he wasn't as fortunate."

"Anti-law? What's that?"

"The power to defy the laws of nature," she explained. "The common and simplified term is magic, though it's not really the same."

"Wait," said Darek, "does that mean you're stuck here too?"

Azura shrugged. "Pretty much."

Darek was at a loss for words. There was no place for him to go, and from her description of the situation, it seemed it wouldn't be safe anywhere.

Azura saw that Darek was pretty upset over the matter and pitied him. "It's not all hopeless. Come with me. There might still be some human villages. It's always possible."

"Really?"

Azura smiled and said, "I'm sure we'll run into someone eventually. If worse comes to worst, my friends will come for me when they find out I haven't returned."

Darek found comfort in her words and presence. Before she had mentioned that the Legion of Heroes had sent her to this planet. Ever since he was little he was taught to trust the Heroes. They were the protectors of good. He had heard courageous tales of how they fought against monsters and villains, all for the sake of keeping the peace. He also had witnessed the greatness of her strength first hand.

Then he took a moment to briefly think about his situation. Did he really want to be stuck in this cave alone in a dangerous world full of man-eating monsters? The answer was an obvious no. Darek quickly grabbed his satchel and said, "All right, I'm ready. Let's go."

Azura snapped her fingers. "Yeah, that's the spirit! Let's go!"

CHAPTER 8
Lost Memories

Faint birdcalls echoed along the dense wall of trees. The leaf canopy blocked out all of the sun's rays, bathing everything in darkness. However, there was one tiny spot in the forest where sunlight was able to penetrate: it was the crash site of a shuttle.

After breaking through the atmosphere, Sorren had reversed his thrusters at maximum power to negate the momentum. The final result was a relatively safe landing; despite the heavy damage to the hull, the interior of the ship was intact.

The jerky ride caused blood to rush to his head. Sorren kicked open the shuttle door, staggered out and toppled to the ground. Grimacing, he crawled into the dusky shade of the trees. The darkness felt good—incredibly good. He slouched against a tree trunk, gripping his temple. While resting there, he felt a surge of life return to his body. He examined his shuttle. The impact wasn't too severe. The canopy was sturdy enough to break the fall. The systems were operational, but it would still require extensive repair before it could fly again.

He faced a dilemma. The black ship they had encountered was quite adamant about not wanting them to land on the planet. He had an idea about who those assailants were; and if he was right about them, the mercenaries were most likely all dead by now. His pursuers would undoubtedly try to track him down. And a shuttle on a primitive planet such as this one would stick out like a sore thumb. Time was of the essence. If he wanted to erase any traces of his position, he'd have to do it now.

Without hesitation, he walked into his cockpit and initiated the self-destruct sequence. The only thing he needed was his sword; everything else was unnecessary. Unlike electronics, a sword was not easily detectable, and with it he'd be able to defend himself. Sorren snatched up his sword, slid into its scabbard, and tied it along his back with a rope.

Sorren fled from his shuttle. As the loud explosion shook the forest, causing billows of smoke to flow outward, he ducked and fell to the dirt. He looked back at the gray smoke in the forest. His shuttle was gone, blown apart into dust. With his shuttle turned to scrap, no one would be able to find him. While this may have saved him from an unwanted encounter, this also meant he had no way off the planet or any method of communication.

The situation did not disturb him, however. He did not panic or despair. If anything, he felt indifferent to the ordeal. Whether he lived or died, whether he returned or not, none of that really mattered to him.

A cool breeze ran across the forest, howling and whistling through the trees. Sorren could feel its gentle touch tingling the hairs on his skin. He breathed it in deep, filling up his lungs, and could smell the fresh scent of grass. He walked in the direction of the wind, hoping it would be the fastest route out of this forest.

The tops of the trees truly made it difficult for light to spread into the forest. There were several cracks in the canopy that let a few rays slip through, however it was not enough to allow the growth of grass and other lowly vegetation on the forest floor.

While it was normal for vegetation to be stifled in this environment, he found it disturbing that the forest was quiet. After all, any forest with a moderate climate should be teeming with life. When he had first entered the forest, he had noticed several noises, but as time went on, he heard less and less of the birds and bugs.

As an assassin, his senses were sharp; he would normally notice even the slightest movement of a bird that flew above. But in this forest it seemed like nothing moved. A forest devoid of life seemed impossible to him, so his next thought was that there could be a deceptive air. Something could be confusing his senses. A bit of worry strained his face because he'd be unable to avoid danger without his heightened senses to guide him.

Sorren kept on walking, but the forest continued with no visible end in sight. He passed by broken tree branches and brushed aside the thick black vines that hovered over the ground. Sorren followed a straight path, and even if he had to walk across rivers, giant rock formations, or even deep chasms, he would not stray from it. For the straight path, while difficult to tread, was the easiest way to avoid getting lost.

Hours passed and a concern became deeply rooted in him. At first he believed his senses were not functioning properly, but now he knew there had to be more to all of this. Every log and stream he examined was not abounding with small creatures, as he would have expected it to be. Maybe his senses were fine after all, and his inability to sense animated life was because there was none—or because they had left in a hurry.

Then, out of the blue, he could feel a slight presence hiding from him, almost playfully. It shifted places erratically, disappearing and reappearing all over; Sorren could not pinpoint which direction it was coming from. Sorren played it calmly and acted as he had before, trying not to draw attention to himself. He feared that the presence was watching his every move. Though his face did not show it, his thumping heart was in a state of anxious anticipation.

Sorren stumbled after taking a step. On bended knee, he held the palm of his hand to his forehead and closed his eyes. His head throbbed painfully. His breathing was sporadic. He had been perfectly fine just a moment ago, so he wondered what was happening to him.

Sorren got up and made his way to a nearby stream. He lifted his hood and dunked his face into the stream; the cool rush of water eased the pain. Sputtering, Sorren wiped away the water from his mouth and gazed at his reflection. Though he had naturally white hair, his face looked young. He turned away from the clear waters as a glare blinded his green eyes.

When he turned back to look upon his reflection again, it was no longer his own. A familiar face appeared over the surface, a face he never thought he'd ever see again. Sorren's face darkened and, in haste, he thrust his hand through the stream, splitting the face in half; the image was distorted with ripples and waves. He simply disregarded it as a trick of his mind. Then, ignoring it completely, he cupped water in his hands and washed his face.

"Taking your time, I see."

The voice startled Sorren. He spun around to find someone standing behind him. It was the same face he had seen in the water. The man was young and had short, but thick brown hair. His visage was full of vitality and his clothes gleamed like lucent silver. He smiled gently at Sorren, and Sorren bowed before him.

"Is that really you?" asked Sorren skeptically.

"Of course," said the mysterious man. "See, I am what you have made me into."

"What do you mean?" Sorren looked puzzled.

"I'm hurt," the man said. "Look at what has happened to me." All of a sudden many bloody scars were rapidly cut upon his face until he was no longer recognizable. "You were the one who did this," he said softly.

"I-I didn't," stammered Sorren. "I didn't do anything!" Sorren fell with his face to ground. "I'm sorry," he whispered. "I didn't mean to." Tears flowed from his eyes and moistened the dirt below. Even though Sorren turned his eyes away from the man, the image of the scarred face was burned into his mind. Sorren slammed his fist against the ground.

"Oh, then why do you still…"

Sorren looked up and the man was gone.

"Where did you go?" Wiping the tears off his face, Sorren stood up and ran past the trees, searching for the man. There was a small clearing in the forest and Sorren examined it. In the middle of the clearing was a stone well—a peculiar sight considering there was no cabin or encampment around.

Something about the well beckoned to him and he could hear a calling, though it was not in the form of a voice. He drew near to it and peered inside, only to find another face that he recognized. This time the reflection was of a man dressed in golden armor, wielding a sword of light. He glared at Sorren and grinned mockingly at Sorren's surprise.

Sorren's sadness instantly turned to hatred. Drawing his blade from its sheath, he furiously stabbed the surface of the water. He gripped the top of his head as the pain in his forehead became increasingly stronger. Staring into the well, a vivid image flashed in his eyes: a deceptive light, emerging from the darkness, gathered the hundreds of lesser lights in the sky and lit up the infinite space with its brilliance. The headache left him.

The memories of the past were things that he had intentionally forgotten. But why did those harsh and painful memories return now? The man he hated no longer roamed the surface. There was nothing for him to worry about, he thought.

Sorren stared at his own reflection in the water for a little while and then turned to leave. But the moment he shifted away his attention from the well, he could feel slight vibrations coming from the water. His instincts drove him to try to escape a lunge from behind. He was not fast enough and was knocked into a tree.

He lifted his head to get a good look at what had managed to land a fierce blow upon his unprotected back. It was a sea serpent! Or to be more precise, it was a serpent of the well. Regardless of what it should be called, the reptilian monstrosity was there before

Sorren; the beast eyed Sorren and insatiably licked its lips with its forked tongue. The creature had a slender body like a snake and it towered over Sorren, stretching its long neck nearly twenty feet high; it arched over, looking intently at its prey. Its skin was covered with masterfully sculpted scales, which were tightly woven across the flesh of its body in a colorful pattern of blue, red and green.

The overgrown water snake got ready for another lunge; a wide grin spread across its face, revealing its large fangs. Sorren took a stance, wielding his blade. The snake lashed out with a loud snap, trying to catch Sorren in its jaw. Sorren barely managed to escape from its clasp, but once again bounced off painfully from the impact.

His body sprawled on the grass, Sorren panted for air. Though his body was in the present, his mind was stuck in the past. The pain and sadness of the past burdened his heart.

Are you going to let yourself die here? A voice spoke into his mind. *You've killed serpents before! How can you be so weak now?*

"It is all my fault," Sorren murmured, delirious. "I've failed him."

You are a fool. I had noticed it when we first set foot into this wretched forest. The air is poisoned and so is your mind. That man would never blame you. Do not listen to the wicked lies of the serpent! It only seeks to leave you distraught, so you will be as defenseless as you are now.

Sorren gasped, "Will I die a worthy death?"

In its jaws, you will not even die a dog's death, scum.

"What do you mean by that?" asked Sorren angrily.

A dog will at least die for its master. But you—since you gave up so easily—are a disgrace. You are worse than the scum of the earth.

"I can't help it! I'm useless…"

I suppose I can help you. The voice snickered. *Your mind is heavy. Let me lighten things up a bit. I will only leave the memories you need. But since I haven't done this before, I am not aware of the side effects. Beware. It could be fatal.*

Sorren's eyes opened wide. His mind was open and clear. No longer did he regret the past or worry about the future. He got up, dusted himself off and took up his sword. The serpent tried to strike him again, but before it reached him, Sorren vanished, leaving only a wisp of darkness.

Fear struck the serpent like an iron rod against its skull. Terrified, it quickly tried to retreat back inside the well. But before the serpent could pull his head back under the water, Sorren reappeared behind the serpent and, with one earth-shattering slash, severed the serpent's neck. The upper half of the serpent's body fell limply to the ground, while the rest of the body dropped down the stone well and never resurfaced.

Sorren looked over the well in silence. After a short period, two men jumped down from the trees and approached Sorren. Both of them wore very plain tunics and simple sandals.

The man on the left was large, strongly built, and carried a giant club. He was for the most part bald, though he did have a few short strands of hair that he did not bother to deal with. His face had this dumbfounded look. The other man was terribly short and thin, and he also appeared a bit silly because his head was somewhat pointy. He held in his hand a large but elegant scythe.

"Welcome," they said, as they bowed down before him, "it is a pleasant surprise to see you here."

Sorren cocked his head. "Who are you? Do I know you?"

The men looked at Sorren strangely, surprised by his question.

"I suppose not," said the smaller one. "You may call me Windzer." He pointed to the burley fellow. "This big guy here is Hortmel. He doesn't like to talk much, so if you have any questions, please ask me. Since the path is quite dangerous, we'll be your escorts to the capital."

"Capital? How far is this capital?"

"With our rides," Windzer replied, "the trip shouldn't take more than several days."

"Rides?" Sorren looked around but saw nothing that they would be able to ride.

Suddenly, massive vibrations came from the earth. Sorren wondered what was going on. The earth cracked and split open. Something large jumped into view. Out of the dust rose several giant bird-like creatures. Their heads resembled an eagle's head, their beaks looked powerful enough to crush rocks, and the yellow feathers on their backs were soft and sleek, glistening with an amber glow. Unlike an average bird, however, it had four legs instead of two. The monster, short and plumpish, crept close to the ground.

"What are they?" Sorren asked.

"We call these monsters Kajins. They're tamed so just hop on," said Windzer.

Sorren mounted the Kajin and it let out a gleeful cry. It jumped around playfully, forcing Sorren to hold on. The Kajin romped around the stone well until Windzer patted it on the head to calm it down.

"Sorry about that," Windzer apologized. "He's a playful one." Sorren stared at Windzer, exhausted from holding on.

When all three of them were on the Kajins, the birds let out a shriek. With their huge talons clawing at the ground, they dashed away, breaking down tree trunks as they ran. They galloped onto the plains, leaving the forest behind in their wake. The majestic Kajins zipped along with incredible speed, keeping in line with each other.

"Why were you expecting me?" Sorren shouted because the galloping was quite loud. "Are you with the mercenaries?"

Windzer thought for a second. "No, we work as law enforcement on this world. We saw several bright lights fall from the sky, so we came to investigate."

"Several bright lights? How many did you see?"

"I can't say for sure. I'd say about six or seven."

"Six or seven?" Sorren became quiet, wondering if the mercenaries had survived or if his pursuers were hot on his trail.

Daybreak. The sun rose from the east and the sunlight dispersed its rays all across the surface of the southern plains. A morning wind forced its way through the six-feet tall grass and caused drops of dew to go rolling down the sides, like toddlers on slides. Sorren and his escorts proceeded along a dirt path that cut through the grassy plains. After several long hours of traveling, Sorren could understand why they would need rides to traverse the land. Aside from the complications of walking through tall grass, the land was rocky and rough, making it difficult to cross on foot. They stopped at the entrance to a long canyon near the desert valley.

Windzer turned to Hortmel. "Are you sure we're at the right place?"

Hortmel pulled out a map from his tunic and took a minute to study it. He scratched his cheek, looking rather confused. "I'm not sure. Something's not right."

"Let me see that." Windzer grabbed the map and looked at it. His eyes wandered back and forth from the map to the landscape. "Doesn't make any sense."

"Is there a problem?" asked Sorren.

"According to the map, this canyon shouldn't be here," Windzer replied, showing the map to Sorren. "I suppose this map is a bit old."

"There's no other way across?" Sorren glumly gazed at the treacherous terrain.

The canyon was fairly large and had a strange appearance. It looked like two smaller canyons were put side-to-side to form one big canyon. The center of the canyon had a long but thin bridge of land that ran straight across. The bottom looked safe. There was only a small stream of murky water. But climbing down and up the canyon walls would be terribly difficult because the incline was almost completely vertical.

Sorren glanced around. A dense forest covered the sides. The trees were so closely knit that they almost appeared to be hugging. "What about going around?"

"No can do." Windzer shook his head. "The way that forest looks is no illusion. The trees there are no more than a foot apart from each other. It's a very tight squeeze."

"What about the Kajins? Maybe we cut through the forest or fly across."

"They're land birds. Can't fly," explained Windzer. "Asking them to cut through the forest is too much, even for them. They'd be too tired to move after an hour of trying to break down such a thick forest." He then pointed to the strip of land in the center of the canyon. "If we just walk along that land bridge it should be no problem. The other end looks far, but we should be able to cross over by sunset."

After looking at the bridge, Sorren said, "It's too small for the Kajins."

"That's fine," said Windzer. "We'll leave the birds here. It won't be much farther until we reach the desert anyway and Kajins hate arid regions. They get dehydrated quite easily."

The three of them walked across the strip of land slowly. Although it was wide enough to have them walk across one by one, the ground felt unstable. Sorren's foot slipped, causing a few rocks to fall into the deep chasm. He peered over the canyon and was surprised by what he saw.

"There's so little running water down there," said Sorren. "What could have caused a canyon like this to form?"

"I'm not sure myself," Windzer replied. "Probably one strong flood cut through it. Could happen. Lots of crazy things happen around here."

A loud screech reverberated off the canyon walls. Sorren was at the front of the line and couldn't turn back to see what was going on.

Windzer, standing at the back of the line, looked behind. The Kajins were minding their own business, nibbling happily on tree bark.

"False alarm."

But Sorren noticed the sound coming from different directions. The abrupt noises sounded like they were getting closer and closer. His concern prompted him to look up.

"What's that?"

Giant flying lizards soared above. The red reptiles had thin beaks and long, leather wings. Though they were lizards, they also had a distinct black mane on the back of the neck. These lizards let out a shrill screech that made everyone cover their ears.

"Nothing to worry about," said Windzer. "Zortzels. Common beasts."

Despite his confident reply, it was difficult for them to move properly on the land bridge. They fumbled around with their weapons, swaying in an effort to maintain their balance. Falling would not be pretty, for the plummet would be of several thousand feet. Before they could get into a defensive position, two lizards dove straight at their backs and clamped onto Windzer and Hortmel with their massive claws. The two men vehemently resisted being caught in their clutches, but the strength of the claws restrained all movement. In a swift gliding motion, the lizards swooped off the ground, taking the men high into the sky.

Disappearing from view, Windzer shouted, "Don't worry about us. Go on ahead!"

Sorren wasn't fazed by the pronounced sense of urgency. The thought of falling all the way to the pit of the canyon made him hesitant to pick up the pace. More screeching rang through Sorren's ears, and he braced himself, expecting to be attacked by more of those odd flying lizards. Nothing happened. Sorren turned back and found it was the Kajins that were screeching this time. The Kajins galloped in circles, screeching at the top of their lungs. Sorren wondered what had their feathers all ruffled.

The canyon walls shook back and forth, forming rockslides all over. The savage trembling showed no signs of stopping. Sorren hugged the ground. Boulders came tumbling down to the left and right of him. Even the land bridge started to crumble. Realizing he'd fall if he didn't make a break for it, he ran as fast as he could across the thin strip of earth. With the canyon in an uncontainable convulsion, it looked as though everything would collapse.

The canyon suddenly burst apart. A massive creature emerged from the rubble. It resembled an earthworm—except its size was absolutely mind-boggling. Nothing around them was left intact as the gargantuan worm tore through the earth, engulfing whole mountains of rock with its insatiable appetite. The worm was as large as the canyon itself, nearly several thousand feet high. It didn't have eyes on its head, but it didn't need any because of the hundreds of feelers and grooves across its skin that acted as its sensory receptors. Its mouth stayed open as it traveled; Sorren could see that the inside was lined with several hundred layers of tiny teeth, too innumerable to count. The layers of teeth just rotated over and over, continuously breaking down and consuming everything in its path.

Watching the situation fall apart, Sorren began to doubt the credibility of his escorts. It was quite apparent that this worm had created such an odd-looking canyon in the first place. A worm of this immense size would be hard to overlook and was bound to create hundreds of canyons over its lifetime. How could Windzer have overlooked this?

In the midst of the ensuing chaos, Sorren didn't have time to think about anything else, but instead he tried to stay standing to the best of his ability. However, he helplessly lost his footing when all of the earth under his feet gave way.

The worm swerved randomly through the canyon while feeding. It was not targeting anyone. It was merely following its daily routine of digging through the soil, looking for nutrients to fill its appetite. Sorren and the others were like ants, too insignificant to be noticed.

The larger conglomerate mass of boulders disintegrated into a sea of rocks, and Sorren fell into its tumultuous waves. He swam through the rolling dirt with all his might, trying to force his way up because, unlike swimming in an ocean of water, he would not float. A giant wave of the worm's excrement came crashing down. He narrowly escaped it.

After the worm had finished accumulating a sufficient intake, it disappeared back into the bowels of the earth and flicked its tail contently as it left. The old canyon was gone and a newly formed canyon had replaced it. From the hole where the worm left came a loud rumbling. A flood of water flowed out. Sorren, completely exhausted from his ordeal, could not move. He gritted his teeth, bracing for the impact. *Whoosh!* Then the rushing stream carried him away.

Meanwhile, Hortmel, still caught in the claws of one of the flying lizards, swung his club aimlessly and, by a stroke of luck, managed to land a single blow on the Zortzel's leg. The reptile, whimpering in pain, released him from its grasp. Before Hortmel started to fall, he quickly grabbed onto its leg and climbed up its back. The Zortzel banked side to side, attempting to shake off Hortmel with sharp, speedy maneuvers. Hortmel remained steadfast in his grip and would not let go. He acquired control over the reptile by taking hold of the mane on its scaly neck and using it to steer the lizard in whichever direction he desired.

Hortmel drew close to Windzer and smashed his club against the other lizard's skull. The Zortzel let out a shriek. Freed from the grip of the claws, Windzer also followed Hortmel's lead and hopped onto the back of his own Zortzel. He drew his scythe forward. With a snap of his wrist, he straightened out the blade, turning his scythe into a spear. The head of his spear glowed; Windzer struck it into the lizard's spine.

"Give it another hit!" Windzer shouted to Hortmel.

Hortmel closed in on the Zortzel and struck the body of the lizard with an explosive blow. The violent assault on the Zortzel forced it to let out a weak cry. It could no longer fly straight and dove toward the ground as it was losing consciousness.

"I am now your master," Windzer whispered into its unsuspecting ear. "You will obey all my words. In return, you may have a fraction of my spirit."

Windzer twisted the spear like he was twisting a key, and a yellow glow surged from his hands, through the spear and into the body of the lizard. A spark of energy flowed through the veins of the Zortzel and spread through all parts of its body, revitalizing it instantly. The lizard, now feeling vigorous, easily glided out of the near fatal drop and hovered over the rubble, taking flight once again. Windzer pointed down to a safe spot. "Land over there."

The lizard screeched in reply and flew down. Hortmel was already standing on solid ground and waved back to Windzer. Once Windzer landed, he told the Zortzel to stay put.

"Do you think he's still alive?" Hortmel asked, staring at the running water.

"I sure hope so," said Windzer, motioning to him. "Come on, let's go for a swim."

CHAPTER 9
Abandoned

As the distant sun slid down the sky, it illuminated the atmosphere with its multicolored splashes of orange and red. An ominous sandstorm wreaked havoc on the desert's serene afternoon. It soon passed, but the face of the landscape was forever disfigured. A breeze changed into a strong gust, hoisting small clusters of sand into rough swirls that resembled tiny tornadoes. Small kangaroo mice retreated to their burrows to hide from the fickle winds.

Darek felt sick. The meals he had been forced to ingest over the last few days were far from delectable. The menu had consisted of roasted lizards, bugs, and a few other things he couldn't identify. Azura was an expert on determining what would be safe to eat. But even if the things they ate weren't poisonous, he had never felt so disgusted in his life, so much so to the point of vomiting whenever Azura cheerfully said, "All right! Time to eat!"

It was also never enough. It was impossible to fill his stomach from such nasty little critters. Every night he'd go to bed hungry. He regretted rejecting Azura's first invitation at a filling meal. If only he had known he was going to be eating nothing but gut-wrenching oddities, he would have filled his stomach in the first place.

But it was not all bad. Occasionally, he'd find some nice succulent cactus fruit to hold him over. That was the only highlight of his day, and while they walked on, he kept on praying for more.

Darek followed Azura the whole time and could barely keep up with her rapid pace. Though they divided all the food and water equally, slept the same amount and walked the same distance, Darek could not comprehend how she kept on going without even looking tired. Even so, he still had his pride. If she was not going to take a break, there was no way he would suggest it. But that didn't keep him from watching her movements closely, waiting for her to make a stop. Then the unthinkable finally happened: it was not time to sleep or rest but she stopped walking regardless.

"What's wrong? Tired?" wheezed Darek, as he crouched over, catching his breath. "Don't push it. It's been a long day. You don't look so good. I can see you're sweating like crazy. Maybe you should take a break. We have a long way to go, you know."

"Look over there." Azura pointed to the horizon. "What does that look like to you?"

"Look at what?" Exhausted, Darek straightened up and tried to match his view with the direction she pointed at. "What are you talking about? I don't see anything special."

"You don't? But it's right over there—clear as day. That thing that stands right out on top of that sand dune." Azura squinted her eyes. "It looks like a large city."

Darek squinted at the same spot for a minute but the best he could see was a little black dot. "Are you sure? That could be anything..."

"But look at all those structures," said Azura, "I don't see how it could be natural."

When she turned back, she found him already passed out on the sand, snoring deeply. She shook her head in disappointment. "You should have waited until we reached the city before going to bed. Kids these days are just too impatient." She took hold of his ankles and, dragging him across the sand, went about her way toward the city.

By the time they entered the city the sky was dark. The evening was young yet no one was on the roads. The only voices around were the whispers and howls of the wind. The only faces were the blank stares of abandoned buildings. The city was an empty shell.

The city, in spite of its death, still was a wondrous sight to behold. Covered in dust and ashes, the city's towers were like majestic giants. Untended gardens were strewn along the rooftops of apartments. The grandiose roads and buildings, elaborate in design, were impressive feats.

Azura walked through an empty boulevard, marveling at the sight. She was awestruck by the complexity of the architecture. She had been to several worlds and had seen many cities along the way, but this was one of the most elegantly constructed cities she had ever laid eyes on.

There was one thing that stood out in particular: a large waterway. It was still running. "Amazing," she muttered. "A system of transport using water, and it's connected to the river. Water must have played an important role in this civilization. This system is so large and extensive. I bet it could transport small homes." She looked around. "I wonder how far it goes."

She reflectively gazed at the city. By all accounts and considerations, the civilization on this planet should have been primitive, but judging from what she could see, this was not the case. How could such an advanced civilization have collapsed without a trace?

"Are we there yet?" Darek shot up and stretched. His back was aching and sore, though he wasn't sure why. Then, when he looked around, he was stunned at the masterpiece of a city. "Looks way nicer than the slums. What do you suppose happened on this world? A genetic experiment gone awry, or maybe a crazy evil dictator left everything in ruins?"

Azura was not amused by his questions. "Let's look for survivors."

"Wait a minute." Darek looked at her strangely and waved his hands, gesturing for her to look across the cityscape. "Why bother? There's no one here! Look at how old this place is. Even if there were survivors, they would've moved on by now."

"As a Hero, it is my duty to make sure no one is left behind." Azura ran to windows of the buildings, checking each one to see if she could find anybody inside. Azura opened up one of the doors and motioned for Darek to follow. Darek didn't budge. She asked, "Now, are you going to help me or not?"

"Help you?" Darek sat down defiantly. "I'm staying here. Those buildings look like they could collapse any moment. I don't see why I need to risk my life for nothing."

Azura shrugged. "Fine, suit yourself."

Azura disappeared through the entrance of the building. When she was no longer around, the city fell completely silent for a few seconds. No chirping, whistling, howling or any other nocturnal noises could be heard anymore. Had it not been for the sound of his own breath, Darek would've believed he had gone deaf. The city started to seem like a much scarier place. Colossal shadows waned left and right along the front of vacant residences. Speeding objects zoomed overhead without a sound. Enigmatic lights flashed chaotically in the sky from time to time. There were so many strange things going on around him, yet he couldn't tell what was causing all those unexplainable events to happen. It could be nothing...but then again, there could also be some humongous, ferocious man-eating monster just hiding around the corner! Darek gulped. He could feel the hairs on his neck—and maybe even atop his head—prickling up.

He glanced left and right, twitching at every single thing that moved. Frightened, he called out, "Azura? You still there?" There was no response—aside from a cricket chirp that enjoyed answering him.

Because of the near-absolute silence and the impenetrable darkness, his senses became highly responsive. He believed he was hearing the footsteps of beetles marching on the fence behind him. In the corner of his eye, he thought he caught sight of several shadows running amok through the windows. Darek plugged his ear and shut his eyes. He figured he might be going crazy. But by covering his ears in this eerie silence, he could hear the incessant drumming of his heart. Fearing for his sanity, Darek got up and ran to the door where he last saw her enter.

Darek scanned the dark hallway from the outside. He didn't really want to go in, but he'd much rather be inside with Azura than outside alone. Taking in small breaths of courage, he slowly tiptoed into the building.

"Azura," Darek whispered several times as he went along, "where are you?"

It was too dark to tell where he was going; keeping one hand along the wall, he headed straight down the corridor. The floor was littered with debris, which brushed against his feet. He wondered what all the stuff on the floor was. Since he couldn't see anything at all, his curiosity was piqued. He tried stepping on whatever was on the ground, and it made a loud crunch. Bugs? The thought unwillingly crossed his mind, but the shape didn't seem right; it felt more like plaster or hard wood. But as long as he couldn't see it, it would be for the best. He would probably feel better if he stopped thinking about it all together.

Darek walked past each room, peeking inside each one as he went. She was nowhere to be found. He took one deep breath and then boldly shouted, "AZURA, WHERE ARE YOU?"

Azura slapped him across the face. "You don't have to be so loud, I'm right behind you!" She tapped his shoulder to show him where she was. "You almost blew out an eardrum."

"You were here the whole time?"

"Yes, I was."

"Why didn't you answer me the first time?"

"I did. I nodded and waved my hand to show you where I was. You looked right at me."

"I can't see anything at all!"

"Well, I'm checking upstairs."

"Wait! I'm coming with you." Darek chased slowly after her, following the wall. He waved his hand steadily ahead to avoid bumping into things. "I won't be able to keep up with you if you move too fast. Azura? Did you hear me?" She didn't reply.

"Oh great," grunted Darek. "Left me all alone again." He groped around in the dark and found the railing that led up the stairs. Ascending the stairs was a shaky experience because every step he took made the boards creak. He stayed along the very edge of the stairs, fearing they would break at the middle.

When he reached the upper floor, he inspected the nearest room. At the window he saw the blurred silhouette of a person. But when he blinked, the person disappeared. Startled, Darek reached into his bag for his daggers. His trembling fingers lifted them out of his bag, but they slipped out of his hands and onto the obscured floor.

Darek shuddered. He now had to deal with two fears. Should he face the shadow before him unarmed, or would it be better to search for his daggers in an unknown darkness? He panicked and dropped to the floor, feeling the ground and pushing aside the unknown junk.

"What are you doing?" Azura turned on the light in the room.

"Oh, thank God, it's just you." Darek was relieved to see her. "I dropped something on the floor and..." Blood drained from his face when he looked down.

"Bones!" Darek shrieked. He stumbled back and gasped. The floor was literally littered with hundreds of skeletons. Darek kicked them away. "Everywhere! They're everywhere! What's going on here?" Terrified, Darek said, "Did the monsters do this?"

Azura held a skull in the palm of her hand. "I don't think so."

"Why not?"

"No signs of struggle. No dismemberment. Even their clothes are okay. Their clothes would be ripped if they were eaten. This is...unusual. It's like they...died on the spot."

"Whatever it is, I don't care! I just want to get out of here!"

"Are you hearing yourself talk?" Azura placed the skull down gently on a table. "What if there are people still out there? How can we abandon them in this nightmare?"

Frustrated, Darek said, "What don't you understand? Monsters are everywhere and everyone's dead! There's no one to save!"

"If you want to leave, go right ahead, if you can. I'm not going to stop you." Azura's temper flared as she digested his words. "But I'm disappointed in you. I thought you'd be glad to help, but—" She stopped abruptly. "Stay inside this room," she said in a hushed voice.

"Whatever." Darek was leaving but froze when he noticed something moving outside the window. "I've been meaning to ask you this, but were you in here when I came in?"

"No." Azura carefully stared out the window until something suspicious caught her eye. "There!" she exclaimed. Azura opened the window and jumped out.

Darek gestured with his hand for her to stop. "Don't—we're on the second floor!" He ran to the window and saw that Azura had landed safely. She then disappeared into the dark alley.

She survived that without injuring herself? She can't be human.

Darek hastily grabbed his daggers and hurried to the stairs, but the moment he stepped down, he heard a loud crack. He screamed. All of a sudden, the wooden stairs crumbled beneath him. He fell through, landing clumsily on the first floor. His head felt woozy. Getting to his feet, he dusted his clothes off. His whole body was in pain. He staggered away from the rubble. *Crunch.* There was a strange sound. His eyes ran across the broken staircase. Something stirred beneath the broken boards.

Darek's eyes widened as a large wolf emerged from heaps of broken wood and stone. Shaking off the dust, it eyed Darek angrily and pounced at Darek with such a force that the both of them broke through the crumbling wall and into the city streets.

Darek scrambled to his feet and faced the snarling predator. The big black wolf glared at Darek. It grunted and growled while saliva uncontrollably dripped down its gums.

With his daggers in a cross-like fashion, Darek took a low stance and watched the wolf's movement warily. Blood stained Darek's shirt because the claws had scraped some flesh off. *It doesn't look too happy,* he thought. *But there's no way I can outrun a wolf.* While keeping a close eye on the approaching wolf, Darek retreated slowly. The wolf followed his every step, making sure the distance between them would not widen. Without realizing it, Darek backed into a wall. It was fight or die, and he would much rather put up a fight. Darek wasn't exactly a student of martial arts, but Slade had taught him a thing or two at the orphanage. Even in the slums, he had his fair share of brawls. A wild carnivore would undoubtedly be stronger, but in the best situation, Darek might be able to scare it off.

Darek dashed at the wolf. He slashed with his right blade and then with his left. But the wolf danced side to side, dodging his swipes, and then jumped back and away. Darek stiffened.

Darn, I missed!

While Darek was occupied in thought, the wolf launched an attack of its own. The wolf leapt a great distance, closing the gap between them in an instant, and charged at Darek. Darek skillfully sidestepped the rush, thinking it would be enough. But the wolf, sensing his ignorance, stopped its charge and used a smooth rotation of its body to launch its foot into Darek's face.

Darek responded by blocking its foot with his arm, but the impact still knocked him back several feet. His forearm throbbed from the bloody bruising. The more he thought about it, the more ridiculous it sounded. The only logical conclusion was that this had to be a bad dream. Regardless, it was undeniable: the wolf had kicked him. The black wolf was standing upright like a man. It motioned with its claws, almost as if to say, "Come and get me."

His courage faltered in front of this strange beast. But even so, Darek forced down his feelings of running away. That girl had already saved him once and he was not about to go to crying for her help. He was going to show her that he could handle his own problems. He readied himself for another exchange. This time, he thought, they were on more equal terms.

Once more, he ran toward the wolf, no longer hesitating. He slashed several times but the wolf blocked all of his strikes. The wolf tried to chop and claw at him with his paws but Darek blocked its attacks as well. For nearly a minute, they traded blows in rapid succession. Each attack barely hit and both of them began feeling exhausted from the pressure of the attacks.

Darek was rather impressed with himself. He never knew he had it in him to fight this well. But he was more impressed by the wolf.

What's going on here? Darek thought. *This wolf only punches and kicks!*

The wolf dropped its guard a little and triggered Darek's battle instinct. Darek tried to use that opening as the turning point of the fight and, with the last of his energy, unleashed several close stabs. Sadly, Darek missed. Taking a strong stance, the wolf smashed the brunt of its paw against Darek's chest, launching him several feet in the air. Then the wolf pounced after Darek's body in midair, grabbed Darek's arm and tossed him like a rag doll against the ground.

Darek had the wind knocked out of him, leaving him writhing on the road. While the wolf approached him, Darek recovered, but remained on the ground, faking injury.

The wolf winced, showing a painful expression. Without drawing much attention, Darek glanced around its body and noticed that splinters of wood had penetrated its thick skin. It had been injured from the falling staircase from before. Darek thought, *This is my chance!* The wolf flinched again; Darek sneakily threw his dagger at the wolf's unsuspecting eye and managed to graze it just enough so that it bled. The wolf howled in pain and wiped away the blood from his eye while Darek darted away. Desperate for help, Darek scanned the surrounding area with his eyes. W*hat could Azura be doing at a time like this? Why'd she leave me alone with that monster?*

Darek ran into a long dark alley. It was a suitable place to hide. He took refuge there and found some large crates for cover. *Ugh, what's that smell?* Darek held his nose. There was a powerful stench that came from inside the crates; though it was mildly revolting, he thought it might help to hide his own scent. While huddled up, Darek heard a loud crash coming from above. Azura jumped out a window and landed right in front of him.

Darek exclaimed, "So that's where you were! And here I was thinking you might've been doing something important! While you were having fun, hopping out of buildings, this wolf monster nearly killed—"

"What are you still doing here?" said Azura, furrowing her brow. "Get out of here!"

Crash! Nearly a dozen wolves sprang from the windows, sprinkling glass and splinters of wood from above. The wolves landed all around them, snarling and growling. Their eyes were red with blood and fury; their rancid breath, steaming from their mouths, was clearly visible in the cool night. These wolves looked a little different than the one Darek had faced. They sported a fuzzy gray coat of fur and were smaller, though they were still about as big as Darek.

After corralling Darek and Azura into a tight spot, they charged, thirsting for blood. However, they completely ignored Darek. Instead they focused and coordinated their efforts against Azura. In succession, the wolves pounced at Azura, but she deflected them with a strong fist at every turn. Seeing that their rush had no effect, all of the gray wolves stood upright and began to take fighting stances. An all-out slugfest erupted. The wolves launched punches and kicks, but Azura dominated them, crushing them completely with her fast and furious blows. Before the wolves could even respond, she pummeled them into the walls and crates. They rebounded, but Azura smashed them into the ground relentlessly.

In the middle of the fray, Darek screamed. Azura looked over her shoulder. A black wolf was scaling the building, taking Darek with him. She chased after them, leaping from windowsill to windowsill to reach the roof.

Azura saw them by the edge. The black wolf was grinning maliciously, holding Darek by the collar over the side. Darek, his feet dangling, gaped down in horror. The waterway was below him—far below.

"Don't—" Azura began.

It was too late. Darek was plummeting toward the water. Azura ran to the side of the roof and jumped. She reached out for Darek and grabbed him as they both fell into the current with a loud splash. Their shouts could be heard echoing throughout the city as they drifted along, struggling to stay afloat.

CHAPTER 10
Hidden Mansion

S prawled on his back, Darek blinked. It was cold, dark and damp. He heard the loud sounds of rushing water. He ran his fingers across his shirt. It was soaking wet. He searched his satchel and found his daggers—both of them, which he found somewhat odd because he distinctly remembered losing one. Darek sat up and groaned, holding his head. He found himself in an enclosed cavern. Water cascaded down from an opening above and flowed into a running river that cut into a lightless tunnel.

Azura was lying next to him. He jostled her by the shoulder. Azura shot up, looking dazed. Suddenly, she jumped to her feet and said, "We're alive!"

"You're lucky to have survived," said a mysterious voice.

Darek was surprised to see a new face. Sitting on a rock, the stranger looked to be somewhat young, possibly in his thirties, but had gleaming silver hair. His long white robes were clean and bright, like freshly fallen snow. The man had a pleasant smile upon his face. Darek immediately was at ease in the man's presence. Darek knew nothing about this man yet, by appearances alone, the man looked trustworthy and friendly.

"Let me introduce myself," said the man. "I am Rathos. And you are?"

"A human!" Darek exclaimed cheerfully.

Rathos raised a brow. "Yes…I could tell that much…"

"No," said Darek, shaking his head, "I mean, you're human!"

"Yes…I'm pretty sure I know what I am. But you're still not answering my question."

"Oh right," said Darek, turning slightly pink at his own excitement, "the name's Darek."

"I'm Azura," said Azura, gesturing toward herself.

"Darek?" Another man stepped out of the shadows. "I've heard of that name."

Rathos glanced at the other man. "Let me introduce—"

"I'll introduce myself," said the man curtly. "The name is Sorren."

"Yes," said Rathos. "This man also came from the river. I must say—it's the first time I've ever seen so many people come down a river unexpectedly."

"Ah yes," said Sorren, "I remember now. Darek...that's the name of the target."

Darek blinked for a second, and to his surprise, a sword was held close to his throat. Sorren had unsheathed his blade and pressed it against Darek's neck in an instant. Darek never even heard the sound of the sword as it moved.

"You're the Judge everyone's been talking about," said Sorren icily. "To tell you the truth, I'm actually on a job to hunt down the Judges myself. What a coincidence, huh?"

Sweat poured down along Darek's cheeks, and possibly even a few tears. He remained rooted in place, afraid to even take a step back. Azura grabbed Sorren by the wrist and twisted it, forcing him to release his sword.

"Don't point that wherever you please," said Azura.

Sorren looked at Azura, studying her for a moment. He turned away, picking up and sheathing his blade. He muttered to himself, "Hmm, looks like trouble. Well, there's no point in killing him *now*." He glared at Darek. "I won't be able to get any reward unless I get off this rock."

Rathos cut the tension by clearing his throat. "Now that we've had our very *pleasant* introductions, I'd like to ask a question. And if I'm satisfied with your replies, I'll provide you with food and warm beds."

Darek said, "Are you blackmailing us?"

"With food and warm beds? I sincerely doubt it," said Rathos, beaming. "It's incentive for the truth." He paused. "Now, my question is...where'd you come from? Another continent? You certainly don't seem like you're from around here."

"This may be hard to swallow," said Azura, "but Darek and I are from outer space. I guessed you'd call us aliens. Whether you believe us or not...that's our answer."

"Ah," said Rathos, "very intriguing. So you are like Sorren. He too has said that he does not belong on this planet. That's just perfect." He clapped his hands in joy. "If you'll come with me, I'll take you to my master. I'm sure, as beings from other worlds, you must have many questions about our world. My master will answer all." Rathos gestured. "He's down the river."

As they followed Rathos, Azura nudged Darek in the arm. "Hey, why didn't you tell me you were a Judge? I thought you looked familiar…but I never expected to see you here."

"Um…" Darek cleared his throat. "That's because I'm not really—"

"Oh!" Azura sounded like she remembered something important. "Oh yeah…I see how it is. Judges are supposed to hide their identity." She winked. "It completely slipped my mind."

Darek knitted his brow. "What? No…I didn't—"

Patting him on the back, Azura smiled. "Don't worry, your secret's safe with me. I know. You're not a Judge." She winked at him again.

"Uh…right—exactly…or not…" His face buried in the palm of his hand, Darek felt confused. He wasn't sure if she really understood. Curious, he said, "Do you know much about the Judges?"

Azura shook her head. "Not much. We learn very little about Judges at the Academy. All I know is that the Judges have always been our allies. But because they're intended to be a secret to everyone else, only Archlords and the Overlord ever get to see and speak with them."

They're allied with the Heroes? Darek was bewildered by the concept. During the trial, being labeled a Judge was almost a criminal act in and of itself. When his best friends had come to rescue him as Judges, he had mixed feelings about their intentions. But now that he listened to what Azura had to say, being a Judge didn't seem like such a bad thing. Then again, with Sorren intending to kill him, it would be too dangerous to continue carrying this title. How could he possibly clear up this misunderstanding when no one seemed willing to listen?

The trip through the woods took a good half hour before they came upon a large villa. A mansion stood up on a hill by the water. Torches were lined up in several rows that lit up the dirt path on the way to the iron gates.

Darek stamped his wet shoes on the dry ground. His clothes, completely soaked, were even starting to smell funny. Darek arduously flung out the excess water, though he wondered if it would make a difference at this point. He couldn't wait to dry up. Keeping his arms close to his chest, Darek groaned and glanced around.

Aside from the light from the torches, the whole place was shrouded in darkness.

"Where are we?" he asked.

"This is the cavern," Rathos replied. "It may seem strange, but the forest is underground."

Azura couldn't believe it. "How can anything, especially trees, grow underground?"

"This cavern was formed long ago when large rocks fell across the ravine. The trees were already here before we built the mansion." Rathos lifted one of the torches high and walked up to the tree trunks. "How this forest continues to exist makes it a bit special."

The light from the torch radiated over the forest and revealed its form.

"They're white!" Darek was shocked at the sight.

"These trees stay white in the darkness." Rathos led them up the hill toward the castle doors. "There is never much sunlight here. However—well, I guess it'll be easier to explain if you just saw it. It is almost time anyway."

Rathos blew out the torch. Darek caught a fleeting glimpse of several wolves running down the hill, blowing out torches as they went until all the flames had been snuffed out. Everything turned pitch-black.

Darek felt very uncomfortable. "Wolves? What's going on here?"

"They are friends," said Rathos. "Be at ease. They are not going to harm you."

"But they're wolves! Are you sure it's safe? I don't like how this is—"

Azura silenced Darek with a wave of her hand. She could see faint glowing lights twinkling about. "Glowing bugs?"

Rathos chuckled. "It's quite amazing isn't it?"

Darek snorted while restraining a laugh. "Glowing bugs aren't that amazing."

"We call them Sun bugs," said Rathos. "They are a rarity on this planet. They have a special adaptation for their survival."

The Sun bugs buzzed all around them. A few hundreds lights became several hundred thousand. Their faint glows grew stronger and they attached themselves to the ceiling of the cavern. They littered the ceiling like stars in the night sky. Over a short period of time, the light grew so strong that the entire cavern became fully illuminated with a bright yellow glow.

Unable to hold back his astonishment, Darek's jaw dropped. "Never saw that before."

"It's beautiful," remarked Azura.

They watched as the forest became immersed in the light; the white leaves on the trees became green. The cavern, once dead in darkness, was now alive in the light.

Azura turned to Rathos. "How does this happen?"

Rathos explained, "The rocks that make up the ceiling have many tiny cracks in them. This serves several purposes. While it is difficult for sunlight to come through, raindrops will flow quite steadily down. The cracks also serve as a way for the Sun bugs to go back and forth from the surface. The Sun bugs rest outside on the rocks during the day and bask in the sunlight. When evening comes, they return to the cavern to feed on the leaves of the trees. The trees are then fully nurtured from the sunlight and rain. Though it was never intended to truly work like this, it's amazing how they can take a situation like this to their advantage. They have created a symbiotic relationship to overcome their problems."

"You know a lot about this place, don't you?" asked Darek.

Grim-faced, Rathos said, "Well, I have lived here for a *long* time."

Upon reaching the top of the hill, they met a small pack of wolves, which were guarding the entrance. When they saw Rathos, they nodded to him, welcoming him back. Rathos opened up the front door and the others followed him down the main lobby.

Though Rathos may have called it a mansion, Darek would have more appropriately termed it a castle. The entrance hall was enormous and the inside of the building was full of many twists and turns that never seemed to end. In spite of its impressive size, the inside of the castle was rather ordinary. Simple paintings of black and white shapes, monotonous doors, and identical torches were all placed in a simple repeating pattern. Because everything was so similar, Darek felt like they were walking through the same hall, over and over again.

"Rathos," said Azura, "I want to know…were you the ones that attacked us in the city?"

"You are perceptive." Rathos answered, "Thedes, one of our wolves, was in charge of that. He was eager to bring you here—by force. I had nothing to do with it, but I must apologize all the same on behalf of all the wolves here. It was not a good first impression."

Darek studied him for a moment. "So you're a wolf too?"

Rathos glanced back and smiled. "I can become one, yes. We are human, but we have the ability to transform. I believe the terminology would refer to us as werewolves, though we never considered ourselves as such."

After what seemed like an extremely long detour, Rathos stopped in front of a large scarlet door. "This is the room where my master resides. Please be respectful." Rathos opened the door and brought them inside.

Aside from the throne that seemed to have a spotlight shining down upon it, the room was as black as a cloudy night. Immediately upon entry, they could feel many eyes watching them from the shadows. Darek knew they were not alone. He clearly heard the soft snarls and growls that echoed all around.

Rathos gestured to the large chair before them. "Here is our master."

Darek examined the seat. A young boy was sitting upon it, stroking the fur of a black dog that rested peacefully beside him. The throne was so big that the child barely took up any room on the cushion. The boy looked no more than seven years old. His blond hair was neatly combed to the left side; his clothes were formal and clean, consisting of a neatly ironed suit and necktie. His mature style of clothing did not match the youth of his body.

Darek tapped Rathos on the shoulder. "Is your master a dog? That's kind of ironic."

The dog sat up and growled at Darek. His fur shot up and the length of his body stretched out as he stood on his hind legs. It was not a dog at all. It was the same black wolf he had met in the city. It seemed to be able to shrink and grow in size.

"Oh no, it's him again!" Darek tried his best to appease the wolf with short apologies and incessant bowing. But everything he did only served to infuriate the black wolf even more.

"I cannot stand such insolence any longer!" The black wolf said to the boy beside him, "Please, Master—I beg of you—let me tear that raggedy boy apart. Such filth is not fit to live! Give me the order and I will end his miserable life."

Aware of his mistake, Darek said, "The boy? Isn't he a little young to be the master?"

"Calm down, Thedes," the young boy told the wolf. "It's all right. You should really control that temper. It's not good for your health."

"Greetings travelers," the boy raised his voice as he addressed the group. "You may call me Merdon. Welcome to my mansion." He paused. "Then again, I suppose I should welcome you to our planet of Kedaro as well. I've heard from a messenger sent by Rathos that you are not of our world."

Azura stepped forward. "I am Azura of the Legion of Heroes."

Sorren bowed down humbly. "I am Sorren from the Assassin's Guild."

Not to be outdone, Darek patted himself in the chest and said, "You can call me Darek. I'm a...delivery boy." He felt a little bit embarrassed with his simple title but added as much as he could. "But I'm also currently the most-wanted criminal in the galaxy..."

Merdon coughed so as not to laugh too loudly at Darek's self introduction. But he fixed his mood to become quite serious shortly after. "Well, as impressive as your titles sound, they have no meaning here. We have never heard of other worlds or other peoples. But you all do sound very *distinguished* in your backgrounds." He brushed his hair back. "Rathos has probably not told you much of anything."

"No, he only told us to speak with you," said Azura.

"Then there is much to talk about," Merdon said solemnly. "Does my appearance startle you? Do you wonder why I, a mere boy, am considered the master here?"

Darek flushed red because he was the only one who made the mention. "Not at all! It's unusual to me, but I don't think it's anything *that* startling. You just look a little young."

Merdon shook his head. "No, no, there's no need to apologize. I find it only natural that you would think that way. After all, you would not have known how old I truly am."

Darek began, "What do you—"

Scowling at his own hands, Merdon hissed, "Cursed! This planet is cursed! We have all been cursed! I may look like a boy, but I have..." He slammed his fist against the armrest. "I have already lived more than one hundred years."

"A *hundred* years?" Darek studied the boy from head to toe. The boy had the appearance of a six-year-old. "Impossible..."

"Immortal," said Sorren. "When you become immortal, you always stay the same."

Merdon eyed Sorren curiously, amazed that he knew of such things. "You are correct. We are all immortal. Most of everyone on the planet, or what's left of them, has become immortal, cursed with these bodies that never age."

"Cursed?" Darek said, "How is that a curse? Living forever would be pretty cool!"

"You would think so," said Merdon. "But there are other permanent side effects."

"What kind of side effects?"

"Lack of appetite. Stomach cramps. Insomnia. Infertility. Just to name a few. Though it may sound mild, together, they really make life miserable. Not to mention…I can't grow anymore. It's a little depressing to remain a child my whole life."

"Infertility? You mean, you can't…um…"

"Reproduce. Our population stays the same for the most part."

"How did you all become immortal?" Azura asked, sounding skeptical. "I've heard of them in myths and legends. I find it very hard to believe so many could be gathered in one place."

"Sadly, even I do not know how such a thing came to be." Merdon lowered his head in grief. "It all happened on that ill-fated day. I remember it all too vividly. The day seemed to begin ordinarily enough—but soon all of that changed.

"That day I was woken up by the alarm clock at the usual time to prepare for school. My parents would always be waiting for me at the dining table, but that day was different: my parents were still asleep in bed.

"School was a short walk away. I skipped breakfast and left. I was not allowed to walk to school alone, but I didn't care; I was going to be late. However, on the way to school I was met with a sight of horror that I would never forget: people lifelessly sprawled on the streets, vehicles slamming into each other, angry mobs, and widespread panic. Left and right, people would suddenly fall down and die. The government tried to control the situation. Calling it an epidemic, they quarantined whole cities and called the best scientists to research a solution. But in a few days, even the governments of the world perished. No one ever found out what happened."

"How horrible…" Darek wiped away a tear. "I'm so sorry about your parents."

"My parents are fine," Merdon said flatly. "They currently live in the capital."

Sounding confused, Darek said, "Huh? But you said—oh, never mind. So you really don't know anything about it?"

Merdon shook his head. "No. This is all I know: billions of people died and those that survived became immortal. Even the emergence of monsters began happening then. The only conclusion I came up with is that it could have been some kind of mutational virus, or—dare I call it—an evolutionary step."

That explains the mountain of skeletons we found at the old city, thought Darek.

Merdon continued, "But that is something of the past. Even though it still pains me to remember it, I have gotten over that incident several decades ago. There is nothing I can do to change the past. What are important to me are the present and the future—which is why I invited you to my mansion."

Merdon got up from his chair and clapped his hands together. Sprinting out of the shadows, a wolf hurried to Merdon's side, bringing a huge scroll in its mouth. Merdon grabbed the scroll and threw it on the ground. It unraveled, revealing a large map. "This is the map of the continent, it will help me explain some things." He pointed to a black dot near the northern edge of the continent. "This is Duraskull, our capital. It is the only city that exists today. Most of the immortals live there, though it is not mandatory. The ones who live there do so because they want to relive the past, a world of life, though it is merely an illusion. In the entire world, the population only amounts to around ten thousand."

"Ten thousand," Darek repeated, lips trembling. "Out of billions, ten thousand survived?"

Merdon nodded. "It is even hard for me to call it a city since the population is so low. It is more of a town than anything else. Now aside from those that live in the city, there are several others who prefer to live alone or within small groups. They, like me, have built mansions in different parts of the continent where they live in general solitude. However, all the immortals, regardless of where they live, must gather at the capital for special occasions."

"What kind of special occasions?" Sorren asked.

"Once a year we have an annual celebration to celebrate the...demise of our previous civilization." Merdon scrunched his face and abruptly kicked throne in a fit of fury. "Excuse me, but I get angry every time I think of it. It's mandatory to go. I only go to show my face so they don't get suspicious of my hatred for it."

"They? Who would you be speaking of? The population?" Sorren pressed Merdon for answers, for he was inexplicably interested in the subject.

"The elders," Merdon replied. "The elders were the first immortals, the ones who existed before the great change. Their ages are unknown, though I suspect some of them to have lived over six hundred years. When that fateful day happened and every last living human passed away, they took charge and established a government in which they rule over us. The elders explained what happened to us, how to use our new abilities and acted as if they were our saviors in a moment of crisis. They created our organization known as the Immortal Alliance."

"From outcasts to rulers," Sorren remarked.

Merdon agreed, nodding. "All they desired was power over us and we willingly gave it to them without a moment of thought. They do as they please and force labor over the lower classes. I would try to revolt, but few would aid me. The populace has been disillusioned for years. To attempt a violent takeover would not be so simple. Contrary to human beings, who have a limited life span and grow weaker after a certain point in time, immortals gain more power and strength as they age. Nearly all the immortals, save for the elders, have lived about a hundred years. Even if we confront the elders, the might of my small group cannot hope to overpower the five of them. Still, we must wait for the right opportunity. Our group here intends to overthrow them at all costs, which is why we need your help."

Intrigued, Darek said, "So that's why you're out here in the middle of nowhere? You guys are using this as some kind of secret base for your rebellion?"

"Not quite," Merdon replied. "This is sort of a secret base. But the reason for our location was because of a human village nearby."

"What?" Darek scratched his cheek. "I thought you said only the immortals survived."

"Yes, that is what the immortals believe. But, by luck or destiny, we discovered a remote human village here several decades ago. Since then we've established ourselves here and relocated them in order to hide them from the elders. Who knows what they'll do when they find out some humans survived." Merdon smiled wryly. "And that is where you come in."

"I don't get it." Azura said, "What do you mean?"

Merdon said slowly, "To put it simply, you can be an...*experiment*."

Darek grunted, "I don't like the sound of this."

Sorren asked, "Why us?"

Merdon explained, "Several reasons. For one thing, you make for a good story. You dress modernly and understand technology that we cannot, which helps to explain that you are from other worlds. If we gathered a few of the natives from around here, the village might get discovered, and we cannot accept that great a risk without knowing how the elders would respond. We cannot afford to lose our chance of restarting the human civilization.

"And secondly, we are curious as to how they would respond. A human has not walked inside the walls of the capital for a hundred years. If a human arrived, would they kill them since they have no place in the society, or would they be glad to see a new face and accept them as they are? This is something we do not know. If they accept you, we may in time reveal the other human tribes that live around here and work together to rebuild human life. Even if I do not trust the elders, they may no longer be in control if such a thing happens.

"The other thing is that you are capable of handling yourselves quite well. You might make for good spies. If the experiment is something of a success and they accept you, we'll need you to do a little investigation in the restricted areas of the castle. I believe the elders are hiding something—something that could cause uproar in the populace. So the more capable you are as fighters, the better off you will be. Rathos has told me that the girl, Azura, has bested my strongest warriors easily. He also told me how Darek has potential, judging by the way he managed to hurt Thedes."

"Rathos, how could you have told them such a thing?" Thedes's face flushed red through his fur. "That little worm was practically begging for his life! He only grazed me by luck!" Amused, Rathos just smiled back silently at Thedes.

Sorren ignored them and said, "So basically, because we are strangers, you feel more at ease using us, especially when you are expecting something bad to happen."

"Your wording concerning the matter is harsh," Merdon said, "but true. We must consider failure as a possible option. It would be of no consequence to us and we can have another attempt at a later date. If we were to get directly involved, it'd be the end of our little operation here."

"You know, you can just be honest with me," said Sorren. "I don't care about your reasons. You don't have to lie about your desire to help humans. You don't have to try to get us to sympathize with your cause. We just need a reward. Whatever your plan is, it has nothing to do with us."

Merdon shook his head. "Think what you will. But I sincerely desire to see humans repopulate the world." He paused. "But I see that you in particular just want to know what you'll get out of this. That's fine. If you want a reward, I'll be quite reasonable about it. Especially since there is a chance you might not make it…"

"Good," Sorren said, "then this is our situation: we are trapped on this planet. Do you have any method of space travel?"

"Wait, wait, wait!" Darek interrupted their conversation. "What good is a reward if we might not make it? What good is a reward if we're dead!"

Sorren shrugged. "I don't see a problem. Just don't die."

"That's ridiculous!" Darek shouted, "You make it sound so easy when it's obviously not! We're dealing with powerful and dangerous immortals here! Telling me not to die is like throwing me off a five-hundred-foot cliff and telling me not to break a single bone! I don't even know why I'm letting you speak on my behalf! If these are the circumstances, I want no part of this!" He began to storm out of the room, but Azura blocked his path.

Azura said slowly, "Darek, I understand it sounds unreasonable. But we need you. We have to work as a team. Don't you want to get off this planet? I don't know when or if anyone will come looking for me. This could be our only chance."

Darek shoved Azura out of his path.

"Such a coward," Sorren said, snickering.

Darek looked back, glaring at him. He bit his lip, fighting the urge to say something back to him and proceeded to exit the room.

Rathos squeezed Darek by the shoulder. "You are welcome to stay at the mansion for as long as you like. Let me show you to your room."

Darek bowed his head in appreciation. "Thank you." He followed Rathos out.

"So," Sorren continued his conversation with Merdon, "do you think you can help us?"

Merdon quietly thought for a moment. "Is there anything specific we can help with? Our society in the past was never concerned with space. We have no knowledge of space travel."

"How about power? Do you have energy—like electricity?" Azura asked. "Darek has a teleportation device. We just need an ample supply of electricity to make it work."

Merdon said, "Electricity is something we can do. We have artifacts for that."

"That's the option we'll take," said Sorren. "But before we're in full agreement, I must ask, how can you trust us when we say that we're from other worlds? We could be lying to you."

Merdon said, "Since there're only about ten thousand immortals who live on this planet, we know them all by name and face. When the fall of mankind occurred, my group and I have searched through this planet and have found only a few last vestiges of pure humanity. The ones who survived were the ones who lived in isolation. These small tribal communities are uneducated and primitive. Although, when we first found you, we had hoped you did come from this world."

Sorren nodded. "I see. Then I accept your mission."

"That's great!" Merdon beamed. "I didn't think you'd accept. You must be confident."

"That is not the case." Sorren shook his head. "There is just no other way. When there is only one right visible way, you take that way, regardless of how hard it may be." Sorren gestured toward the map. "Now, if you will, please tell us the details of our mission."

CHAPTER 11
Slumber

Darek thought he would pass out on the soft, clean bed prepared for him—but that was not the case. While his eyes were closed, his mind would not shut down. He rolled in the sheets for hours even though he was dead tired. His face half-buried in the pillow, he glanced around the room, his eyes shifting from the ticking clock to the door. He watched the hour hand move ever so slowly across the unnumbered dial. Finally, he gave up on sleep. Darek got to his feet and paced back and forth in the room, thinking about many things.

His life, as he knew it, was no more. He could no longer see his friends; some of his friends even ended up betraying him. What was he supposed to do now? He originally wanted to get off the planet. But even if he did so, there was no point. There was no place he could go.

Now that he had met Merdon, this planet wasn't as bad as he thought. That was one of the reasons he didn't feel like risking his life on some crazy mission. He could start a new life on this planet. He could become one of Merdon's subjects. He didn't mind being a servant. It sounded like a simple life. If they needed someone to help out the human village, then he could work there. It all sounded good—but was that what he really wanted, or was there something else?

As he continued to ponder, he regretted his actions in the throne room. *I shouldn't have done that*, he thought. *I was the one who asked her to help me in the first place. In the end, I refused to help them.* He hung his head. *Maybe...I'll help them, just this once.*

He paced around several times more, trying to gather up the courage to apologize. As much as he hated the idea, the best way to say sorry would be to offer help for their endeavor. Maybe the mission wouldn't be so bad after all. It's not like it was the end of the world.

He left the room, but he wasn't sure where to go. It was already late, so the others were probably resting in their rooms. Darek figured that if he wandered around, he might find a wolf on guard duty and ask him for directions.

Darek proceeded down the corridor, which was now dimly lit by evenly spaced torches. Peering out a window, he saw that the Sun bugs were now gone from the cavern. The cave was now pitch-black. It must have gotten late. Rathos had told him before that the Sun bugs only leave a few hours prior to the rising of the sun in order to reach the surface in time.

Darek tried to get an understanding of the layout of the mansion, but the more he walked, the more he became confused. Every hall looked exactly the same. He could not tell where he came from or where he was going. After walking for a long time, he caught a colorful painting from the corner of his eye.

The painting was of a man who was striking a rock with his staff. In the background were a hundred more rocks; some were smooth and polished while others were rough and edgy. It was a pretty distinct painting, beautifully drawn and lifelike; none of the other dull paintings remotely resembled it. However, something was odd. He remembered walking past a painting similar to this just a moment ago. Could he have been walking around in circles?

Darek began to panic. He didn't have to worry about being embarrassed about it since he was alone, but he never thought he'd ever get lost inside a building. Morning was near. If he couldn't find them in time, he might never get a chance to apologize to Azura.

Then he recalled a tale about children who left a marking wherever they went so they could avoid getting lost. Darek whirled around, making sure that no one was watching, and then pulled out his dagger. *I hope no one sees this.* He took the tip of the blade and made a little scratch on the wall, near the floor. He inspected his handiwork and grinned. *There. This way, I won't get lost.*

Darek walked several more steps and crouched over, cutting a small bit of the wall in a different and more elaborate design. He proceeded to do so repeatedly to ensure that he would know where he was going. The hallways looped around with stairs heading down, then back up, and back down again. Sometimes he came across troublesome obstacles: two-way forks along the path, hidden trapdoors, and even giant springs that bounced him up to the next floor. After walking for an hour, he got tired from constantly crouching over.

"When is this ever going to end? I haven't seen anyone at all!" Frustrated, he started to run through the hall. However, no matter how much he ran, there was no one to be found.

After running around for another half hour, he was exhausted and his feet were sore. He had forgotten to wear shoes. He screamed at the top of his lungs and punched the wall several times to vent his anger. "What is up with this place?" Panting for air, he leaned on the wall.

While resting, he heard a distorted female voice.

You...it is you...

"Wh-who's there?" Darek's jumped up, his knees quivering.

The voice spoke louder. *You are the key to...come...I'm waiting...*

"Oh...I get it now!" Darek snapped his fingers. "I'm dreaming!" He smacked himself in the forehead. "Man, I'm such an idiot. I should've realized it earlier. I haven't seen anyone after such a long time, I was stupid enough to cut and punch someone else's wall, and now I'm even hearing weird ghastly voices!" Darek clasped his hands together. "Now...how do I wake up?"

The paint...

"The paint? You mean the painting?" Darek took a gander at the nearest painting. It was the same one he had seen before: the painting with the man and his many rocks.

"What do I do to wake up?"

Touch...for you are...

"I am what? I'm him?" He chuckled at the thought. "How stupid. The guy looks nothing like me. Dreams never seem to make any sense." Then he lifted up his hand and saw that his palm was glowing brightly. Darek placed his hand on the painting. Suddenly, the wall crumbled away and shattered like glass, revealing a hidden stairwell. All the broken pieces of the wall and painting vanished without a trace. "How disappointing, that didn't wake me up." He shrugged. "But I guess I might as well enjoy this strange dream." Darek followed the winding staircase down into a basement. Without any source of light, he descended into the darkness, feeling carefully for the next stair before stepping down. However, as he neared the final steps, he noticed some light through an open door at the bottom.

The door led into a small laboratory. "So far it doesn't look like a nightmare..." Darek wandered around. With so many different, interesting things, it felt like a playground. He peeked into the rainbow-colored test tubes, messed with the weights on the scales, sniffed some weird slime-filled Petri dishes, fiddled around with the t-shaped devices, melted a few pens with the burners and even checked out a working computer system.

Open your eyes…see me…

Darek shook his head while playing around with the computer. "I've been trying to wake up, but it doesn't look like anything is working."

Wake up! Not from dreams but from reality!

The voice was strong enough to make Darek's head rattle. There was a sense of urgency in its tone that was hard to ignore.

"It's starting to give me a headache. I wonder if it's trying to tell me something else."

Darek got up from his seat and felt another presence in the room. A mysterious radiance came from the back of the lab, covered by a cloth curtain. Curious, he pushed away the curtain. He came face-to-face with two giant crystals, one blue and one red. They towered over Darek; Darek was rooted in place, gaping at their captivating beauty. Imprinted along the exterior were several inscriptions and markings in a language foreign to him.

"Wow, even the markings are amazingly complex and beautiful. I can understand why they'd want to cover up something like this. It looks valuable." While Darek was busy gazing at its wonder, he noticed something within. "What's this?" It was hard to see at first glance. Darek went up for a closer look, squinting as he tried to make sense of the enclosed objects. The more he stared, the more he understood what he was looking at: the dark silhouettes were actually human figures. There were humans inside! Each crystal housed a person.

Shocked, he stumbled back. As he darted out, he hit something, or rather someone. It was Rathos.

"Oh, it's just you!" Darek exclaimed, wiping away some of the sweat from his face. "You scared me there for a second."

Rathos said sternly, "You shouldn't be here."

"You're not going to chase me until I wake up, are you?" asked Darek. "I hate those nightmares. Always leaves me in a sweat."

"What are you talking about?" Rathos cocked his head. "Anyway, this is a secret lab. I'd appreciate it if you didn't tell anyone about it."

"Only if you promise not to chase me," Darek begged him.

Perplexed, Rathos said, "I don't understand why I would. But I'll give you my word. I'm not going to chase you. Now tell me, why would I chase you?"

"Well, that's because this is a dream. Like if I pinch myself, it won't hurt." Darek pinched himself as hard as he could. "Ouch." He stared at Rathos in an awkward silence, and then pinched himself again. "Ouch."

"So…does it hurt?" Rathos asked.

"Yes…" Darek stood there dumbfounded. He had made a complete fool of himself. His face blushed with embarrassment. Thankfully, only Rathos was around and he didn't even crack a smile at Darek's mistake; if anything, Rathos acted genuinely concerned. But there was a more pressing matter that held his interest. He turned around to see if the crystals were still there, and indeed, they were right there before him.

"What are they?" Darek asked, pointing at them. "Those aren't real people, right?"

Rathos walked up to one of the crystals and placed his hand on it. "I don't know what these crystals are. We found them several miles south of here in a large network of underground caverns. My master thought it'd be good to study them, but we have learned nothing. We even tried to break them open, but we can't even scratch its surface."

"You aren't performing any *strange* experiments here, are you?"

"Well, I suppose everything around here is strange," Rathos said, beaming.

Darek furrowed his brow. "Hmm, I'm sorry for asking such a weird question."

All of a sudden, Darek realized there were so many things that couldn't or shouldn't be, if everything he was experiencing was never a dream. A mountain of questions piled up in his head; all in a rush he blurted out, "Why would you have a secret laboratory under the mansion? Where do you get the electricity to power everything? And what about that wall? How come it disappeared? Why would you have the same picture in your hallway, over and over again? And whose voice is inside my head? Why is the—"

Rathos motioned with his hands for Darek to calm down. "It seems to me that you have a lot of questions. I suppose I can explain some things." He led Darek out of the small chamber.

When they were seated near the computer, Rathos said, "In regards to the technology, we are using relics from our old civilization. We tried to salvage as much as we could. For the past century, we have been studying the technology, although it is very difficult to learn everything."

Darek said, "Where does the electricity come from?"

"From a waterfall. We have several turbines hidden from plain view. My master is the one who designs these things. He has studied engineering extensively." Rathos paused. "I'm surprised you found our laboratory. We were sure no one would be able to detect the barrier. My master wanted to hide our secrets from the elders. So I must ask…how'd you find this place?"

"There was this voice inside my head that guided me here," Darek explained. "I don't really understand it myself."

"A voice?"

Come…

"There! There it is again! Can you hear it?" Darek exclaimed.

Rathos became silent, trying to hear anything out of the ordinary. "I hear nothing."

Am I the only one who can hear the voice? Darek wondered.

The voice beckoned Darek again, *Come closer…*

Darek could almost sense the direction of the voice. It was coming from the back room. He walked past the cloth again and looked at the crystal. Could the voice be coming from inside?

You are the key to…

"I am the key." The blood vessels in Darek's hands were surging with warm blood. Darek looked at his hand again. It gleamed. Placing a hand on each crystal, he watched as they melted away like ice. Vapor filled the backroom. When the vapor cleared, the crystals were gone and two strangers, a man and a woman, were standing in the room with them.

Unsure of their intentions, Rathos backed out of the room, pulling Darek with him.

The strangers followed them out. The man looked mature. He had the appearance of a fierce warrior with his stalwart body, honed to perfection. He had a roughly shaven beard, very short red hair, and rugged mean looks. His clothes were sewn from animal hide. The woman, on the other hand, was elegant. Her bluish green hair ran down her back, stopping just above the back of her ankles. Her body was wrapped in loose gray cloth.

They knelt on the ground before Darek.

"Who are you and what do you want?" Darek demanded quickly.

The woman replied, "I am Reza and this man is Drey, my bodyguard. You have freed us from our slumber, so we will follow you. May we know the name of our new master?"

"Um, I'm Darek. Why were you in those crystals?"

"Long ago a powerful and evil sorcerer cast a spell on us."

Darek tapped his feet in a long drawn out silence. "That's it? That's your story? There has to be more! Who's the evil sorcerer and why did he trap you?"

Reza pursed her lips. "We don't know. He trapped us because he was powerful and evil."

Darek narrowed his eyes. They were clearly hiding things from him. With quick thinking, Darek said, "Okay, you can follow me. I could use a few extra hands."

Rathos whispered to Darek, "Are you sure? Do you not find them suspicious? I've never heard of any legendary sorcerers in our history who could do such things."

Darek replied, "They look harmless enough. I also can't help shake this feeling that they really need our help. I'll test their sincerity myself. Haven't you heard the saying, 'Keep your friends close, your enemies closer, and strangers even closer?'"

Rathos said, "I don't think it quite goes like—"

Darek said curtly, "Same idea. We'll find out soon enough who they really are."

Meanwhile, in the midst of their conversation, Windzer and Hortmel snuck out of the basement.

"What do you think?" asked Windzer.

"This place is nice. They built it well."

"I'm not talking about that," said Windzer, sounding annoyed.

"Then are you talking about Merdon being a traitor?"

Windzer shook his head. "While that is useful to know, I wasn't referring to that either. I'm more concerned about those crystals and those people in them."

"What about them?"

"I feel like I've seen them before but I'm not sure where."

Hortmel rubbed his chin. "You might be right. But we've lived a long time. It's hard to remember everything."

"Well, I'm sure it'll come back to us soon enough, but now is not the time to ponder," whispered Windzer. "We must leave before anyone discovers us. Now that we've caught wind of Merdon's plan, we can be sure that we were lucky to have come to this place."

CHAPTER 12
Hesitation

The sizzling aroma of steaks diffused out the kitchen door. Just a single whiff of the smell aroused the delicate stomachs of the soldiers in the cafeteria. It was time for dinner on board the *Vagrant,* and soldiers that were late to the cafeteria found themselves standing on the back of a line that stretched all the way across the room.

Rex was at the very front of the line. It was difficult to be first in line every time, but he managed to do so anyway. He hated waiting on line, watching the people in front fill their plates. To avoid such a situation, he made it a priority to reach the cafeteria first, even if it meant sneaking off early from his duties to do so.

After receiving the last portions of food on his tray, he politely nodded to the kitchen staff and took his usual seat near the back window. There, in that far removed spot, he could enjoy a quiet meal with the view he loved.

"Is this seat taken?" A woman tugged on the chair next to him. It was the same woman who had helped him capture Darek. Her name was Layne.

"Don't know." Rex took hold of his fork and knife and licked his lips as he looked longingly on the tender, juicy steak.

"Don't ignore me." She slammed her fist against the table.

Rex sighed, placed his utensils down and turned to her. "What do you want?"

"You enjoy playing dumb?" Layne cracked a cruel smile. "Maybe I should just tell Dionus that you rejected his offer."

Rex laughed and said, "At least I'm the one who's only *playing* dumb…"

Layne's smile disappeared. She grabbed him by the collar and breathed, "I'm sick and tired of your attitude. Lately, you've been skipping work. Do you know how bad you're making Dionus look? And to top it off, Dionus gave you a *very* important assignment just yesterday, and you somehow managed to screw it up!"

"So? Why should you care? It's not your problem."

"It is my problem—more than you realize. And I want to settle this now. How about a duel?"

Rex shrugged. "A duel? You're kidding. No one duels in this day and age."

"You're pretty spineless," said Layne. "How about a wager to sweeten things?"

"A wager? What's the wager?"

Layne revealed her wicked smile. "Our lives."

"You're crazy!"

Rex backed away as Layne drew her sword.

Everyone in the cafeteria fell silent. Instead of focusing on getting their fill of meat, they watched the argument between Rex and Layne escalate. While they couldn't help but satisfy their curiosity about how the fight would turn out, they kept their distance apprehensively.

Layne gestured to him. "Shall we make things fair? I'll let you have the first strike."

Hesitating, Rex looked around the faces of the cafeteria. It didn't look like anyone was willing to help him out. He was on his own. There was no way out of this fight. Even if he didn't agree to it, he knew she would still attack him regardless. She had that kind of reputation. She had been on his back for over a week, hassling him and threatening him. He had to settle things with this crazy woman sooner or later. But that was fine with him. He had been practicing anti-law for the past year. All he needed was one powerful attack…and it would be over.

Rex felt his spirit flow like a mighty rushing flame coursing through his body. Power accumulated in the tips of his fingers. The cafeteria became noticeably hotter. He pointed his fingers at Layne and lashed out with a bolt of fire. The stream of flame soared across the room; Layne drew her sword and effortlessly blew out the flame with the swipe of her blade.

Layne laughed. "That's it? I guess I shouldn't have expected much. I don't even know why they allow street scum like you to join the military."

"Street scum?" This infuriated Rex even more. The temperature began rising ever more rapidly and everyone in the room began pouring out buckets of sweat. Rex spread out his fingers; a ring of light appeared before him.

"Now that's more like it." Layne smiled slyly.

"So that's what you were doing." Dionus stormed into the cafeteria, displeased to see that they were fighting. Rex withdrew his hand and the ring of light faded away.

"I thought I told you to deliver a message," Dionus said to Layne.

"I'm sorry," apologized Layne. "I have no words to express my regret. Please excuse me." She hid her sword and left the room.

"I'm sorry about her behavior," said Dionus, patting Rex on the shoulder. "It shouldn't have turned out that way. I'm not sure why, but she causes trouble from time to time."

"No, sir. It is I who should apologize. I was partly at fault." Rex stood at attention.

"Please, take a seat," said Dionus amiably. "Enjoy your meal. We can talk here."

Rex took his seat but refrained from eating.

Dionus could tell that Rex was a little stiff. "Do you have something to say, Lieutenant?"

"As a matter of fact, I do." Rex straightened. "I don't mean to question your motives or anything. But I still don't understand why we arrested Darek. He's harmless."

"You don't need to worry," assured Dionus. "It was an accident. I had circumstantial evidence and made a decision in haste. But that is no longer my concern."

"It isn't?" said Rex. "Then what did you come to speak with me for?"

"I see potential in you, Lieutenant. Even in the face of suspicion and doubt, you followed your orders blindly like a true soldier. I could use someone like you."

Rex raised a brow. "I don't understand."

"Rex, how would you like to be my escort? I'm going to the city of Fallence to have an audience with the Overlord. If you agree, I'll only be taking you and Layne."

"With all due respect sir, I do not get along with that woman, and I don't see this working well, especially on a diplomatic mission."

"Rex, listen to me. Underneath her cold exterior lies the gentle heart of a sweet girl."

Rex couldn't believe his ears. "Are you serious, sir?"

"That's for you to decide." Dionus started to leave. "Now, you don't have to give me an answer immediately. Just make sure to tell me by tomorrow. I need to make arrangements."

"I understand, sir."

Rex watched him leave without so much as a goodbye. He sighed and wondered what Dionus was thinking. Visits to Fallence were not routine for Federation officers. Fallence was the city of Heroes. It was their headquarters and capital; it was a symbol of their power. Fallence was the home of the Sanctuary, where the Overlord reigned. Only the most honored kings or officials would dare go to speak with the Overlord—the undisputed leader of the Legion. Any blunder or embarrassment that took place in front of the Overlord would spell certain death.

It would be best to avoid that place altogether. After all, the Legion was the most respected establishment in the galaxy. Before the Federation was ever conceived, the Heroes were the ones who kept the peace. With sword in hand and peace in mind, they fought valiantly to prevent wars from erupting. A little trouble with the Heroes could hurt the Federation in a big way.

Setting that issue aside, he debated in his mind whether he should go or not. His main concern was Layne. Layne. Rex never knew her personally and never hated her until recently. She had joined the ranks of the Federation at the same time as Dionus. They have been together ever since. She was kind of Dionus's lackey, always there for him, waiting on him hand and foot. Whenever Rex saw Dionus at a meeting, she would be right there by his side. Rex supposed it was admiration that she was the way she was. She would be right on the tail of anyone who spoke ill of the commander. Layne had gotten into so many fights that Rex was surprised she hadn't been kicked out, but that was most likely the commander's doing.

His stomach grumbled. He had almost forgotten about his meal. Rex picked up his utensils again and looked down on the steak. He cut a morsel off the meat and shoved it in his mouth. As he chewed, only one thing came to mind: it had gotten cold.

CHAPTER 13
The Journey Begins

It was late in the morning when the group decided to set off. Since it was going to take several weeks to reach Duraskull, Rathos prepared some rucksacks for them. The sacks were filled with rationed food, knives, clothing, medical supplies, and useful tools.

Darek lay lazily in bed, still drowsy. Shifting in and out of consciousness, he dug his face into the pillow, engrossed in every last second of rest. Too lazy to look at the clock, he wondered about the time. He had lost the concept of time when he first came to the planet. Even if he did look at the clock, he wouldn't be able to really understand what time it was. The days, months and years were different for each planet.

To make things easier for space travelers, the Federation standardized the time to correspond with their home planet of Teraskai. Other planets within the Federation would keep their own days and years but would have to use a formula to convert their time to Federation time when dealing with traveling merchants and other intergalactic affairs.

At the moment, he had a feeling similar to jetlag, but more disorienting. Darek was energetic and tired at all the wrong times. It would take a few days to adjust to the abnormal day and night cycle, but until then he'd have to suffer with this annoyance. And the fact that the Sun bugs lit the cavern at night rather than day only further complicated things.

There was a brisk knock on the door.

"Darek, are you awake?"

Darek sluggishly went to open the door

Rathos was standing there, bowing. "Sorry to disturb, but the others have been *hounding* me to wake you up. It is almost noon."

Darek nodded and, with a sense of urgency, grabbed his things and left. Everyone was already waiting for him at the gates. The group consisted of Thedes, Rathos, Sorren, Azura, Darek, Reza, Drey and a few other wolves that would assist them. Darek was surprised to see that while Rathos preferred his human form, Thedes preferred to stay as a wolf. Darek had not seen Thedes's human form yet and wondered why he preferred being a wolf. If Darek had that ability, he'd much rather stay human. The thought of walking naked in the forest and being swamped by bugs was disturbing. Clothes offered him a feeling of protection from the wild.

Azura crossed her arms in disapproval. "What took you so long?"

Bags under his eyes and hair disheveled, Darek looked like a mess. He staggered, trying to maintain his balance. "You have no idea what I went through last night. I'm really tired. I'm only human for crying out loud." He slapped himself on the cheeks to liven up. "You sure we can't stay a little longer? I want to wake up first."

"Let's go," said Sorren irritably. "We've wasted enough time."

"How about we go over the details one more time?" Rathos suggested. "Darek missed out on what we talked about last night. It might be best to brief him on the plan."

Sorren agreed. "We might as well…even though that was his own fault."

Rathos said, "The continent is not that big. Even with the fastest rides available, it'd take one to two weeks to reach the capital. However, the fastest rides would be too noticeable. I want to avoid being seen together by other immortals if possible. We must arrive at Duraskull separately to avoid suspicion." Rathos pulled out the map from his bag and unfolded it. Then Rathos rubbed a finger along the path they planned to take.

"We'll take the most direct path across the forest. It should take two weeks to clear it. After that, we'll reach the southern edge of the largest desert. We'll be heading east toward a mountain range that cuts through the side of the desert. There should be a railroad tunnel that runs through the mountains. I'm not sure if the train or the tunnel is usable. If we can get the train running, we may save a great deal of time. If not, we can expect more weeks of traveling."

"Weeks and more weeks? I'm not liking this at all," groaned Darek. He glanced at the faces around him and realized something. "Where's Merdon? Isn't he coming too?"

"Merdon is getting ready to leave, but he won't be coming with us," Rathos replied. "He'll go ahead of us and wait for us at the capital. The immortals have their own personal ride in order to travel around the continent at great speeds."

"What kind of ride would that be?"

Before Rathos could answer, a bright light flashed and a loud thunder clapped behind the mansion. The cavern was so bright it nearly blinded them. A chilly breeze and strong air current flooded across the white forest, sending dust in their faces; it was so strong that Darek struggled to stay standing. Crouching, Darek flung his head back and saw the bright light zoom past, spiraling around. Then it disappeared as a white streak across the ceiling.

His eyes wide, Darek steadily rose. "That was crazy. What *was* that?"

"That would be the ride," Rathos explained. "Merdon has a thunderbird, which is very rare. Night or day makes no difference because the lightning it emits allows them to see for miles at a time. The lightning also makes it dangerous to ride, so it's roped to a fully insulated chariot. At its maximum speed, Merdon will reach the capital city within a matter of days."

"What?" Darek exclaimed. "Then why didn't we ride with Merdon?"

Rathos said, "As I've said before, we don't want to be seen together. A thunderbird is easily seen. And if you haven't noticed, we have certain social standards. When the mutation had taken place, we were not all the same. Most people only gained super-human strength. They are still significantly stronger than your average human, but with no true special abilities to speak of, they became the lowest class and are forced to perform the labor as necessary. They construct buildings, farm and hunt, and even serve as butlers and shopkeepers.

"The class above that includes us, the ones able to transform into different animals. We are the warrior class, used as bodyguards or soldiers. We can transfigure ourselves into any animal we wish, but the wolf's form is the most practical and easiest to learn. It takes years of practice in order to attain other forms such as the bear or the lion.

"And the class above us would be the noble class, which is the class that Merdon is a part of. When he became immortal, he gained strange and powerful supernatural abilities that set him apart from most other immortals. As Darek has seen before, one of his abilities is to create an illusionary barrier to hide what we need to keep secret.

"The last and highest class in the social ranking would be the elders. I do not know much about them. They have kept their abilities and their ages a secret. Only nobles are allowed to associate with them, and even then, the elders usually isolate themselves.

"So with that explained, you should understand that based on social ranking we are not to be seen riding around with Merdon. Under no circumstances are we allowed to act as equals. Also, due to the social ranking, as Merdon is on his way, it is possible other nobles will want to speak with him. Merdon must reach the capital alone so that no one will suspect a thing."

"Time is of the essence," Sorren said impatiently, "Let us be off."

Rathos nodded, leading the group with a torch. "Come. We need to follow the river out."

Darek interlocked his hands and rested them on the back of his head, humming as they walked along.

"You're in a good mood today," said Azura. "Did something happen?"

Darek shook his head. "Nothing in particular. I'm just glad. We got some good meals, some *decent* rest and a few new companions."

When they reached the outside, Rathos transformed back to his wolf form. "Before we continue, everyone should find a wolf to ride. Four feet are better than two, and we have the stamina to handle long distances."

Everyone looked for a partner to ride on. There were just enough wolves for everyone to ride. While Darek enjoyed the idea of riding wolves—it did sound pretty cool—there was only one problem for Darek.

"Something is terribly wrong about this arrangement," Darek complained. "Why do I have to be with *him*?" He pointed at Thedes, who chuckled sinisterly.

"You don't want to be with Thedes?" asked Rathos. "I thought this would be a good time for you two to reconcile any past issues. After all, Thedes was the one who requested for you."

Darek glared at Thedes. He knew something funny was going on.

"If you're that much against it, I can't force you," said Rathos. "But I can't force anyone to trade with you either."

"That shouldn't be a problem." Darek was pleased with the suggestion. "Does anyone want to trade partners?"

However, his question did not garner the responses that he was expecting. Everyone sat cozily on the wolves and stared blankly at Darek.

"Oh come on," whined Darek. "No one wants to make an exception?" He turned to Reza and Drey and said, "Hey, didn't you guys say you were going to serve under me? I demand that one of you trade places with me."

After she cleared her throat, Reza said, "Should I or should he?"

"Well I guess I don't want to be mean to the girl." Darek pointed at Drey. "You should trade places with me."

Drey shook his head.

"Hey! You can't refuse! That's against the rules!" grumbled Darek. "Now come on and help me out here."

Drey said, "I can't…I have a bad back."

"What? And what difference would that make—"

"Just shut up and get on," snapped Sorren, his voice icy. "All you're doing is wasting my time. I don't feel like staying on this planet any longer than I have to. If you aren't going to cooperate, then you're better off staying than coming with us."

Darek bit his lip. He wanted to say something back but the words wouldn't come out. It was true he wanted to stay. That was the real reason why he slept in. Lack of sleep was just an excuse to delay things. Though he told them he would go with them, he really didn't feel that compelled to go. Somewhere in his heart, he was still afraid to begin the journey.

In the deserted city, he could barely defend himself. He wasn't like the others. He wasn't an immortal, a Hero, or an assassin. He wasn't strong. He wanted to help…but he wasn't sure if he truly could.

"Hey," Azura said to Sorren. "Can't you tell he's troubled? He's got a lot on his mind."

Sorren replied, "Is that a proper excuse for him to waste our time? No. I don't care if he is a Judge." He sneered, "For a Judge to finally get caught after all these years, their standards sure have fallen. It looks like they're all just a bunch of snotty brats now."

"Age has nothing to do with anything!" snapped Azura. "Just because you're a little older, it doesn't mean you're better than him!"

"It's all right, Azura," interrupted Darek. "I understand what he's saying."

Without any more hesitation or grumbling, Darek took his place on Thedes. It wasn't as uncomfortable as he expected. The saddle they strapped on was built to absorb shock. In a hurry, they dashed off, cruising down a long slope that went into a forest at the bottom of the mountain.

Darek held on tightly; he wrapped his arms around Thedes neck to avoid slipping off. The wolves zipped through the trees, dodging tree trunks with ease.

Thedes thought that this was the perfect time to get his revenge for the scar on his eye. Darek would now feel the full force of his insurmountable wrath. As Thedes zoomed toward the trees, his keen eyesight picked up on lower branches that would be just the right height so that he would be able to barely run under it without getting harmed. He darted at those low tree branches with utter anticipation.

Thwack.

"Ouch!" yelled Darek. His nose was bruised with a sharp slap in the face by a tree branch. "Watch where you're going!"

Thwack.

"Gah!"

Thwack.

"HEY, THAT HURTS!" Outlines of tree branches were marked across Darek's face. "Now you're pushing it! I know you're doing it on purpose!" Darek screamed. "Let's see how you like this!" Darek started to pull clumps of hair off Thedes's back. The wolf howled in pain.

Thedes retaliated by slamming Darek into the thickest tree branch he could find. Darek was knocked out cold, falling unconscious on Thedes's back. Thedes grinned with satisfaction on his lips.

"No hard feelings," Thedes growled. "Just an eye for an eye."

Azura had seen the whole thing from behind, and while she felt a bit sorry for Darek, she had to stifle a laugh. "This is going to be one long journey."

CHAPTER 14
Paths to Power

Upon hearing frantic shouts in his ear and feeling painful slaps on his cheeks, Darek woke up and said, "Wh-what's going on?"

"Someone's coming," said Azura. "I don't know who it is, but we need to be ready for anything."

Darek got to his feet and looked around. No one else was with them. He wasn't sure how long he'd been asleep, but it couldn't have been more than a few hours. "This is weird. Where'd everyone go?"

"They split up to gather things for the camp," replied Azura. "Stay focused right now and don't do anything offensive. We don't know what we're dealing with."

A pair of surly faces came from behind the underbrush. Darek observed them. The woman had short unkempt brunette hair and long thin eyebrows. She appeared a bit scrawny, but her rolled up sleeves revealed strong arms. An iron headband was tightly buckled across her forehead, holding up her messy locks of hair. The rest of her clothing constituted of dark gray leather and blended in quite nicely with the early evening. The most conspicuous aspect about her was the giant metal pipe she carried on her back; it looked cumbersome to bring along, yet she walked around with it easily.

The other fellow was calm, but had an unpleasant, steely gaze. A slim metal helmet covered the top of his head to the lower part of his face, leaving only his lips visible. Darek had never encountered anyone like him, but Darek knew what he was through books and stories. The man was a cyborg—a man turned machine. His body was fully plated with wires running through. His breathing was hard and heavy, like he was suffering.

Cybernetics was common within the Federation, though certain people would consider the integration of man and machine to be dangerous and unethical. When it became available for public use, it was believed to be a miracle cure. People who lost a part of their body could now easily replace it. However, it was confined to civilian use and was banned from the military. It was only meant for medical treatment, not for war. All cybernetic enhancements were weakened, allowing people to only carry out basic functions similar to an average human.

But this cyborg was different. Darek only needed to catch a glimpse of its hydraulics in action to be able to understand that his cyborg was built to be well beyond the limits imposed by the Federation. He was a living weapon—something Darek thought he'd never see.

"We don't want any trouble," Azura told the strangers. "We're just travelers."

The unstable woman stared at Azura for a few seconds without even blinking. "We got something good. Must be our lucky day." Her voice was low and hoarse, like a scratchy hum.

The armored man asked in a monotonous voice, "Both or one?"

"That girl," the woman said, as she cracked her neck. "She's a Hero. I don't have much data on her. Must be new."

"Uncertainty is perilous," the cyborg said.

The strange woman snapped, "It shouldn't matter. Most Heroes aren't that great anyway." She pounded her fist into the palm of her hand. "Like Xavius. It's surprising how that weakling is an Archlord. He couldn't hurt an ant if he accidentally stepped on one." Anxious, she flexed the fingers in her right hand. "The boy is a nobody. I have nothing on him. Scans show his abilities are above average, but that's not saying much. Kill him only if he gets in the way."

"I don't think they're immortals," Darek whispered to Azura. "The immortals here shouldn't know about the Legion."

"You're right. I've got a bad feeling about them." Azura gripped her fists and inched her way into a fighting stance as a precautionary measure. Azura said to them, "I don't know what we did to offend you, but I wish to settle this peacefully."

"Peacefully?" the woman replied. "It will be quite peaceful…when we have your head."

Azura whispered to Darek, "It sounds like it doesn't concern you, but you can help me if you want. I've always wanted to see how a Judge handles things."

Darek stood there, looking confused. He wasn't sure if it was because he was feeling woozy after waking up, but nothing made any sense. These people, not even natives of the planet, popped out of nowhere and started looking for a fight for no real reason. They even knew Azura was a Hero, and they still wanted to kill her. That just seemed very odd to him. Heroes should be revered and respected for the good that they do.

"The cute Hero wants to play." The woman smiled at her companion. "Wardon, you're up. Let's see what this Hero's got."

"As you wish, Kaye." The armored man crouched over and slammed his fists against the ground, causing a minor tremor. Steam blew out from his joints as he let out a deep bellow.

Darek was startled by the display of force, and though he had the urge to run away, he didn't. His pride held him firm.

"Hey, kid," Kaye shouted. "You're in the way. I don't really have anything against you, so I suggest you get out of here."

Darek swiftly whipped out his daggers from his satchel. "What kind of man runs when his friend is in trouble?"

Azura's stern face broke into a smile. "Thanks, Darek. To be honest, this is my first real mission since I graduated from the academy. I could use the help."

"No need to thank me," Darek said. "This is one of those things I have to do."

Wardon jumped up and landed near them, crushing the ground beneath as he walked. He bolted his iron fist at Darek. Darek tried to block the attack as fast as he could. The block was useless. He was slammed straight into a tree. He heard all the bones in his arms crack simultaneously. Shards of broken bone protruded from his skin.

"My arms!" Darek howled in pain and collapsed on the ground. "Crap...how did he..." Dazed, he tried to stand up, but without his arms to support him, it was an overly strenuous task. Grunting, he squirmed against the tree, working his way off the grass.

"Darek, hold on!" Azura pushed the armored warrior back with furious attacks. She tried to best him with incredible speed, squeezing in two to three punches in a second. But Wardon, despite his bulky size, was able to dodge each attack. Kicking off a tree, Azura jumped into the air. She let loose a flying roundhouse kick, slugging Wardon over the head; Wardon tumbled into the ground. Now that the cyborg was out of the way, Azura ran to Darek's aid. She gently pressed her fingers on his arm. Darek cried on contact.

"Your arms..." Azura said, grimacing. "I can't do anything. They're shattered. I can't set them back together. We have to find a doctor to handle this—and fast." She thought for a second. "Maybe Rathos can help. They shouldn't be far off. If we can just—" Before Azura could help Darek up, Wardon grabbed her arm with a solid grip and swung her across the forest, sending her almost twenty feet in the air. She plummeted into the nearby lake.

There was an initial shock after her bad dive, but Azura quickly recovered. Though in fine condition, she didn't rush for the shore, thinking it would be safer in the water. Since the lake was rather deep, she figured the cyborg wouldn't be able to reach her here. This was a good time for a short rest—or so she thought.

Her hopes were unfounded. Wardon plunged into the lake and swam, forcing his way through the water by brute force. He would undoubtedly sink if he stopped moving, and so he swam perpetually like a torpedo, carrying his weight by pulling through the waves. Wardon pierced through the currents and made his way over to Azura as fast as he could.

The two engaged in an underwater battle. Azura gave it her best by following the current and cutting through the water with sharp chopping motions, but even so, the two combatants looked like they were fighting in slow motion. Their attempts to strike one another failed horribly because their slow movements were too predictable.

"Azura!" After stumbling in excruciating pain, Darek finally was on his feet. He ran through the forest to the edge of the lake and looked out, attempting to locate Azura across the rippling surface. Darek yelled at the top of his lungs again, "AZURA!"

Azura made her way up out of the water and Darek breathed out a sigh of relief when he saw that she was still okay. However, he held his breath as she was immediately dragged back down into the water. Darek could still make out the bubbles of air that rose from their position.

Then he overheard Kaye mutter, "She's much stronger than I thought. Wardon can't handle her. How could a nameless Hero beat Wardon in a fight? Unless…could she be the Aenarian?"

Azura surfaced from the water with a big splash and flung back her drenched hair. Exhausted from the struggle, she walked up the shallow part of the lake.

"Azura, you're okay!" Darek ran to meet her with broken arms.

The mud below Azura's feet suddenly burst in a loud explosion. The blast volleyed her back into the lake, rendering her unconscious and wounded. The gentle waves around her were stained red by her blood. Darek froze at the sight of Azura floating on the top of the lake, motionless. He swung around to see the cause of the explosion. The woman, Kaye, had nestled herself on top of a strong tree branch. Strapped to her arm was the giant pipe that she had been carrying on her back. Smoke and rising heat scattered out of the hollow barrel from the pipe. Darek immediately understood it wasn't a pipe at all—but a cannon!

"Looks like she's still breathing," said Kaye.

Kaye strengthened her grip on the handle and pulled a small lever on the cannon to prepare her large weapon for a second shot. Her stoic gaze was focused on the laser sight aimed for Azura; she slowly tightened her finger around the trigger.

"NO!" Darek shouted. "DON'T SHOOT!" Darek struggled to raise his broken arms. *I can't let this happen! I'm supposed to help her, not watch her die!* He grabbed his broken arms with his own hands. Doing so inflicted excruciating pain, but he did so anyway. His hands glowed; a warm feeling flowed through his arms. At that moment, he thought he was going crazy because it felt like the shattered pieces of bones were rearranging themselves. But then he realized he wasn't crazy when he discovered his broken bones were made whole again. "My arms...they can move!" he uttered in amazement. He didn't understand what had just happened, but he didn't care.

In a hurry, Darek grabbed one his daggers and the dagger mysteriously burned bright red. He hurled his dagger up towards the cannon without Kaye even noticing. Kaye fired again but the explosion—caught by the flying dagger—erupted in midair.

"I missed? How'd that happen?" grunted Kaye, disappointed.

She cocked back the cannon, priming it for another shot. But as she peered through her scope, she only caught sight of the pool of blood. The body of Azura was gone. Through her scope, Kaye scrutinized the surrounding area of the lake and found a trail of blood leading into the forest. She sighed. "She got away..."

Kaye jumped off the tree branch and approached the shore. Something emerged from the lake. It was Wardon. Unlike Kaye, who was absolutely furious that her target had escaped, Wardon stayed mellow, not even twitching.

"First we let that mercenary shuttle get away, and now we let a Hero get away!" growled Kaye. "This is really frustrating. Even the boy is gone." She paused, raising a brow. "Wait, wasn't he injured?"

"He was...I'm sure of it," said Wardon. "The boy is a normal boy. Not an immortal. He could not even withstand a single punch. But the woman is different. Her capabilities are strange—erratic even. She is definitely Aenarian."

"So you've confirmed it?" said Kaye.

"Yes. Her strength kept…shifting. She was able to allocate muscle strength at will."

"This is vital information! There was a rumor about an Aenarian joining the ranks of the Heroes, but I never thought it was possible. This is dangerous. She must be eliminated."

"What happened to you?" Sorren asked plainly. "You don't look so good."

Darek slipped and fell to the ground, holding a bloodied Azura in his arms. He cried out, "She's coming! You have to stall her while I get Azura out of here!"

"What are you talking about? Who's coming?" Sorren scanned the forest.

"I don't know. They just spouted something about Azura being a Hero and started attacking us." As soon as Darek heard the sound of footsteps behind him, he stumbled along the ground and turned around. Darek was surprised and scared to see that Wardon was operational again; the cyborg walked alongside Kaye as if nothing had happened.

"So there was another one." Wardon asked Kaye, "Is he immortal?"

Kaye's right eye flashed like a laser and analyzed Sorren through the computer chip implanted in her brain. "An assassin," she said, surprised. "Low ranking. Nothing impressive."

"I'm not at optimal condition anymore," said Wardon. "He could be dangerous…and they may have other allies around. Should we take the chance?"

"Of course," said Kaye haughtily. "We need that Aenarian dead."

Sorren observed them closely. "Normally I wouldn't care about you, but you've already caused me quite a bit of trouble by hurting this girl." Sorren raised his hand; out of his palm was a black spot. The black spot grew into a hazy shadow that coiled around his fingers like worms. He flicked his fingers at them and the shadow shot forth, hovering across the ground.

"Anti-law…" Wardon dodged the shadow. It wrapped around a tree behind him, forming a thin black stripe around the trunk. Shaken, Wardon stared at the tree as it shriveled up and died. "I've never seen that kind of anti-law before."

A drop of sweat fell off Kaye's forehead. "The reading on that greatly exceeds normal levels. I must say—I'm quite surprised. This could prove to be an invaluable experience."

"Not bad," Sorren said, sounding amused. "Let's try this." He wiggled his fingers and waved his hand. Large swirls of darkness came from the earth, rolling around like smoke. The billows of darkness formed a perimeter around Wardon and Kaye and slowly closed in on them.

Wardon and Kaye both put one knee on the ground and ripped open a patch on their left shoulders in unison, revealing a small button. After they tapped the button, a large white force field ballooned around them and dissipated the darkness that surrounded them.

"That was a close one," Kaye said. "This is the strongest anti-law I've seen in a while."

"A dispelling barrier," said Sorren icily. "Hunting down Heroes with some powerful devices. I should've known. You're the Anarchists that chased my shuttle down, aren't you? I've changed my mind. I'm going to *kill* you right now." He licked his lips.

Kaye said, "But your magic is useless against us."

"Useless?" said Sorren. "You haven't even seen the *full* might of the darkness." The ground trembled around him as vaporous shadows began spewing out from newly formed cracks. A chunk of the earth split open, revealing vehement streams of darkness; it was like a violent tornado and it withered all the trees and grass within reach.

"Retreat!" Kaye ordered Wardon. "This is not worth the trouble."

The two Anarchists bolted out of there, desperate to escape with their lives intact.

Sorren took a deep breath and wiped the sweat from his brow. The darkness vanished and everything became peaceful again. "I think I went a little overboard. But at least they won't be back." Sorren turned around to see Darek tending to Azura.

"Where's Rathos?" asked Darek. "We need his help! Azura could die!"

"She'll be fine," Sorren replied.

"Look at her! She was almost blown to pieces!" Darek snapped, angry at Sorren's reply.

Azura said softly, "No. He's right. I'll be fine." Azura managed to sit up with her last ounce of strength. "More importantly, we have to help Darek. His arms were shattered."

Sorren shot her a look of disbelief. "That's impossible. *He* was the one who carried you here. There's no way he could've done that with broken arms."

"What?" Looking surprised, Azura seized Darek's arms and inspected them. "They're healed! How's that possible?" She looked Darek in the eye. "What kind of ability is this? Is this the Judge's power, or is it some form of anti-law?"

"You're asking me if I have weird abilities or magic powers? I got nothing!" Darek shook his head, insisting that he didn't understand it himself.

"That's fine." Azura breathed a sigh of relief and fell on her back to rest. "As long as you're okay..." She broke off. Utterly exhausted, she fell into a deep sleep.

"Is she really okay?" Darek said, sounding unconvinced.

"Of course. She's Aenarian," Sorren replied.

"That's what the strange woman said. But I don't get it. I've never heard of them before. What's an Aenarian?"

Sorren took a seat next to Azura. "They are humans from the planet of Aenaria. Aenarians don't rely on modern ways. They live in peace with nature. Their population as a whole is very small. But they're special. They have the innate ability to control their bodies completely. For example, you can move your arms and legs, but she has control over her own heartbeat. Azura can increase adrenaline flow, regenerate damaged parts, and strengthen muscle fibers all at her own will. Every involuntary muscle can be voluntary for her."

"Sounds pretty convenient," said Darek.

Sorren nodded. "It is convenient. Because of their abilities, they make excellent warriors. By disabling nerves, they can dull pain in the heat of battle to keep up their reaction time. By refining the lens in their eyes, they can see for miles at a time. By increasing the growth of their hair, they can keep warm in winter."

"Sounds creepy too," said Darek. "Oh—you mentioned something about Anarchists too. Who are they?"

Annoyed by Darek's questions, Sorren sighed but answered him anyway. "The Anarchists are the perpetrators of chaos. They believe in freedom for all people from the dominance of the more powerful factions. They don't really care about local governments. But they do harbor hatred against the United Federation. They'll hunt down

Heroes and Judges, but they'll also attack underworld organizations alike."

While seating cross-legged, Darek angrily punched the dirt to vent his frustration. "So that explains why they were after Azura!"

"That's only part of the reason," said Sorren. "They also don't like it when people like us travel to primitive worlds like these. They've got their own sense of justice." Sorren rubbed his temples. "Anyway…were there more, or were there only two?"

"Only two."

Sorren's expression became grave. "Huh. That's odd."

"What is?" Darek cocked his head.

"Every way I look at it, Azura shouldn't have been defeated by those two. She's strong…very strong. Even I wouldn't want to mess with her. Did something happen?"

Darek swallowed. "It might've been my fault. I was trying to help her fight, but all I did was get hurt. And then when Azura tried to help me…she was caught off guard."

"I see." The mood changed. Sorren stood up and said bitterly, "You overestimate yourself in too many ways. I know you're a Judge, but it seems that being a Judge is nothing special anymore if someone as pathetic as you became one. You seem to not comprehend how weak you truly are. You endangered the mission and your allies. Azura was almost killed because of you. In fact, if you didn't find me, both of you would've been dead."

Darek muttered under his breath, "I'm not really a Judge. It's not like I could've done much of anything."

Sorren heard him. "What?" He scowled. "What do you mean you're not a Judge?"

"I was framed!" Darek shouted. "Everyone thinks I'm a Judge, but I'm not! And every time I try to explain my situation, no one listens to me!"

"I don't remember you trying to explain anything to me," said Sorren scornfully. "You didn't say anything at all! If you'd told me beforehand, we wouldn't have gotten into this mess. I would've divided the teams more evenly!"

"But I…" Darek wasn't sure how to respond. He wanted to say excuses. He wanted to blame his failure on his young age, his weak body, and the turmoil he was suffering after running away from the Federation. But were those valid excuses? Why didn't he explain that he wasn't a Judge? What was holding him back? Every time he wanted to say something, he backed out. Was it because he enjoyed the attention from Azura? Was it because he thought no one would listen to him just like the judge that ignored his pleas of innocence? Or was he still wishing unconsciously that Sorren would help him end his misery when this was all over?

"I'm going to go find Rathos," said Sorren. "It's getting late and we need to set up camp. You can just stay here and watch over her. That's about all you're good for anyway."

Darek watched Sorren disappear into the trees. He slumped to the ground and stared at Azura's peaceful face. From dusk till dawn, he stayed in that place and gazed upon her.

The next day, as they continued northward, Darek remained depressed. He looked over his shoulder to see Rathos, in wolf form, carrying Azura on his back. Sorren's words rang over and over again in his ears. It was most likely his fault that Azura was now in this condition. Sighing, Darek regretted it, and the more he dwelled on this regret, the more he came to regret everything he had done.

"Hey, Sorren." Darek tapped him on the shoulder. "You think you can teach me how to fight? Not that I would fight in that situation again, of course not. I know I caused trouble, so I shouldn't have fought, but maybe if I could fight and maybe if I weren't weak then it would have been an option. But you know, if I ever come to a point where there's no way out and I have to fight, then I think that it would be great if—"

"Please," Sorren interrupted, "just get to the point."

"Oh, the point. Right." Darek dropped to his knees and grabbed onto Sorren's legs, begging. "Please teach me how to fight! I saw how strong you were! Teach me how to be strong like you! I'll do anything! I'll wash your…well, maybe not…that's disgusting. Okay, I'll cook for… actually, I'm kind of bad at it. You know what? I'll make Reza and Drey do something for you! I'm sure they can do something useful! Or at least…I hope so."

Sorren tried kicking him away but Darek held firm. "I'll do it. Just get off of me."

"Really?" Darek said. "You aren't just pulling my leg?"

"*You* are pulling *my* leg. Besides, I was going to teach you as long as you asked. Your weakness will be a disadvantage to our mission," said Sorren. Then Sorren cleared his throat and told everyone, "It's getting dark. Even though we're already behind schedule, Azura would fare better if we rest now. I'll stay here with Darek to watch over Azura. You guys can set up camp."

The others left to handle the menial tasks while Darek and Sorren were left alone. Sorren quickly started a campfire. Darek sat down by the fire, facing him.

Sorren said, "This may sound sudden, but are you ready to begin? I don't want to waste time. We only have a few months to bring you up to a respectable level."

"Yes," Darek replied. "Please teach me."

Sorren sat cross-legged near the fire and Darek imitated him. While the sun descended behind the towering trees, the fiery glow upon Sorren's face became more apparent, creating new shadows along the curves of his face. Darek watched Sorren intently.

"We'll do this step by step," said Sorren. "First, I'll begin by teaching you about the paths to power. You need to understand this to be able to fight accordingly." As Sorren spoke, the fire crackled. A strong breeze rushed across, blowing leaves into the wavering fire. Embers, leaping off the burning sticks, rose into the air and faded away. "I will not teach you about all the paths. There are only three paths to power you need to be concerned with: body, mind and spirit. These three elements make up the human being and can intertwine to form our different abilities.

"The body represents physical ability, mind is your mental ability, and the spirit is your inner being. The spirit is something only humans have and thus separates us from the animals and monsters. It is our essence. It is eternal. The path of spirit is much more elusive than the mind and is difficult to gain control of…but can be powerful."

Darek groaned, "Do I really need to learn this?" Darek wasn't expecting a lecture. Sorren had only begun speaking, yet Darek couldn't stop yawning. "Can't you teach me some moves?"

Sorren whipped Darek in the arm with a stick. "You asked me to teach you and I am doing so," Sorren snapped, waving the stick around. "Stop asking such pointless questions."

"Ouch." Darek rubbed the stinging pain in his right arm, wondering where that stick came from. "Sorry. Please continue." Darek held a few doubts in his mind, thinking this could just be some superstitious nonsense.

Sorren continued, "Now, one who trains his body will become strong in body, fitting for a warrior. One who trains the mind may attain new heights such as psychic powers where they can manipulate the outside world through their thoughts. One who trains the spirit may even be able to separate the spirit from the body.

However, the paths are not always straight. You can cross paths to attain new abilities. I'll give you some examples.

"The paths of body and mind can intersect. Take Azura for instance. Aenarians are born with this ability. I've explained this before, but I'll explain it again. By using her mind, she has achieved the power over the parts of the body that most people have no control over.

"The paths of the mind and spirit can also intersect. You saw me fight the Anarchists. My power to control the darkness is the result of these paths. Most refer to it as magic since it is something they can't explain, but others call it anti-law, as it goes against the laws of science. Simply put, this power is a manifestation of the spirit through the will of the mind.

"These are the most basic and easiest to understand paths, but aside from these there are other paths that are harder to use. Take for example the path of soul. The soul is your life. Everything that lives has a soul. Every human is born with a maximum potential lifespan of around a hundred and twenty years. The soul user can shorten his lifespan in order to gain power beyond human imagination. Theoretically, when a soul user is newborn, he is at the height of his power. But even so, few have the innate ability to control it and even fewer dare to use it."

"How few are we talking here?" Darek became interested in the path of the soul.

"I'd say the chances of finding one would be...one in one billion. At most, only a hundred of them would exist in the entire galaxy. But..."

"But?" Darek wished that Sorren wouldn't talk so slowly and hold him in suspense.

"It is rumored that the ability to use the soul's power is available to everyone and only needs to be unlocked. It's just a rumor. I've never seen anyone achieve it."

Sorren went on, explaining every single aspect of the three paths. But the more Sorren talked, the more Darek became confused; it almost felt like his head would soon lift off and spin around in circles. Darek tried his best to pay attention and acted as if he understood. But the intricate details that Sorren spoke were lulling him to sleep. Slowly, Darek began to weave about. His eyelids soon became as heavy as iron and they clamped shut.

A stagnant mist rested upon his face. It rapidly grew into a massive torrent that uprooted the forest around them. The dirt below crumbled and fell into a bottomless pit of vast emptiness. The sky shattered like glass and was sucked up into a vacuum above leaving only nothingness. Everything, aside from the fire in front, disappeared.

Feeling a nudge against his back, Darek opened his eyes. "What the…" He spun about and saw only the darkness that encompassed him. "Where am I?"

"This is a deep layer of your consciousness. In other words, you're asleep." Sorren said as he sprung up from the darkness, "Your will is weak, as expected, but I can use this to my advantage. Prepare yourself."

"Wait. If this is a dream, then why are you in it?"

"Well, you asked me to teach you and we don't have much time," replied Sorren. "From this point forward, I will now teach you as much as possible when we are awake and asleep. The dream is a great place to train. We don't have to worry about getting injured and I don't have to hold back. But in a dream you will be unable to train your body, so we'll focus on technique. I will hone your mind with experience by showing a few techniques. Are you ready?"

Darek shrugged. "Sure, whatever."

Sorren unsheathed the sword from his back and pointed the tip straight at Darek. He then swung his sword in a wide semi-circular motion forward. The tip of his sword hit the ground, causing a shock wave to burst forth. The wave rode along the ground in a straight line to Darek. When the wave hit his feet, Darek was catapulted back several feet from the impact. Though it was only a dream, Darek felt a painless emulation of being knocked back; he even felt a little dizzy. But other than that, he was perfectly fine.

"That is the Earth Wave," Sorren explained. "Make note of it. It's a common technique. Heroes favor it because it will not mortally wound anyone except under extreme circumstances. It may even scare some people into submission with its display of force. To properly execute it you need longer weapons—like swords or spears. Your daggers won't work." Sorren slid his sword back into the scabbard and took a fighting stance. "Now I'll show you something simple that the Immortals are likely to use. I believe they will rely on strength and power rather than weapons, though some may not be as arrogant."

Sorren kept his right fist tightly locked back. He sped forward and shot his punch straight to the pit of Darek's stomach, knocking the wind out of him, leaving him writhing on the ground.

Sorren helped Darek back up to his feet. "Simple, right? However, it is made lethal when you consider the strength of an immortal. Do you remember what Merdon said? They have super-human strength and their strength grows greater as they age. Remember this well, most immortals will be relying on brute strength. Use their arrogance to your advantage. They will leave themselves open to attack. When they do, strike them with whatever you can. In spite of their name, they can be killed. Immortality only describes their unending lifespan."

Sorren said, "Lastly, I suppose I could show you one of my own techniques."

"Your own?" Curious, Darek goggled at him. "What kind of techniques are they?"

"The techniques of a Black Raven Rogue," Sorren replied gravely.

"Black Raven Rogue?"

Sorren nodded. "It is the clan I was originally from. If you've never heard of it, that's understandable. Few would ever know of the Black Raven Rogue because it is now extinct. We perfected killing techniques with the sword." Sorren added, "I will only show you this once. Before I do, you must promise not to tell *anyone* that you have seen this. The techniques of an assassin are *not* to be shared."

"I promise," said Darek, nodding. "Please continue."

Darek was surprised that Sorren would show him something so secretive. Even if Sorren was teaching him about combat, there was no need to go so far as to reveal his own techniques. In fact, Darek was still having trouble understanding why Sorren was helping him out. Sorren said he wanted to kill Darek because he was a target for assassination. What exactly was Sorren's motive in all of this? Darek was left bewildered and grateful, an odd mix of emotions.

"Good," said Sorren. "The only reason I am showing this technique is to inspire you to create your own style. You will not be able to learn this or even learn how to counter it by watching it once. Since this is an assassination technique, I can only show you in a dream. Otherwise..." Sorren's cold visage became a sinister grin. "You'd be dead."

"Assassination technique?" A once in a lifetime experience, Darek thought. The more Sorren spoke of it, the more anxious Darek became. He stared at Sorren with a ravenous gaze.

Sorren unsheathed his sword once again and held the blade vertically in front of his chest. "This is Melody of the Wind." He stood silently with the cold blade held closely to his face.

Darek stared at Sorren in immense anticipation. All of a sudden, a shrilly high-pitched sound began to ring. It started soft, but grew so loud that Darek had to cover his ears. He even tried shaking his head to get the sound out. But no matter what he did, the sharp ringing remained inside his skull. The atmosphere grew impenetrably thick. Darek clutched his own throat, aware that he was suffocating; it was as if his nostrils were afraid to breath in the poisonous air. Darek collapsed onto his knees under the tremendous, agonizing pressure, feeling like he had been trapped at the bottom of a deep ocean. "Is this...the technique? I haven't...been touched. Is this...really a dream?" He barely breathed out, "It's a...nightmare!" He searched for Sorren but couldn't find him. "Sorren left me here to die? No. What's this feeling?"

He could feel another presence close by, but he didn't see anyone at all. The ringing quieted down into a dead silence. *Thump*. Darek heard a slight step. *Thump*. There it was again, a few seconds apart, but he still couldn't see anyone around. Then, an abrupt noise overwhelmed the silence in an instant. *SHRRRRRRRRK!* It was the sound of a thousand blades clanging together. At first it seemed far away, but for every second that passed, it drew nearer until he came face to face with these chilling swords. Without any hands brandishing them, these swords violently swung back and forth in midair. Then they vanished before his eyes in a wisp of smoke.

Darek couldn't restrain himself any longer. He screamed his lungs out. He could feel his body being shredded away, piece by piece, by hundreds of invisible blades. He lost sensation in his fingers and toes, then up his arms and legs, and finally, it was like his body was gone.

"No more! No more! Please stop! STOP!" he cried, whimpering. He opened his eyes. The campfire was before him. Whispers surrounded him. Glancing around, he saw that everyone had already returned and was sitting around the fire. They had been uncomfortably watching him scream in pain for the past few minutes.

"Are you okay?" asked Rathos, approaching Darek out of concern.

Breathless, Darek began saying, "It was horrible! I was..." But Darek immediately stopped himself from continuing. He wiped off the cold sweat that tingled his skin and steadied his breathing. Darek searched the faces around the fire and saw Sorren sitting there, prodding the fire.

Darek calmed down. "No, never mind. I'm fine. I think I just had a bad dream."

Darek remembered his promise. If he kept his training a secret, then he wouldn't have to worry about blurting out something he shouldn't have. But even so, the technique that Sorren showed him instilled in his heart a sense of fear and a deeper respect for Sorren. This was a dangerous man, and Darek was glad that Sorren was on his side—at least for now.

CHAPTER 15
Mother

T he journey through the forest took many days, but Darek never noticed it at all. If anything, his time in the forest felt very short because every day was spent working towards his goal of becoming strong enough to defend himself.

Sorren had told Darek that the most important task for the day was to train his body. Darek would practice by swinging his daggers. This endless repetition helped to tone his muscles and increase stamina. While he rode on Thedes, he even got good at slicing off tree branches that Thedes would purposely put in his way. Once in a while Sorren made Darek get off Thedes and run with the wolves, which was, needless to say, impossible. Darek would be left so far behind that everyone was in bed by the time he arrived.

Sleep provided no solace for Darek because it was during the dreams that Sorren would take the time to instruct him. Sorren made it a priority for Darek learn the proper stances in order to achieve the highest combat potential. Though most of the time was spent learning how to fight, Sorren also felt that sparring would provide the needed experience for practical application.

When they had first begun, Darek couldn't understand why they would bother training during their sleep. After all, it was fake and merely an illusion. However, he came to understand that with Sorren's help, dreams were indeed useful.

Darek wasn't able to grasp how he did it, but Sorren managed to take full control of the dreams while he slept. In this dream world, everything had to be established and created. Sorren had to apply the laws of science that would be relevant to their training.

Sorren took the training very seriously, and with his preparation, he went above and beyond anything Darek had come to expect. Sorren unleashed his creativity, going wild with his imagination such that no two dreams were ever the same. He would fabricate a number of breath-taking environments for them to practice in. Over the course of his instruction, they would train anywhere, from the depths of the sea to the tops of mountains.

Under the ocean, Darek was forced to hold his breath and every time he imaginarily drowned, they would have to start over. On the mountains, the air was thin and left Darek breathless.

But even though Sorren seemed strict during the dreams, he did give Darek some periods of rest. Darek would sometimes meditate under the roof of a dojo to maintain his concentration and focus. Darek would also sometimes lie in the summer meadow and experience the beauty of nature.

These dreams that Sorren crafted for Darek were amazing. Even if it was only for a few nights, Darek felt like he had spent an eternity traveling the galaxy, training and meditating. However, it was a bit embarrassing because, while he tried to keep his training a secret from the others, almost everyone was concerned to see him sleepwalking throughout the nights.

This exhausting routine continued until they finally made it out of the forest.

Rathos sniffed the air. "The scents are changing. The desert is not far from here."

"Oh, great. I finally get to walk around in the wonderful desert—again," said Darek. "At least I won't have to deal with these pesky bugs anymore." He checked his clothes for squirmy little bugs. Whenever he found one, he'd be grossed out and would flick it away with a dagger. "Why the desert? Isn't there an easier route?"

"We can't avoid it because the desert spans across the continent," replied Rathos. "However, we are merely passing by. We'll reach the mountain range soon."

Darek glanced back. He was most interested to see how Azura was faring. She had fully recovered several days ago, but he was still worried about her. Any normal person would take weeks, if not months, to recover from the damage she had suffered.

"Are you okay?" Darek asked her, "Is something bothering you?"

Azura slowly shifted her gaze back and forth, watching the forest warily. "Hasn't it been a little too quiet? I know we're not being chased or anything, but what about the monsters? Ever since we stepped into this forest we haven't had a single encounter. That has me worried."

Darek beamed. "It's never too quiet for me. Maybe we're just lucky."

"Ah, about that," replied Rathos. "Over the past century our group has been working to get rid of the monsters from this region. You'd be hard pressed to find any lurking around."

Azura wasn't satisfied with his reply. "I don't know. I have an uneasy feeling about this."

Sorren asked her, "Is this coming from your intuition?"

Azura shook her head. "I don't rely on intuition." She pointed to a few smudges along the dirt path. "Look at this trail. Something went ahead of us."

"Nice observation," said Sorren. "I don't think it's anything we have to worry about, but we might as well proceed cautiously."

Just as Rathos had said, the desert was not far off, and soon the group began their dismal trek through the sandy wasteland. Rathos sent the rest of the wolf pack back to the mansion; from the group of wolves, only him and Thedes were to continue on this journey. Rathos transformed into a human for the trip across the desert; there was no longer any need to run long distances. Thedes, however, refused to be human. Despite the rising temperatures, he stubbornly remained as a wolf, but he decided to walk upright since no one would be riding on his back.

The blistering heat wore Darek down. Dragging his feet in the sand, Darek was thankful that Rathos had insulated their shoes with rubber, but it was not enough to stop the heat of scorching sand from seeping in.

"Too hot," Darek grumbled. "Can someone pass the water? I need to cool off."

"The water?" asked Azura, sounding a bit concerned. "Weren't *you* supposed to have the water?"

"I was? But I don't have it."

Azura rolled her eyes. "Then *who* has it?"

The group stopped and rummaged through their bags of supplies. They found everything that they would normally need—except for the water. No one had any water.

Agitated, Thedes grabbed Darek by the neck. "How could you forget such a vital thing? We reminded you over and over again in the forest. You were the one who was supposed to stock up!" He tightened his grip; Darek choked and gagged.

Azura was about to interfere but, to her surprise, Sorren went ahead of her.

"Let him go," said Sorren. "No use in fighting over it now."

Thedes growled, "Why should I listen to you—you feeble human?"

"Because if we move quickly, we might find an oasis up ahead," said Sorren. "The faster we solve our problem, the less painful it will be." Sorren glared at Thedes. Immediately, Thedes could feel a fear rising in his chest. Backing away from Sorren, Thedes released Darek and went back to minding his own business.

"Thanks," Darek said, gulping air. "I thought he was going to snap my neck for a second there. But, honestly, I never expected you to back me up."

"I take responsibility for my actions. Seeing that it is partly my fault, I couldn't just ignore it," replied Sorren.

"Your fault?" Darek blinked, looking perplexed.

Sorren took Darek aside and whispered, "The training we've been doing has some side effects on the mind. If you haven't properly rested in a while, you may become absentminded."

"Ah, is that so?" said Darek. "But even with a semi-valid excuse, we're still in a heap of trouble. Maybe we should head back. We could die out here." Darek took special notice of Reza and Drey. Unlike everyone else, they were strolling through the sand without any complaint or worry. Darek walked beside them and said, "What's your secret? You guys don't look thirsty. Are you hiding some water from us?"

"No. We just have a higher *tolerance* for heat," replied Reza.

Unsatisfied by their reply, Darek returned to Sorren and asked him, "Do you think they're hiding something from us?"

"It doesn't matter," replied Sorren. "Even if they are hiding something, it's not good to try to force it out of them. Just leave it be."

Darek agreed with him and dropped the subject. After all, it was only speculation; to accuse someone of something without evidence would dissolve any thin bonds of trust they might have. Darek had already experienced being framed for something he didn't do, and it made him reconsider judging people by what they look like or what they have supposedly done.

The desert was a place of solitude that these travelers could not enjoy. A slight wind rustled about, shooting sand into their weary eyes. The loads of sand spread out before them in plain sight only served to dampen their spirits, as they had no idea when they would ever reach the end of it. Their dry throats only served as a pesky reminder for their perilous situation.

"Look, a cave in the mountain!" exclaimed Azura, pointing. "A good place to cool off."

Rathos nodded, wiping off the sweat from his chin. "But water is still a pressing issue. We must find an oasis soon or we will die regardless of how much shade we find."

"Should we turn back?" asked Darek. "It's only another hour of walking back."

Rathos said, "We should. Even though we'll waste time, it's necessary."

Stepping into the crevice of the small rocky mountain, they went inside and found that it was fairly shallow. It appeared to have been used as a shelter in the past. There were remains of a snuffed out fire, some soft cloth on the floor and a simple wooden table. There were also other assorted useful items, including barrels for storing water.

"Do you think someone still lives here?" asked Darek.

"Highly unlikely," said Rathos, sniffing the air. "The scent of fire and ash is not strong."

When Sorren walked in, his knees felt weak and he slumped to the ground. Darek, who was next to Sorren, took hold of him and laid him on the ground.

"Hey, is something wrong?" asked Darek.

Moving sluggishly, Sorren grimaced. "I'm f-fine. Just a little tired."

Rathos looked worried. "Place him on the mat. Let him rest." Placing his hand upon Sorren's forehead, Rathos ran a quick check for a fever. Sorren was burning red hot. "I'm not a doctor...I can't say much. But he has a fever, that's for sure. It could be a heat stroke or some kind of infection," said Rathos. "Whatever it is, he's suffering and we need to help him relieve it. He's in no condition to go with us."

"Talk about bad timing," said Azura. "What should we do? He'll dehydrate rather quickly. We don't even have water for ourselves. Going back to the forest will take too long."

"Then maybe there's nothing we can do for him." Rathos stared at Sorren, searching for an answer to this new riddle.

"We just need to go straight out there and bring back some water," said Darek, suddenly brimming with energy. "It's as simple as that! We can't just sit here and think about it!"

"I like your enthusiasm." Rathos smiled. "And you're right. We should try to find water. That is the only solution, regardless of how impossible it might be. If we're going to do this, we do it efficiently and safely. Anyone who is tired should rest here for now and help us later.

"For the rest of you, we'll split from this central point and search every direction except where we came from. Only move in a straight line. The desert can be disorienting, so you have to go in a straight line and return in a straight line. Drag your feet in the sand if you have to. You should only walk out for about half an hour so you will return in an hour. Anyone who does not return in an hour, we will search for you. The main priority is water." Rathos dug out several used water flasks from their bags. "I will give everyone a flask in case you find some. Second priority is food and travel. If you happen to stumble across any herds of wild animals or monsters, let us know." Rathos paused. "Are there any questions?"

"None," said Darek, as he stood outside, ready to start. This was his chance to help out Sorren and repay him for his teaching. Not only that, but he was beginning to think that Sorren was a pretty decent guy. At first Sorren appeared heartless and wooden. But after getting to know him some more, he didn't seem that bad at all…unless it was some kind of trick to get him to trust him.

"Good." Rathos assigned directions for everyone to explore. "Try not to exhaust yourselves, we don't want anymore cases like Sorren on our hands. One is plenty."

"Should someone stay with Sorren?" asked Darek.

"I'll do it," said Azura.

"No," said Reza, interrupting her. "Let me handle this task. I won't be able to cover as much ground as anyone else here. I should stay and watch him."

"Be sure to do a good job." Darek eyed her suspiciously, still unsure of her intentions.

"If that is your wish, my master," replied Reza with a pleasant smile.

The rest of them set out on their search for water, leaving Sorren and Reza alone in the cave. Sorren lay there, breathing like every breath was his last, his face scrunching with misery. Reza watched over him in silence.

Fifteen minutes passed and Sorren's condition had grown worse. Beads of sweat began streaming down his flushed red face. His body shivered at short intervals. His bloodshot eyes were tearing. He raised his feeble arms and brushed away the tears with his fingers.

Reza just sat there, watching him suffer. Her compassion was stifled by her decision not to interfere. But there was only so much she could take.

I'm sorry, a man's voice spoke into Sorren's mind. *I thought blocking your memories would help. But now it seems you are suffering the consequences.*

You don't sound like your usual self. Don't be sorry, Sorren replied. *I exhausted myself by entering Darek's dreams. This is my fault. Do I have much longer to live? Will I make it through this?*

Unfortunately, if they do not return with water soon, you will die.

Ah, is that so, said Sorren. *Then it doesn't matter anymore. I'll accept my death.*

Will you really? Your mind changes all the time. But you will undoubtedly want to live once I release your memories.

"Listen to me," said Sorren, wheezing. "If I lose consciousness, tell Rathos to leave me here with my sword and clothing. This will make a fine grave."

"What are you saying? Everything will be all right," Reza assured him.

"I'm going to die. I can feel it." Sorren closed his sleepy eyes.

"Just wait," she snapped. "Open your eyes!"

"I...can't..."

"You have to!" Reza stood up and paced around the room. "I can't help you. Not now."

Just then a flood of memories stormed his mind causing his pupils to twitch and bounce around uncontrollably. His mouth gasping for air, he fixed his cold gaze towards the ceiling. His eyes fell on Reza and he remembered whom she was. Tears flowed down his cheeks. It had been a while since he had last seen her, but she still looked the same.

Sorren raised his hand and she took it. "Mother, I don't want to die yet...Help me. Give me one more life to live!"

"I'm not your mother," Reza said. "There's nothing I can do."

"I figured as much," Sorren said, lamenting. "If even the truest words of my heart are not enough to move you, then I am glad to have at least seen you one last time." Sorren said nothing more. He closed his eyes, trying hard to focus on something else other than the unrelenting pain.

Reza chewed her lip as she got up and paced again. "Why do you have to give up so easily?" She stopped and turned to him. "Fine, I shall grant you this favor—but only for this time and this time alone. I shall never aid you again."

Kneeling down, Reza laid her cold hand on his brow and from the pores of her hand came a cleansing mist that washed off the sweat and tears from his face. She drew a deep breath of air into her nose. The she blew out a small stream of clear, glistening water out of her mouth. The water paraded around the cave like floating globs. Then, with a flick of her wrist, Reza commanded the stream to slide down into Sorren's throat. Sorren's anguished face became relaxed. Refreshed, he could feel the fever leaving him and strength returning to his body. The pains and aches were washed away.

"Thank you, Mother. I can now rest easy." Sorren closed his eyes again and fell asleep.

Reza walked out of the cave into the harsh sunlight. She twirled her hands around in a little dance and small droplets of water formed and swirled around her. The droplets of water came together to create a small puddle of water that she caressed in her hands. Reza then flung the water in the air and it shot forth in a direction like an arrow released from its bow.

"So that's where the nearest oasis is," she muttered.

"You found one?"

Startled by the sudden voice, Reza looked to the side. Darek was running back towards the cave. The others were right behind him.

"You saw?" Reza asked Darek, sounding rather cautious.

"Saw what?"

"Never mind," said Reza. "More importantly, I found an oasis about ten minutes away."

"You did?" exclaimed Rathos. "Great! I'm glad somebody was able to find one! We better tend to Sorren right away."

"I already did," replied Reza. "He's doing all right now. But he drank all the water I brought back. We'll need to get more."

Rathos said, "Show us where it is. We should stock up with whatever we can carry."

But when they followed the trail that Reza was leading them, Darek noticed something peculiar. There were no steps in the sand. Darek thought about it for a moment, but decided it was not worth looking into. She had saved Sorren, and for that, she earned his trust.

CHAPTER 16
Into the Tunnel

Sleeping in the cave was something of a bad experience. The cave itself was fine, but it was not made for six people and a wolf to sleep in. They had been able to stand and sit around comfortably without a problem, but by the time they stretched out their legs to sleep, they discovered the cave was suitable for at most three or four, but seven was pushing it. All through the night Darek got kicked in the face and punched in the stomach. At first he thought it may have been an accident, but he figured there was more to it when he saw all the claw marks on his clothing.

After they had rested up, the next morning felt like a fresh start. Sorren was back to his old self again. And Thedes was in a good mood, appearing pleased with the much-needed refreshment. It was awkward for Darek to have to replenish Thedes's water bowl, but no one else would do it. Whenever Darek was looking for Drey's assistance, Drey would seemingly disappear at all the right moments, much to Darek's disappointment.

As soon as everyone was ready to depart, the group went back to the oasis for a quick stop and then proceeded onward to the mountains.

Rathos pointed into the far distance. "I think I can see the peaks from here."

"Finally," exclaimed Darek, "we're almost there!"

"The sun is high and there are a few trees up ahead," said Sorren. "Why not rest now under the shade and finish the journey through the cooler night?"

"That's a fine idea," Rathos said. "I'm sure everyone will agree."

Darek nudged Drey. "Hey Drey, do you mind keeping watch?"

"Not at all," he replied.

Utterly exhausted, Darek didn't bother sleeping on a mat. The sand suited him just fine. His only relief was that Sorren had stopped the training. Ever since they had reached the desert, Sorren no longer entered his dreams. Darek wondered if it was because Sorren was still recovering.

Darek glanced at the others and saw that everyone else was fast asleep. Then he curled up and shut his eyes. When he opened his eyes again, he was in another place—one he did not recognize. It looked like the inside of a huge building with walls that stretched high above. There were hundreds of doors in the walls; all of them seemed quite randomly placed with no rhyme or reason.

Darek knew this was no ordinary dream. He turned around, expecting to find Sorren behind him as usual. Just as he expected, Sorren was standing there, looking at him. Yet there was something different about him. Sorren's face became twisted in agony. Coughing up blood, the focus of Sorren's eyes fell on his own chest; the tip of a sword came slowly piercing out of his robe, right where his heart was. Sorren staggered and collapsed facedown with a thud. His body was lifeless. The sword stood out of his back in the shape of a cross.

Darek couldn't stop shaking. Did someone just kill Sorren before his very eyes? Staring at Sorren's dead body, Darek was rooted in place. The shock was unbearable.

"SORREN!" Darek ran to Sorren's body and knelt down to pick him up. When he held Sorren in his arms, the body crumbled away like powder and slipped through his fingers.

Someone emerged from the shadows. Darek screamed, glaring at the man with a spark of hatred in his heart. But his hatred was smothered and his feelings changed to bewilderment when he realized whom it was.

"You! You're the judge that sentenced me to death! Did you do this? Were you the one who killed him? ANSWER ME!"

"Please, you can call me Dionus," the man said. "Your friend, Sorren, is fine. He's not hurt in any way. After all, this is only a dream, a place where people will never be born and will never die; it is a place where all things are possible and impossible."

Darek froze. Dionus was right. The image looked so vivid and real that he had almost forgotten he was inside a dream.

"He's okay? He's really okay?" asked Darek.

Dionus assured him, "Yes, don't worry. I can't really kill anyone inside your dream."

"Then why—I don't understand—why'd you stab him?"

"I'm sorry you had to see that," said Dionus solemnly. "I wanted to speak with you, but the moment I tried to enter into your mind, Sorren tried to stop me. I couldn't even explain myself to him. So I forced him out. But I'll let him return soon enough."

"You want to speak with me?" It was then that Darek remembered the humiliation he had suffered at the hands of Dionus when he was put on trial. "That's why you forced your way in? There's nothing to talk about! If Sorren doesn't want you here, I don't want you here either!"

"Please calm down," said Dionus. "I can understand your anger. That is why I came to apologize. I was an ignorant fool. I thought I was doing the right thing. I was only trying to uphold justice to preserve peace within the Federation. Even now, because the Judges roam free, the Federation is in a state of panic. But, ever since I discovered you were innocent, my conscience has been bothering me. Convicting the innocent is unforgivable. For that, I am truly and terribly sorry. I hope you can forgive me."

"Oh," said Darek. "I...don't know what to say. I guess I can forgive you." But then he realized something. He said eagerly, "Wait a minute. Does this mean I can return home? I can finally go back?"

Dionus nodded. "You have been pardoned. There's no longer a bounty on your head."

A big grin spread across Darek's face. "That's great news! Thank you so much!"

"No," said Dionus. "Thank you." Dionus vanished in the blink of an eye.

Bit by bit, the dust on the ground molded itself into a human body. Finally, as a last touch, it sculpted the face of Sorren upon its head and Sorren was whole again. He stood and looked at Darek; Darek expected Sorren to say something about the situation, but he didn't. Frowning, Sorren turned away and vanished.

When they finished resting, they made their way through the final steps of the desert, crossing into a grassy plain. Since the whole trip was done through the early hours of the morning, they managed to reach the station by sunrise. During this time, Sorren stared at the sky as if he was engrossed in his thoughts. Darek was worried. Sorren was usually quiet, but now he was absolutely silent. Darek thought about talking to Sorren about what happened, but decided against it, thinking that it wasn't really any of Sorren's business.

They entered the train station. Darek wandered through the building. The train station was grand. The walls were comprised of stacked bricks. Black steel poles provided necessary structure. It was like a small self-enclosed town, featuring an assortment of stores and inns. Though the overhead lights would not turn on, there was ample lighting from the windows to be able to walk freely around without clumsily running into things. But the emptiness of the station gave Darek an ominous chill. Visions of huge throngs of people bustling from gate to gate flashed before his eyes with each step that he took. He even thought he could clearly hear the sounds of trains pulling in and out of the station, though Rathos assured him that it was only his imagination.

Rathos checked to see if there were any usable locomotives along the tracks. All of ones available were powered by electricity, a resource currently unavailable. He searched extensively for anything else but returned empty-handed.

"There's nothing here," Rathos said. "We'll have to walk." He led them through a gate that took them outside to a dark tunnel. "We can still follow the tracks, I suppose."

Darek studied the entrance of the tunnel, hesitant to step inside. "I don't know about this. It's really dark in there."

"Well, it is a big tunnel," said Azura. "And there's no electricity. Of course it'd be dark."

"I know," snapped Darek. "I'm just saying it doesn't seem like a good idea to walk through a dark tunnel like this."

"He has a point," said Sorren. "We don't have any flashlights. Makeshift torches without good fuel might not last the whole way. And it could be dangerous to go in blind."

Azura frowned. "Don't tell me we came all this way for nothing!"

"I was really hoping we'd find some old engine to carry us," said Rathos. "But now, I'm not sure what we can do. If worse comes to worst, we can still take the long way around."

Darek suggested, "How about breakfast? We can think things over while we eat."

"Darek's right," Azura said. "It'll be hard to think on an empty stomach."

They all agreed. The group took this time to eat and rest before proceeding. They started a fire near the entrance of the tunnel and hunted around for small bunnies and squirrels. When they cooked the meat, the aroma dissolved into the air.

"That smells really good," said Darek, as he tried to hold back the stirring in his stomach.

"It's ready," said Rathos. "Just dig in."

Darek held the piece of cooked meat in his hands and stared at it longingly, licking his lips. As he was about to take a bite, a huge gust of wind began blowing. The wind was so strong that the fire was blown out. Everyone was completely surprised.

"Is that normal?" said Darek.

"I don't believe so," answered Rathos. "But it's probably nothing."

Darek's belly growled, a reminder of the empty void inside. The wind started up again, rustling the trees in the distance. Darek ignored it; a little wind was not going to stop him from taking a bite. The gust of wind kicked dirt in his mouth and he vehemently spat it out. He groaned in frustration. This juicy piece of meat was right in his hands, but the wind kept getting in his way. He tried to bite into it again, but this time, his shirt flew right up, into his face. Darek grunted. His meat was now sullied with grains of sand. But he didn't care. This time, for sure, he was going to take a bite! The wind kept getting stronger and stronger, smacking him in the face left and right with twigs and rocks. Then, by one powerful gust, the entire group was blown away—as though they were weightless feathers—straight into the heart of the tunnel.

Getting tossed in the air by a strong wind was something Darek had never experienced before. Initially, he thought it was another dream. But soon enough, he discovered that everyone else was around him, though it was too dark for him to actually see anyone.

"Is everyone all right?" Azura asked, shaking out the leaves in her hair.

Darek devoured the meat in his hands before saying, "I guess that decides it for us." Darek fumbled about in the darkness, trying to look for the wall. "How far did we go? I can't even see the entrance of the tunnel, much less my own hand."

"Rathos," said Sorren, "care to fill us in on that strange wind?"

"I apologize, but I know nothing about it," replied Rathos. "I'm not very knowledgeable about this region. Thedes goes exploring here, but even he has never gone inside this tunnel. Concerning this wind, it may or may not be a natural occurrence. Honestly, I haven't a clue."

"Who cares about that?" said Darek. "We need to get out of here."

"Search around," said Sorren. "Maybe there's a flashlight or something on the ground."

"That sounds impossible, but fine, whatever," Darek grunted.

They crawled along the ground searching for anything they could use, bumping into each other and into the walls of the tunnel. They ran their hands across the dirt and didn't find much aside from leaves and sticks.

"This is hopeless," Darek said, saddened. "There's nothing here. Let's just go in one direction and hope to reach an exit. Thedes, can't you tell where to go with that nose of yours?"

Thedes took a few sniffs of the air. "The air is strange. The scents are all mixed up."

"Azura," said Darek, "can't you see in the dark?"

"Not this dark," said Azura. "I need at least a small amount of light to see."

"I have a suggestion," said Reza.

"What is it?" asked Sorren.

"Maybe we could use Drey's magic ability. He can light the way for us."

"What? You guys know anti-law?" exclaimed Darek. "Why didn't you say so earlier?"

"Drey—use it," Reza commanded him.

Drey was reluctant to obey her command. "But I thought you said specifically to—"

"Never mind that," snapped Reza. "Can't you see the circumstances we're in?"

Drey nodded. He raised the palm of his hand and it ignited. Drey held it forth and waved it around. The flame expanded, lighting up the tunnel. Now that they could see, they found it was not as simple of a tunnel as they thought it would be. Rather than a long and straight tunnel that would run through the mountain, what was before them was a huge chamber with many smaller tunnels that seemed to go into every direction. It was like a maze. There were small tunnels above them and around them and even below them. It was a miracle they didn't fall down any of the pits.

Darek gawked at the open room. "This is a lot worse than I thought."

Rathos crouched over and examined pieces of the broken train tracks that were scattered along the ground. "I wonder what happened. Mechanical weathering? Or could it be chemical?"

A small tremor echoed across the interior of the mountain. Heaps of tiny pebbles slid down from upper tunnels, overflowing the room with a thick dust.

"Whatever it is, it must still be going on," said Darek.

A massive boulder fell out of one of the numerous tunnels and landed with a thud, cracking the ground beneath it.

Rathos observed the boulder curiously. "It's perfectly round! Where'd this come from?"

"Be careful! It's still moving!" Darek shouted.

The boulder started to roll across the dirt towards another tunnel.

"The ground isn't uneven," said Sorren, staring at it. "Why would it roll?"

The group peered around the back of the boulder and saw a strange little creature nudging the boulder forward.

"Cute," gasped Azura with glazed eyes.

Darek rolled his eyes. "Cute? It's just a little freaky-looking monster."

The little creature, no more than half a foot in length, had a head, thorax and abdomen. It bore some resemblance to an ant, but each part of its body was of equal size, like three flattened balls tied together. A thick green fur rested only across its back, leaving its soft, squishy belly exposed. The creature had long flat bunny-like feet and two wire-like antennae jutting from its forehead. With big green endearing eyes that were slapped on the front of its face, it gave the group a dirty look.

Darek laughed at its face. "Look at that! Trying to intimidate us? What a cocky fellow."

"Hmm," said Rathos. "Very intriguing. I've never encountered this species. From what I can tell, it must've made its home here by burrowing. I shall make a record of it and name it—"

"Hey," interrupted Azura, "I saw it first, so I'm naming this one. In fact, I think I'll keep it. I'll call it Currie." She picked it up and carried it in her arms.

Darek shook his head in dismay at Azura's horrendous name. "It doesn't look anything like curry! We should leave the naming up to Rathos."

"No!" Azura strongly stamped her feet, leaving well-defined footprints. "It's cute—it's furry—so it's Currie!"

Sorren brushed his hair back. "Does anyone care to notice that there are lots of these little weird things staring at us right now?"

Hundreds of the little Curries had dropped into the chamber. Taking small steps, they cautiously approached the group.

"What do you think they want?" asked Darek.

"We're intruding," replied Rathos. "This is most obviously their home."

"They don't look friendly," said Darek.

"I think you're right," said Azura, still hugging the Currie in her arms.

Darek snapped, "Throw that thing away! That might—"

Darek was interrupted by the sound of a low growl. The hundreds of little Curries started to hum and shiver in unison. Suddenly each one curled up into a little blue ball and, with a mighty force, they bounced around the room like bullets ricocheting off the walls. Darek tried to slip and dodge past the speeding Curries. He couldn't fully dodge one and, the moment it grazed his side, it launched him into the wall. Darek clutched his side, grimacing. The blow had nearly crushed his rib cage. Though the outer most layer of the Currie's skin was soft, the inside was as hard as steel. It was like being pelted with a cannonball.

"Don't let your guard down!" warned Sorren. "They're dangerous!"

"We need to get out of here!" shouted Rathos. Rathos stooped and transformed back into a wolf. He growled, "Try to find the exit while we slow these things down. If we don't get out of here now, everything might collapse on top of us!"

"Right," said Sorren. He scanned over the different paths in a hurry and something caught his eye. "Look, all boulders are being pushed toward that tunnel over there. It could be the exit!"

"Better check it out fast," said Darek. He winced sympathetically every time he saw Rathos get bowled over like a bowling pin. "Or they won't last."

Rathos and Thedes stayed behind to keep the Curries from following after the others, but it was not an easy task. Since Drey had left them, the wolves were left stranded in darkness and had to rely on their sense of smell and hearing to keep up with the relentless barrage of bouncing Curries. Unable to avoid their attacks, the two of them were bashed from head to toe.

Meanwhile, Darek and the others urgently dashed down the path they believed was the exit. They ran along the path for some time, but because the tunnel didn't seem to end, they started to have doubts about the path and wanted to turn back. Sorren pointed to the fragments of railroad tracks and dusty lanterns as evidence that he was not wrong.

"I can see light at the end of the tunnel," said Azura. "It's faint, but I'm sure of it."

"Good," said Sorren. "We should wait for the others before continuing."

"I hope they get here soon," said Darek.

While everyone was waiting for the wolves, Darek noticed something strange about the exit. The light that poured in from the opening was rapidly disappearing, and within seconds, the exit had disappeared. "It's gone," uttered Darek, astonished. "The exit is gone…"

"It collapsed?" asked Azura.

"I don't know. I don't think so. I mean, I didn't hear any rocks fall or anything. It was silent—totally silent." Darek walked up closer to where he remembered seeing the exit just before it had vanished. "Drey, bring the fire up closer so I can get a better look."

Drey followed Darek to the wall and together they inspected it.

"It's definitely not a collapse. There's just one big boulder here." Darek placed his hands on the boulder, tapping and pushing it to see if it would move. "Do you think someone blocked it on purpose from the outside?"

"Now why would someone do that?" Azura said, "There's no else around."

"Maybe…someone doesn't want us to go to the capital," answered Darek gravely, his lips quavering.

Azura chuckled. "Now, you're just paranoid." She touched the rock with her hand. "It's not a problem anyway. If someone pushed it in, I can push it out just as easily."

Like the stirrings of an earthquake, the inside of the mountain began to shudder. Rathos and Thedes came striding across the dirt on all fours. Both of them were bloody and bruised, but still recognizable; there was a bit of a limp in their step from the beating they had taken.

"Did you find the exit?" growled Rathos, looking quite concerned. "The tunnel looks like it could come down any moment now."

"Yeah, we found it," said Azura. "What happened to the Curries? You lost them?"

Rathos said, "Those little beasts just stopped coming. They didn't even try to follow us."

"They sure give up easily," commented Darek. "Then again, they shouldn't have any more reason to pursue us. I think they attacked us because Azura touched one of their buddies. Now that we've left them alone, we should be okay."

"I see. That might be it." Azura petted her Currie on the head.

Darek's jaw dropped when he saw that she was still holding the fuzzy monster in her hand. "You still have that? Are you really planning on keeping it? I bet you don't even know what it eats. Return that thing immediately before they come storming down here!"

The Currie curled up into a ball and snuggled into the embrace of her arms.

Azura smiled contently. "Aww, look at that! It already likes me."

Realizing he couldn't get his point across, Darek scoffed, "She's in her own little world."

The mountain began stirring again, causing large piles of dirt and rock to fall from the ceiling. Some of the rubble was moist and splattered all over them like mud.

"It's coming down," said Rathos. "We should leave now!"

"The exit is down here." Darek pointed toward the end of the tunnel. "It closed up, but if we work together, we might be able to push it out."

The blood drained from his face as Rathos set his eyes on the boulder. "That's not a rock…"

"What?" Darek sounded confused. It looked like a rock to him. "What else could it be?"

Rathos said, "That's a Rock Worm. A really big Rock Worm…"

The Rock Worm opened its round mouth, which appeared as a large hole in the rock. It began sucking in the air with such a force that it created a massive vacuum. Smaller rocks were easily lifted up and flown straight into the dark pit, which was its stomach, with no escape.

Everyone tried to stay firmly in place so they wouldn't get sucked in. Sorren thrust his sword deeply into the floor and held onto the hilt. Thedes and Rathos gripped the wall and ground with their powerful claws. Azura spared no time to dig her fingers into the earth; the Curric hopped into her jacket and stayed there. Darek took his daggers and smashed the blades into floor. However, Drey and Reza had no means of hanging on and, though they crouched closely to the ground, were steadily being sucked in.

"Hang on!" shouted Darek. "I'm coming!" Darek tried to inch forward by pulling out a dagger, moving it a step ahead, and shoving it back into the ground. But he was too slow; within seconds the vacuum grew strong enough to suck in Reza and Drey. Once they were sucked in, the mouth closed up without warning.

With the vacuum gone, Darek ran up to the Rock Worm's mouth and began furiously stabbing it, but his daggers couldn't even scratch its hard skin. "Let them go!" he yelled. "Spit them out now! If you don't, I'll—"

Azura said, "Let me handle this." Though she spoke calmly, Darek could see that she was quite shaken and angry. Azura pulled back her arm and made a fist. Then she took one deep breath and unleashed a powerful punch. *BAM!* By using the momentum of her body and the spring of her knees, the punch knocked the face of the Rock Worm back out of the tunnel, unveiling the exit.

Startled by the impact, the worm wildly swerved its head and neck around. It bellowed an earth-shattering roar that made the grass sway. Its conglomerate skin was covered in smooth and shiny minerals that made it sparkle a multi-color rainbow in the sunlight. It was almost one hundred feet in height, and it towered over the group; to the worm, the people looked like little grasshoppers, easily crushable in a single strike.

"Now look what you did!" said Darek, utterly frightened. "You angered it! Why did you have to anger it?"

"Wasn't that your intention?" Azura countered.

The Rock Worm slammed its bulky head against the side of the mountain, causing a massive rockslide to begin its descent. Dozens of giant boulders came tumbling down. Everyone tried to run outside to avoid getting caught underneath the rocks.

During the calamity, some of the heavy rubble landed on Rathos's tail; he howled and winced as his tailbone broke rather painfully. Understanding the dire situation that Rathos was in, Thedes came running to his side to aid him.

Darek turned back and also wanted to help Rathos, but Thedes growled at him, "Go on! Get out of here! You must complete the task at all costs."

"No! I'm not leaving anyone behind!" Darek refused to listen to Thedes, but Azura forcefully dragged him out of the way of the crumbling ceiling. The immense landslide from the mountain landed, covering the side of the mountain with large immovable boulders. The tunnel collapsed and Azura, Darek and Sorren were the only ones to make it outside.

"No, we have to go back!" cried Darek. He pulled himself away from Azura and ran back to the mountain. "They're still in there! They're still alive!"

Darek climbed the heap of rubble and scrambled to toss aside the smaller rocks that were in his way. But when his hands reached the larger rocks, he couldn't even make them budge. His determined face covered in tears and mud, Darek kept pulling on the rocks. Then, gritting his teeth, Darek punched the rocks until his knuckles bled. All his efforts were futile. When he realized there was nothing he could do to save the others, he broke down and cried out.

The gigantic worm thrashed about once again, smashing its head against the mountain.

"GET OUT OF THE WAY!" Azura screamed. "IT'S COMING FOR YOU!"

Darek spun around to see the head of the Rock worm before him. The one-eyed worm scrutinized Darek, determining whether or not Darek was suitable prey. The shock from the sight made Darek freeze in place. Speechless, he stood there and gazed into the Rock Worm's glare in overwhelming fear. Darek felt like he was staring at the embodiment of death itself; one bite from the powerful jaws of the worm was sure to end his life in an instant. His body was not discreet about his current feelings: while hyperventilating, his knees kept knocking together.

"My legs…won't move," Darek whimpered.

Sorren tried to divert the monster's attention by slashing at its body, but he could not penetrate the worm's rocky plating. In fact, his sword was starting to crack.

The worm twirled its head around and came close to Darek; it opened its mouth wide and stooped down as if to swallow Darek whole. Azura ran toward Darek, hoping to reach him in time. Seeing that she was too far to rescue Darek, Azura picked up a rock and threw it at the worm's body. She knew it wouldn't do anything, but she was so frustrated at their inability to stop this monster that she didn't care.

However, at that moment, the worm stopped aiming for Darek and began to act strangely. The worm twisted around and swung its head left and right, as though searching for something. Darek quickly took the opportunity, now that the worm was distracted, to run away and rejoin with Azura and Sorren.

Azura raised a brow. "Did throwing the rock do something?"

"No." Sorren turned his attention toward the ground. "Something…"

"What happened?" asked Darek, his legs still unable to stop shaking.

"Something big is coming," Sorren continued.

Darek pointed at the giant worm. "Big? There's no way it could be bigger than that!"

The land began to shake violently. Huge shock waves rolled along the ground, shearing it apart. The tremors knocked everyone off their feet and they wondered what was going on. The ground opened up, and this time a giant earthworm appeared; it was similar to the one Sorren had seen at the canyon before.

"You weren't kidding! Another giant worm? And it's ridiculously bigger than the other ridiculously big giant worm!" exclaimed Darek in a panic. "THIS IS ALL SERIOUSLY SCREWED UP! WE HAVE TO GET OUT OF HERE!"

"With a height that incredible, it could probably see everything for miles! There's no place for us to run or hide!" said Azura.

"It doesn't matter where we go! It's too dangerous to stay here," said Sorren. "Just run!"

Azura agreed and they all ran as fast as they could away from the area. While they were running, Azura tugged on Darek's sleeve and pointed toward a small patch of trees along the plains. Darek nodded. Together, they all snuck into the shade.

Sorren and Azura climbed up the tallest trees and hid among its branches; from this place, they could watch the worms and their behavior. Darek had other ideas. He was not at all interested in seeing what the worms were doing. Instead, he found a giant log and crawled under it. Scrunched inside the tight area, he then scrounged up leaves from around and used them for more cover, leaving no piece of him exposed.

The two colossal worms engaged in a battle of cataclysmic proportions. The Rock Worm tried to chomp down on the earthworm's side but its hide proved to be too thick to penetrate. The earthworm began its relentless assault, bashing his head against the Rock Worm. After being hit several times, the Rock Worm roared in fear and started to run away. But before the Rock Worm could escape, the earthworm opened its mouth as wide as it could and snatched onto the Rock Worm's tail. It then sucked up the Rock Worm like a string of spaghetti, engulfing the worm whole.

Azura saw the entire battle between the worms and watched in awe as one worm swallowed up the other. But her awe turned to bitterness as she realized that Reza and Drey were now impossible to rescue.

"What's happening?" asked Darek. "I can't see a darn thing down here."

Azura said, "The larger worm swallowed the smaller one."

"What? But that means—"

"Yes," said Azura bleakly, "there's no hope for them."

Darek clenched his teeth and furrowed his brow. How could they have lost so many of their friends in such a short time? In his frustration, he let out a sharp, bitter scream. He just wanted to let it out, all of his feelings in one shout.

"Hush," said Sorren. "Now is not the time."

The giant earthworm began scanning the plains. When it saw the lone patch of trees in the middle of the plains, it stared at the place curiously, tilting its head.

"It's looking this way," Azura said.

Darek hugged the ground tightly and inched his way deeper under the log. "If we stay out of sight, maybe he'll forget about us."

But as they stayed hidden, they could hear the worm crawling slowly on its belly, getting closer and closer. The shaking of the earth became stronger and louder as the worm closed in on their position. Then it stopped. And everything fell silent.

The worm should be on top of us, thought Darek. *What's it doing?*

"Hey, is there anyone in there? Anyone at all?" said a voice above.

Darek scratched his head. *Am I hearing a human voice? I must be imagining things.*

"Yes," replied Sorren as he jumped out of the tree branches. "We're here."

Why's he revealing himself? Darek ran out from under the log. "What's going on? Is the worm gone?"

Windzer, Sorren's escort, was standing out on the field. The worm was there too, and it observed everyone calmly.

"Sorren, it took a while but I finally found you." Windzer looked at the others and asked, "Who are they?"

Sorren replied, "I found them around the area. They are travelers from space, like me. He is Darek and she is Azura. They also want to go to the capital."

"More space travelers? This is perfect!" said Windzer. "We can all go to Duraskull together."

Sorren looked at the worm. "Is that the same worm from the canyon?"

"No," said Windzer. "This one's only a baby. The one at the canyon was much bigger. I caught this little one while I was looking for you."

"Caught it? How can you catch something like that?" asked Darek skeptically.

"I'm a Caller," said Windzer. "With my spirit that I impart, I bend their will to mine. I can do this with all animals and monsters. But let me tell you, this worm wasn't an easy catch."

Sorren unsheathed his blade and placed it forward.

Windzer smiled. "Ah, so you do remember me. I was wondering about that before." Windzer touched the tip of his scythe on Sorren's sword and Sorren grinned.

Darek had no clue as to what they were doing. But Darek didn't care. It didn't concern him. Darek's gaze shifted from the mountain in the distance to the belly of the worm. He sighed. Was Rathos fine? This was a question that bugged him, but deep down he was optimistic about it. They were immortals. They wouldn't die that easily—or at least they shouldn't. But the situation of Reza and Drey was a different matter. They were not coming back. He didn't know them for long, but that only made him feel worse. Darek kind of teased them about their commitment to serve him. But now, they were as good as dead. He had set them free only to let them be gobbled up by some living rock monster. Why did such a thing have to happen? If only he were stronger, he would never let such a thing ever happen again. If only he were stronger…

CHAPTER 17
Overlord

"**A**ttention all passengers," the captain announced through the PA, "we'll be arriving at Salhades shortly."

Rex eagerly stared out the oval window of their small shuttle to see the planet as they approached it. This was the first time he'd ever been to the home world of the Legion of Heroes, and he could finally take the time to confirm the rumors about the extravagance of the place.

Rex immediately took notice of the odd white orbs floating in space. There were hundreds of these round space stations that were strewn along the orbital path, forming a white ring around Salhades. The space stations were armed to the teeth, having numerous gun placements. Rex was sure that there were also hundreds of space fighters tucked away in their docking bays, ready to be launched at any time. Then Rex turned his gaze toward the gallant white fleets that nearly blinded him with their reflection of the nearby star. These fleets consisted mostly of the Legion's elegant Valorian cruisers, which were usually fitted with SKAR cannons in order to quickly disable hostile ships.

After seeing everything for himself, he could tell that the security, even before entering the planet itself, was nearly impenetrable, as he had heard it was. With such a large fleet and several protected checkpoints, it'd be impossible for unknown ships to drift toward the planet without being captured in seconds. Even the Fedcration, with the strongest fleet in the galaxy, would have a difficult time breaking through the defense.

But there was more to the security of Salhades than just the numerous defense forces in space; the planet also had a tough shell to crack. Massive dark-green shield generators hovered just above the uppermost region of the atmosphere. The whole planet was wrapped in several layers of some of the most advanced shields known to man. People, who were not among the highest-ranking Heroes, could only enter or leave the planet during certain hours. Whenever someone would request to go through the shields, only a small hole would be opened to prevent any possible large-scale invasion force from coming in. The Legion spared no expense when it came to the protection of their world and their glorified Overlord.

The city of Fallence, however, was completely different. While still magnificent, it was nothing he imagined it to be. He was used to industrial slums and the modern world of the Federation. However, walking through the city of Fallence was like a walk into the past. Much of the city was preserved from the start of the millennium. The buildings were antiquated and the roads were of stone. The city was like an ancient work of art. It remained true to its history.

While the Heroes were revered across the galaxy, it was here in their city of Fallence that they were most celebrated. Statues of stone, portraying the most venerated of Heroes, were situated at the steps of large temples that overlooked the countryside. Near the center of the city were coliseums where fierce tournaments were routinely held; they were so popular that citizens from all over the world would come to experience them once a year in their annual pilgrimage. It all looked amazing. Rex's heart skipped a beat at the prospect of sightseeing.

The place where they were going to meet the Overlord was a ziggurat in the middle of the city known as the Sanctuary. The roads that led into the temple were paved in gold. The temple itself was constructed with fine cedar and adorned in gold. Even in a city that prided itself on its pleasing architecture, the temple's majestic appearance stood out like a sore thumb.

When they walked up to the front gate, several guards stopped them from proceeding. The guards, clothed in silver armor, carried long spears.

"Do you have an appointment?" asked one of the guards.

"Yes," replied Dionus. "The three of us are scheduled to have an audience with the Overlord. We are ambassadors of the United Federation."

The guards nodded. "We've been expecting you." They led Dionus, Rex and Layne into the main hall. It was wide open and spacious, with lion-faced fountains along the walls. Images of past heroes and their feats were painted along the ceiling and walls comprising one large mural that seemed to tell the history of the Legion. Rex looked over the mural, trying to see if he could make connections between the pictures and the history books he had read.

Most of it was familiar to him, such as the first Overlord, Ellik, who was portrayed in golden armor, wielding the sword of victory,

Quezectur. However, there was something he couldn't recognize no matter how long he stared at it. He couldn't recognize the strange creature that Ellik was fighting. The early days of the Legion were filled with wars against human factions. Encounters with monsters were rare, but the Heroes did deal with them, and when they did, it would always end up being written down as a legend for years to come. Yet in this picture, Ellik was attacking a two-headed shark, and it was nothing that Rex had ever read about. Surely something like this, concerning the first Overlord himself, would be a famous legend.

"Excuse me," said Rex. "May I ask a question?"

"Go ahead," grunted the captain of the guard.

Rex pointed. "What is that monster? I don't remember that legend."

"Sorry, I don't know," the guard said. "The one who painted that picture long ago never made a record of it. It is a forgotten legend, most likely nothing important."

"Nothing important?" Dionus set his eyes on the beast that Rex was talking about and, breaking into a smile, turned his gaze away.

As they approached the end of the hall they were presented with three large wooden doors. All doors were painted black and each one had a different sign above them.

Rex read the signs out loud, "Birth…Life…Death? What's this for?"

"The trials." The guard cleared his throat. "Anyone who wishes to speak with the Overlord must pass one of the trials. So each one of you must complete a trial."

"What's the difference?" asked Rex. "Or are they all the same?"

"The first door leads to the trial of Birth. It is also known as the trial of the Mind and of the Past. It is the longest trial, but also the simplest. An examiner will examine your mind and intentions and see if you are fit to meet the Overlord. The second is the trial of Life. It is also known as the trial of the Body and of the Present. It is a test of a physical skill. For this trial you will fight one of our greatest warriors. The final door leads to the trial of Death. It is also known as the trial of Spirit and of the Future. It is a test of will. It is the shortest trial and will only take a few seconds. But beware of this trial, for you may lose your life quite easily. This is the trial for those who cannot chose among the other trials. Now choose a door. May you succeed and may all the Heroes of the past guide you toward your success. If you fail…you'll never set foot in this place again."

Rex groaned, "I did not sign up for this." After pondering about it, he asked the guard, "Can we all take the same door?"

"You can, " replied the guard. "But you'd have to take turns. You cannot take it all at once. We may need to prepare the trial every time."

"Let's just each take a door," said Layne. "That's the fastest way. I'll take the trial of Death. I can't allow Dionus to take—"

"No," said Dionus curtly, "this is my choice. I'll take the trial of Death."

"But—"

"No. I will do it. End of discussion."

Furrowing her brow, Layne agreed. "Fine, then I'll take the trial of Life. Since Rex is the youngest, let him have the trial of Birth. It suits him."

"What's that supposed to mean?" grumbled Rex.

"Do you have something to say?" questioned Layne.

"Not at all." Rex shook his head. "Let's get this over with."

Rex walked into the first door not knowing what awaited him. The door slammed shut behind him and he followed along a narrow lit path into a small room. It was an ordinary room with a creepy little old man who sat on a cushion with his legs crossed and his eyes closed. A little candle was situated in the center of the room, in front of the old man.

"Welcome," said the man, "to the trial of Birth. My name is Walter Rollworth. I am a G-Rank Hero, Psionic class. I will be your examiner. Please take a seat here with me."

Rex silently sat in front of the candle. The light from the small flame created spooky shadows that pranced about the walls, even though there was nothing else in the room with them.

"Close your eyes and clear your mind," instructed Walter. "I will do the rest."

The instant he closed his eyes, he could feel a tingling sensation in his head. At first he only saw the darkness, but soon a small light came into the center of his vision. The light erupted into a deafening explosion that tore a nearby city asunder. Hundreds of these massive explosions lit up the night sky, overlapping into the cries and howls of weeping children. Suddenly Rex heard many voices—familiar voices.

"Stop the child from crying or else they'll hear him!"

"It's too late! Just hide the child!"

"They're coming! Open fire! Don't let them get inside!"

Gunshots pierced the walls of buildings and blood flowed into the streets. Soldiers hiding among the trees opened fire blindly; it was too hard to see what they firing at, but at the same time, they didn't want to see.

Sitting up from his bed, Rex screamed. Sweat and tears were smeared all over his face. A young Darek ran into the room and laughed at Rex.

"Pull yourself together," said Darek. "It's already noon."

Surprised to see Darek around, Rex gawked at him and then he looked at his clothes; he was no longer in his uniform. His hands and feet looked smaller than normal. He was no longer at the Sanctuary, but was now inside his shabby old bedroom.

"Come on." Darek grinned. "It's almost time for lunch."

"This is...the past?" Dumbfounded, Rex stood up and said, "How old am I? Why am I back in this orphanage? Why am I at Whardhime? What is going on here?"

Darek ignored him and left the room. "Must've had a pretty bad nightmare."

From that point forward, Rex relived the moments of that day in his past, but he couldn't help but wonder if it was real or not. Was this a part of his memory? Or could it have been actual time travel? If it was time travel, then maybe he could change the event—the event that changed his life forever.

"Hey Rex," said Slade. "Want to see who can make the best paper airplane?"

"You're on." Rex beamed. He couldn't best Slade in sports, but when it came to making things, they were on equal ground.

That afternoon, Rex designed many prototypes in order to see which one would fly the farthest. He didn't really think too much about it, all he did was try different things until he made twenty different kinds. After they were all made, he ran to the backyard. One by one, he threw the paper airplanes; one by one, they fell across the field. Some of them were no good and fell backwards. Most of them were decent, making their way near the center of the field. But he wanted one that would shock Slade, one that would totally blow him away. After nineteen tries, he nearly gave up on that idea. None of these paper airplanes were going to impress anybody.

The last paper airplane rested in his hands. After taking a deep sigh and muttering a few prayers, he tossed it into the air. It soared higher than any other plane and was caught up by the wind, taking flight high into the sky. Happy with its performance, Rex ran under it and followed it all the way across the field. This was it. This was the plane that would help him win.

But as it floated down, Rex looked stunned. His look of joy turned to horror. Beyond their backyard was a steep cliff, and his plane had drifted over the cliff and into the valley below. The valley was a place they often had to roam through because it was not unusual for things, like a ball they were playing with, to fall in. However, they were only allowed to go there when the sun was high. But now, the sun was nearly setting.

Slade ran out of the house. "All right, let's fly our planes now or we'll be late for dinner."

"Wait," said Rex. "My plane fell down there."

"Oh, come on," Slade said. "Stop making excuses. I see your planes are all over."

"It's not just any plane! My best plane really went all the way down!" Rex pouted.

Slade sighed. "Don't get all teary on me. I'll give you time to make a new one."

"It's not the same," said Rex. "That plane was really amazing!"

"That's what I'm saying. You can make it again."

"I don't know how I made it," admitted Rex. "I don't remember. I have to see it again."

"Look, do you want to have this contest or not?"

"I do! Just let me go down to get it first."

"Dinner in ten minutes boys!" Miss Kurt shouted from the window of the house.

"We have ten minutes," said Slade. "Let's find it quick."

The two of them ran down a slope into the valley and searched as fast as they could for the airplane. With their sticks they prodded tree branches, hoping the plane would fall out from somewhere. But no matter how much they looked, they couldn't find it.

"Let's go back," said Slade. "It's getting late. Miss Kurt is waiting for us."

"But I know I can find it," said Rex. "Just a few more minutes."

"You said that several times already. We can come back tomorrow."

"But what if it gets blown away? It might be gone tomorrow!"

"You can make a new one," said Slade.

"I keep telling you it's not the same! It has to be that one! That one really flew!"

Slade looked Rex in the eye and saw a small tear. "We'll come back tomorrow. If it's not here, then we can call the whole thing off. It's just a game."

Rex nodded. But to him it wasn't just a game. He wanted to prove his worth. He wanted to prove to everyone that he wasn't just a good-for-nothing crybaby; that it was not a mistake for him to be born. This was now a lost opportunity, just one of many. But to him every single one mattered.

Seems to me you have a lot of guilt, said a voice in his mind.

"Who's there?" asked Rex.

Don't be afraid. It's just me, your examiner.

"Oh, so this is a dream—one that you conjured from my past."

Yes, said Walter, *this is the trial of Birth. This trial is the simplest because all I want for you to do is face the ghosts of your past. From what I can tell, you blame the death of your parents on yourself.*

"If I didn't cry, my parents might still be alive. The soldiers wouldn't have found them."

But you were only an infant. What could you do?

"That doesn't change the fact that I was at fault. I am lucky to have lived, but I was better off not being born! My family was sacrificed that day. Yet, I still don't think it was worth it. They shouldn't have—"

Whether it was worth it or not, is not for you to say. Let us continue.

"No." said Rex. "Not anymore…please…I don't want to see what happens next."

You've been hiding it all along. You have forgotten or rather, you have chosen to forget. But don't worry, after this, you will have passed the trial.

Layne entered the second door to take her test. What awaited her was a stone bridge that was suspended over a deep pool of water. A well-dressed woman was situated on a high platform that overlooked the bridge.

"So what is this?" asked Layne.

The woman replied, "I am Wyra Avins, a G-Rank Hero and a master of archery. I will only be the judge for this match. The one you are to fight is this man before you."

A man walked out onto the bridge and faced Layne, glaring at her. His body was covered in padded armor that bore the colors of the Hero: white, yellow and blue. He wielded a two-handed sword with a blade that was a head's width. He strapped on a chrome-plated helmet that covered his face and had a slit for his eyes to see.

"His name is Harry Grimstone, W-Rank Hero. He is the grand champion of the fall tournament. He will be your test. Killing is not allowed. Anyone who kills will be disqualified. If you fall off the bridge and into the water, you are disqualified. If you wish to forfeit, you may do so by saying, 'I give up.' Do you have any questions?"

"Yes, as a matter of fact. I have one question," said Layne smugly. "What if I kill him accidentally? I'll try my best to hold back, but I can't guarantee anything."

"A kill is a kill," replied Wyra, her eyes narrowing. "You'll be punished. Is that all?"

Layne was disappointed, but she nodded in reply.

"Very well," said Wyra, "you may begin."

Layne drew forth her blade. A ghoulish-white glimmer flashed from its surface. As she waved her sword around, tiny white wisps fled from her sword in the image of skulls.

Wyra looked astonished when she saw Layne's sword. "Is that a legendary sword?" she mumbled to herself, "I've never seen anything like it…"

"Try not to die," Layne said to the warrior with a vicious smile. Her hair still covered her left eye, but her right eye glared back at him. "I cannot fail Dionus."

Layne sprinted across the bridge, dragging her sword behind her. With a leap, she launched several slashes down at the Hero. The Hero confidently parried each attack with his sword. After she had slashed fifteen times, she turned her back on the Hero. The Hero looked at her curiously, wondering why she had given up so soon.

"I've got you now!" he shouted, aiming to strike her in the back.

But before he could lift up his sword, he felt weak and knelt on the ground. He watched his hands as blood dripped down his elbows. Then he looked at his armor and blood flowed through fifteen new cracks on his chest. His face was distorted with confusion, and from the shock, he passed out on the ground.

Even Wyra, who was carefully watching the match so that there wouldn't be any cheating, didn't understand it. With her hawk-like vision, she had a clear view of the fight, yet her mind could not comprehend what had happened. The swordsman, Harry, had clearly blocked every attack, yet surely enough, her blade had cut his armor.

There was nothing she could hold against Layne. There was no trick, or if there was, Wyra couldn't see it.

Dionus had walked through his door at the same time as everyone else. A middle-aged man greeted him at the other side.

"My name is Ruwan—"

"Spare the small talk," Dionus interrupted. "Just tell me what I have to do."

"How rude," Ruwan whispered to himself. He said, "Then stand in the room behind me."

Dionus stood in the room as instructed. The floor of the room was painted with black ink in the form of a strange glowing seal, complete with foreign markings and inscriptions.

"This is a summon seal," remarked Dionus. "Are you a Summoner?"

"I am," replied Ruwan, surprised. "You are familiar with these arts?"

Dionus nodded. "I've seen them before. A manifestation of the spirit in a beastly form."

Ruwan smiled proudly. "Well, this is one you've never seen before. The Heroes of long ago poured out their spirit to create this summon…the lord of all summons!"

Ruwan placed his hands on the floor and the seal shined with intense light. The seal came to life, tore itself from the floor and became three-dimensional; like the pieces of a jigsaw puzzle, the parts of the seal folded and fit together, forming an odd, mythical creature.

The creature had the head of a lion, the body of a bear, the wings of an eagle and the legs of a leopard. It was clothed with fire and the flames engulfed the room. Its eyes were proud and overbearing, demanding absolute attention and respect.

"I am the great spirit Arthrun," the beast bellowed. "I shall give you the trial of Death."

Scratching his head, Dionus stood before the beast undaunted and unimpressed.

"This is a trial of sacrifice," said Arthrun. "Tell me what you wish to sacrifice and if it seems right to me, I shall take it from you without fail. If your sacrifice is lacking, I shall take more from you than necessary. Now tell me, what is it that you wish to sacrifice?"

"I will sacrifice my left arm," replied Dionus flatly. "I have no use for it anyway." He lifted his left arm, presenting it to the beast.

"Your left arm?" The beast scoffed. "You will not sacrifice your ambitions, goals or dreams?"

"Of course not. Those are my life's purpose. If you take those away, you might as well take my life."

"Then what of love? Will you not sacrifice that and live a life of loneliness? Or how about your joy? I can take away your joy and leave you bitter for the rest of your life. And what of peace? Peace would be small price to pay. You can stay worried and in fear. Are those not wonderful choices for your sacrifice?"

"No," said Dionus, his eyes fixed on Arthrun's. "My left arm is all I will give and that is all you will accept."

"Your left arm is not enough," Arthrun thundered. "What a foolish man you are! You have insulted my gracious offer. For that, I shall not only take your left arm, but I shall take your right arm, your vision, your hearing and your tongue as well! Then I shall strip away your love, peace and joy! You will no longer have ambitions, goals and dreams! I SHALL TAKE IT ALL!"

Dionus stretched forth his left arm and Arthrun chomped down on it, the serrated teeth sank all the way into the bone. Dionus said, "My left arm is worth more than your existence. Eat it and perish."

"It can't be," whimpered Arthrun, as he tasted his flesh.

While chewing on Dionus's arm, the flames around Arthrun were blown away into a billow of smoke. Swiftly, Dionus released his sword from its scabbard and thrust it between the beast's eyes, piercing straight through its skull. Arthrun roared in anguish and pulled away from Dionus, ripping off his left arm in the process. Arthrun squirmed and writhed on the floor for a while. Then, without a sound, it burst into bits of black paint, disintegrating into nothing.

Ruwan was paralyzed in horror. Arthrun was supposedly invincible; it was the greatest creation and symbol of power given by the great Heroes from past generations. But it was now reduced to nothing more than chips of paint.

"Am I done here?" Dionus picked his sword up and slid it back into its scabbard.

Ruwan trembled. "Yes, the Overlord will see you now."

After Dionus left the room, Ruwan fell to the ground and said, "How could the immortal Arthrun be defeated? When the Overlord finds out about this, I'll be exiled—or worse yet, I'll be killed! He will strip away the Fate that was given me! This is my end…"

CHAPTER 18
Celebration

The enormous earthworm squirmed across the landscape, ruining all of the vegetation along its path; as it wriggled, it flattened hills and raised valleys, causing alteration on a global scale. The creatures that stood in its path made no mistake of hanging around; they ran away in droves when they heard the rumbling of the worm's coming.

While the worm went on its way, Darek and the rest of the group rested on the back of the worm's giant head. Windzer was busy controlling the worm; he tapped its neck in the direction he wanted to go, and the worm followed his wishes. Sorren and Azura had fallen quickly asleep, for they were exhausted. The little Currie rested under Azura's arm, using it as a blanket. Darek was also tired, but as he lay on his back, he kept his eyes open and watched the clouds pass him by.

Darek sat up and jostled Sorren. "Hey, are you awake?"

Annoyed, Sorren opened one eye, glaring at him. "I am now."

"Can we talk?" said Darek.

"There's nothing for us to talk about."

Darek ignored his protest and said, "I'm still regretting what happened to Drey and Reza...and Thedes and Rathos. It was so sudden. It all happened so quickly."

"Regret?" said Sorren. "What is there to regret? There was nothing you could've done to save them."

"I *know* there's nothing I could have done, but in my heart I still *feel* like I could have done something..."

"That makes no sense." Sorren pretended to go back to sleep.

Darek jostled him again. "Come on, Sorren. Stop trying to sleep. I need to talk to someone about this."

Sorren turned around, sighed and said, "Fine. What else did you want to say?"

"Why did you choose to be an assassin?"

"*What?* What does that have to do with anything?"

"You may be thinking I'm going off on a tangent, but I'm serious," said Darek. "I've been doing a lot of thinking lately. About death and stuff. It's a pretty depressing topic, but it happened, you know? I can't stop thinking about it. And I thought maybe if I talked it over, I'd feel better. Most people choose…normal jobs—ones that involve business, or law, or health. Why would anyone want to be involved in killing?"

"I doubt such a talk would ease your mind. Do you *really* want to know about me?"

"Sure! I mean, we're friends now, aren't we?"

"Allies," Sorren said dryly, "not friends."

"Whatever."

"My reasons are my reasons," said Sorren. "All assassins have different motivations. Some are forced into it. Some need the money. Some enjoy the thrill of the hunt."

"But what about you?" Darek asked.

"I enjoy the freedom."

Darek raised a brow. "Freedom? Isn't assassination…illegal? Don't you get chased by the Feds?"

"Well, yes—I'm talking about a different kind of freedom. As an assassin you get certain benefits. Information is easier to come by. Get in connections with the right people, do them a few favors, and you can go anywhere without much trouble. I'm looking for something…and these kinds of benefits help with my search."

"Hmm? What are you looking for?"

Sorren simply gave him a blank stare.

"Ah," said Darek, understanding. "I see. None of my business. So I take it that you don't really do many assassinations?"

"A few now and then," said Sorren, "just to get a decent meal. I guess you could call me a small-time assassin. I'm not really wanted for much."

"So what's the biggest job you've done?"

"What do you mean by biggest job? Most dangerous? Highest pay?"

Darek grinned. "Most dangerous!"

It looked to Sorren as though Darek was enjoying this talk more than he should. "I'll tell you only if you can keep a secret."

Darek hesitated. "A secret?"

Sorren made sure he had his full attention. "That's right. If I tell you this, you must *never* mention a word of it to Azura."

Darek didn't particularly like to keep secrets from people who were nice to him. However, he was dying to know what the secret was. Darek said uncertainly, "I think I can."

Sorren's face darkened. "I've killed a Hero before."

Darek pressed his hand against his chest and felt his heart racing. "Okay—*now* I'm starting to wish you never told me this."

Sorren ignored Darek's response and continued, "It was a job I took several months ago. I was wandering through the countryside of the planet Raleign. When a man found out I was an assassin for hire, he pleaded with me to stop someone. There was a Hero who was taking advantage of the people living there. He would eat without pay, take things without asking, and sometimes even punish without fault. A Hero is one that, in most cases, will not be disturbed by police or Federation forces. Heroes are feared and trying to tell a Hero what to do is considered taboo of sorts. And, of course, those Judges wouldn't do anything about it."

"Wait. Why wouldn't the Judges do anything? Isn't that what they do?"

"The Judges have an alliance with the Heroes," Sorren explained. "Because of that alliance, the Judges do not monitor the activities of Heroes. The Judges would never dare do anything that would harm its alliance, for they rely on the Heroes for cover. It is only because of a powerful public presence such as the Heroes that the Judges have never been discovered…until now. In return, the Judges deal with the extreme cases; the Heroes would have a bad reputation if they couldn't stop certain villains from continually committing crimes.

"Well, anyway, that stuff happens often. People with power abuse it. And because they have power, everyone is powerless to stop it. The only ones who would ever bother fighting the Heroes would the Anarchists, but they tend to stay away from Federation territory. I felt bad for the villagers and told the Hero to stop whatever he was doing. When he refused, I ended his life."

"So it was a really tough fight?" Darek asked. "The Hero was pretty powerful?"

"No," said Sorren. "It was a nameless Hero. One slash did him in. He didn't even have time to draw his sword."

"That's your most dangerous job? No offense, but that sounds kind of…lame."

"The fight itself may not sound impressive, but picking a fight with the Heroes is suicide, even more so than with the Anarchists. If the Heroes discovered my hand in it, they'd send the whole Legion after me and would never rest until I was captured."

"The Heroes are that scary? But they're nice, aren't they?"

"I wouldn't call them scary," said Sorren. "But the Heroes are special. Every one of them carries something known as the Fate of the Hero. It makes them a real pain to deal with."

"Fate of the Hero?" Darek's interest was piqued. "Is that a sword...or an armor?"

"No," replied Sorren. "Swords and armors are nothing. The Fate is supernatural, something beyond human understanding. It's hard to put into words. The only way I can explain it is that it forces luck to be on their side. If I try to slice off the head of a Hero, he may slip accidentally. If I have him cornered, a friend of his may randomly show up to save him from certain death. It's the unpredictability that makes it a dangerous force to be reckoned with."

Darek grumbled angrily, "How could a Hero do bad things and be fine with it? How could they violate that trust? Everyone respects the Heroes because of the good they do for us."

"That's the way of the universe. No one can truly be trusted. Some Heroes are more trustworthy than others."

The worm stopped crawling.

Darek stood up, vigilant. He glanced at Windzer and asked, "Why did we stop?"

"The worm is tired," Windzer said.

"Really?" Darek didn't think that was possible, or rather he never considered it. They had taken breaks, but it was usually for them and not the worm.

"No," laughed Windzer, "I'm kidding. We're here!"

"Already?" said Darek. "Wow...that was fast. We've only been out here for a few days!"

Everyone hopped off the back and Windzer waved a goodbye to the worm. The earthworm went on its way, contently crawling across the land on its belly. Darek could see the walls of the city in the distance. After sauntering down the dirt road, they reached the city gates.

"Wait here for a little bit," Windzer said. "I must announce your arrival. I don't know what they have planned for you. I'll be right back." Windzer entered the city.

While waiting, Darek decided to get a good look at the outside of the city. Even at first glance, Darek was impressed. The city walls were incredibly sturdy, built from solid stone. What was most impressive was the size of the stones. Each individual rectangular-shaped stone was nearly twice Darek's height. Seeing such a large wall of gigantic stones made Darek think that they were visiting a city of giants. These stones were also tremendously thick and heavy that Darek imagined them to be impossible to be moved by any normal means. When Rathos had said that they used most of the immortals for labor, Darek could now understand why; he shuddered at the thought of their incredible strength.

Many minutes passed and Windzer had yet to return.

"What's taking him so long?" Darek kicked a pebble at the wall out of boredom.

Azura and Sorren didn't respond. Unlike Darek, who was quite impatient, they were enjoying this time of peace and rest. After another hour of silence had gone by, a sudden noise caught their attention. The neighing and trotting of horses could be heard through the gates; Windzer was driving a chariot.

As Windzer drove his chariot near, he pulled on the reins and stopped in front of them. "The elders have informed me that there will be a parade to honor this event and to show everyone the faces of our guests." Windzer gestured for them to hop on. "I'll take you to the center square where you'll be able to meet the elders."

The group was sluggish; they had gotten lazy after lying around for a while. But since Windzer was in a hurry, he rushed them to their seats. When everyone was seated, he started the chariot off. The horses pulled the chariot down the center of the road. Even before they entered the city, they saw hundreds of people crowding near the gate.

To celebrate the arrival of Darek and the others, the local band played exuberant music. The horns and trumpets blared over the uproarious throng. They pounded their drums feverishly and clashed their cymbals. Beautiful female dancers lined up in rows and led the way for the chariot. They moved about and danced as if they were possessed, weaving and shaking at the heavy beats of the drums. Their frenzied motions looked as if they had been driven mad in their delirium. Confetti fell like the heavy downpour of rain over the roofs of the buildings; the sky couldn't even be seen because the confetti blanketed over them like thick clouds. Many bottles of wine were popped open from people standing in balconies, and the foamy liquor was sprayed all over the city streets. An innumerable amount of flowers were tossed such that a wild fragrance overflowed the senses. As they went along, more and more people swarmed into the city streets, waving their hands and cheering as the fanfare resounded.

Darek wasn't sure how to react. Merdon had kept them in the dark about what was going to happen, so all of this was a big shock for him. Why were they so happy to see them? From the way Merdon had spoken, he thought they'd be in big trouble, possibly locked up and branded as outcasts. But instead, they were being celebrated as heroes, as champions over a glorious victory. It was a momentous occasion that shocked Darek speechless. With such applause and excitement, it was hard for him to contain himself. He accepted their celebration and raised his hands to acknowledge the crowd, and they responded in turn with even greater shouting and wilder dancing.

"Come on, Sorren, give them something to respond to!" Darek screamed over the loud noise. Sorren declined, shaking his head.

Darek continued to embrace the jubilation. It was the first time in his life that he had ever experienced this for himself. He had seen parades back at home, but he was always in the audience looking into the streets. But now that he was able to experience it on the other side, he had mixed feelings about it. There was a sense of joy and wonder from the collective excitement, but there were also some doubts in his heart about whether he really deserved such celebration. After all, it was not like they were planning on doing anything great for these people. If anything, they were going to be assisting Merdon in his desire for a revolution, which would sadly lead to bloodshed.

The chariot followed the parade through the main street of the city, taking them all the way to the center square of the capital. It was there that Darek saw a large balcony that protruded from the majestic castle and overshadowed the square. The chariot stopped at a close distance to the balcony and Darek could see several people up there, looking down at them. Then the entire city was hushed into silence.

One of the men on the balcony moved forward to address them. This man looked quite distinguished, exuding an air of authority. He had a long chin and curly black hair. His apparel consisted of a black Victorian coat and hat.

"Welcome to our city, travelers," he said. "We hope you enjoy your stay. I'm sure you will find that this place is a slice of paradise on this forsaken planet. Be sure to enjoy the sights and sounds of our beautiful city. We have already prepared lodging for your stay.

Tomorrow there will be a great ceremony that I hope you will attend, and following that, you are invited to join us at the castle for a banquet in your honor." The man tipped his hat and took a bow. "Now if you'll excuse us, we have important business to tend to. Please direct all questions to your escort, Windzer." The man clapped his hands together. "Let the festivities continue."

The trumpets blasted as the men on the balcony disappeared into the castle. The rowdy crowd let out a roar the moment the men were gone. Explosions burst in the sky, turning Darek's attention to the magnificent display of rainbow-colored fireworks. These flower-like fireworks were large, blending the once bland sky with its bright flashes to become like an artist's palette, vivid and unpredictable with its blazing fusion of colors.

Darek gaped at the marvelous scene, uttering, "This is awesome…"

Darek whistled a cheerful tune as he dropped his things along his bedside. He had a little dance in his step ever since the jubilation ended. Darek jumped into his bed and embraced its soft comfort. He let out a sigh of relief and curled up by his pillow, squeezing it.

Azura put her sack on her bed. Currie leaped out of her arms, rolled up into a ball, and bounced around the mattress. Azura took out her clothes, one by one, trying to decide what to wear for the banquet. When she encountered a piece of clothing that she thought would be appropriate, she placed them out, folding them neatly in a pile.

Sorren tossed his belongings on his bed and said, "I'll be in town." Then he left the room as quickly as he came in.

Darek jumped off the bed and headed for the door. "I'll be out too."

"Where do you think you're going?" Azura asked, putting her hands on her hips.

"I don't know. I was thinking of exploring. The city has so much to see."

"No, you're not."

"I'm not? Why not?"

Azura's face was split by a grin. "With all the training you've been doing, aren't you itching to spar? It's not like there's anything better to do."

"I can think of tons of better things to do!" Darek rushed out the door. The very thought of sparring with Azura appalled him. The only way he would ever agree to spar with her was in a dream. That way, there wouldn't be any accidental deaths—not any permanent ones anyway. He had already experienced too many imaginary ones during his sessions with Sorren, and it made him understand the huge difference between his ability and theirs.

However, his fear of Azura's brute strength wasn't the only thing that made him leave the room in a hurry. The truth was he did have an objective in mind. He wanted to spy on Sorren.

Sorren was a mysterious character to him. Even though they had trained together for weeks and had several talks along the way, his past was still shrouded in secrecy. For an assassin, he wasn't all that bad. He didn't appear to take pleasure in killing. If anything, he seemed to be quite nice. In his story, Sorren may have killed a Hero, but he apparently had done so to help some villagers. Was he a nice guy then? Why would a nice guy choose to be an assassin? Could his story have been a complete lie to make Darek trust him more?

Sorren had amazed Darek, but had also frightened him. Sorren had killed a Hero, killed him many times in his dream, and could possibly still have some plans to kill him now. Aside from working together to get off the planet, there was no other reason for Sorren to help them. He was a powerful ally that had protected them from the Anarchists, but in time, he could also prove to be the most dangerous foe. Was it wise to trust Sorren? Darek sure didn't think so.

While pondering on many things, Darek searched for him, but Sorren was nowhere to be found.

"He got away," said Darek, sounding disappointed. "Maybe I should just see if there's anything to do before dinner." Darek took out a map of the city that he had stashed in his satchel and examined it. He figured the place for him to be was the shopping district.

Darek explored the city. It had a very simple layout and was easy for him to understand, which was good because he hated getting lost. The gigantic walls of the city made him think the city itself would be huge, but that was not the case. The outside walls were much taller than the highest buildings within. Darek couldn't guess why they would have walls bigger than the smaller city. It left most of the town under its heavy shadow. Noon was the only time the city could be fully illuminated. Because of the lack of sunlight, sufficient lighting was supplied by the streetlamps that littered the city.

The bulk of the residential areas were located near the inside of the wall, surrounding the castle in the center. All the houses were like five-story mansions. As the roads neared the center of the city, they grew much wider and these streets were absolutely packed with people. The center square of the city was bustling with so much activity that Darek had to push his way through to walk a single step.

Occasionally, as he walked, people would come up to him and greet him, welcoming him to their city. Some people, however, kept their distance. He decided there were bound to be a few gloomy people no matter where he went.

Darek spent his hours walking through several shops, though not much of what they had was of any interest to him. Some shops sold small monsters as pets, others sold jewelry, and the most popular shops were hobby-related. After looking around for an hour, he found one shop that he enjoyed perusing through: an antiques shop, which had artifacts and relics for sale.

To him it was almost like a museum. The technology they had was still impressive. They may not have achieved space travel, but they still had many breakthroughs in compact, renewable energy sources, hover technology, all-in-one home appliances, and weather control. He was astonished by everything that was available and wanted to take a few things with him, but he didn't have anything to barter with and was sure that credits would be worthless here. There was a lingering regret incited by greed, for he knew that if he were to sell some of this technology to intergalactic merchants, he'd make a hefty sum.

While he was still looking through the store, he happened to spot a familiar face. Sorren was walking down an aisle. Darek hid himself carefully and tiptoed around, stalking him. While stalking Sorren, he then spotted yet another familiar face. It was Windzer. Could this be more than coincidence? Darek observed them without being noticed. But he found it peculiar that, even though Sorren and Windzer passed by each other, they did not even say hello.

Sorren went up to the shopkeeper. "I'd like to buy this."

The shopkeeper stepped back, a bit startled and excited to see Sorren. He cleared his throat and tidied up his clothing to look slightly more professional. He observed the item carefully and said gruffly, "Is that all? You just want this sword?"

"Yes," replied Sorren.

"What do you have to trade? Do you have anything otherworldly? I've heard stories that you aren't from this planet." The shopkeeper almost squealed in his low voice, if that were possible.

Sorren thought for a moment. "Is gold worth anything?"

The shopkeeper frowned. "It's worthless."

"How about this?" Sorren unsheathed his sword and presented it to the shopkeeper.

Now the shopkeeper was even more bewildered. "A sword for a sword? And furthermore, yours is chipped. You don't have *anything* else?"

Sorren searched his clothes and found a little device. "What about this?"

The shopkeeper's eyes sparkled. "What is it?"

"I have no idea."

"I'll take it!" shouted the shopkeeper. He ripped it out of Sorren's hands and began analyzing it immediately.

Windzer left the store without so much as a glance at Sorren. After sliding his new sword into his sheath, Sorren left as well. All of this was suspicious to Darek, so he tailed them. They moved rather quickly, but Darek was lucky enough to catch a glimpse of Sorren as he went into an alley. Darek peered around the corner of the building and saw Sorren speaking with Windzer. *Aha! I knew there was something going on between them*, thought Darek. But while he wanted to listen in on their conversation, he couldn't hear more than a mumble from where he was standing. Darek rubbed his chin and frowned, trying to think of some way to listen in. He knew he had to do something fast. Without even reconsidering, he hurried into the building and climbed the stairs to the roof.

Darek looked down from the edge. Sorren and Windzer were still chatting below. The alley was narrow, but it was big enough for him to fit. Darek climbed down, pushing his hands and feet against the walls of the buildings. His arms and legs stretched out, he descended slowly. The bricks of the wall were rough; the trip down was long, difficult, and painful. After having an excruciating time, he finally made it so that he was directly above Sorren and Windzer by no more than a few feet and could hear the last of their conversation.

"No, Sorren. You're the only one who still thinks that way," he heard Windzer say. "The others don't care anymore. I don't care anymore."

"Then I will do it alone," said Sorren.

"You will not survive."

"Not that it matters to you. I thought it was fate that we met here." Sorren leaned against the wall. "So that's it…"

"Hey," Windzer said, "stay away from the wall."

Sorren backed away from the building. "Something wrong?"

"Sort of," said Windzer. "We had a little infestation problem recently. Carnivorous ants. They're quite dangerous and problematic. We exterminated most of them, but there are still a few colonies around. You should stay away from the walls for the time being. If they feel tremors along the wall, they will come out...to *feast*."

"Is that so? I'll be careful."

Darek furrowed his brow. Then he quickly ran his eye along the walls and, sure enough, could see some ants crawling about. As he realized he was now in deep trouble, he tried to get back up the wall as fast as he could. But to his disappointment, the ants crawled along at a crazily fast pace. It would've been faster to drop down, but Sorren and Windzer were still hanging around below. Darek's arms and legs started to wobble as he moved up the wall. Next thing he knew, a massive swarm of ants lined the area directly above him so that he couldn't go up any further. *Get away you stupid ants,* Darek screamed in his mind.

The mass of ants slowly walked down the wall. Darek noticed their shift of movement and inched down slowly to avoid being caught by them; the ants followed every move he made.

Windzer smiled. "Darek's quite an interesting fellow, isn't he?"

Sorren nodded. "It's faint. But I see something special in him."

Darn it! Just stop talking and go away! Darek wiggled around, hoping for the situation to start getting better.

Sorren and Windzer continued talking for an hour. They rambled on and on while Darek held on for dear life. The ants didn't move at all. They just stayed there, as if they were waiting for Darek to make the first move. Darek started to consider dropping down and letting the whole thing go. But Darek feared what Sorren might do if he found out about this.

Darek cracked open the door of the room they were staying in. "I'm back."

Azura said, "I'm surprised you went out for so long. It's been a few hours. I was beginning to think you weren't coming back. Did something happen?"

Darek couldn't say a word. He was too tired to speak. His arms and legs were sore from top to bottom. Every move he made hurt so much that he almost cried. He plopped onto the bed and shut his eyes.

"Did you do some training without me?"

While lying on the bed, Darek turned to face Azura. "Don't ask."
Azura shrugged. "Fine."

"What are you doing anyway?" Darek watched Azura, as she moved her hand up and down a wall.

"I found something neat," she replied with a grin. "I saw some ants that were wandering around our room and asked the locals about them. They're pretty harmless and fun to play with. They'll actually follow you around but won't hurt you. They're great because they collect the oil, sweat and dead skin that you leave behind. It's very useful for keeping everything clean." She moved her finger up and down the wall and a small ant followed the motion. "Neat, huh?"

Recognizing the ants, Darek sat up and exclaimed, "WHAT? ARE YOU SERIOUS?"

Curling his lip, Darek grunted, "That Windzer! He tricked me! He knew I was there and tricked me!"

Someone rapped on the door. Darek and Azura exchanged glances.

"You're closer," said Azura.

Darek crawled into his sheets. "Can't you see I'm dying here? I can barely make a fist with these sore hands."

Another brisk knock alerted them. Azura stared firmly at Darek, telling him with her expression that she was not going to move. Darek groaned as he got out of the bed. He walked up to the door with a slight limp and opened it. A man was at the door. His skin had a dark complexion and his long hair was slicked back. It was no one that Darek recognized.

"Read this." The man handed Darek an envelope and walked off without another word.

"Who was it?" Azura had caught a glimpse of the man, and he seemed familiar, but she couldn't quite understand why.

"I don't know," admitted Darek. "Do you think I should open this?"

"Is it addressed to anyone?"

"No."

Azura shrugged. "Might as well. Like Rathos said, they should know everyone's face by heart. No case of mistaken identity."

Darek ripped open the envelope and found a letter inside. He read it out loud:

Dear People That I Know,

I'm glad to see you have safely arrived. My spies have informed me about the ceremony tomorrow and I've decided to send you this letter as a warning. It is believed that sometime during the ceremony they will have a process in which to convert you into immortals. This is still speculation, but I really believe this to be the case. This initiation ceremony may very well be some kind of disguise so that we would not be able to figure out how the process works.

As you well know, I am not aware of how a person becomes an immortal, so we must be on guard and carefully analyze everything that goes on around us during that time. Do not back out of the ceremony! This will only lead to suspicion and the elders won't be so quick to let you go. Do not fear the ceremony tomorrow. We will try our best to ensure that you survive. Trust in us.

    From,
You Know Who

"Must be from Merdon," said Azura.

Worried, Darek said, "Does Merdon really expect me to put my life on the line like this?"

"Don't worry about it," assured Azura. "I'm sure Merdon's got everything under control. I just wonder when Sorren will get here. He should probably read this."

"No," said Darek. "We can't let Sorren know about this."

"Why not?"

"There's something fishy going on with him."

"Hasn't he been helping us all this time?" asked Azura.

Darek said, "Today I saw him talking with Windzer. They know each other. Sorren could be a hired spy for the elders! He could be searching for evidence to bring against Merdon!"

"You don't trust him?" said Azura.

"Of course not! That guy tried to kill me!"

Azura laughed. "Oh yeah, I remember that. Good times."

"Azura!" Darek shouted. "This is serious!"

"Fine, I won't tell him. But I still think you're getting paranoid."

CHAPTER 19
Ceremony

The beating of drums thundered at dawn, violently waking everyone from their slumber. These loud drums were made with the thick, resilient hides of Doarocks, the brutish herbivorous beasts that roamed the plains. The drums were all around the city, so that everyone would be alerted to the start of the day. With their superhuman strength, the drummers pounded away; the deafening impact of each hit shook the foundations of the buildings and rattled the windows. Screaming and shouting permeated the streets as the immortals anticipated the ceremony.

Darek tumbled off his bed, shaken. During the night, he had nothing but nightmares pertaining to a rather sudden death at the coming ceremony. He was not happy about this. He had signed up for a daring mission, for infiltration and spying—not suicide.

Azura and Sorren were waiting for him at the door.

"Are you ready?" Azura asked.

Darek yawned and scratched a few morning itches. "No. Just give me a few hours."

"Everyone out there is so excited," said Azura. "They are waiting for us. You don't want to disappoint them, do you?"

"Actually, I don't mind disappointing them," said Darek, climbing back into bed. "Just tell them I didn't wake up. Let them be disappointed."

"You have to go!" Azura shouted. "Don't you remember what the letter said?"

"Letter?" asked Sorren. "What letter?"

"Um, I meant…the leather…" Azura coughed and cleared her throat. "Anyway, Darek, you can't back out now! Everything's going to be all right."

"No." Darek pulled the covers over him. "Just leave me alone."

"Come on, Sorren." Azura elbowed him in the chest. "It's your turn to convince Darek to come. We need the extra hand in the mission."

Sorren sighed. He didn't want to get involved. He just stood by the side of the bed and said, "Just go or Azura will be angry. Don't worry. It's not like there's anything weird going on. They aren't going to *sacrifice* you or anything."

Darek shot out of bed and snapped, "That's exactly what's going to happen!"

"He's not going to change his mind," Sorren told Azura. "Let's leave him and go. It should still be fine with the two of us."

"No!" Azura scowled. "You barely even tried!"

"If it sounds like I don't care, well…I don't," replied Sorren truthfully.

"And I do care," Azura said. "Now convince him! I'm not leaving without Darek. And without me, you're on your own in the mission."

"Getting pushy," mumbled Sorren. "Fine." He tapped Darek on the shoulder; Darek's eyes rolled up as his breath momentarily left him. Darek fell back onto his bed, unconscious and helpless.

Concerned, Azura asked, "What'd you just do?"

"I clouded his mind. He'll have trouble trying to collect his thoughts." Sorren tried to make Darek sit up on the bed. "I'm surprised he didn't put up much of a fight."

"How could you do such a thing?" Azura shrilled, exasperated by his actions. "I told you to convince him, not put him to sleep! I want him to come to a decision on his own."

Sorren grumbled, "Darek doesn't listen—you yell at him. I help subdue him—you yell at me. Make up your mind. You're totally unreasonable."

"I'm unreasonable?" Azura glared at him. "You're the one who does whatever he likes! You can't justify your actions any way you want!"

A knock came from the door and it opened up halfway. Windzer stuck his head in. "Are you guys going to come out soon? It's time." He looked at Darek, whom Sorren plopped back on the bed. "Partied a little too hard last night?"

"Not quite," muttered Sorren, as he pulled the door wide open and left in a hurry.

"What is wrong with him?" Azura said with a sigh. "He didn't even bother to help me."

"He's just that kind of guy." Leaning on the doorframe, Windzer watched Sorren disappear into the crowded street. "Always aiming for the goal. Always willing to handle his problems alone if need be."

"It almost sounds like you know him," Azura said, remembering what Darek had told her the night before.

"Huh?" Windzer looked startled. "I was just saying that everyone is different. And that he seems to me like someone who handles things alone. Some people are just like that. You can't change everything about a person. You have to just understand them and learn how to work with them."

"You're right," said Azura, nodding. "That's true. I guess I just have to put up with him for now."

Then Windzer gestured for Azura to leave. "I'll carry Darek. You need to get to the square."

The main square was already packed by the time they arrived. Most of the people there could barely contain their excitement; the horde of immortals waited impatiently for the starting horn that would signal the beginning.

"Make way for the guests!" Windzer raised his voice above the crowd.

Heads glanced back, and when they saw Darek and the others, the crowd parted. The anxious onlookers watched as Sorren and Azura made their way to a special platform. Darek lagged behind, still out cold; he had to be carried on Windzer's shoulder the whole way.

Azura scanned the faces of the crowd and grinned when a familiar face caught her eye. She pinched Darek in the arm; Darek jumped up and rolled off Windzer's side. Darek was feeling woozy for a few seconds before becoming fully aware of where he was. He opened his mouth and almost let out a panicking scream, but Azura urgently muffled him, clasping her hand over his mouth.

"Shush!" Azura pointed over the crowd and said, "Tell me what you see."

Darek squinted and saw Rathos standing among the other immortals, appearing perfectly fine. "He's okay! How'd he get here so fast?"

"I don't know," said Azura, shrugging. "But now you don't have to worry anymore. I'm sure Rathos has everything under control."

Darek let loose a big smile, overjoyed to see Rathos alive and well.

Special elevated seating was arranged for the nobles. These cushioned stands were positioned close to and around the center stage. Merdon took his place there, inspecting the various aspects of the ceremony with utmost scrutiny. This was the only chance for him to find out how the transformation from mortal to immortal took place, and he was not going to let this chance slip away.

Rathos nudged him and whispered, "Master, please read this." He handed Merdon an envelope.

"What's this?" Merdon tore open the envelope and found a letter inside that read:

> *Reign of the King*
> *You see by night.*
> *Do not wave, for*
> *He will be waiting.*

"A poem?" Merdon read the letter several times, analyzing it. "And a poorly written one at that. It does not make sense. What is this for?"

"I haven't the faintest," said Rathos. "I found it in my pocket just now. Could it be a warning from the elders?"

"I hope not," said Merdon. "If this fails, we may never get a second chance. But I don't see this as a threat from the elders. They could simply get rid of us if they wished." He held the letter in his hand with a firmer grip. "No, there's more to this. We have here an anonymous writer, one who possibly seeks to aid us."

"A clue?"

"Most likely. We can't be sure but…we'll take what we can get."

Merdon fell silent as several other nobles took their seats next to him.

He whispered to Rathos, "Keep it in mind. Tell me if you discover anything. We must come up with the solution before it is too late."

When several trumpet blasts signaled the start of the ceremony, the crowd became quiet.

"It is now time for us to begin," said an elder. He stepped in front of the platform near a pedestal and introduced himself to the group, saying, "I am Elder Zid and I will be leading this ceremony. You may remember me from yesterday. We will start with a special piece performed by our orchestra."

Rathos asked Merdon, "Could it be the music?"

"Impossible," Merdon replied. "It would mean that people who are deaf are immune, but I know of several people who were deaf before they became immortal."

The song played without interruption and it was a beautiful piece that everyone enjoyed. At the end of the performance, the orchestra got up and took a bow, and the crowd showered them with applauses and flowers in appreciation.

"I want to thank you all again for coming to our humble capital," said Zid. "It has been exactly one hundred and three years since the fall of our civilization. But no matter how hard it has been for us, we survived in the end. We fought back the monsters and rebuilt our world together! It was glorious. But it was also sad that we were alone. Today you have showed us it is not the case. We are not alone! For that, we graciously thank you." The Elder Zid bowed his head. More loud applauses followed after his speech. Some of the people in the crowd even shed tears.

"For coming here," Zid continued, "I shall give you my blessings in accordance with our traditions." Zid walked up to each one of them and placed his hand upon their shoulder. He then passed on some sayings for prosperity, peace and unending life.

"Your thoughts?" asked Rathos.

"Nothing seems out of the ordinary," said Merdon. "Words are the same as music, won't work on a deaf person. Touch, however, is different but still unrealistic. I'm sure either you or Thedes have touched the humans on your travels, yet nothing has happened."

Rathos thought for a moment. "But what if the immortal needs some sort of technique. Maybe casual touch would not activate the Ascension—but an imparting of power can do that. A special touch."

Merdon said, "Even if that were the case, the few elders would had have to touch millions of people in the world for the catastrophic event to occur. That's not possible in a few days, let alone a lifetime. Even if they spent forever trying to touch every single person, people would be getting born in places they've already visited, leaving many untouched children."

Zid waved his arms at a group of servants that stood at attention nearby. The servants acknowledged the elder with a brisk nod and wheeled out carts toward the raised platform.

"Next," said Zid, "we have some delicacies prepared for this momentous occasion."

Zid removed the lid off of several pans to reveal cooked dishes.

"This could be it!" said Rathos, deeply concerned. "The food could contain something!"

"Don't be so alarmed," said Merdon. "While this is indeed a possibility, I find it hard to accept that they could achieve this on a world scale. In the past, food was distributed by many different retailers and was produced by many companies. Achieving control over this would've been impossible unless they were dictators."

Darek ate whatever was placed before him and he was pleasantly surprised to find out how good it tasted. It was incredible. He especially liked the thin slabs of delectable meat coated with breadcrumbs and sugary orange syrup. There must have been a master chef who had spent his immortal life dedicated to the preparation of food.

Zid smiled. "I'm glad to see you enjoy it. Tonight you will experience more, but for now let me quench your thirst with a drink." Zid said to a servant nearby, "Tell them to bring the water." The servant nodded and headed through the crowd.

Merdon stood up nervously. "Give me that letter!" Rathos sensed his master's urgency and handed the letter to him. Merdon looked it through once more and said, "This is it! This letter is not a poem, code or riddle. The diagonal words are a simple clue. Not reign, but rain; not see but sea; the waves are the waves in the ocean; the waiting is similar to wading. The writer is hinting at the water! In the past, the distribution of water was done by only a handful of major facilities. Not to mention, water is easily contaminated! Spread the word."

In haste Rathos walked down the steps and recognized a group of his subordinates. Passing by them casually, he whispered in their ear, "There should be cups of water up ahead being prepared. The water they use is special. See to it that it is replaced with normal water." The men made a soft guttural grunt in response and took off into the crowd. Rathos snuck around the crowd and approached a building that overshadowed the platform. He transformed into a wolf and, with graceful leaps, he jumped from ledge to ledge, scaling the building.

While the crowd was waiting for the water to be brought to the platform, Rathos knew what he had to do. He caught sight of a large gong that lay beside the floor on the rooftop. With a fierce growl, he shoved the gong off the roof. People screamed and moved out of the way when the gong came tumbling down. Rathos let out a resounding howl.

Zid scowled. "What does that crazy dog think he's doing? He's ruining everything! Someone stop him!"

Several immortals ran up to the building and climbed it all the way to the top, but Rathos managed to knock down each and every one that approached the roof's edge. While Rathos made a commotion, his friends sneaked behind the people who had the cups on a cart. Seeing that the gazes of the servants were firmly locked on Rathos, Merdon's men swapped one of the cups. They wanted to replace more of the cups, but the servants regained their focus on the cart, making it difficult to do another switch.

A lion reached the rooftop that Rathos was on. The lion growled, "Rathos, I don't know what you are doing, but I will put an end to your foolishness."

Rathos quaked in fear for the lion was none other than the elder Rendall. With a pounce, the lion butt his head into Rathos's chest, crushing his ribcage. The immense strength of the lion made Rathos's face become disfigured in pain and bewilderment. Rathos struggled against Rendall and they brutally wrestled each other on the roof. Rendall forced his way toward the edge, hauling Rathos with him. Interlocked, the two of them rolled off the side and fell from the rooftop. Rathos tried to break away in midair but Rendall remained steadfast, clutching Rathos in his claws. Rathos was slammed into the ground. The road cracked beneath them. Rendall got up and walked away as Rathos lay there, paralyzed. The servants of the elders whisked Rathos's body away from the ceremony.

One of Merdon's men walked back up to Merdon and delivered a secret message to his ear. "I'm sorry, Master. Only one cup has been changed."

Sorren looked directly at Merdon. Merdon raised his index finger as a sign.

"One," mumbled Sorren. "Either one cup was switched, or one cup remains."

"Did you say something?" asked Azura, turning to him.

"Just talking to myself," said Sorren, shaking his head.

"Excuse the intrusion," Zid told them. "I assure you that nothing like that will ever happen again. Let us continue." Zid motioned to his servants. "Bring out the cups."

A servant rolled a cart down to the platform, revealing three cups, one for each person.

"Please," said Zid, "take and drink of the cup. Think of it as a toast."

Sorren analyzed the cups, searching for some kind of detectable difference.

Darek walked up to his cup.

"Wait," interrupted Sorren, holding Darek back by the shoulder.

"Is something wrong?" questioned Zid.

"Nothing really, but I think we should do it one at a time so we can savor the moment. Do we have your permission to do so?"

Zid eyed Sorren suspiciously but replied, "You may do so."

"Darek, take the cup on the right," said Sorren with a short wink.

Darek glanced at Azura, wondering what was going on. Azura nodded back at him and gestured with an open hand for Darek to take the cup.

Darek picked up the small porcelain cup with his finger and thumb. It was like a tiny teacup. Darek examined the inside. It appeared to him as ordinary water. He didn't smell anything weird, and when he took a sip of it, he didn't taste anything weird either. Seeing that it was fine, Darek downed the whole thing.

Sorren watched the pleased expression on Zid's face.

"Azura," said Sorren. "Take the middle cup."

Azura picked up the cup and drank from it. Nothing happened. She was fine.

Sorren smiled and picked up the leftmost cup in his hand. "Before I drink to this ceremony, I would like to say a few words." He looked over at Zid for approval. Zid nodded.

Sorren turned to Azura and Darek. "Thank you. I had no idea what awaited me on this planet. These past weeks have been eventful, to say the least. Though it may not have seemed to be the case, I have enjoyed our adventures together."

Sorren swallowed the water in one gulp. The cup slipped out of his hand and fell to the floor, shattering into tiny fragments. Much to the speechless astonishment of everyone, Sorren clenched his fingers in the center of his chest as though grasping for his heart. Panting and heaving, he suddenly collapsed and began a series of short convulsions and seizures that lasted for seconds. When it ended, he was motionless.

The crowd gasped. Darek's visage was frozen in despair. What had just happened? He had no idea and a part of him never wanted to consider the possibilities.

CHAPTER 20
Moving on

Darek silently sat on the floor of their room, leaning back against the wall. Darek thought Sorren was faking his death—but he wasn't. Elder Rendall had inspected the body and Sorren had been pronounced dead. Was there no way to avoid it? Darek was supposed to be the one to take the leftmost cup. If Sorren hadn't switched cups with Darek, the opposite would have happened. Darek just couldn't understand why Sorren did that. Sorren was a killer, one who couldn't be trusted, and yet he decisively took the cup and drank, knowing that he would die. Why did he do such a thing?

The door opened. Azura entered and found Darek looking as glum as ever.

"Where have you been?" Sounding uninterested, Darek asked simply for the sake of asking.

"I had to throw up the water, just in case."

"Throw up water?" Darek blinked. "Can you do that?"

"Of course," said Azura, beaming. "Sorren was hinting something to me when I took the cup, so I held the water in my esophagus to keep it from going any further. It's a complicated process, but definitely something you shouldn't try unless you're Aenarian."

Darek said nothing in reply to that. Azura thought Darek would still be curious or disgusted by it, but he remained silent. Then, all of a sudden, he began to repeatedly bang the back of his head against the wall. She could tell he was still bothered by Sorren's death.

"I can't believe someone dies every step of the way," said Darek. "First Reza and Drey—and now Sorren! Am I bad luck? Am I some stupid curse? I thought I'd be helping out the mission, but it's almost like everyone's dying because of me!"

"Don't say that," said Azura. "It's not your fault! They…had their circumstances. There was nothing you could've done. Even if you weren't around, it wouldn't have changed a thing!"

"You're wrong…" Darek smashed his dagger into the floor and yelled, "It is my fault!" He bashed his dagger into the floor, over and over, leaving many deep marks in the wood.

"Darek…" Azura whispered, shocked to see that he was so affected by this.

"Do you not understand?" Darek breathed. He made a pinching gesture with his index finger and thumb. "I was this close to death! I was the one who was supposed to die! ME!" He beat his chest in anger. "It's *my* fault you were hurt by the Anarchists! It was *my* decision that allowed Reza and Drey to come along with us in the first place! It was *my* cup that killed Sorren! I'm sick of this being all my fault!"

Consoling, Azura said, "Everyone who came on the mission knew it would be dangerous. Things happen. It's not like you didn't try to help us. It's not like we never wanted you on this mission. You still handled everything well in my opinion. You did manage to save me from the Anarchists. And Sorren trusted you enough to leave the matter in your hands."

"He trusted me?" Darek buried his face in his arms. "Do you think so? I didn't trust him. I didn't like him. For him to trust me…it makes no sense. He was the skilled assassin. I'm just…a pathetic delivery boy…who can't even handle deliveries. Now we have no hope. Without him, we can't finish the mission."

"That's not true!" Azura said. "We can still do this!"

"Maybe you can." Darek stood up and said to her face, "But I'm only a normal person. I'm a *normal* human being! You don't even seem shaken by his death! Death is not something I can just brush off. If I see someone die before my very eyes, I can't forget it so easily! I can't be tough like you! I bet you don't even feel a thing! That's why you think it's all right!"

Azura slapped him across the cheek; she slapped him so hard he could feel his jaw crack. His right cheek was burning red and swollen. Stunned, Darek almost retaliated, but refrained from doing so when he saw Azura in tears. With one hand, she grabbed the collar of his shirt, lifted him off the ground and slammed him into the wall. He stared apprehensively at her.

"Death hurts. I know," Azura said. "Don't think for a second that I'm immune to things like pain or sadness. I'm human too! But you don't have to feel responsible for his death. *You* did not kill him. You had nothing to do with it! And there was nothing you could do to stop it. But there is something you can do now. You can stop acting like this and focus on finishing what he couldn't! Why do you think he did it in the first place? He knew the transformation had consequences! But he trusted you. No one willingly sacrifices themselves for something they don't believe in. He believed in you. He believed you would continue the mission…and live on. Are you going to just waste his effort by moping around like this?"

Darek hung his head, abashed. She was right. He couldn't let Sorren's death go in vain.

Azura dropped him and faced the other way. She wiped away the tears with the sleeve of her shirt; using her Aenarian ability, Azura stopped the tears from flowing.

"More importantly," said Azura, turning back with a halfhearted smile, "don't you want to see how Rathos is doing?"

With the shock of Sorren's death, Darek forgot what Rathos had gone through. He asked, "Where is he now? Is he okay?"

"Windzer should know," said Azura. "Let's go find him."

"You want to see *him*?" Windzer nearly jumped out of his shoes. They caught Windzer at the food court, scooping up some fried fish for lunch.

"Yes," snapped Darek. "No matter how you rephrase the question, the answer is yes!"

Windzer ignored them and quickly ran away from the buffet table, taking his seat under the shade of a nearby umbrella. He hoped they wouldn't follow him to the table. They did.

"Come on," shouted Darek. "Take us to him!"

Windzer told them, "It's just that I don't think it's a good idea to see him now. He really doesn't want to be disturbed. He's had a very rough morning. Visitors aren't welcome!"

"Nonsense! Just take us to him," said Azura. "We're the guests of honor."

Windzer scratched his neck and loosened the collar of his shirt. "Getting on your high-horse, eh? That is that and this is this. You can't expect me to give in to *all* your demands!"

Darek got close to Windzer's face and spat, "I wonder what the elders would do if they found out we weren't treated properly."

Windzer backed away, wiping the spit off his nose. "So you're going to play that card, huh?" Windzer glanced nervously at the other tables, making sure no one was listening in. He motioned for Azura and Darek to get close and muttered, "I guess I have no choice. Just promise me that you won't talk of him. Not a word about Rathos to anyone whatsoever."

Azura and Darek exchanged glances and said, "What do you mean by that?"

"There's no hidden meaning!" snapped Windzer. "Stop making things complicated!"

Windzer approached a small fortress near the elders' castle. The walls were heavily reinforced; thick barbed wire was stretched over the fort like a massive net of prickly spikes. Watchmen were positioned on all sides of the walls. The captain of the guard opened up the front gate and ran out to meet Windzer.

"Have you come to question the prisoner?"

"Yes," Windzer replied. He looked over his shoulder and motioned to the two others behind him who were in hooded robes. "These are my servants. They will be accompanying me. I'd like to go down."

The captain nodded. "Of course, my lord. Anything you ask for will be granted."

The captain led Windzer and his servants past the gates and into the main building. While in the first room, he grabbed several keys from his desk and took hold of a small torch on the wall and handed off another torch to Windzer. The captain opened up the barred door and led them down some stone steps into what seemed to be a dark, foreboding world. It was the dungeon created by the elders, a place of vicious punishment and inexplicable torture. It was the existence of this building that ensured that the rule of the elders was absolute.

The dungeon did not consist of the usual prison cells. There were no bars to peer through, only solid walls to hide the faces of the victims who were imprisoned. Each prisoner had his or her own room. While it may sound accommodating, nothing was farther from the truth. There were no comforts provided for them. They had no bed or blankets; ventilation was poor, making it hard to breathe in fresh air; the food was served charred, cold and heavily salted; the only water given was bitter. The dungeon had no windows and no light. It was utter darkness and pure silence. There was only one prisoner who had to suffer within these walls. Very rarely did anyone come here, for no one would willingly anger the elders.

The captain of the guard led them to the far end of the corridor. There was a revolting odor that lingered in the darkness. As they walked, their shoes squeaked from a layer of sticky, oily filth on the tiles. They stopped at a solid wooden door.

"Here he is. I'll be waiting at the steps. When you're done, please come see me."

Windzer gave a slight nod in reply.

When the captain left them, Azura and Darek took off their hoods.

"What is Rathos doing in this horrid place?" asked Azura, feeling disgusted by everything around them.

"It's the only jail we have," replied Windzer. "Not much of a choice for lawbreakers."

Darek grabbed the torch from Windzer, kicked open the door, and entered the room, clearing away the darkness that encompassed them. As he raised the flame, Rathos slowly came into view. Darek gasped when he laid eyes on him. Rathos was standing there, frail and sickly, his hands and feet chained to the wall. As the light hit his eyes, Rathos flinched. Though tired, he could not sit. His body was beaten and bruised, with flowing blood that streamed down like rivers across his back.

"Rathos!" Tears dripped off Darek's cheeks. His compassion oozed out when he saw Rathos in so much pain and suffering. Darek passed the torch back to Windzer and approached him. "What happened?"

"Darek, is that you?" Rathos huffed, "Sorry, I can't see well…"

Darek turned to Windzer. "We have to get him out of here!"

Windzer shook his head. "Doing that would only bring more trouble."

"But he'll die!"

"He won't die. They won't let him die. Every immortal is important to them. If he dies, it'll be a loss, a grave loss. Not to mention, they only want to exact punishment."

"He's right," exhaled Rathos. "Don't worry about me. This pain means nothing to me. Now leave this place. The banquet will soon start at the castle. You must go and show yourselves. Do not be late. And please…do…not…fail…" He fainted.

"I understand," said Darek, brushing away his tears. "I will do as you say."

The streets that led to the castle were getting swamped with activity as people trickled in. Broad smiles were on the faces of the immortals as they headed toward the castle. It was almost time for the banquet to begin. The immortals usually had nothing to do with their time. After a hundred years of living, they had already explored their original hobbies and sought after new ones. Aside from several household chores and simple jobs, the immortals would spend their time creating fine arts in the day and partying at night. But even so, they still felt excited to go to this banquet because there was now a reason to celebrate.

Darek and Azura took their time to walk to the castle. They weren't in a rush. Even though they were the guests of honor, they'd much rather be fashionably late.

Darek didn't have anything fancy to wear. Rathos had packed him several long sleeve shirts and pants, which he had used during the journey for cold nights, and he hoped that long sleeves would be more appropriate for such an occasion. While the clothes were better than anything he had, there were still shabby and dirty from the trip. He was a bit nervous because he looked so out of place.

Azura was also nervous. While Azura did have some personal sets of clothing on hand, it was all meant for combat. Her clothes were rather plain as their main purpose was to withstand tearing and offer protection. She had on a purple, protective blouse, which she would usually dress underneath a vest; Azura didn't have a skirt, so she wore silky black shorts.

Azura stopped abruptly. "Do you hear something?"

Darek shrugged. "I hear lots and lots of footsteps if that's what you mean."

Azura said, "It sounded like an animal crying."

Darek perked his ear up and listened carefully. "You're right," said Darek. "Now that you mention it, I hear a dog whimpering over in that alley."

The two of them wandered into the back street to investigate. They found a little puppy standing on its hind legs, scratching the brick wall. When it saw Darek, it stopped and stared at him.

"What's it doing in a place like this?" Darek crouched over and stuck out his hand. "Come here little puppy. I won't hurt you." The puppy had an innocent look on his face and it strode over to Darek's fingers, sniffing and licking it. It grinned maliciously and chomped down on Darek's hand, nearly engulfing it. Upset, Darek jerked back his bloody hand and shouted, "Bad dog! Bad dog!"

"Oh, shut your whining," said the puppy. The puppy started to rapidly grow in size before their very eyes until it was larger than Darek. It was the black wolf, Thedes. Apparently, he had the ability to change the size of his wolf form; it was something Darek had witnessed in the mansion, but back then he had thought it was merely a trick of the mind.

"Thedes?" Azura was surprised to see him. "You survived too?"

"Of course I did!" growled Thedes. "I visited you yesterday!"

Darek tried to recall everything that happened the day before. "No…I think I'd remember something like that."

Thedes grunted, "I was the one who gave you the letter! Did you even read it?"

"Th-that was you?" Darek stammered. He quickly recovered from the shock of remembering Thedes's human form. "How did you and Rathos make it back?"

"We found another exit soon after," Thedes explained. "And conveniently, we found several tame Kajins—these birdlike beasts—waiting there for us. We rode the Kajins back here, arriving shortly after you did."

"Ah, it must've been Windzer," said Darek.

"Windzer?" Thedes asked, "What does Windzer have to do with anything?"

Looking bewildered, Darek said, "Isn't he a part of your group?"

"No," said Thedes. "Though he's a noble, he's a servant of the elders. Lower class immortals are forced to be servants, clerks, and the like. Nobles do not usually bother with that, but he went directly to the elders and requested to be their servant. He'd make a great spy if he did join our group, since he's so close to them. But he is not affiliated with us in any way."

"He still is helping you guys," said Darek. "I'm sure of it."

"How can you be so sure?"

Darek leaned against the wall and thought about it. "Okay, maybe I'm not that sure. But he did save us from the Rock Worm at the right moment, which means he was in the area at that time. And when we asked him to take us to Rathos, he did! It was almost as though he knew we were working with Rathos."

"If what you said is true, we may have to back out," growled Thedes.

"What? Isn't it a good thing?"

"It's not like we can trust Windzer so easily. Yes, he could be on our side—but he could also be helping us as part of an elaborate scheme to bring us before the elders."

"Darek said the same thing about Sorren, calling him a possible traitor," said Azura. "We all know how that ended."

Thedes ignored Azura's comment. "Did we not tell you the whole purpose of this mission? The whole point was so that even if you failed, there'd be nothing to tie us together! If Windzer, who is so close to the elders, knows of our connection, he may be waiting with a trap to corner us in. Once we are inside the castle, we might fall into their hands."

"I don't care if it's a trap," said Darek. "We're doing this."

"Oh?" Thedes looked surprised. "You sound confident. Where does all that confidence come from?"

"I'm not that confident," said Darek. "But look where we are! We've passed the ceremony and earned the trust of the whole community! We've come so far. It'd be a total waste to back out now. I mean, how often do you get a bunch of aliens that you can try this with? This is like a once-in-a-lifetime opportunity!"

Thedes crossed his furry arms. "Sure, you may have gotten quite far. You have dealt with the biggest hurdle. But aren't you forgetting something?"

"What?"

"Sorren is no longer with you. He was the greatest asset to the team. He was the main reason we wanted to do this mission in the first place. I have seen first hand how great his skills are at stealth and combat. Now that he is gone, my master's faith in this mission is wavering."

"You trusted Sorren so much," said Darek, looking Thedes in the eye. "Yet he placed his trust in me, even to the point of death. Doesn't that give me any kind of credit?"

Thedes nodded, smiling at Darek's attitude. "I'm surprised. Very surprised. Darek, maybe I was wrong about you. You might just pull it off. Very well, I approve of tonight's mission. You may continue as originally planned."

"Tonight's mission? You mean—at the banquet?"

"Yes. The banquet will be more than just a party for you."

"Isn't it dangerous to do it tonight?" asked Azura. "Everyone will be there!"

"I know," said Thedes. "But we have no choice. Tomorrow will be the test of your abilities to determine your social rankings. Because you faked the first test, I'm assuming you'll have no abilities to show, which will cause problems."

"I could fake it," said Azura, beaming. "Superhuman strength is my forte. I'm pretty sure I could pass for one of the lower class."

"But Darek wouldn't be able to," said Thedes. "If we do this mission tonight, we won't have to worry about tomorrow. There are other reasons we must do it tonight. For one, our spies have found out that many security guards will be taking off for the evening so they can attend the feast. This negligence on their part is our gain. Moreover, since it'll be crowded, it'll be easier for you to slip away unnoticed. Lastly, the main and most obvious reason is because the place we must investigate is inside the castle. Rarely does anyone get a chance to go inside the castle. Only the elders and their servants live there." Thedes paused and frowned. "However, because this is working out a little too perfectly, I still feel that a trap is likely."

"Even so," said Darek, "trap or not, we have to do this. Once we finish this, the elders will be exposed for who they are, and Merdon will be able to take control."

Thedes nodded. "I'll take you to where you need to go, but from that point forward, everything else will be up to you. You can die if you want, but whatever you do—do not fail. The future of our planet rests in your hands."

The festivities were so loud that, at times, the uproarious music and crowd could be heard outside of the city walls. Darek already had high expectations for what he would experience in their greatest celebration, but his expectations were thoroughly surpassed. He didn't know if it was because he never really expected much in life, or if this was just way above his imagination. For one thing, the moment he entered the dining hall, he froze and gaped at the immense size of this one hall alone. The castle seemed large on the outside, but the inside felt much bigger than it should be. The ceiling of the hall had to be nearly twenty stories high; massive columns supported the weight of the beams above them.

The town band was there in full form. It was focused mostly on percussion. A hundred drums of each and every size filled the stage and twenty skilled artists manned them. Each drum had a particular note and it seemed they were able to play beautiful melodies with this vast array of drums.

Long mahogany tables were lined up along the walls for the people to sit, leaving space for small circular tables to be placed closer to the center of the room where food was served. Servants strode in and out of the kitchen, carrying platters of treats for the guests.

Everything was excessive. Chandeliers were suspended overhead, and when a strong gust of wind rushed through a network of air ducts, the chandeliers swung from side to side like dancing pendulums. All of the eating utensils and plates were forged of gold. The walls were ornamented with hundreds of perfectly cut diamonds.

Darek said, "What do we do now?"

"Eat and enjoy," responded Azura, almost swooning. She was absolutely famished and did not spare a single second before digging into the feast. She voraciously slurped up any food within reaching distance of her hands.

The music stopped for a short moment as Elder Zid stood upon the center stage and announced, "The banquet will run through the night. Please enjoy yourselves till dawn."

"Dawn? They're crazy," commented Darek.

Azura laughed, "That's a good thing for us."

A servant approached Azura with cookies on a plate. "Please take one."

"Thank you." Azura picked up one of the cookies. It was light and most likely hollow.

"Looks like a fortune cookie," said Darek, sounding eager to crack it open.

"Go ahead," said Azura, handing it over.

Darek cracked it open and found a small piece of paper that read:

> *Twenty paces forward will lead you to a door.*
> *Head down that hall until you see a four.*
> *Pull the rope to go to the next floor.*
> *Be prepared for a prize in store.*

"How's this a fortune?" groaned Darek, disappointed. "Fortune cookies never have fortunes anymore! They should say things like 'You're going to get rich soon!' or 'You'll soon find the love of your life!' How lame. Did it even have to rhyme? Super lame."

"Give me that!" Azura tore the note from Darek's fingers. "Of course it's not a fortune—these are directions! They must be from Merdon."

"Oh," said Darek. "I better grab another one then."

Darek was about to wander off, but Azura grabbed him by the shoulder and pushed him to a door that seemed to be twenty steps away. No one was in that area. Just as the note had said, they found the number four on a door at the end of the hall. Right beside the door was a quaint rope.

"So this rope unlocks the door?" Darek jostled the doorknob. It wouldn't budge.

"There's only one way to find out." Azura yanked on the rope and they heard a loud rumbling. The door clicked open and revealed a pitch-black room.

Darek entered and fell right through a trapdoor beneath his feet. "WHAAAAA—"

"Darek!" Azura jumped down into the hole after him.

After tumbling down a slide, the two of them stumbled into a beautiful garden full of shrubs, flowers, bushes and small trees.

Darek got up and shook off the dirt and leaves from his clothes. "Where are we?"

"Seeing as we fell down," said Azura, "this would have to be under the castle."

"Under?" Darek couldn't believe it. There was a blue sky above them and all of this vegetation at their feet. How could they be underneath the castle? It didn't even look like a room. There were no walls, nothing to enclose them in this open space. "Looks like the outside."

"It's fake," she replied. "Take a closer look. Only the dirt is real. Everything else is fake."

Darek inspected the leaves of the leaves and they looked like they were pinned to the branches. "Hey, you're right!"

"I can't believe you didn't figure that out sooner. I was sure the sky was a dead give away. It was completely dark outside an hour ago, but it's sunny in here. That's impossible."

Darek gazed at the sky and said, "No wonder the clouds don't look like they're moving. But why would someone bother with this?"

"Probably just an over-extended hobby," replied Azura. "Bored people do all sorts of crazy things."

"Or someone could just like to have perfect weather all the time," growled a voice.

"Who's there? Is that you, Thedes?" Darek inquired.

A lion crept slowly behind them. It stood tall on its hind legs and turned back into its human form. Not surprisingly, the man still resembled a lion after he transformed. His long golden hair was like a lion's mane and his stalwart body was intimidating to say the least.

"I have not introduced myself, have I? I am Elder Rendall."

"Isn't this the guy who hurt Rathos?" hissed Darek. "The lion *punk*."

"Calm down," Azura whispered to Darek. "We don't stand a chance against him."

"It seems you picked up the note," said Rendall. "Congratulations! You are the lucky winners of the event for tonight!"

"We won? Seriously? What did we win?" asked Darek.

Rendall smiled cruelly. "A trip to your own private dungeon."

Rendall wasn't lying. It was something of a dungeon, but it wasn't that bad. The walls were a vibrant white color and the floor was soft and cushiony. It reminded Darek of a crazy house, one of those places where they keep people who had lost their precious marbles. Darek and Azura were held in separate rooms next to each other. A barred door kept them from escaping their prison cells. They both sat on the floor with their backs against the same wall in such a way that if the wall weren't there, they'd be sitting back to back. But even though the wall separated them, they didn't feel lonely. They could hear each other through the wall.

"So…I guess it was a trap after all," said Darek.

"Yeah," said Azura gloomily.

"Can't you break out of here?"

"I've tried. I can't. It's hopeless," she grumbled.

Darek cleared his throat and said, "You don't sound so good. Is something wrong?"

"I *hate*…being locked up." Her voice quivered. "I *hate* it…" She buried her face in her arms. "I HATE IT—HATE IT—HATE IT!" she screamed.

This was a side of Azura that Darek had never seen before. From the sound of it, she was panicking and breathing unsteadily; he thought he could hear her sobbing. The noble, mighty Azura was now scared. He always believed she was absolutely fearless; after all, she fought terrifying monsters and made death-defying leaps with no less than a smile on her face. Azura seemed like the type to laugh in the face of danger. Yet, at this point in time, even though he couldn't see her face, he could imagine her terror as if she were right next to him.

"I don't know why," said Darek, "but even though we're locked up in this place, I'm not worried or scared. Maybe I've gotten used it to." He forced a laugh.

Azura was silent.

Darek continued, "It's weird. I want to be free, but every now and then I seem to end up behind bars for no reason. At the same time, I figure I always get free in the end. Maybe that's why I'm not scared." He paused. "So don't worry Azura. I'm sure we won't be in here long."

After a long period of silence, Azura said, "Thank you, Darek. I appreciate it." She took a moment to think. "Did I ever tell you about why I became a Hero?"

Sounding excited, he responded, "No."

Azura's frown broke into a slight grin upon hearing Darek's enthusiasm. "I suppose you don't know much about Aenaria either. It's similar to this planet except, instead of terrifying monsters, we have frightening animals. The animals on my planet are fiercer and stronger than most of the monsters here. They are gargantuan beasts. With great strength they rule the land, sea and air. You may have heard of some of these creatures, some which are called dinosaurs."

"You still have dinosaurs on your planet?" Darek gasped.

"Yes. To survive such a dangerous world, we worked together. Luckily for us, despite their immense size, dinosaurs rely on instincts, and such instincts are predictable and easy to turn against them. But even so, a slight miscalculation in trapping them would lead to death.

"Every day is a fight for survival. We hide in small caves and mountains. We strike when the opportunity arises. Because of that, there are no cities and no towns, only small nomadic tribes and clans. If a clan is too large to survive, it splits. That is the only way for us to live. And that is the way we did live—until *they* came."

"They?" repeated Darek.

Azura said, "Our primitive planet was deep within Federation territory, very close to their home world of Teraskai. Unlike every other inhabitable planet around us, our world never took off into the space age. Mining companies, slave traders, and other opportunists saw our world as a gold mine. The law was supposed to protect us, but the law was weak in the face of greed. Thirteen years ago, our world was invaded. The more our world was exploited, the more other groups wanted to exploit it…It was like a snowball effect and soon the situation was too big for the Federation to ignore."

Darek asked, "So what happened?"

"The Federation requested the aid of the Legion of Heroes to use all means necessary to slow them down and to help the Aenarians. At that time, I was only seven. I can't remember much. All I remember was how slave traders had kidnapped me. I was locked up in cage far from home for a week with no food or water. It was then that destiny intervened. Heroes stormed the encampment and freed everyone who had been taken captive. Even though I can't remember much, I grew up with this thought in mind: I was going to be a Hero. Just as I was saved, I was going to save others. Whether from natural disasters, villains or even themselves, I would save them all. From the moment I was saved, my life was no longer my own. I was forever indebted to the Heroes and the Fate bestowed upon them. So when I turned eighteen, I left my clan behind. I left everything behind to join the Heroes.

"It's a pretty simple story, right? It's even a little ridiculous. I was the only one of my kind to ever leave our world. Everyone thought I was crazy for leaving. My dad tried to persuade me to stay, but I refused. Did you ever have something you wanted to do and maybe felt you had to do, but everyone seemed against you on it?"

There was no response.

"Darek?" Azura put her ear up close against the wall and soon heard a deep, guttural snore. She chuckled, "Honestly, if you want to cheer me up, you shouldn't be falling sleep."

Azura also felt her eyelids getting heavy. Without resisting, she snuggled against the wall and dozed off.

CHAPTER 21
Great Discovery

"**D**arek, wake up!"
Darek tried to swat away whoever was shaking him and yelling into his ear. "A few more minutes," he mumbled in his sleep.

"We don't have a few minutes!"

Darek felt someone slap him in the face furiously. "I'm up! I'm up!" Feeling a stinging sensation on his cheeks, Darek opened his eyes to see Azura in front of him. He blinked several times and scratched the back of his head, trying to put his thoughts together.

"Why are you here?" he asked.

"To wake you up!"

"No, not that," Darek said. "More like—how'd you get in here?"

"All the doors were open when I woke up," replied Azura.

"What?" Darek scrambled to his feet and ran to the door. Azura was right. There were no signs that the lock or door had been broken. It was simply unlocked. But who could've done it? "Let's get out of here before they find out!"

"Aren't you worried?" asked Azura.

"About what?"

"The doors are opened and even the guards were knocked out," said Azura. "The person who freed us didn't even stick around to wake us up or anything. Isn't that strange?"

"What are you getting at?" Darek folded his arms. "Are you trying to say this is another trap? Why would they bother?"

Azura groaned in frustration. "I don't know, but something's not right."

"Look, we're free," said Darek. "Who cares about the details? Let's just get out of here."

"Wait," said Azura. "This might be a good opportunity…"

Rendall walked into the prisoner's hall. "Let me see how they are doing."

His servant bowed and said, "Yes, sir. Right this way."

As the two of them walked toward the prisoner's rooms, they stumbled upon the bodies of the guards as they lay on the ground, beaten and bloody.

Rendall thundered, "What is the meaning of this?"

The servant trembled and said apprehensively, "I'm not sure. I will find out at once."

"Wait," Rendall told his servant. He bent over and examined one of the bodies. "They're not dead, only unconscious. Wake them up."

Rendall opened up the doors of the prisoner's rooms and saw that Darek and Azura had disappeared. After the five guards had regained consciousness they lined up against the wall and stood at attention.

Rendall asked them, "What happened here?"

The leader of the guards replied, "S-sir, to be honest, I'm not sure what happened. Something ran in and moved like a blur...I think it was a monster or a beast. That's all I know."

"That's it? That's all you know?" Rendall curled his lip at their incompetence. "The prisoners must be trying to escape! Tell all the men on this level to search above. We must catch them before they get too far. We can't let anyone know we captured our guests."

The guards obeyed his orders and left the hall. Rendall, now alone, looked back at the hall and sniffed the air. Then he went on his way, following the guards.

Azura poked her head out of a door and looked around stealthily. "They're gone."

Darek exhaled. "That's a relief."

Azura smirked. "See? If we tried to escape, they'd be on our tail."

"But now we're trapped down here."

"Merdon did want us to look for some kind of hidden secret inside the castle, and so far, I think this fits the bill quite well."

Darek shrugged. "I don't see anything out of the ordinary. It's a basement."

Azura shook her head. "Look how big their castle is already! They don't need a basement. The only reason, just as Merdon suspected, is to hide something from the public."

"Ah," exclaimed Darek. "Merdon has a secret basement too. I guess it's pretty popular here to make one."

"But something still bugs me," said Azura.

"Again? What is it this time?"

Azura furrowed her brow. "Rendall sent *all* the guards to look for us in the wrong direction. Isn't that weird? Why didn't he send a few in this direction?"

"Maybe he didn't really think about it," said Darek. "Most prisoners do try to escape."

"Or maybe, there's more to this than we realize," remarked Azura.

Darek and Azura ran deeper into the basement. While running, Darek reached for his satchel and could still feel the handle of his daggers through the opening. Azura did have some valid reasons for suspicion. He found it odd that they didn't even bother to disarm him.

They did not see a single soul the entire time they sprinted to the end of the hall. They came to a dead end. There was only one thing there: a massive vault door.

Azura yanked on the handle. It didn't budge. "It's stuck."

"Stuck is not the word for it," said Darek, pointing at a keypad for entering passwords.

"Seeing as we don't have the code, can you pick the lock?" asked Azura.

"Are you kidding? The only thing I pick is my nose," said Darek sharply. "Why don't you try smashing it? That always works in the movies."

"People don't design security systems so that people can just punch them to unlock," said Azura. "Besides, if I break it and it doesn't work, we'll never get inside."

Darek sighed. "Then should we go back?"

"Whatever's behind this door must be important," said Azura. "We have to get inside."

"Ah," said Darek, realizing something. "Whenever I get to this point in videogames, you have to find the code somewhere. People always leave the code out so they can remember it. It could be on a computer system or a piece of paper lying on a desk."

"Videogames don't imitate real life," said Azura, frowning.

Footsteps echoed in the narrow hall.

"Someone's coming," said Azura in a hushed voice. "We've got to hide."

"Hide?" said Darek. "There's nowhere to hide…"

There was only one thing they could rely on in this situation. Even though there weren't any places to hide in that open hall, it wasn't very bright. Dim, flickering lights hung from the ceiling.

Azura pushed Darek over to the side and motioned for him to stay there quietly. The two of them fanned out their arms and legs and flattened their backs against the wall; they remained absolutely silent and still.

This is not going to work, thought Darek nervously. *This is silly. He's going to see us.*

A hooded man appeared in the darkness of the hall, steadily walking to the door.

I'm a wall, Darek thought to himself. *I'm brick and mortar. I'm a piece of construction that is not, in anyway, out of place. I'm just a part of the building.*

As the man got closer and closer, Darek clenched his teeth and swallowed loudly. The man spun his head towards Azura, and then swung his head back at Darek. As Darek looked into the man's eyes, Darek felt his heart start racing.

Is he looking at us? Darek gulped, sweat pouring off his brow.

The man ignored them and walked up to the keypad. He entered in a code and the door cracked open. This was their chance to get inside. Darek and Azura leaped from the wall and simultaneously tried to the strike the man while he was still unsuspecting. Azura launched a flying roundhouse kick to the head and Darek thrust his dagger at the man's side.

The man parried their attacks and said, "What do you guys think you're doing?"

"Huh? It can't be..." said Darek, recognizing the voice. "Sorren?"

"Yeah." Sorren took his hood off. "What grudge do you have against me this time?"

"Sorren!" exclaimed Azura, elated. "I thought you were dead! Are you a ghost?"

"I'm not dying that easily," said Sorren. "Still got things to do."

"What happened?" asked Darek, looking confused. "How are you still alive?"

"I faked my death," explained Sorren. "It was a risk I had to take to throw them off. If all three of us lived through the ceremony, someone was bound to be suspicious."

"Was all the water okay?" said Darek.

"Only Azura's was the real deal," said Sorren. "The others were switched."

Darek said, "But Azura could've died!"

"There was that possibility," Sorren admitted. "But I believed that Azura could handle it, so I hinted for her to be careful. And look at us now. We're all here, alive, and ready to go." Sorren led them beyond the door and into another room.

"Were you the one that freed us?" asked Azura.

"Freed you?" said Sorren. "From what?"

"No, nevermind," said Azura quickly.

The room they entered was very different from what they thought it would be. It did not match the corridors or the castle; instead, it appeared much more modernized. Computers were built along the walls and digital cameras were suspended in the corners of the ceiling. The room was a perfect square and inside this room was another smaller square chamber in the center. This small chamber was encased in strong, thick glass. Darek looked through the glass and all there was inside was a large hatch on the floor.

"Sorren, how'd you get the code to enter this place?" Azura stared at the room in awe.

Sorren replied, "I looked around. Found it lying somewhere."

Darek had a smug look on his face and glanced at Azura. "See, I told you so."

Azura turned away, refusing to admit defeat over something so trivial. "Whatever. Let's try to grab as much information as we can."

"Be careful what you say," said Sorren. "If you haven't noticed, there are cameras that are watching us. They've already caught our faces, but that's okay. We just need to make sure no information ties in with our…client."

While Darek and Azura went about inspecting and investigating, Sorren spared no time to begin looking through the items within cabinets. He reached his hand into drawer after drawer, and he grinned when he found what he was looking for.

"What'd you find?" said Darek.

Sorren lifted it up in plain view for Darek to see. "Goggles."

"Night vision?" Darek's interest was piqued.

"No," said Sorren. "These are for blocking harmful rays of light."

Darek was disappointed. "What do we need those for? We're underground."

"You never know." Sorren opened the door to the glass chamber. "Come on, get inside."

Darek shrugged and went inside after Azura. "Do you have any idea what this is for?"

Sorren replied, "I have a pretty good idea." Sorren pressed a few buttons on a keypad and the large hatch on the floor clicked. The pressure from the hatch was lifted and a small elevator rose from the floor.

"There are more floors to this place?" exclaimed Darek. "I'm impressed."

Sorren went inside the elevator and the others followed him in. Something struck Darek as odd. The elevator did not have many floors listed on the buttons. In fact, there were only two buttons for the elevator: up and down. What was even more odd was that the elevator was perfectly symmetrical. Even the ceiling looked exactly like the floor.

"That's silly," Darek snickered.

"What is?" asked Azura.

"Why would you need an elevator for two floors? The whole purpose of elevators is for multiple floors. They should have built stairs."

"Stairs wouldn't be practical for where we're going," said Sorren.

Long handlebars were screwed onto all sides of the elevator. Sorren promptly took hold of one of the bars and held on.

Vroom! The elevator rapidly descended down the shaft like it was freefalling. The speedy descent caused Azura and Darek to become weightless and float several feet off the ground. Sorren floated a bit, but he hung onto the bar to avoid floating too high. In a panic, Darek thrashed his hands about and seized a handlebar.

"What's going on here?" Darek shouted over the roaring engine. He screamed as the elevator descended for miles into a never-ending chasm. "Don't tell me we're going to go splat on the bottom!"

The elevator suddenly eased up and began decelerating. As it did so, Darek could feel the gravity reversing and his body falling towards the ceiling. When the elevator came to a full stop, all three of them were now standing on the ceiling as though it was the floor.

Darek felt nauseated and wanted to vomit. He took deep breaths to settle his stomach. Azura patted him on the back to comfort him. The elevator doors opened up and the sight astounded Darek, making him forget he was ever feeling sick.

"This can't be real," Darek uttered, letting his jaw drop. "Wow, what is this place?" Darek gawked at the strange landscape.

They stepped out of the elevator to find themselves in a place that they were not familiar with. It was not a floor of a building, but rather, they found themselves almost seemingly in another world. It was similar to the surface of a planet. There was a giant blue grassy field that stretched like a fluffy rug across the land. Thousands of lonesome trees dotted the field like blemishes. Hundreds of serene green streams were networked through the land like connecting blood vessels. But unlike the surface of the planet, there was no sky and no sea. The entire place consisted of one large landmass, as if they were enclosed inside a hollow ball. The land began from where they stood and stretched all the way around.

The air was tremendously thick. Though fairly clear and nothing like fog, the air was still partially visible, as if they were looking through a very thin sheet of water. The density of water in the air made it excruciating to breath. Darek clutched his chest while panting for air.

In the very center of the space was a bright and shiny sphere as bright as the sun, and it filled the vast open space with limitless light. The sphere was a brilliant orange; splashes of molten magma spurted and oozed from its surface. It pulsated like a heart and the streams of water on the land swayed back and forth, following the rhythm of the beat.

"Don't look directly into the core without shades. It'll burn your eyes out," warned Sorren, as he passed everyone a pair of goggles. "Wear these while we're in here."

Darek strapped on the protection for his eyes and marveled at the sight of this other world. "This is the core? So that means we're—"

"Yes," said Sorren. "This is what you'd call the center. Every planet is structured similarly to this one. The planet is hollow, except for the giant core in the middle. As you can see there is no sky, because we are within the planet. There is only land all around."

"But gravity would pull us down into the core, right? How can we be standing up?"

"Didn't you feel it in the elevator? The force of gravity was pulling us towards the bottom of the crust. After we passed the threshold, the gravity flipped. So in other words, gravity is keeping us to this floor."

Azura turned to Sorren. "You've been here before, haven't you? You knew about the goggles so you knew we would be going to the core. Merdon never said anything about going inside the planet. How do you know all this?"

Sorren turned away and glanced for a moment at the core. "I've never been here, at this place, before. But as I've said, every planet has a core. I've been inside another planet."

"Is this common knowledge?" asked Azura. "I never learned this at the Academy."

"No one knows. No one cares. And if you tell people about it, they'd think you're crazy."

Azura agreed. "You're probably right." She couldn't help but smile at that moment. "But to think that something like this is possible. It's amazing."

Darek stood over a running stream of water and kneeled. He dipped his hands into the water and felt the warm current against his palm. He then cupped the water into his hands and was tempted to take a drink. Even though the water was a little warm, the water still looked so pure, crisp and sweet.

"Don't do it," said Sorren. "You mustn't drink of the water on this side."

"And why not? I'm pretty thirsty right now," said Darek.

"You could die."

Darek immediately let go of the water.

Sorren explained, "That's the same water that was used during the ceremony. This is where they get it. You've heard the tales of the fountain of youth, haven't you? People desperately search for the drink of immortality. And only those people who survive the many perils will find the entrance to the underground. This would be the so-called fountain of youth. If you don't have the absolute will to live, you will die if you drink it."

"You couldn't have learned that from Merdon." Darek turned to Sorren and shouted, "So you knew all along about the water? Why didn't you tell us? Why didn't you tell Merdon? It could've—"

"It could've what? Made a difference?" Sorren said, "Do you really think so? Wouldn't Merdon be more suspicious of me if I actually knew the secret of immortality? And if you knew of it, wouldn't you hesitate to drink the water, unsure of whether or not it was still contaminated? There were too many things to consider."

"So you always keep us in the dark on purpose?" said Darek bitterly. "You didn't warn us when you pretended to die. You didn't tell us about the water. You didn't tell us about this place. You don't tell us anything! That's ridiculous. It's like you don't even trust us."

"Does it seem that way? Well, it's true. I cannot put my full trust in you. You've done nothing to prove to me that you can handle a situation like that."

Darek grabbed Sorren by the collar. "You've never given me a chance! How can I prove myself if every time a situation like that comes along, you always deal with it yourself, acting like we aren't even part of this. We're working together, aren't we?"

Sorren analyzed Darek for a few seconds. "Do you trust me?"

Darek released him and said, "I do."

"Then you will be the one to suffer the consequences," said Sorren. "Now, we must get moving. We'll end this meaningless discussion now."

"No," Darek snapped. "I'm not ending this discussion because you say so. This is important! I'm trying to work as a team here, but it's more like everyone's doing their own thing!"

Sorren narrowed his eyes. "Then we'll continue this discussion as we walk."

Darek made direct eye contact with Sorren. "Why are you in such a hurry? You're hiding something again, aren't you?" Darek sat down on the ground. "I'm not moving until you tell me what's going on."

Sorren groaned, "Oh, all right…I'll tell you." He pointed at a gargantuan mechanical tower. It was the only building on the land and was fairly near to the elevator's location. The tower was staggeringly immense. It was tall enough to reach all the way to the core. "Take a look for yourself. What do you think that is?"

"I don't know. A tower, I guess—and an impressive one at that."

"Yes. It's not a natural structure. It didn't just pop out of nowhere. Someone built it. The real question is: why is there something like that inside this planet? It's not normal, and seeing that it even extends to the core, it has me concerned. Whether they are trying to study it or harness its power, the core is something that should not be disturbed."

"And why is that?" asked Darek.

"The core is dangerous. It could have disastrous consequences."

Darek got up. "Now that wasn't so bad was it? I mean, it is kind of bad, but in a different sense. But now that we know a little bit more of what's going on, I have some motivation to hurry up. See how a little explanation can make things better?"

"Right. Whatever."

There was a concrete road that went from the elevator to the entrance of the tower. Giant slabs of stone were held up above the road by tall pillars, and these stones served as a roof that sheltered the concrete road from the dazzling core.

"Does anyone else feel that?" whispered Sorren.

"The heat?" muttered Darek. "Not so much. Sure it's crazy humid but…"

"No. I'm talking about those watchful gazes."

"It doesn't seem hostile though," said Azura.

Darek looked around the pillars, and sure enough, he caught sight of several small embers that floated around. "I don't think it's anything to worry about."

The embers floated around and slowly came together, consolidating into a ball of fire. The ball was then molded, as if by invisible hands, into the form of a human—an old hag to be exact. Her complexion was pale and her hair was bordering white. Her body was small and frail and she beamed at them.

"Hello," said the elderly woman in a garbled vocalization. "Who might you be?"

Darek opened his mouth to speak, but Sorren quickly interrupted and spoke first.

"We may answer you depending on who you are," said Sorren. "If you refuse to tell us first, then we'll just be on our way."

"What a cautious fellow," the woman cackled. "I am a resident of this place. Is that good enough for you?"

Sorren thought for a moment. "Yes. As for us, we're just a few people passing by."

The woman smiled. "Why do you think I appeared to you?"

"How should I know?"

"Because you are different than the others," said the old hag. "The foolish immortals have wrecked this place by building that horrific monstrosity. You are different from them." She paused. "I need your help. The immortals are on the path of destruction. If nothing is done, misfortune will befall all."

"That's not our problem," said Sorren coldly. "Unless you have something to offer."

"How dare you ask for something from a helpless old lady?" Azura scolded him. She then said to the elderly woman, "Don't worry about a thing. We'll help you. What do you want us to do?"

Sorren grumbled to himself, "This is why I *hate* working with Heroes. What kind of helpless old lady appears out of thin air like that?"

The old lady continued, "My request is quite simple really. All I ask is that you destroy the Tower of Legai—the tower before us— and the elevator that leads to the surface world. It all must be destroyed."

Azura laughed nervously. "Are you sure that's what you want?"

"What? Is there something wrong with my request?"

"Wrong?" said Azura. "I wouldn't say there's anything wrong. More like, it's totally unreasonable to ask us to just destroy a massive tower."

"Is that so?" Sniffling, she broke into tears and covered her face with her hands. "Then...I must live in torment and in fear for the rest of my life!"

"Save your act," said Sorren. "Even Azura's not going to change her mind about this."

The old hag glared at Sorren. Sorren stepped back, startled. Tongues of fire erupted at the feet of the old woman and burned their way up to her head. When the flames were snuffed out by the wind, the old hag was gone but now a cute young girl was standing there. Her hair was tied in a little ponytail and she sported a pink dress with flowery frills along the sleeves and skirt.

Sorren gave her a dirty look. She was trying to play them for fools.

The cute little girl began to bawl her eyes out with tears that flowed like a fountain. Pearly tears rolled off her soft face, and wherever her tears wet the ground, roses sprang up and blossomed.

"Look here," said Sorren. "I've already told you—"

"Please stop crying," sobbed Azura. "We'll help you!"

"What's wrong with you?" Sorren snapped at Azura. "She's not even human!"

The girl stopped her tears and said to Sorren, "Don't worry. If you want, I'll give you something in return."

Sorren looked at her, trying to understand her intent. Then he said, "I'm listening."

"You want to go in there anyway, do you not? I will help you get inside. With my shape-shifting capabilities, I can lead you through safely."

"Hmm," said Sorren, crossing his arms. "That sounds good to me...only if you can get us through undetected. If you pull any nonsense or do anything stupid that jeopardizes our mission, you can sure I won't be very forgiving."

"Once again," grumbled Darek, "no one ever talks to me or wants to know what I think. I think this is stupid. I think we shouldn't do this. No one ever listens to me. I bet you guys don't even realize I'm here."

The little girl ignored Darek and wandered over to the stream that flowed nearby. "I need to refresh myself first. All that transformation has drained me dry." The girl burst into flames and out of the flames came a tiny fairy. The fairy had glimmering white hair and a cute white dress.

The fairy dove into the stream and playfully swam in it, drinking the water and bathing in it. She then enthusiastically popped out of the stream; with the flapping of her powerful, yet tiny wings, she bounced around in the air sporadically like a humming bird, excited to begin.

"What should we call you?" asked Sorren.

The fairy beamed and squeaked, "You can call me Ios. I'm the one and only. Nice to meet y'all! I'll be your fairy guide! Let's go and knock that tower down together! Okay?" The fairy flew in front of Sorren and gave him a warm smile and a hug on the nose.

Sorren wrinkled his nose and blew her away with a puff of air, muttering, "I liked you better when you were an old lady."

Guards, armed with short swords and dressed in leather armor, were stationed at the entrance to the tower as sentries. Two stood at the main gate. The other eight were divided into two sets of four; each set was positioned on either side of the gate. The guards rested upon the palms of what appeared to be giant stone hands.

Darek and the others hid themselves from plain sight by sneaking through the row of giant pillars. Darek peered from behind a pillar, observing the guards from afar.

"How do we get past these guys?"

In a squeaky voice, the small fairy Ios said energetically, "I've got the perfect plan! You didn't think I'd try this without knowing what to do, did you? I've studied them for many years and I have analyzed their movements, their reactions. Anything you need to know, I know it!"

Aggravated, Sorren said, "Just tell us your plan."

"Oh right," said Ios, turning away, pretending to blush. "We'll do this step by step. First we need to lure three of them to us."

"It has to be three?" asked Darek.

"Yes," she said firmly. "No more, no less."

"And how do we do that?" said Azura.

"I don't know," admitted Ios. "That's for you to figure out."

Azura frowned. "That's not a plan…it sounds more like a basic idea."

Ios shrugged. "Be careful though. Even if you pass the guards, there're cameras behind their backs."

Sorren suggested, "If it doesn't matter which three, we can split up. One person on each side of the tower and someone will stay here. Ios will relay messages between us."

Sorren sneaked over to the left side of the tower. He moved so quietly that no one suspected a thing. Azura wasn't as stealthy; she had to walk all the way around so she wouldn't get noticed. Darek stayed at the pillar.

Sorren motioned for Ios to come. Then he whispered to her, "Have Azura try to lure the guard on the right side." Ios nodded and flew to the other side to inform Azura.

Azura roared like a tiger, startling the guards as they kept watch. The guard on the right side of the tower left his seat and tiptoed over to inspect the cause of the sound. As he disappeared from view of the guards, another guard heard a scuffling sound from that direction and asked, "Is everything all right?"

Hidden from their sight, Ios replied with a perfect imitation of the guard's voice, "Yes, there's nothing to worry about."

Azura had quickly knocked out the guard with one swift jab. "How'd you know the voice of the guard? He didn't even say anything."

"I've already told you," said Ios. "I've been observing these guards for a long time. These guards have been working here every day for the past several decades."

"What do I do now?" asked Azura.

Ios replied, "You impersonate him."

Ios sprinkled a glowing powder from her tiny hands and patted it on Azura's face. Azura's face became contorted and convoluted. All of her facial features twisted and bended until it looked exactly like the unconscious guard's face.

Ios showed her a tiny mirror so she could see her own reflection. "Nice, right?"

Azura scowled. "Are you for real?"

Ios glanced back. "What?"

"You only changed my face!"

Ios giggled, "That's all I can do. Isn't that enough?"

"There's a big difference in our bodies. If you haven't noticed, I'm not even a man!"

"Hush up," Ios snapped. "Quickly put on the clothes and get out there."

Azura reluctantly strapped on the guard's suit. She dipped her feet into the boots and scrunched her lips as she heard a gross squishing sound coming from it. There was a nefarious odor emanating from the clothes and, because her nose was extra sensitive, it almost felt like she was trapped in an airtight room filled with reused soggy, sweaty socks. Ios was serious about how long the guards have been guarding this place. It seemed to Azura that they have never taken a shower or washed their clothes the entire time they've been put on duty here. Azura was compelled to pass out and barf, but Ios slapped Azura around a bit to keep her going.

Azura walked back to the other guards, pretending like nothing happened.

"What was it?" A guard asked her.

"A cat," Azura grunted.

Ios pinched Azura in the back of the neck. "Let me do the speaking!"

One of the guards looked at her and said, "Is something wrong?"

"No," replied Ios, using the guard's voice.

"Your voice was odd and your cheeks are red. Maybe you should stop by the infirmary."

Ios realized this was also a good thing. "Yes, you're right. That's a good idea. I'll be back." Azura couldn't mouth Ios' words very well and one of the guards rubbed his eyes and cleaned out his ears thinking there was something wrong with his senses.

Ios whispered in Azura's ear, "Try to find a place to wait for the others. I'll—" Before Ios could finish her next sentence, red lights flashed chaotically inside the building.

"Emergency alert," said a computerized voice. "Intruders have breached the perimeter. All security personnel must be on duty at this time."

"Intruders?" said Sorren. "Did they discover us?"

Azura rushed to the entrance but a barred gate came crashing down, sealing it off.

"What's the meaning of this?" Ios asked the other guard. "I'm not feeling well."

The guard studied Azura for a moment and said, "We are not allowed to leave our post during emergencies. You should know that very well."

"I guess it's my turn to scare them with something fearsome," said Darek. Darek began making shrieking noises in an attempt to divert the guard's attention.

"What's that horrible sound?" said one of the guards, clasping his hands over his ears.

Disgusted and annoyed, another guard said, "Sounds like a dying cat."

Darek jumped out from behind the pillar and confronted the guards. "It does not sound like a dying cat!"

All of the guards stood there surprised by Darek's sudden appearance. They drew forth their blades with an enraged look upon their faces.

"Look, an intruder!"

"Fine, whatever," said Darek, fuming. "I'll be your intruder!"

In a fit of rage, Darek pounced on the nearest guard and the two of them rolled around on the grass, exchanging blows. The other guards jumped into the fray, but no one could tell what was going on; everyone was aimlessly punching.

"Darek seems to have snapped," said Azura, amazed. "I guess if his opponent still looks human, at the very least, he thinks he has a chance."

"Good for him," said Sorren. "He's faring well. I guess all that training paid off. Now help me open up this gate."

"You still want to continue on?" Azura was taken aback by Sorren's reaction. "I thought you'd want to retreat now that we've been discovered."

"I don't think they're looking for us," said Sorren. "The intruders could be someone else. If so, we can still pose as guards. Chaos may be a good cover."

"Hey, guys?" said Darek, barely able to defend himself from the nine guards. "Can you two stop talking and help me out?"

CHAPTER 22
Tower of Legai

The elevator doors of the Tower of Legai opened, and Darek and the others stepped inside. After the doors closed behind them, Darek took a deep breath to relieve the built up tension. The disguises they wore were decent at best, and walking through the guard-infested lobby was a nerve-wrecking nightmare. Though the guards didn't find them suspicious, every glance aimed his way still made him want to find a corner and hide.

They removed their goggles because it was practically impossible to see with them on.

Sorren pushed the button for the first floor. "They are looking for someone else."

"How'd you come up with that idea?" asked Darek.

Sorren replied, "Because they didn't bother to inspect us. My guess is they've only discovered one or two intruders *and* they know what the intruders look like. This leads me to believe that there must be a centralized way to get detailed information. It's speculation, but if true, we'll be safer if we move as a group of three."

"The tower is huge though," Darek whined. "It'll take forever to explore if we stick together."

"You're exactly right."

Darek raised a brow. "I am?"

"Which is why we're splitting up."

"W-we are? B-but I thought you just said we should stick together!" Darek stammered.

"No," said Sorren. "I merely said it would be safer. Besides, look at the number of floors." Sorren pointed to the sequentially numbered buttons. "Even though the tower itself is quite large, there are only thirty floors. Its size is only because they need to reach the core. Most of the tower is probably empty space. We'll divide it up. Each person gets ten floors. We must do it fast to avoid getting caught up in the intruder situation."

Darek said, "Are you crazy? You're asking me to go alone in a tower full of hostile immortals! That's like suicide! Besides, our disguises aren't even that good. Look at me! My sleeves are way too long and my armor looks big enough to slip off any time! Azura's even worse off. Her voice doesn't match his face and her body doesn't match—"

The doors opened up at the first floor.

Sorren said to Azura, "Go to the top floor when you're done. We'll meet there."

Azura nodded and left the elevator.

Darek stretched out his hand, reaching out for Azura to come back.

"See you at the top!" Azura, thinking he was waving goodbye, waved back at him as the doors shut.

"Wait! Don't go!" Darek cried out to her, but the doors were already closed and the elevator resumed its course upward.

"Darek," said Sorren, pulling him away from the closed door. "I saw how well you handled those guards at the entrance. You have surpassed my expectations and my teachings."

Darek backed away in shock at Sorren's words. "You mean that?"

"Of course," said Sorren, beaming. "You might be so powerful now that I wonder if you may have already become an immortal yourself. You might even be the most reliable person we have on the team right now. You might just be able to handle yourself in this place."

"Really?" Darek's mood swung all the way up. "Why didn't you say so before?"

"I didn't want you to become too full of yourself. But now is the time for you to understand that you might be able to do this."

"You really think so?"

The elevator stopped at the eleventh floor and Sorren urgently left. "That's all. Good luck—have fun." The doors quickly closed again and Darek hesitantly put his thumb on the button marked for the twenty-first floor.

Wow, thought Darek. His heart sunk after Sorren left. I have this nagging feeling that I was just duped. Shouldn't I be able to tell if I've become immortal? Come to think of it, he kept using the words 'might' and 'may.'

Thud. Something fell on the floor. Darek glanced down. He gasped. Ios was on the ground, wheezing and feeling faint. Darek stooped and gently lifted Ios up with his hands.

"Hey, are you alright? Hang in there." Darek used his little pinky to tap Ios on the shoulder. "What's wrong?"

"Sorry," breathed Ios. "I should've…realized. I spent…too much energy…illusions. Strength gone…thought I could handle…without light from core…"

"Wait…don't tell me you're going to die!" exclaimed Darek. "Hang on for a while longer! I'll try to find some light from the core!"

The elevator eased to a stop at the twenty-first floor and the doors slid open, revealing the corridor before him. Several armed guards just so happened to be standing there, and they watched as the elevator opened up. Darek snuck Ios into his bag and slid the bag behind his back, out of view. Darek froze, not knowing what to do or how to react.

"Are you getting out or not?" asked the guard, staring at Darek's dumbfounded expression.

"Oh, sorry," apologized Darek. Walking out, he calmly said, "Did you want to use it?"

"Where are the rest of the reinforcements?" said the guard, his brow furrowing. "Why are you alone?"

Darek's hands got all sweaty and he rubbed his palms on his pants. Now was the time for a little improvisation. "We got a little tied up with something. The others will be here shortly."

"What could be more important than dealing with the intruders?" The guard demanded.

"Oh," Darek tried to think of something more and blurted out, "we caught sight of the intruders! Yes, that's why everyone was hung up. They sent me ahead to tell you this."

"Is this true?" said another guard, stunned.

"Yes?" Awkwardly enough, Darek's statement ended up coming out as a question.

"How could this have happened?" said the guard. "That means there are more intruders!"

"No!" Darek said, "They're the same ones as before!"

"But we have those intruders trapped on this floor! We've been watching this elevator and no one has gone through here. We haven't received reports from the stairwell either."

"The intruders are on this floor?" Darek realized the grave error of his mistake. "Oh…then there must be more intruders. I'm sorry, I thought you already knew about the…um…*other* intruders…"

Sorren is so going to kill me, thought Darek, panicking. *Now we've lost our advantage.*

"There was no announcement on these new intruders. I better go alert the others," said the guard. He asked Darek, "Can you give a description of the other intruders?"

Ah, this is my chance to redeem myself!

"Yes, I can," said Darek. "There is only one other intruder that I saw. He's very short; I suppose about four feet tall. He's also very...fat. He's not wearing any disguise of any sort, not dressed up as a guard at all. Um...that's all I can think of."

"Right..." The guard pulled out a handheld device from his pocket and entered in the information that Darek gave him. "The others should now be informed..." The guard's voice trailed off as he uncomfortably gazed upon Darek's face. "Are you okay?"

"Excuse me?"

"Your nose..." said the guard, staring at Darek's face. "It looks like it's falling off."

Darek swung around and saw his reflection on the elevator door. *He's right! My face is getting all messed up. Could this be due to Ios' weak state? I have to get out of here before they find out who I really am!*

Darek said to the guard, "I have to go to the bathroom really quick. Sometimes my nose just starts to *run*." He laughed weakly but no one else was amused by his poor joke.

"Looks like something serious," grunted the guard, his suspicion awakened. "We better get you to the infirmary as soon as possible."

Darek backed away, trapped between the armed guards and the elevator door. There was no way for him to explain his way out of this. His cover was blown. He inched his hand across the door and pressed the up button of the elevator.

The tension between Darek and the armed guards was cut by shouts and cries from deep within the hall. Soldiers were screaming.

"They're coming!"

"Stop them at all costs! Don't let them get away!"

Two figures blazed through the hall. As they zipped by, their sporadic movement ripped gaping holes in the walls and cracked the cold hard floor beneath their feet. The guards drew forth their swords, but before they could react, the intruders slipped past them.

One of the guards writhed about, screaming, "My arm's on fire! Someone help me!"

"What are these monsters? They can't be stopped!"

Utter chaos broke out. The guards slashed and slashed but their blades only managed to cut each other. Several men, fearing for their lives, hid inside rooms. The braver ones still could not lay a finger on their mysterious opponents no matter how hard they tried.

Darek stood with his back against the elevator door, praying that whatever was out there would not notice him. After what seemed an eternity, the elevator door finally cracked open and Darek fell backwards into the lift. The two intruders pushed all the guards out of the way and squeezed into the elevator just in time for the doors to shut.

Covering his face with his hands, Darek crouched in the corner of the floor, afraid to make eye contact with whoever or whatever else was with him inside the elevator. He could hear the sound of the button being pressed. The lift began cranking its way up the shaft.

"Well, well, well…if it isn't our old master. It's nice to see you again, Darek."

Darek looked up and saw Reza and Drey. "You guys! But—you're dead—" Darek gasped in fright, "Real gh-gh-ghosts!"

"Hey, calm down," said Reza. "We're not *exactly* ghosts. See? We're not transparent, and look at this…" She grabbed Darek by the wrist and with a firm grip, helped him to his feet. "We can touch. That's not something a ghost can do, right?"

"Really?" Darek's expression changed into excitement, but there was still some uncertainty tucked in the back of his mind. He never really knew what ghosts looked like or what their limitations and abilities were, so everything she was telling him didn't really strike a chord. But there was a distinct sincerity sewed within her voice that was hard for him to ignore.

"Don't worry," replied Reza. "It's not like we came back from the dead to haunt you."

Darek wiped the sweat off his brow and said, "So if you aren't dead, then you really must have been—"

"What?" Reza stared at him, wondering what he wanted to say.

Darek continued, "For you to leave the worm's body, could you have been pooped—"

Blushing profusely, Reza clawed her fingers at Darek's open jaw and clamped his mouth shut to prevent him from finishing the sentence. "I know what you're going to say. You were going to say that we were pooped, right? Yes. We were very *tired*." Darek nodded, his eyes goggling at her ferocity.

"If I'm correct," said Drey, interrupting, "I'm pretty sure he's saying that we were—"

"I TOLD YOU, I KNOW WHAT HE'S TRYING TO SAY," snapped Reza. "I will not go into details, but I will say that our escape from the worm is nothing you could imagine."

"Really? Because I can imagine quite a bit," said Darek.

Reza scowled.

The lift abruptly paused, the cables outside screeching. Everyone nearly tumbled over from the sudden stop. They glanced around. The blue and red lights within the lift flickered and a smug voice came from the speaker.

"Did you intruders really think you could escape that easily?"

Without warning, the elevator rocketed upward to the top floor; the rapid acceleration flattened everyone to the ground. Once it reached the top of the tower, the lift was shot back down, hurtling everyone up to the ceiling. Again and again, the operator of the elevator was bent on torturing Darek and his friends by firing them straight up and down the extent of the tower, over and over, at roaring, breakneck speeds as if he were violently jolting a soda bottle.

"Hopping—in—here—was—the—worst—idea—ever," gasped Darek in short intervals.

This outrageous outburst went on for several minutes until the gears and mechanisms came grinding to an unexpected halt. The power was cut off and all the lights fizzed out.

"Oh shoot," said the voice on the speaker, grumbling. "It's broken. Can't get the darn thing moving anymore."

"Looks like we're saved by stupidity." Drey pried open the elevator doors.

"What floor is this?" said Reza.

Darek wobbled out of the shaft, stumbling over his own foot. He had suffered a number of bruises and small injuries.

Drey directed Reza's attention to the sign on the wall. "Thirtieth floor."

They heard voices in the distance say, "The intruders have landed on this level! This time, don't let them get away!"

"They're coming! What should we do?" asked Darek, still attempting to recover from the violent elevator ride.

"Darek, can we count on you?" said Reza.

Darek shrugged. "I don't know, depends on—"

"It's settled then," said Reza in a hurry. "We'll let you handle this."

"Huh?"

Drey suddenly combusted into a hovering flame that dawdled for a bit before zipping into an air vent in the ceiling. Reza's skin became ice blue and she staggered every step toward a locked door. Her body liquefied into a puddle of water that splashed about as it hit the floor. The lively puddle of water slithered across the tiles of the ground as one adhesive mass and trickled underneath the bottom of the locked door, disappearing from the hall.

Standing alone, Darek grumbled, "Duped again..."

Seeing that he only had a few minutes left before the guards came storming down the hall, Darek fearfully jostled each doorknob, hoping to find a suitable place to hide. It just so happened that one of the doors was unlocked. Darek stepped inside and closed the door.

Darek found himself in a control room that overlooked the core. The room was fairly small and was filled with computers, tables, chairs and, oddly enough, dirty, smelly dishes and clothes, as if someone had been living inside for a while. Because of all the clutter, there was just enough space for one or two people to move about. There was one large window on the end of the room. Looking out the window, he could see a huge platform, which had a massive marvel of engineering on top. This colossal machine was able to touch the core with its tip. The windows were heavily tinted with a dark color, blocking out most of the light from the core.

It took Darek a few seconds to notice that there was someone inside. A lonely-looking old man was sitting in front of a computer screen with bloodshot eyes. He was a grim old man with shaggy white hair and a pair of brown goggles around his neck.

After a brief silence, the elderly person faced Darek and said, "Who might you be?"

"I just was stopping by," said Darek, startled by the sudden question.

The old man said quickly, "Oh? I'm intrigued. For you see, I don't go to the surface very often. A visitor comes every now and then, usually to inform me of new happenings or messages from the other elders. Today there was supposed to be some sort of celebration going on. Most of the other scientists in the facility have already left. Ah, but I cannot leave this place. No, there is something of great importance to be done here. Everything must be perfect. Oh, by the way, where are my manners? Before I forget to introduce myself, I am the sixth elder, Liam."

"I thought there were only five elders," said Darek.

"Now there's a cruel joke," Liam hissed, "one I do not find amusing at all."

"Ah, sorry. I sometimes go a little overboard with my jokes." Darek thought things over. This old man, though odd, did not appear threatening. With the guards roaming about outside, this room could be a temporary safe haven. But would he be safe for long? The guards knew he was on this floor. There was no doubt in his mind that they would comb the entire floor, checking out each room and closet. After all, there wasn't any real place for him to hide.

"So then, why are you here?" Liam said, "Excuse me if I come off a little rude. Do you have an important matter to discuss with me, or have you come here to waste my time?"

"Right," Darek muttered, "I definitely didn't want to waste your time, when you apparently seem to be doing nothing to begin with."

"I didn't quite catch that whisper of yours." Liam cupped his hand by his ear. "What'd you say? You'll have to speak louder than that."

"Well, the thing is..." Darek suddenly remembered something. "Liam. You're Liam?"

Liam nodded. "Yes, that is correct."

The name seemed familiar, Darek thought. Why did it seem so familiar? Darek searched his pockets and pulled out a beaten up envelope. It had experienced quite a bit: it had been drenched, crushed, bitten, stabbed, clawed and smashed several times. But thankfully, due to good packaging, the envelope was still in fair shape. He checked the name on the envelope and indeed it was for Liam. "I don't believe it...this package that I've been carrying all along is for you—an elder."

Liam hopped out of his chair and snatched the package right out of Darek's hands. "Oh? I rarely get anything nowadays from the surface." He tore an opening and dumped the contents on the counter; his face lit up when he discovered a small bottle. "The necessary ingredient!"

"All right," said Darek. "Now if you'll just give me my pay, I'll be on my way." Darek froze. He was so used to asking for payment that he forgot he was speaking with an elder.

But before Darek could say anything to correct himself, Liam said, "Your pay? How about I reward you with the most spectacular thing you'll ever see? We must begin at once!"

"But I really must be going," insisted Darek. "You know what? Forget the payment. I'll just head out now."

Jumping up and down, the man joyfully screamed, "Yes, it's time, it's time! Time to begin the operation! Young man, you have no idea how much this means to me. Oh, how I have waited for this day. It seems like forever. Let's get started. I'll need your help."

"You want my help?" Darek rolled his eyes.

Liam's eyes narrowed. "Is there a problem?"

"Well, I'm in a hurry. I have other tasks to take care of." Darek walked away.

"What?" The old man's face became grave. Curling his lip, Liam snapped, "What could be more important than this? Do you dare defy me?"

Darek considered making a quick escape but he knew he couldn't properly leave without consent from the elder. This was an elder before him. Though his appearance would seem like a fragile little old man, he remembered from Merdon's words that appearances are deceiving when it comes to dealing with immortals. He figured the best way to handle this would be to get on the good side of this elder and maybe an opportunity to escape would present itself in time.

"I could help," Darek yielded.

Liam patted Darek on the shoulder. "That's my boy! Now don't worry if you don't know what to do, I'll lead you through the process. The two of us will be enough to get the engine started." He situated Darek in his chair and turned on the computers. As the monitors flickered on, millions of intricate calculations began to roll along them.

Darek tried to excuse himself one last time. "I really know nothing about how to operate this stuff. Maybe this isn't such a good idea for me to be here."

"All you have to do is just push this red button right here when I tell you to." Liam pointed to a large red button. "Simple, right?"

"I guess. But it's still confusing for me. I thought red signified stop. Maybe I—"

"Don't think about it!" Liam was tired of hearing excuses. "Just do as I say! I'll tell you when to push the button." Liam left through a small elevator shaft.

As soon as the strange scientist left the control room, Darek got up from his chair and tiptoed to the door and cracked it open. Peering outside, Darek saw his pursuers in the hall. Oddly enough, the guards seemed to have skipped over the room he was in. He wondered if it was because the room belonged to the elder. Maybe stepping inside this room was even more dangerous than staying out. But there was a possibility that this elder might be different from the rest. He certainly didn't seem as dangerous as the others. By helping this elder, he may be granted a favor in return, Darek thought.

Darek sat back down and saw Liam tinkering around with several machines. Liam was standing on the elongated platform that extended itself out from the tower, far towards the core. The place was shielded from the radiation by something that looked like a glass bubble. The old man ran here and there, inspecting everything and ensuring that everything was in working order. He then took the bottle and emptied its contents within a small tube on the large machine. Liam spun around to face Darek and gave the thumbs up.

Darek hesitated. Darek didn't know if he should go through with this or not. On one hand, helping the elder would allow him to escape, and on the other, he didn't know what would happen if he pushed the button. Sorren had told him that messing with the core was a bad idea.

While Darek was thinking, he felt a tingling feeling on his shoulder. He looked at his left shoulder and there it was—a large spider. It had dropped down from a spider thread.

"Eek!" Darek shrieked. With excessive force, he brushed it off with the back of his hand.

Darek was able to get a good look at the bug, which was scampering away the moment it hit the floor. At first he thought it was a spider, but after looking at it, he couldn't tell anymore. Its body was long and thin with spiky bristles protruding; its legs looked like crab legs, but hairier and plumper. Beady eyes were all over its back, giving it full vision of the room.

Darek snatched up some paper he found lying around. There were reports and charts and all of them were suitable for spider whacking. Distracted by the spider's presence, Darek ignored everything around him and focused on the bug's demise.

With this roll of paper, Darek chased after the spider all across the room; Darek was hot on its tail as it jumped up the table and ran circles around the controls. Then Darek had the greatest opportunity before his eyes. The spider stopped moving. *Wham!* Darek slammed down with all his might! But when he lifted the roll of paper, which was now smothered with spider entrails, he realized he had slammed down on the red button. Nervous about his mistake, Darek walked back up to the window to see what would happen.

The machine started to crank into gear. The top of the machine was long and thin, built like a massive syringe with a needle. Through a series of complicated, automated procedures, the needle was injected into the core. The outside of the machine had many transparent tubes; Darek watched with full attention as fluids were constantly pumped through these tubes into the interior of the core by powerful pistons. The core, which was originally orange, became a dark crimson red. Like an enraged ball of hot magma, the core expanded and shook feverishly in place.

Liam cackled and howled with laughter and shouts of joy. He paraded around his machine and exclaimed, "It is finished! It is finished!"

CHAPTER 23
The Elder

The elder returned to the control room and found Darek with his hand on the exit, looking like he was about to leave. He had returned so soon that Darek didn't have time to escape. Darek shrank away from the door, pretending to be stretching his arms and legs. Ignoring Darek, Liam sat down and began typing away commands on the keyboard.

"Is it all right if I leave now?" asked Darek.

Liam's eyes were glued to the computer screen. "Sure thing."

Darek hurried to open the door. It wouldn't open.

Liam turned in his chair to face him. "Did you really think you could take me for a fool?"

"I had nothing to do with the package," said Darek nervously. "If it's the wrong stuff, it's not my fault."

"The package was fine. Your presence here is not."

"What do you mean?" Darek averted his eyes.

"Just who are you?" Liam demanded, "Where did you come from? Speak!"

"Just transferred here," Darek lied. "I'm Darek. I was initiated through the ceremony."

Liam snickered. "Oh, is that so? Even if you were new, you have no excuse to come into this room. No one except the greatest of scientists can enter this room without permission! And now that you've outlived your usefulness—it'd be proper to dispose of the trash."

This guy is crazy! Desperate to escape, Darek grabbed the doorknob, shaking and jostling it, hoping that it was only a little stuck. However, no matter how hard he pushed and pulled, it wouldn't budge.

"It's no use." The elder had a smug look on his face. "The door is sealed."

"That's what you think!" Darek whipped out a dagger and smashed it against the hinges of the door, weakening and breaking them. He then tried to kick down the door with all his might. To his embarrassment, he didn't even dent it.

Darek remembered Merdon saying something along the lines of how elders were not opponents they could face. It wasn't like he had much of a choice. He twirled the dagger between his fingers and moved forward to attack. He slashed fast and hard. But the elder parried his attacks with ease. There was no way for him to win. His only thought was to try to act aggressive and divert the elder's attention away from his true aim.

"Wait," said Darek, stopping his attack, "You don't have to kill me. You said I outlived my usefulness, but isn't that just a nearsighted approach to things? Anything can be useful."

Liam scoffed, "Are you proposing that you're willing to be my slave—that you will aid me in any way conceivably possible?"

"I don't really like to be called a slave…but something like that, yes."

The elder took a moment to think about it. "I do have need for a paperweight, but you are too big for that. Either way, you'd be better off dead. I'm not going to bother feeding a paperweight."

"I didn't mean it that way," said Darek. "Let's say I am a spy. I may have accomplices."

"So what are you proposing?"

"I'll help you locate them and stop them. In return, let me go and I won't ever return."

"That does sound like a pretty good proposal."

"Doesn't it?" Darek cracked an unconvincing smile.

"Not really, no. I was only kidding. You shall die now. To tell you the truth, I hate proposals and I hate compromises—too much of a hassle. Killing you is much, *much* easier."

Darek shuddered. "You won't know what my friends are doing! I guarantee you they're up to no good! Terrible things will happen if you don't stop them!"

Liam cackled, "A pity, but it no longer matters, for the operation is already complete. Everything is meaningless. Now that we have injected the final solution into the core, it'll only be a matter of hours before we witness an amazing event."

Curious, Darek asked, "What amazing event?"

Ecstatic, Liam closed his eyes and raised his hands high, as though he were reaching for something. "The destruction of the world and the birth of a new era! Once the solution has spread itself within the core, this planet will explode and flood nearby planets with massive amounts of the special radiation, creating a universe of immortality!"

Shocked at the plan, Darek shrieked, "You want to mess up more planets?"

"No," snapped Liam firmly. "Perhaps you misunderstood something or did not hear me correctly. I want to *perfect* more planets."

"What will happen to everyone on this planet?" Darek protested, "Everyone will die! Are you really willing to kill your friends to achieve this? This is wrong and you know it!"

Liam slammed his fist against the counter in fury, bending it. He picked up a desk full of heavy equipment with one hand and tossed it across the room. The electrical equipment heated up and exploded all around them. His blood boiled and his eyes were full of scorn. "You understand nothing! It hurts to do this, but it must be done! I cannot expect you to understand what it truly means to be immortal in a mortal universe. You are only a baby; you have only been birthed recently. Even most of the other immortals, aside from the elders, cannot understand the way we lived before this perfect world came to fruition.

"As you live for eternity, your family and friends grow old and pass away, while you still remain the same. Everyone you know will die, yet you still live and meaninglessly so! In the distant past, when humans found out about the powers I possessed, people labeled me a filthy monster and hunted me down. They destroyed my homes and creations! They came after me with pitchforks and torches, calling out for my death to come quickly!

"Why do you think it was so hard to see an immortal in those days? It's because we had to live in fear and in the shadows. We were killed without mercy from people who called themselves saviors of the world. We six elders were the only ones to survive.

"But though we have an immortal body, we are still human at heart. We are hated, therefore we hate! This curse—the pain, the sadness, the loneliness—all of it is just too much to bear and it eats away at your soul. Hundreds of years we have lived in secrecy, preparing for the day of glory when we could be considered the dominant race! And it came! No longer were we discriminated against; no longer were we hiding in fear. We were the heroes, not the villains. We were the people to help, lead and judge the society—we were the ones to bring happiness.

"If you understand what I speak of, then and only then, you would realize the small price to pay for what we will accomplish! Our perfect eternal universe will finally be born. We will no longer be alone. We will live together for eternity, in peace and harmony. There will be no mourning and no death. Can you still not understand how wonderful this concept is?"

"Wow, you sure had a lot to say," said Darek. "But you know what I think? I think you paid the price for your own mistake. And now you want everyone to suffer as you did. What's the logic in hurting everyone because you've been hurt? Shouldn't you want to help them so that they'll never experience your pain?"

"As I expected," replied Liam, "you cannot possibly understand."

While Liam had been talking for so long, Darek moved into position for his escape. He slammed the button behind him and it opened the doors that led outside. Darek snapped on his goggles and jumped into the shaft. Then it whisked him to the outside, onto the outer platform. He tried to lock the exit of the shaft to keep the elder from following him but it was useless. The window above, where the control room overlooked the platform, shattered. The elder jumped out of the tower and landed on the platform.

Liam said, "Let me see the extent of your abilities, child. I'll apologize first. I have not used my powers in such long a time. I may be rusty."

Darek wasn't sure why, but now that he was finally face to face with this powerful elder, he didn't feel as scared as he thought he would be. Facing Sorren in his dreams was much more terrifying, even if it wasn't real. Perhaps it was because he had accepted the fact that he would stand no chance against this elder.

With daggers in hand, Darek confronted the elder with all of his courage. Darek lunged into Liam and pierced his side. A look of horror was etched upon Liam's face as he staggered back, bleeding.

Clutching his wound, Liam gasped, "You wounded me…?"

"I didn't expect it," said Darek, shaken. "I've never actually landed a clean hit before."

"Just kidding," chuckled Liam, straightening. "You can't hurt me like that."

Liam drilled his fist into Darek's chest. From that one punch Darek could feel his entire body being launched off the ground. Darek tumbled into several crates, but rebounded. Crouching on one knee to rest, Darek thought his body would waste away into nothing. He dropped his daggers and coughed up blood.

"What's this?" said Liam. "I barely touched you. Are you really an immortal?"

Gulping air, Darek said, "Can't we talk this over? If it wasn't for me, you wouldn't have gotten the package!"

Liam grinned. "Did you think you were the only one?"

Darek cocked his head. "What do you mean by that?"

Liam replied, "There are many packages. In order to ensure that we will eventually receive the package, you were not the only one. There were others sent before you, and others would have been sent after you if you had failed."

Sent from where? Sent by whom? Darek couldn't help but think that what was going on here was only a small fraction of a bigger picture. But that was not his main concern. He could speculate, but unless he escaped from this elder, he may very well be dead within minutes.

Darek stood but soon lost his balance and stumbled back. Losing his orientation and sense of control, he slipped on the cold metal floor. Before he knew it, Darek was already hanging on the edge of the platform. Darek clung on desperately with both hands. The grasp of his fingers was weakening. He looked up, only to see the condescending creep stare back down at him.

"So you intended to kill yourself?" said Liam. "I congratulate you on your wise decision. As pity, I'll give you a few minutes to live. Enjoy it." Liam took a seat on a crate, waiting for Darek to fall.

This is the end, Darek thought. It was at this point he wanted to cry, but the tears would not flow. *I guess that's all there is to it. Though the government pardoned me, there is nothing more I can do. I'm sorry, Jenson. To everyone who wanted to see me again, I'm sorry.*

Boy, do I feel stupid. Darek laughed, almost hysterical. *I went through all this trouble just to die by falling off a tower. I came to this perilous planet, tread across the suffocating desert, stood face to face with terrifying monsters, and even trained day and night with Sorren until my hands bled and my body was torn apart. But in the end...the result is the same. Death.*

Darek's fingers lost their grip. His descent had begun. To him, time had slowed down. Second by second, he could see his fingers get farther away from the platform. There was nothing below that could save him. The ground was inconceivably far away. This was it.

In a few moments, he would make contact with the ground and it would not be pretty.

Just when he thought it was all over for him, he stopped falling. Looking up, he saw he was only a few inches below the platform. Yet there was nothing to hold onto. His right hand was being held up by something. He wasn't sure what was going on…until he heard a voice.

"Darek, put some effort into it!" shouted Ios. She firmly held onto Darek's fingers; fluttering her wings frantically, she fought hard against the gravity to keep them both aloft.

"Ios…" Darek had forgotten all about her.

Being so close to the energy of the core had rejuvenated her and now she was able to fly again. She tried so hard to pull Darek up that her face became as red as a cherry.

"There's no way you can lift me," said Darek. "Just let me fall!"

Ios cried, "No! I didn't bring you here to die! I brought you here to help me! So help me by showing some effort!"

"But what can I do?"

"Flap!"

"Excuse me?" said Darek, puzzled by the advice.

"Flap your hands as if they were wings!"

Darek looked at his free hand and shrugged. What did he have to lose? Then he beat his hand against the air. Ios's power flowed into his fingers and across his body, making him almost as light as a feather. His continually beating of the air slowly gave him lift and he managed to hover his way back up a few inches, just close enough for him to reach the platform. He grabbed onto the platform with every last bit of strength he had.

Ios was tired and started plummeting. Darek stretched out his hand to grab her, but missed. When she had fallen too far out of view, he gaped in sadness and horror. Staring down the side of the tower, he grimaced. She had sacrificed herself for him because she believed in him. How could he betray her by letting her down?

Darek would not let her sacrifice go in vain. Seeing her try so hard had inspired him to try hard as well. It was then that he remembered how Officer Bellum had risked his life for him; he remembered how Rodney had lost his store because of him; he remembered how Jenson had risked everything to rescue him. And ever since he had walked on this planet, Azura, Sorren and Rathos helped him and saved him from danger. If everyone else risked their lives for him, the least he can do is risk his life *with* them!

Darek wanted to change for the better—that's what he really wanted. But he never truly did and this angered him greatly. He was not angry with Liam. The one Darek was most angry with was himself! Darek used all of his might to crawl back onto the platform.

Liam was still on the crate, scratching his nose. When he found Darek standing before him, he was struck with astonishment…but also a hint of delight.

Darek began, "Now listen here—"

"RAAAAAAAAAAAH!"

A harsh scream wailed and reverberated within and throughout the planet. It was so deafeningly loud that Darek immediately covered his ears and fell to the ground. It seemed to him as though everything was shaking, or at least his head was.

When the screaming finally stopped, Darek looked up. "W-what was that?"

"Once again, I do not find your antics amusing." Liam had not heard anything at all.

The scream began again and Darek felt that the limits of his sanity were being stretched and strained to the point of snapping. Darek turned to face the core.

Trembling, Darek muttered, "What is *that*?"

The core had a face of a man. The face was contorted in agony and cried out in pain, "It hurts! It hurts! It hurts so much I could just die!"

Darek looked back at Liam and then to the core. He hoped the face was just a product of his imagination. Yet there it was again, and this time, it was staring back at him. If it was his imagination, it was frighteningly real and disturbingly persistent.

"You…" said the core, his tongue still dipped in the fires of agony. "You can see me."

"Wh-who? Me?" Darek spun around, wondering if the core was talking to someone else.

"Yes, you."

"No, no." Shaking his head, Darek said, "It couldn't be me."

"You, the young man in uniform, standing upon the platform, and looking straight back at me through those silly-looking goggles," the face of the core said. "Yes, I'm talking to you."

"Oh," said Darek. "He pointed me out pretty clearly there…"

"You're special," said the core. "I can see it. You desire great power, do you not? The power to save and destroy! I can give you this power if only you'd help me. I know that you have the power to free me, for you are the key to *destruction!*"

Darek's hand started to glow brilliantly, and when Liam saw this phenomenon he could not help but stare at it. The light that enveloped Darek's hand materialized into a thick red glove. "This feeling…I remember this feeling. But why?"

Darek picked up his daggers and as he held onto the handles, the blades were forged anew in searing flames. The blades took on a new form with a symbol of fire embedded on a new red surface.

"So you do have some power after all," said Liam.

"Sorry." Darek flung his dagger at Liam and it fizzed through the air. The blade sunk into Liam's chest. "*Flames of Judgment…*" As Darek said those words, Liam could feel an intense burning in his chest. His body burst into flames, charring his skin and bones in a raging inferno. The flames changed from orange to white and rose higher and higher. Liam yelled out as the fire continued blazing. Then in an instant it all disappeared in a wisp of smoke. Liam, having lost all strength in his body, collapsed backwards gracefully.

"Now this wasn't in my calculations," Liam chuckled softly with his wavering breath, "That last attack was splendid, well beyond my comprehension."

Darek drew near to Liam's weak and dying body. The pained expression on Darek's face was not from his past injury but from a fresh feeling of regret.

"Why the frown?" asked Liam. "You have survived. Enjoy whatever time you have before the end of the world. Every second is precious."

"Why'd you allow me to attack you?" Darek looked at him with sorrowful eyes. "I wouldn't have been able to kill you, otherwise. If you'd tried, you would have killed me first."

"As I said before, you cannot fully comprehend what it means to be immortal in a mortal world. Our desires never cease even when we realize they were futile in the first place. The ideals we had have long grown cold." He paused. "Tell me, do you know of entropy?"

"I think I have heard someone speak of it before. It's like from order to chaos, right? Like if you build a new house it will break down over time."

Liam stifled a painful laugh. "Not the best of analogies, but yes, that is what I'm talking about. My mind was the same. As the flow of time continued, so my mind became more and more twisted. Things that I never would have considered doing years before, I ended up doing later. Immortality is something long sought after, but such immortality is of no use in a mortal universe. Everything will change and there's nothing you can do but watch it as if from a distance." Liam gasped. His final moments seemed near. "But now that my mind is clear, I can see that everything I have done was a mistake. I have nothing but regret."

Darek knelt down, concerned. "Then is there a way to stop the core from exploding?"

Liam shook his head. "We only researched how to stimulate the core to produce this reaction. Get out of here. There's a spaceship in the castle basement. It belongs to me."

"But how do I get out? You sealed the exit of the control room."

Liam wheezed, "You have to enter a code into the panel..."

Darek scratched the back of his neck and waited a few seconds. Then he impatiently blurted out, "Hey, don't leave me in suspense! What's the code?" But there was no response.

"Such a shame." Darek lowered his head. "Rest in peace."

"I'll try," said Liam.

Darek blinked. "You're not dead?"

Liam remained very still and quiet, but his breathing and pulse started up again.

Darek gazed upon Liam's face and saw a glow running across his flesh.

CHAPTER 24
Countdown

The control room was disturbingly quiet. All the computers were shutdown. The burning electrical equipment that Liam had tossed about before had been doused by an automated sprinkler system. No longer did the distraught beeping or the subtle, hoarse whispers of flame disrupt the tranquility. All that remained was the eerie calm.

Darek swirled around and around in the office chair, kicking and dragging his feet along the ground. He stopped and turned his attention to the door. He glanced over Liam's comatose body, then shook his head and started spinning again.

"How do I get out of here now?" he wondered out loud.

As he kept spinning, the chair support snapped out of place. The seat collapsed. Darek fell flat on his face. But he wasn't angry; he was too worried to be angry. Darek picked himself up and rubbed off the pain.

"I have to get out of here and let everyone know what's going on." Darek walked over to one of the computers and turned it on. He searched through the files, seeking a way to unlock the door. Then Darek sung ruefully, "Where is the number? Where is the code? I've got to leave before it explodes." He tapped his fingers along the keyboard. The harder he searched, the more frustrated he became.

Full of anger, Darek got up and tossed the keyboard to the floor. Then he ripped the monitors off the table and threw them against the wall. He kicked a computer across the floor and flipped over a table. "There's nothing here at all! NOTHING!"

Darek walked up to the door and kicked it. "Why can't I get out of here?" He kicked the door again. "I fought an immortal and lived." Darek kicked the door repeatedly. After kicking it so much, his toes hurt, and he slouched to the ground. Exhausted, he put his back against the door and looked across. Through his goggles, he could see the beautiful core through the broken window. It had a bright, furious red color and its flames looked close enough to sear the outer platform. "The world's going to end." He hung his head. "I'm dead."

"No—there must be something I can do!" Darek rubbed his hand against his forehead. But as he was doing so he noticed he was still wearing the thick gloves that had appeared on his hands while he was fighting Liam. He gazed at them. "These gloves are amazing. I don't know what they are but…they can create fire and even melt crystal. I wonder if it's a heat thing." An intriguing notion crossed his mind.

Darek stepped in front of the door. Warmth pulsated through his hands as he gently ran his fingers across the sides of the door. He pushed against the door, and like a piece of cloth, it floated into the hallway; the thick door lay on the ground, contorted. "I guess I'm not totally insane yet." Darek looked at Liam's body. "Let's get you out of here." Darek heaved him up on his back and left the room.

The place was in disarray. Sirens were blaring and lights were flashing on the ceiling. Left and right, people scurried into hall. Some of the guards who were running along even caught a glimpse of Darek and did not appear to care.

"So that's where you were!" Azura met up with Darek. Sorren was close behind her. "We've been going around in circles looking for you. Where have you been?"

Darek asked, "Where's everyone going?"

"Elder Rendall called for a meeting in the city," said Sorren. "He said it was an emergency. Most have already left and the rest are leaving. They won't be bothering us. Now about the mission, Azura and I went through the research laboratories and we saved as much data as we could. We did our job." Sorren paused and pointed curiously at Liam. "Who's that on your back and why's he burnt to a crisp?"

"He's a friend. He just had a little mishap." Darek was afraid of how they might react if they found out Liam was an elder.

A shockwave made its way from the core. The tower trembled so hard that several of the walls were ripped apart and whole chunks of the tower broke apart.

"We'll discuss this later," said Sorren, shaken.

Azura had no complaints. "I agree. Something weird is going on. There was a similar shockwave just a moment ago. I don't think this tower will last."

Sorren led the others down through the stairwell, fearing that the elevator might be too dangerous. As they ran down, they cut corners wherever they could, sliding along the rails and jumping off steps to speed things up. A loud explosion came from above, rattling the stairs; it shook so hard that they couldn't help but wonder what had happened.

"I'm almost afraid to find out what that is." Darek was reluctant to look, but seeing the surprised expression on Azura's face, as she gazed above in awe, piqued his curiosity. He flung his head back and looked up. The upper levels of the tower were all gone; it had crumbled away, most likely from the impact of the shockwave. But that wasn't what had astonished Darek most.

"Is it just my imagination or does the core look larger than before?" asked Darek, frightened. He turned to Azura and Sorren, but they were already down the stairs, going faster than before. "Hey, wait for me!"

The structure of the tower became frail. The stairs began to swerve and bend like a swinging bridge.

"Come on, Darek," Azura yelled back, "pick up the pace!"

"I'm going as fast as I can!" Darek struggled to keep up with the others. A rough tremor made him lose his balance and miss a step. Darek tumbled down. Liam's body flopped out of his grasp. Both of them landed on their backs. Darek groaned, unwilling to move.

A loud creak came from the stairs above. The upper stairs came crashing down one after the other like a domino effect. When Azura discovered Darek wasn't behind her, she ran back up to check on him. She found Darek and Liam on the floor.

"This'll be rough." Azura grabbed hold of both of them, but Darek stared up in horror. Whole sections of the stairs were collapsing down toward their position, and they were about to be crushed under it.

Sorren saw the situation and flicked his wrist at Azura. A small black circular mass appeared above the group and swallowed up the influx of collapsing debris, giving them time to escape. "Keep moving!" he shouted.

Azura took Darek for a piggyback ride and held Liam's broken body in her arms. She followed after Sorren in haste but, with the added weight, was slower than before. Darek gawked at the sight above. Everything was getting worse. The core was expanding at an alarming rate. The core became so large that it started to engulf the higher areas of the tower.

"Hurry!" said Darek. "The core is getting closer!"

"Shut up!" Azura growled through clenched teeth. "I'm hurrying as fast as I can!"

They zipped and zoomed down the stairwell, desperately trying to reach the bottom of the tower as fast as they could.

"We're not going to make it!" cried Darek. "It's too far!"

"I said *shut up!*" shrilled Azura. "Or at least say something encouraging!"

When they reached the bottom floor, Sorren kicked open the door and let Azura run out first. He followed after her and the two of them sprinted across the deserted lobby.

After exiting the Tower of Legai, Sorren spun around, running backwards to see the situation for himself. The massive core had already swallowed up half of the tower. However, for some reason, a thick white layer of molecules formed around the core. Sorren believed it to be the work of spirits, like Ios, that lived in this place. The layer acted like a barrier, holding back the core's growth.

Azura stopped walking and set Darek down as soon as they reached the end of the road. The elevator was not there, most likely because the workers in the tower had last used it to return to the surface. The hole, through which the elevator made its trips up and down through the earth's crust, was still there. Beside the hole was a stand with a button that activated the elevator. She anxiously pushed the button. Nothing happened. Still jittery, she pushed the button several times. Still nothing.

"Maybe it takes a while?" said Darek.

"There's something here," said Azura. She found a tiny flashing screen next to the button. "It says, 'Not Available.'"

"They must've overworked it," said Sorren. "Since it travels at high velocities and rarely gets used, it probably couldn't handle the increased usage."

"What should we do?" Darek quivered at the thought of being incinerated by a giant core.

"What can we do? Not much," said Sorren. " The only thing we can do, I suppose, is jump down the hole. It's better than being out here…"

"Wait." Darek remembered something. "I want to see if Ios is okay. I accidentally—er—dropped her and—"

Go, said Ios. *Don't worry about me.*

"Is that really you?" said Darek, startled by the voice in his mind.

"Who's he talking to?" said Azura.

"Probably himself," said Sorren. "He's weird like that."

The voice continued, *This is my place, my home. The core is my responsibility. I will help slow it down, but you must leave. We cannot keep the core from expanding. In time it will encompass the planet.*

"I'm sorry," said Darek. "This was all my fault."

This was unavoidable. Now leave. You will die if you do not leave right now.

Darek nodded and then turned to Sorren. "Okay, I'm ready. Let's go."

The three of them jumped inside the hole, taking Liam with them as well. At the beginning they were falling normally, the acceleration of gravity caused them to fall faster and faster. After falling for a long time, they slowed down. Then, as if they were held by an invisible rubber band, they bounced up and down from a central point.

"Why aren't we falling anymore?" said Darek, getting a little dizzy in midair.

"This is the between the crust above and the crust below where the two directions of gravity meet. We'll get pulled up and down until we come to a stop in the center."

"Then what?"

"Then nothing," said Sorren. "We'll just end up floating here in the middle."

"We can't do anything?"

Sorren scratched his head. "If you really want to, I guess we *could* try to climb the miles of earth above us."

"You came in here knowing this?" exclaimed Darek.

"I forgot," said Sorren. "When there's an abnormality such as an enlarging core that could effectively lead to our imminent destruction, I can't think straight. Jumping down sounded like a good idea at the time." Sorren paused. "Now that you mention it, there is something I could do. But I haven't done it in so long..."

Two bolts of light came rushing from below them.

"What's that?" Azura was the first to notice with her sharp senses.

It was Reza and Drey. Blanketed in light, these two flew up to meet the group. Though they did not have wings, they were able to control their movement through the air.

Surprised, Reza said, "Still here? Would you guys like some help?"

"Yes! Someone came to our rescue!" said Darek, smiling.

"Hold on to us," Reza told them. "We'll fly you out."

Reza took hold of Azura and Liam. Drey held onto Darek, and was about to grab onto Sorren as well, but Sorren declined.

"I can do it myself," said Sorren.

"Don't wear yourself out," said Reza. "You're not one of us anymore. You're human now. Save your strength."

Displeased at her words, Sorren grunted, "Very well."

Drey took hold of Sorren. Then in a brilliant flash, they took off, soaring upward. After flying for a while, they came to a halt. A massive oozing stream of molten rock obstructed their path. The stream rushed from one side of the tunnel to the other, leaving no gaps to squeeze through.

"I don't remember this part," said Darek in awe.

"Obviously," said Azura. "You couldn't see anything from inside the elevator."

"There's no way around this," said Reza. "It's a long way up. I'll shield the humans. Drey will carry us up."

Drey nodded. "Sure thing."

Reza took a deep breath, and then breathed out an icy cool breeze. She twirled around with the cold vapor leaving her lips. The frosty air encircled them and instantly froze everyone, except Drey, in one large block of ice. Drey drew a deep breath, grabbed hold of the ice and slammed headfirst into the fiery stream. Holding onto the frozen surface of the icicle felt like having hundreds of knifelike needles pierce his chest. But despite this sharp, mind-numbing pain, he pressed on, fueled by the warmth and touch of the magma that enfolded around his body. The sensation of the molten rock on his skin was soothing to him.

It took a while but Drey was able to break out of the magma. Then Drey sailed all the way up through the crust and the shifting plates. Then they finally broke out from the dirt. Drey landed onto the earth and discovered that they were now behind the castle. The ice immediately cracked and shattered, freeing everyone from their frozen state. Feeling weak and faint from the ordeal, Reza fell on her knees, gulping air.

Darek laughed and shook the water out of his hair. "Well, I'm glad it's over."

Drey glanced at him and said, "It is far from over."

Hundreds of brilliant lights zoomed across space. Appearing as comets, these celestial objects twisted and turned as they went along;

their violent rumblings could be felt as tremors across the galaxy. They flew chaotically at first, jumping from direction to direction, unsure of where they were going. But once they heard it—the loud, bloodcurdling scream of the core—they tightened their formation and moved uniformly.

Reza pointed upward, showing everyone the new specks of light in the sky. "Look! They've come. It seems our time is short."

Darek looked up. "Who or what are you talking about? The stars?" Then he realized something strange. "Wait a minute—it's not even that dark out anymore. How can they be so bright?" While gaping at the wondrous sight, he took a step forward and almost tripped over Liam. Liam was so quiet, Darek had almost forgotten about him. Darek took him aside and let him rest on the grass.

Drey said to Reza, "Our fellow Guardians have arrived. No doubt they are seeking war."

Reza nodded. "A war would be meaningless at this time. We must inform them of the situation and convince them to stand down."

"War?" Darek remained rather puzzled. "What are you guys blabbering about?"

Acting strangely, Reza and Drey said nothing in reply and moved away from the rest of the group. Drey began a strange transformation. First there was fire rising from his feet. His whole body burst into a scorching pillar of fire. The flames spun around him like a tornado and his form changed into that of a giant red bull. His horns were ivory in color. He snorted out steam and stamped his feet wildly.

Reza was next to transform. A mist rose up from the beneath Reza's body. Like a fog, it swept over her, veiling her from their sight. When the mist faded away, her appearance was different. A long flowing white robe wound around her body. Her complexion and hair became differing shades of blue and green. She hovered in the air, pretending like she was sitting down.

Darek and Azura stepped back, almost unable to believe what they were witnessing.

"Uhh…" Darek gibbered all sorts of nonsense before finally saying something. "I don't get it. What just happened? Where did Reza and Drey go?"

Reza told them. "Don't be afraid. It's just us. These are our other forms."

Darek couldn't stop shivering at the sight of them. "What's going on here? Other forms? You're aliens, right? Weird, freakish, hideous aliens!"

"We don't have time to explain," said Drey, feeling a bit offended by Darek's remarks. "We must hurry to the others. If we don't stop them soon—"

"Mother." Sorren approached Reza and said, "Do you need my help? What is happening may be out of your control. I could be of some assistance."

"No," said Reza. "I want you to stay. You are needed here. And as I've told you before, stop calling me Mother. I have long since abandoned you as my son."

Reza and Drey both elevated several feet into the air. With a strong burst of energy like the liftoff of a rocket, they soared high into the sky, much to the surprise of everyone standing there.

"Mother?" Darek gave Sorren a suspicious stare, considering the possibility that he could also be an alien. If true, it would help to explain several things. "Nothing makes sense anymore."

Azura said, "What should we do now?"

"We should head for the castle," Sorren replied. "It's the safest place to be."

"Are you crazy?" Darek said, exasperated. "We're going to run straight back into the home of the elders? Don't you know I almost died in that tower? If it wasn't for the giant talking face and these strange gloves, I—" Darek looked at his hands; the gloves weren't there anymore.

Azura crossed her arms skeptically. "Go on. What's this about a giant talking face?"

"Uh...never mind." Darek knew his own words sounded unbelievable. "But I still don't understand why we have to go back to the castle."

"This is going to be a little difficult to explain, but I'll try," said Sorren. "I suppose I should start by explaining who Reza and Drey are."

"You know them?" asked Azura.

"Yes." Sorren turned to Darek. "Darek, where'd you say you found them?"

Darek replied, "In the basement of Merdon's mansion. They were stuck in crystals and said something about an evil sorcerer that trapped them."

"Ah," said Sorren, coming to an understanding. "They weren't exactly truthful. This might be hard to swallow, but Reza and Drey are spirit beings known as the Guardians of the Elements. Since they are spirits, they cannot die. If they're injured severely, they'll turn into crystal, waiting there for eternity. This is their death." Sorren paused. "And since it's their death…they shouldn't be able to get out of their crystals. How did you free them?"

Darek shrugged. "I just touched it. That's all."

"You touched it?" Sorren stared at Darek's hands, looking for something peculiar.

Seeing how Sorren was distracted, Darek faked a loud cough. "Is something wrong?"

Sorren came back to his senses. "Oh, no. What were we talking about again?"

"You said something about Reza and Drey being Guardians of something or other."

"Yes, they are Guardians," said Sorren. "And they are also those *stars* above. They can glow quite bright in space."

"But why would they—" Darek stopped speaking, his mouth still open as though he suddenly froze in place.

There was a drawn out silence. Azura tugged on Darek's jacket. "Hey, are you okay?"

All of a sudden, Darek smacked himself in the forehead. He said animatedly, "Of course! They came for the core! That's why Reza and Drey were inside the tower!"

"The core?" said Sorren.

"Yes," said Darek. He pointed at Liam who was unconscious and sprawled on the grass. "At the top of the tower I met him. His name is Liam. He's an elder—"

"An elder?" Sorren raised his voice in anger. He was about to draw his sword, but Darek quickly gestured with his hands for Sorren to relax.

"Don't worry. Just let me finish first. He's on our side now—I think," Darek said. "Anyway, he explained everything to me. He injected a strange solution into the core. The core will eventually explode and the radiation will transform people on nearby planets into immortals. That's their goal."

Sorren's eyes widened. "Why didn't you tell us this earlier? The core will explode? How much time do we have left?"

"A few hours, I guess. Liam also said that there's a spaceship inside the castle."

"A spaceship…" repeated Sorren, licking his lips. He was now worried. Within a few hours, the planet would explode. It was like a ticking time bomb right under their feet. "Let's go find that ship."

"Wait," said Darek. "Isn't there a way to stop the core from exploding?"

Appalled by his question, Sorren replied, "You're thinking of *that* at a time like *this*? How should I know? Besides, we don't have time!"

A wave of guilt washed over Darek as he remembered that he was the one who had helped the old scientist get that devilish machine working. He had caused the problem so he felt that it was only natural that he should be the one to set things straight.

Darek said, "But it's not right to just leave. How can we even consider running away when everyone else will die?"

Sorren said, "If it makes you feel better, all of the immortals here are already over a hundred years old. They've lived their lives to the fullest—you haven't."

"But other planets will be affected! The lives of billions are at stake here!"

"Darek's right," said Azura. "We should figure out a way to save this planet."

Sorren sighed deeply. "This exactly the reason why I wish I was working with a few more cold-hearted assassins." He grabbed Darek by the shoulders and shouted, "Listen to me! Why waste your time? You don't even know them! Most of them deserve to die anyway."

Darek gasped at Sorren's harsh words.

"It doesn't matter what you think." Azura scowled. "You can't measure the worth of their lives. It's not like there's harm in trying to help—"

"Oh," scoffed Sorren, "come on! There *is* harm in trying. We could save three lives—ours. Or we could *all* die."

"Or we could save everyone," Azura added.

Sorren shook his head. "Impossible."

An idea came to Azura's mind. Smiling mischievously, she said, "Look, how about a deal? You're a man of deals, aren't you? How about I give you all my money?"

Sorren broke out in mock laughter. "I'm gambling my life away for chump change? Do I look that desperate?"

"Then what do you want?" Azura placed her hands on her hips. "If money's not enough, there's got to be at least a favor I can do!"

Sorren pondered on her question for a moment. He pursed his lips and then said with a grin, "Give me your Fate of the Hero."

"My Fate? You want my Fate? I-I can't do that," said Azura. "I don't even have that kind of authority…the power to give the Fate. And even if I did, I can't just give it to anyone!"

Sorren shrugged and then started to leave them. "Oh well. That's too bad. You guys can play around while I get out of here."

"Now wait a minute," said Azura, putting a hand on his shoulder. "I only said that I can't give it to you. But that doesn't mean you can't earn it yourself. If you want, I can give you a special recommendation to join the ranks of the Heroes."

Darek whistled. "Are you sure that's a good idea? I don't really think that'd work out. Sorren doesn't look, act or think like a Hero. He's even killed—"

"I'll do it." Sorren smiled, baring his teeth. "You better be good to your word." He faced her and held out his open hand.

"Look who's talking," Azura countered. "Unlike you, I'm always good to my word."

They shook on it and the deal was sealed.

The three of them rushed back to the castle. There was no time to waste. The end of the world was near. When they reached the front of the castle, they hit a barrier: an impenetrable throng of immortals crowded around the square, shouting and bickering amongst themselves. The streets were locked in chaos. Thousands of immortals flocked to the balcony where the elders were ready to give their announcement.

Rendall approached the balustrade. The crowd quieted down, attentive to what he had to say. Rendall said, "My fellow immortals. Heed my words. You may be wondering what is happening— wondering about those new stars in the sky. The phenomenon above us is not unexpected. We knew this day would come. These lights in the sky are celestial beings that find our existence threatening. They wish to silence us by force.

"I assure you that we are fully prepared for this event. We have been in preparation for a while. However, we will need every man and woman to work together for our cause. For now, no one is allowed to leave the city. I will return soon to discuss the details of our operation."

Rendall and the other elders disappeared into the castle. The pandemonium died down. The crowd scattered as people decided to rest while they waited for more news. Darek and the others were able to sneak into the castle.

"Don't they know the world's going to end?" said Darek. "If everyone's going to die, why would the elders bother to fight?"

"You saw what happened," said Sorren. "It's a form of control. They are telling the people what they want to hear to prevent any armed revolt. But there's also a possibility that the Guardians could stop the process. They'll want to prevent the Guardians from reaching the core."

"So they're actually going to fight?" asked Azura.

"Of course," said Sorren.

"But then, why don't we just let the Guardians in?" Darek grinned with excitement. "If they can stop the core from exploding—problem solved!"

"It's not that easy," Sorren said. "In a war between two nations, who can be trusted? What you are saying is absolutely ludicrous. First of all, the Immortal Alliance needs to surrender openly, because if they don't, the Guardians will attack. But for a complete surrender we would need the consent of the elders. The people will only listen to them. They're certainly not going to listen to us."

Darek grinned. "Then we'll do that!"

"Do what? Are you even listening? The people will only obey the elders."

"All we have to do is make the elders tell everyone to surrender."

Incredulous, Sorren said, "How do you plan to do that?"

"By force! We take over the leadership!" Darek shouted. "There are only five elders and I've defeated one easily. With the three of us combined, it'll be no problem!"

Sorren snapped, "That's—"

"Brilliant!" added Azura. "We should try that."

Sorren massaged his temples. He could feel a headache coming on. "Great," he said sarcastically. "Just great. Let's just do an impossible fight against the elders, which we can't win, and force ridiculous demands upon them, which they will not listen to."

"Oh come on Sorren," said Azura. "I know I'm exaggerating about how good the idea is, but if the Guardians are the only way to stop the destruction of the world, then we need to get them inside as fast as we can. Do you have any better ideas?"

"Hmm…we'll either die by the exploding core, die by the war with Guardians, or die by fighting the elders." Sighing, Sorren looked very depressed. "Nope. Just lead the way."

CHAPTER 25
The Calm Before

Reza and Drey crossed over the ceiling of the atmosphere, and as they did, onlookers from below only saw two shooting stars, jetting across the sky. When they reached the immeasurable blackness of space, high above the surface of the planet, they immediately recognized their fellow kind in human form, floating around in groups. Seeing that the other Guardians were using human forms, they reverted back as well.

One of the Guardians saw the two of them from a distance and flew out to meet them. Because they were now in space, the Guardian used a mental link to communicate with them, but he still moved his lips as if he were actually speaking. "Reza! Drey! You guys are alive! I haven't seen you guys for a year. How've you been?"

"Who's leading this group?" said Reza impatiently, ignoring the Guardian's greeting.

"Your father, Beld," the Guardian replied. "Come, I'll take you to him."

"My father?" Reza was shocked. "Why would my father be leading? He is only of the 75th generation!"

"Take a look around," said the Guardian. "There are only several hundred Guardians from the 66th to 77th generations in this group. While Beld may be of a younger generation, among us there is no dispute that he is most qualified to lead."

"What's going on here? Where are the elder generations? Why didn't they come to deal with such an important matter?" Reza demanded to know.

The young Guardian's face remained grave. "We were caught unaware. Several cases of the same situation randomly popped up across the galaxy. We had to split up to investigate each case. But because we discovered this one last, whoever was left was sent here."

Reza furrowed her brow. "What? More cases? How'd this happen?"

The Guardian shrugged. "No clue. In any case, you must speak with Beld. He'll be happy to see you." The Guardian beckoned for Reza to follow and he led them to where Beld was.

Beld was in a meeting with several of his most trusted advisers. They sat around in a circle, floating in the middle of space, apart from the rest of the larger group. In the center of their circle was a holographic three-dimensional map, which they examined to gain understanding of the land and of the capital city. Several tiny orbs swerved about, drawing the map using thousands of colorful miniature-sized rays.

One of his advisers said to him, "Judging from the size of the city, I estimate a population of a few thousand if not more. Regardless of the exact amount, we are greatly outnumbered. Also take note that they have drunk the blood of the core. As it is, we are at a disadvantage."

Beld replied, "Yes. Though part human, they are not to be underestimated. Direct conflict would be dangerous. The only advantage we have is the element of surprise. They should not know our capabilities. If so, we can exploit their weakness and crush them quickly."

Reza spared no time and interrupted their meeting. "Father, you must stop this. We have investigated the planet. Most of the people down there are innocent! We cannot allow the innocent to perish for the sins of a few."

Beld lifted his head up and caught sight of her with the corner of his eye but he did not he turn his head to see her. "I haven't seen you in a year. Now that you've returned, you tell me this? I'm sorry, but I cannot comply. The attack must go on. If we do not reach the core, many more will perish."

Reza pleaded, "Please, Father. Don't do this. The immortals are stronger than you think! A war will end with unnecessary casualties on both sides. If you give me time, I know I can get us through. Some people are friendly and I'm sure if we explain the situation to them—"

"The humans?" Beld said, "We cannot rely on them. They caused this."

"But Sorren is also…"

Beld grew fierce. "Sorren? I told you never to mention that name in front of me ever again! That wretched fool is the one who started this mess in the first place!"

"No!" snapped Reza. "He's never done anything wrong! If anyone's to blame—"

He motioned for several others to come close and ordered them, "Take Reza and Drey and restrain them. They must not be allowed to interfere. They'll be of no use in the battlefield."

As they took hold of her, Reza struggled. "Listen to me, father! This will not end well!"

Beld shook his head. "I'm the leader and what I say will be. You are deceived so easily, my daughter, by those humans. I, however, will not be swayed."

Meanwhile, inside the castle of the elders, a knock rapped on the door of Rendall's chamber. Rendall sat quietly in his chair with his back to his desk; he gazed through the window to observe the clear, yet ominous, sky with wonder. Rendall was in human form, wearing gallant red garbs. He brushed his fingers across his beard and groaned wearily, deep in thought.

"Come on in," said Rendall.

Windzer opened up the door and approached the desk. "Still star gazing?"

Rendall hummed. "It is quite an amazing sight. Very beautiful— especially the way they move ever so slightly in spiraling shapes as if they were dancing in space. How deceptive when I think of what destruction they're capable of." Rendall swiveled his chair to face Windzer. "I am, at the moment, a bit bitter. I followed your instructions and let those kids roam underneath the castle in hopes they would finally bring enough evidence to start a rebellion. Yet, why is it that we are at this point right now? Why are we in a position where everyone may very well die in a few hours? Can you please explain this mystery to me?"

"Sadly," said Windzer, "this was unexpected. I was unaware that one of them was a package carrier. If they didn't have it—"

"If they didn't have it," repeated Rendall, listless. Rendall closed his eyes and tried his best to relax. The stress had been mounting ever since he learned that the destruction of the core was now imminent. Though he was an elder, he had changed his mind about everything the elders had done and wished for the reign of elders to end. But now, his plan of betraying the other elders had failed. There would be no point in revealing the elders' hand in this dilemma if everyone was going to die.

"What are you thinking about?" asked Windzer.

Rendall said, with his eyes still shut tight, "Right now, I'm debating in my mind whether or not I can still trust you. I know that you are different than the others. You aren't a young immortal. You may even be older than me."

"What a keen observation," said Windzer slowly. "How did you know?"

Rendall chuckled, opening his eyes. "I was in charge of administration when the world was changed anew. I was the one who researched every single person in order to create his or her role in our new society. However, you were different. You had no records. You had no prior life on our world. I believe you were sent by the real Immortal Alliance to monitor us."

"Yet, you did nothing about it," said Windzer with a smirk, "and even came to me for help over the years."

"You're right," grunted Rendall. "Even though you were the most untrustworthy, I find myself continually placing all my faith in you." His eyes became watery and he leaned back in his chair, fixated on the sky. "I don't know what to do. I've always been good at reading people. I could discern their thoughts, their minds, their intentions, and their desires...I even had all the elders figured out. But you, on the other hand, are different. I always feel like I can trust you, when I know I can't."

"That does sound troublesome," remarked Windzer, sounding amused.

"Tell me, what should I do now?" Rendall said.

"Lead your people to fight this war."

Rendall looked Windzer in the eye. "Shouldn't we surrender?"

"I know them and how they think," said Windzer. "After seeing their current formation, I know for a fact that they are planning on striking us without warning."

"But then what? Even if we win, what else is left?"

"I have a way to stop the core from exploding."

Rendall's eyes lit up. "You do?"

"Yes, but it takes time and nothing must interfere. I can't do it now because the attack will soon begin. If you can just fend them off and hide this from the elders. I can set things straight."

"But can we really win?" said Rendall, unconvinced by Windzer's words. "I've fought with two of them nearly a year ago. A man and a woman came to us, telling us to stop what we were doing, but the other elders refused to listen. Individually, they were not much stronger than us elders. But still...that would be like fighting an army of elders."

"I can win," said Windzer. "If you give me authority over the people, I can lead us to victory. I have a plan that will work against them. But it requires everyone to listen to me."

Rendall said, half in jest, "If you can really pull off such a miracle, I'll give you the leadership when we reestablish our government."

Windzer laughed. "I'd run away if something like that happened. Merdon is much more suited for the task."

Rendall removed a pendant from around his neck and placed it in Windzer's hand. "Take this. The symbol of my power. Show it to the chief officers and they will immediately recognize it and will listen to your words as if they were mine."

Windzer nodded. "Will you be joining me on the battlefield?"

"Yes," said Rendall. "But I want you to be in complete command."

"I understand," said Windzer. "Your trust will be well placed."

While speeding through the halls, Darek panted for air. Full of urgency, they had been running around the entire time that they were inside the castle. Corridor after corridor, Darek could hardly believe how large the inside of the castle was. What was most worrying was that they had no idea where to find the elders. They had run into the castle blindly, with no sense of direction or idea of where they were supposed to go. However, luckily for them, there was no one else inside the castle. The castle was empty, making their search easier, but still very tiring.

"This is worse than I imagined," said Sorren. "By the time we find the room of the elders, they'll probably be long gone."

"Who cares?" said Darek with short breaths. "The important thing is we're trying!"

"Save your breath," growled Azura. "Shut up and keep looking."

The castle hallways had been constructed like a maze. Each hall looked exactly the same and they were placed in a grid-like fashion. The group ran into many dead ends, much to their dismay.

"I'd hate to live here," said Darek. "It's so confusing. I'd probably starve while searching for a kitchen. I probably can't even find the bathroom in here. That'd be a nightmare."

"Look," said Azura, excited. "A red carpet! Maybe that'll take us to the throne room."

The three of them followed the path of the red carpet all the way until they found decorated large double doors. The hinges and handles were golden and the wooden door was painted in thick black as contrast. Various red symbols that appeared as hieroglyphics, were embedded on the paint. Though beautiful in design, there was an underlying, nasty odor emanating from it. Darek considered it to be a musty smell.

"This must be it," said Darek, tidying himself. "Do I look presentable?"

Sorren ignored him and proceeded to push open the doors.

The red carpet reached all the way to the six thrones of the elders, which were situated in a semi-circular manner. Though relatively small in width and length, this throne room stretched high in height, symbolizing that though they are small in number, they have reached the pinnacle of power. The zenith of the room was the highest point in the castle—and quite possibly the highest point of the capital. It was the only point of the city visible from outside of the city walls.

Four elders sat upon their thrones, unmoving.

Darek cleared his throat, took a few steps forward and said, "You may be wondering what we are doing here. We've come to stop you from making a big mistake. Tell your people to surrender!"

One of the elders slumped to the ground in a bowing gesture.

Thinking they were appeasing him, Darek said, "No need to bow. We just want peace."

Azura had a shocked expression on her face. "Darek…" She tugged on his shirt to pull him back a step. "They're all dead."

"Indeed they are." A voice came from behind the thrones. "Now you don't have to worry. The elders won't bother you anymore."

"That voice…" said Darek, surprised. "I know that voice!"

Sorren walked forward and stood before the thrones. "I know that voice as well. Dionus—what are you doing here?"

Dionus came from behind the thrones and bowed slightly. "I've come to finish the job."

"And what job would that be?" asked Sorren.

Dionus chortled, "The execution of Darek."

CHAPTER 26
Annihilation

Beld observed the city from far above the sky. He turned to his adviser and asked him, "Are we ready to begin?"

The adviser replied, "Yes. We have seven hundred fifty-eight able fighters. The preparations for our assault are complete. Just give the order."

The small army of Guardians lined up in formation, standing at attention before Beld as he inspected them with scrutiny.

Pacing back and forth, Beld shouted, "I'm sure you all understand why we have come here. In the past we protected the humans and cared for them. But now they have betrayed us. Set aside all hesitation—kill without mercy. We will not let this unnatural, unholy existence run rampant through the galaxy. Before this gets out of hand, we will put an end to their recklessness."

Beld then told Alksorn, his trumpeter, "Blow the first trumpet."

Alksorn nodded in reply. Being a Guardian of wind, Alksorn filled up his chest with a burst of air; putting the trumpet to his lips, he blew on the trumpet with such force that the entire world could hear its echo. That was the signal for the first phase to begin.

Like a raging meteor shower, the Guardians fell toward the planet's atmosphere. The aura from their unified spirits illuminated the blue sky, causing smooth turquoise waves of light to scatter and signal their presence to the planet. The Guardians, while in midair, began the transformation of their bodies. These new bodies came in all varied shapes and sizes. Some resembled the proud beasts of nature: lions, sharks, rays, hawks, bulls, elephants, and bears—just to name a few. Others took the form of colossal humanoid giants surrounded by elements of earth, wind, water, fire and lightning.

They assembled themselves far from the eyes of the capital. After all of them were accounted for, they were divided into three smaller groups. One group took to the sky and veiled themselves with the clouds; another group submerged itself deep under the depths of the ocean; yet another group dug into the earth and were covered by blankets of dirt and vegetation. They positioned themselves close to the city and waited for the order.

Beld did not join them. He remained far above the sky. When he saw that the Guardians were in position, he shouted in a loud voice, "DESTROY THEM!"

Alksorn sounded the trumpet of war again.

All the Guardians—whether they were in the sky, earth or water—let out a massive battle cry that rattled the planet to its already shaken core.

Windzer reached the top of a castle turret and gazed into the distance. "Seems like it has finally begun," he muttered, as heavy winds beat the walls continually.

Peals of thunder sounded out in rapid intervals. Clouds unfolded overhead, laying the entire land with a thick coat of darkness. The seas stirred and waves crashed into the shoreline so hard that the rocky cliffs crumbled. Tremors in the earth traveled along the ground and, as it approached the city, the outer walls began shearing apart; it was being ripped to pieces like sheets of paper.

Windzer waited, taking in all the ominous sights and sounds of nature. "I can feel goose bumps rising on my skin and shivers running down my spine." He glanced over his shoulder and shouted to the citizens below, "Everyone—to your positions! Do not come out until I say so!"

The city had underground shelters for dangerous situations such as these. The shelters were hollow chambers that were several hundred feet deep. There was enough room in the shelters to fit everyone in the city without crowding. The city itself, with its shops and residences, had been built as a shield to cover over these shelters as the first layer of a near impenetrable defense.

After everyone had crawled into the underground shelters as ordered, an eerie silence swept over their fair town. It was dead quiet. People huddled together in their dark asylums, wondering what was happening.

The silence did not last for long. Shortly after, large bolts of fire and lightning came raining down. The rapid artillery from the clouds set the city ablaze in a sea of fire. No cries or screams could be heard as the city was pummeled over and over again. The flames rose up past the highest walls, licking up all of the food, water and wood till there was nothing left but stone and metal. When the barrage had stopped, the smoldering dust and ashes dispersed.

Next, a large shadow was cast upon the sea. A tidal wave, nearly two miles high, walked along the surface of the water, towering over the city.

While the wave was getting closer to Duraskull, Windzer faced the sea and said, "They intend to drown the city!" Then he raised his scythe and slammed it against the ground. "Come forth, Galokys! I command you to rise!"

The waves stirred around a newly formed whirlpool. A giant sea serpent stuck its head up out of the agitated waves. The sea serpent had the head of a crocodile but the body of a stout eel. Its long jaws, full of jagged teeth, were large enough to snap up fifty grown men in one bite.

Windzer said to it, "Galokys! Stop the tidal wave from reaching the city!"

The sea serpent bowed once and made a low clicking sound from its jaw. Then it turned to the oncoming tidal wave and whipped its long tail-like body to unleash a wave of its own. The two gargantuan waves collided with incredible force, causing a massive wake, but the overpowering wave from the sea still managed to weakly creep its way into the city, leaving it drenched from a short drizzle.

Dripping wet, Rendall climbed up the wall to meet with Windzer.

"How's the situation?" he asked him.

"Looks like we are in luck," said Windzer.

"How so?"

"The fiery barrage on the city and the tidal wave coming from the ocean, they were both very weak."

Rendall could not keep calm. "Those devastating attacks are considered weak?"

"Relatively speaking," said Windzer. "Those attacks should be based on the combined force of several hundred Guardians. For several hundred Guardians that is considered weak. They must be of a late generation."

"What? I don't understand what you mean by late generation. What are you talking about?"

"The Guardians are spirit beings," Windzer explained. "So naturally, the process in which they were created is different from humans. According to legend, in the beginning there was only one Guardian that was created. They thought it would be best to create a natural hierarchy to maintain order and delegate power. The first Guardian is the strongest of the Guardians and is considered the 1st generation. Then he gave 'birth' to the 2nd generation; that generation gave 'birth' to the 3rd generation, so on and so forth. The final and weakest order of Guardians is the 77th generation."

Intrigued by the legend, Rendall asked, "So we are dealing with the 77th generation?"

Windzer said, "Maybe. Most of the lower generations are all weaker so we can be dealing with anything around the 77th."

"So because of this 'late generation' thing, we have a chance to win the battle?"

"A chance?" Windzer said, "I'd say so. If everything goes well, they'll tire themselves out before any real harm is done. Then, when they come, we should be able to overpower them." Windzer mused over the sight of the sky. It was starting to clear up. "They've been quiet for a while. They might invade now. Tell everyone to get ready."

Rendall nodded and ordered several of his officers to alert the people. The officers ran across the ruins of the city, shouting, "Get ready, everyone! Come out for battle!"

Windzer continued to watch the sky but felt that something wasn't right. This period of silence was too long and drawn out. It was taking much longer than he expected. In a scenario where the enemy is concentrated in a small area with no escape, a heavy bombardment and rapid invasion was their standard tactic. But several minutes had already gone by; if they wanted to use the element of panic and confusion, the time had already passed. What could they be up to?

Suddenly, the dark clouds overhead began to swirl in a spiral. The thunderclaps were louder than ever and, every time it boomed, Windzer thought his bones would be crushed from the waves of sound. Though the stormy clouds withheld the sunlight from shining on the city, the relentless bolts of lightning filled the area with an eye-opening brilliant blue. This sudden change in the temper of nature made Windzer nervous.

A hole opened up in the center of the clouds, forming the eye of the storm; but the strange thing was that it had, quite literally, the shape and form of a human eyeball. This massive red eye that spanned thirty miles in diameter appeared from above and looked down upon the city in disgust and anger. It scanned the city for any survivors and immediately its attention was drawn to the people who started leaving the shelters.

Windzer was stunned when he saw the eye. His lips quivering, he exclaimed, "The Eye of Beld! This is bad..." Realizing his error in judgment and horrible miscalculation, he shouted at the top of his lungs, "GET BACK INSIDE! DON'T COME OUT!"

"What is that thing?" uttered Rendall, gaping at it.

Windzer grabbed Rendall by the collar. "Tell everyone to get back inside!"

"But I thought you said—"

"It doesn't matter! TELL EVERYONE TO GET INSIDE NOW!"

It was too late. Several hundred people had already come up to the surface, and most did not hear anything that Windzer was saying because the thunder was too loud. With no time left to spare, Windzer dragged Rendall deep into the nearest shelter. The shelter had several floors. He rushed to the lowest floor and fell flat on his face, forcefully making Rendall do the same.

From the pupil of the giant eye came a burst of stunning red light, which shone onto the capital. Then a blue light emerged from the pupil and merged with the existing red light. It ignited into a blazing inferno that wrapped the city and the forests around it in flames hot enough to melt stone. The walls, towers, and buildings of the city crumbled and were melted into the ground.

Windzer screamed a harsh cry as the violent tremors came from above, rattling the shelter. He screamed, not out of fear, but because he knew that those on the surface would not survive.

Indeed, the people above who had returned to the surface were incinerated into ash right on the spot. In seconds, their bodies became tiny particles that dissolved into the air. But that was not all. The tremendous beam of scorching flames was eating up all of the oxygen surrounding the city; powerful vacuums caused by drops in pressure sucked people right out of the shelters, dragging them into the vaporizing flames of destruction.

The eye of Beld laid waste to the entire city, leaving it in shambles and ruins; only the castle remained steadfast and relatively intact.

Windzer crawled out of the shelter on his hands and feet, only to find a mood of hopelessness and despair pervading the remains of the city. Aside from the castle, no stone remained on top of another. The capital had been painted with black and red. Sounds of weeping and wailing permeated out the entrances of the shelters. Hundreds had perished.

CHAPTER 27
Close Call

S tepping back nervously, Darek laughed. "That's um…a joke, right? Didn't you tell me I was pardoned? There's no reason for you to execute me."

"The Federation has pardoned you," said Dionus, placing his hands behind his back rather formally. "That's for sure. But I'm no longer part of the Federation. The Federation has nothing to do with this. I'm here to finish what I started."

"How did you find me way out here?" asked Darek. "The only one who—"

"You may have told him where you were," said Sorren.

"Are you crazy? I didn't tell him anything!" Darek shouted.

"That day when you saw Dionus in your dream," said Sorren. "He was inside your mind. He was able to read your thoughts and memories. Your mistake was that you did not kick him out. It was your mind, you should've had the strongest control, but instead you let him do as he pleased."

Darek snapped, "Then why didn't you tell me anything? Why didn't you stop it?"

"Because it's not like I could tell you anything at the time," said Sorren. "He killed me in your dream to force me out. I had no idea what was going on inside your mind. All I could do was try to enter, but Dionus had it blocked off until he left. I had my suspicions about what had taken place, but I didn't want to worry you with assumptions. Furthermore, I had no idea Dionus wanted you dead."

Darek grimaced. He had spent all that time trying to run away and hide. But in the end, everything begins again. Everything comes full circle.

"Please understand, Darek," said Dionus, "this is nothing personal. I will make it as painless as possible."

"As if we'd let you do that," said Azura, moving into a fighting stance. "If you haven't noticed, it's three on one. I say you should back off and leave while you still can."

"Actually," said Dionus, "it's ten against three."

Nine others walked out of the shadows and stood beside Dionus. Their clothes were made of white and purple linen, glistening in the light of the torches that surrounded the room.

Looking shocked, Azura recognized them instantly. "Vaelthren—What is going on here? This...can't be. Why would they—"

"Who are they?" Darek asked Azura, nudging her in the arm. "Federation soldiers?"

"The Vaelthren Guard," said Sorren. "Bodyguards of the Overlord. They only follow and listen to the orders of the Overlord. All of them are Heroes of the highest class."

"*The* Overlord?" said Darek, surprised. "The Overlord of the Legion is *here*?"

"You're looking at him," said Dionus.

"Where?" Darek flicked his gaze left and right, searching the room briefly, but he didn't see anyone out of the ordinary.

"Right here." Laughing, Dionus patted himself on the chest and bowed. "I'm the Overlord now."

"How dare you say such things," Azura snarled. "Don't insult the great Althair, our glorious Overlord, with your disgusting lies!"

"It's no lie," said Dionus, staying composed. "I am now the Overlord. Althair has stepped down from his seat and has graciously given it to me."

"I won't listen to your lies!" Azura shouted. "Althair would never give up the seat to a sniveling, conniving Federation snake like you!"

"Still your tongue, nameless Hero Azura," said Eir, captain of the Vaelthren Guard. "What he says is true. Pledge your allegiance and bow down before him."

Azura shook her head defiantly. "You can't be serious. There's no way—"

"*Bow*," said Eir again, this time in a commanding voice. "Azura, this is the will of Althair. If you bow, Dionus may forgive you for your wayward words."

"It can't be," she groaned. Though she was in a state of disbelief, she reluctantly obeyed and bowed her head before Dionus. Even if she couldn't trust Dionus, she had absolute faith in Eir and his words. Defying the law of the Heroes was the one thing she would never do.

"I'm sorry, Darek," whispered Azura. "This is out of my control. Run."

Darek staggered back, as confused as ever, and left the room in a burst of speed.

"Dionus—" Azura said.

"That's Overlord Dionus to you," said Dionus, "my young Hero."

"Right," grunted Azura. "*Overlord* Dionus, you cannot possibly execute a person unless they are a rebellious Hero. It is not the way of the Heroes to kill. Even if you are the Overlord, you cannot command us to kill."

"I know," said Dionus. "That is why it is fortunate for us that there is one here who can kill—and without hesitation, I might add."

Though nervous, Azura tried to stay calm. "And who would that be?"

"Why, Sorren, of course," said Dionus, gesturing at him. "Sorren, I know this isn't exactly the best time for a reunion. I have forgiven you for what you did to me all those years ago. I'm a different man now, as you can see. And I've dedicated my life to protecting the innocent. With that said, Darek…must…die. He may look innocent now, but in the future he will bring untold destruction."

Sorren made firm eye contact with Dionus, trying to understand his intent. "I know the stories as well as you do, Dionus. Darek seems special, but I'm—"

"Sorren," said Azura sternly. "He's lying! Don't listen to him!"

Dionus laughed at Azura's words. "Who do you think this man is? Sorren is a man of the darkness. Do you think he cannot tell lie from truth?" Dionus turned to Sorren and said, "Examine him and you'll see what I mean. He is the one we are looking for."

"Dionus," Azura roared, "as Overlord, you dare order an assassin to kill?"

"I don't need to," said Dionus. "All I'm doing is telling Sorren that he needs to see it for himself. That is as far as I will go. The rest of the responsibility is his."

"I understand." Sorren's green eyes stared coldly at Dionus. "If you are right, I'll see to it that he will not be able to cause harm. But keep in mind that we have unfinished business."

Azura said, "Sorren, listen to me! This is Darek we're talking about! We've been traveling with him for a few weeks. You know he's not—"

Sorren ignored her and dashed away; Azura chased after him, sticking closely behind so as to not lose sight of him.

Eir bowed before Dionus. "My lord, we really must be going. It is not safe here. If you are done with whatever you needed to do, we should leave."

Dionus replied, "You are right." He looked at the open doors. "Even if Sorren does fail—it wouldn't matter. The others can finish the job."

Eir said, "What of Azura? Should I send someone to go after her? She might not be able to escape otherwise."

"Leave her be," said Dionus darkly. "I'm sure she'd refuse to come with us anyway."

While they breezed across the massive labyrinth of walls and doors, Sorren was silent and tried to shake off Azura who was right behind, but Azura was able to keep up with Sorren's top speed.

Azura gulped for sufficient air in her tireless run. "Sorren, you aren't really planning to kill him, right?"

"Help me find Darek first," said Sorren.

"Don't tell me you actually believe what he said." She analyzed Sorren's cold expression. He seemed emotionless, as always.

Sorren said icily, "Why don't you? He *is* your Overlord. I thought all Heroes took the words of the Overlord as law."

"I won't recognize him as the Overlord. He was not even a Hero to begin with! How could I possibly accept that?"

Sorren kept his gaze on the corridor ahead, scanning for any sign of Darek.

"Wait." Azura grabbed Sorren by the arm, prompting him to stop. "Let's make this clear. You will not harm Darek. Understand?"

Sorren became uncomfortably silent. He didn't even turn to face her as she spoke.

"Did you not hear me?" snapped Azura. She angrily shoved Sorren into the wall and held him up against it. She hissed, "You're starting to scare me with your strange attitude."

Looking into her eyes, Sorren said, "I'm sorry. But this is what I have to do. Please…please don't get in my way."

Darek did not get very far at all. He was too exhausted to run and so he decided to search for a hiding place. Going through a wide corridor, Darek checked door after door. Most of the doors were locked. The sound of rapid footsteps echoed in the halls behind him. Someone was coming toward him and at a frighteningly brisk pace.

With the sound of footsteps coming closer, Darek ran to the next room and found an unlocked bedroom for guests. He quickly slammed and locked the door behind him, just in case. There were no good hiding spots. Darek decided to check the window to see if he could escape. He peeked out, only to discover he was nowhere near the ground.

Boom! Boom! Boom!

Someone was banging on the door so hard it almost sounded like it would break. "Darek, I know you're in there. Open up!"

Frightened, Darek crawled out the window without a second thought. He found himself walking along a skinny ledge outside the castle. A brief glimpse at the ground made him whimper and close his eyes. But something wasn't right. There was something about the scene that he found disturbing. He slowly opened his eyes to the world before him.

The city was no longer there; it was now a pile of rubble and scrap. Spots of flame and puffs of smoke littered the barren land. Darek searched through the gloomy haze, hoping there would be survivors.

"What happened here?" Though he was fearful of the height, his curiosity forced his eyes to continue watching the dismal picture. "The city…it's all gone…"

"Darek, even if you don't open this door, I'm still coming in after you!"

He heard the person outside start kicking the door. Darek, realizing that climbing outside was a big mistake, remained where he was. Being chased was now the least of his worries. All the strength in his legs was gone and his knees quivered slightly, though he really wished they wouldn't. He was now rooted in place, too scared to move back to the window. He started to panic, huffing and puffing uncontrollably.

The hinges of the door flew off as the door was kicked down. The wolf, Thedes, entered the room. Seeing that Darek was not around, Thedes lifted his nose to sniff for his scent. Thedes stopped sniffing. He stared at the window and said, "Darek, are you out there?"

Recognizing Thedes boorish voice, Darek replied, "Y-yes."

"Get in here," growled Thedes. "Time for you to make your report. Stop running away!"

"I'd come back if I could, but I really can't."

Thedes stormed his way to the window. When he looked out and saw the city in ruins, he gasped loudly, "Oh my goodness…THE CAPITAL! IT'S BEEN—"

"Yes, yes, I know!" Darek said, "Forget about that now. Bring me in first!"

Thedes turned to Darek. "What's wrong?"

"Can't you see I'm a bit scared?" he replied.

Thedes held out his paw and said, "Take my hand and I'll pull you in." His paw was no more than three inches away from Darek's hand.

Darek, overly cautious, slid his hand slowly across the wall to get within Thedes's reach.

"Almost there," said Thedes. "Just a little bit more."

Just when their fingers managed to touch, Darek's lost his footing. He flailed his body back and forth, trying to maintain balance. He could feel himself losing control, but Thedes practically threw his upper body out the window to snatch his hand. Darek was now dangling below the windowsill; his only means of staying alive was Thedes's outstretched arm.

"Hang on," said Thedes. "I'll pull you right up."

At that moment Darek caught a glimpse of a silhouette right behind Thedes. He warned him, "Watch out! There's someone in the room with you!"

"Behind me?" Startled, Thedes loosened up. The rest of his body was dragged out the window by Darek's weight. At the last second, before they both dropped down, Thedes jammed the claws of his feet into the wooden frame of the window. Thedes breathed a sigh of relief. He would probably be able to survive the fall because of his immortal body, but Darek on the other hand was too feeble.

"Now what do we do?" asked Darek, looking up at Thedes. "Are we going to be stuck here?"

All of a sudden, the two of them were jerked upward. "Stop worrying so much," said Azura at the window. "I'll pull both of you up!"

Azura had planted her feet firmly inside. She gradually hauled them in, keeping a steady hand so Darek wouldn't panic or fall. As soon as they were inside, they sat on the floor, taking a moment to rest from the ordeal.

"Thedes," said Azura, "why are you here? I didn't think anyone was still in the castle."

"During the banquet, Merdon was concerned about you," Thedes explained. "We were never able to contact you inside the ballroom. He ordered me to stay behind and wait for you. I waited near the basement's secret entrance all night, but only saw servants leave. It was now that I picked up Darek's fresh scent in the halls."

"Phew," breathed Darek, brushing off the sweat from his forehead. "And thank God for that. I would've been stuck there."

Thedes headed for the door.

"Where are you going now?" said Azura.

Thedes said fretfully, "Don't you see the city in ruins? I must find my master immediately! He needs my help!" He feared the worst and disappeared from the room.

"We might as well leave too," said Azura, exhaling. "There's nothing more we can do. The elders are dead. The city is destroyed. It's all over. Let's just find the spaceship and go."

Looking rather perplexed, Darek blinked. "Where's Sorren?"

"Um…he said he'd meet us at the ship," said Azura. "He's…getting it ready."

"Azura?" Darek observed her strange reaction to his question and became suspicious of her behavior. "You're not good at lying. What happened to Sorren?"

"Nothing!" She insisted. "He's waiting for us. Now let's hurry!" She walked to the door and anxiously gestured for him to leave the room with her.

"Azura." Again, Darek pressed the question, "What happened to Sorren? Is he okay?"

Azura laid her hands on his shoulder and said with an unconvincing smile, "I'll explain everything later. But we have to leave—right now!"

"You're starting to sound like Sorren," said Darek, giving her a dirty look. "Tell me, did something happen?"

"Be careful!" Azura yanked Darek away from the window right when a loud whoosh came from behind.

Darek checked his jacket and there was a clean rip on the back. Had Azura not moved him a few inches away, he would've been sliced in half.

Sorren was standing by the window with his sword drawn.

He said, "Let's make this quick."

CHAPTER 28
Invasion

Windzer knocked on the entrance of an underground shelter, calling out to whoever was within. The metal trapdoor that led to the underground passage was securely bolted from the inside. The latch slowly unlocked, the trapdoor opened, and a man stuck his head out.

"Tell everyone to get out now," Windzer ordered.

The man frowned. His visage was wrinkled with anxiety and fear. "Why continue? We've lost. Let us surrender and end this already."

"Get out!" Windzer barked. "We'll fight until the end."

The man nodded and hesitantly called for the others. Anguish had made him lose heart. He obeyed Windzer because that was the code they always followed. But regardless of his obedience, he sincerely believed that it was hopeless to continue the fight. To him, this war was already over. No matter what they did, it would not change that fact. But to Windzer, this was not the end—far from it.

A sound came from behind them. It sounded like something heavy was being dragged across the dirt. Windzer glanced back. Rendall was limping over rubble. His leg was badly hurt. His skin was burnt all over. He was not able to escape the last attack unscathed.

Outraged, Rendall said, "I thought you knew what you were doing! I trusted you!"

Windzer said, almost mockingly, "Tell me, what did I do wrong? There was a slight miscalculation, to be sure. But I did what I could. Most of the citizens are alive."

"The city is destroyed!" Rendall exclaimed. "There's nothing left! What do we protect now? We now have nothing! Our home, our utopia, is now gone—up in smoke!"

"Is that all?" Windzer took him by the shoulder and waved at the city with his hand. "Look! Look clearly at this world of yours and understand this: the walls, buildings, and the very foundations of this city meant *nothing* from the beginning! I would never waste my effort to protect wood and stone. What is important among this rubble? The lives of the people. As long as the people still stand, my purpose is fulfilled."

Rendall removed Windzer's hand from his shoulder and said, "We're alive for now. If they toppled our fortress in less than an hour, how little time will it take to wipe *us* out? You say you'll protect the people, but with what means? There is nothing to protect them with!"

"Calm down," said Windzer slowly. "This isn't over. Their show of force was merely a bluff. They spent all their strength in one blow to crush our city. They should be greatly weakened." Windzer held up the pendant in his hand, letting it dangle before Rendall's eyes. "You put your trust in me—and I will not betray that trust. So listen to me. We can fight them and win. We have nothing left to lose but our lives."

Rendall lowered his head and rubbed his finger across his temple in thought. "What do you propose we do now?"

"They will be coming in full force from all around," Windzer replied. "They'll attack from earth, sky and sea. I want everyone to hide and pretend to be dead. Their forces will be unsuspecting. Then, when they are all in the city, we will ambush them."

At that moment, the final trumpet echoed across the sky.

"We don't have time to prepare," said Rendall. "They're coming!"

Everything around them was in turmoil. All nature was in chaos. The immortals tripped and fell as the land rattled fiercely. The waves of the ocean rose higher and higher, crashing against the cliffs, overflowing into the fields. The skies rumbled. The winds played a tug-of-war, pushing and pulling everything with powerful gusts that went to and fro.

"Then just make sure everyone is armed and ready to make a stand," said Windzer. "We can still win this without an ambush! As long as the people are willing to fight—"

"Please stop! No more!" cried the townspeople. "We surrender!"

The immortals crept out of their hiding places. Fearing for their lives, they took off their armor and weapons and fell to the ground in reverence. "Don't hurt us anymore! We don't want to die..." They sobbed and bowed repeatedly toward the sky in repentance.

"What do they think they're doing?" said Windzer in disdain.

Rendall said, "It seems you're the only one who wants to keep fighting."

Windzer drilled the shaft of his scythe into the dirt. "That's because I know that these Guardians will not accept surrender! It is too late for that! Are we going to let them destroy us without a fight?"

The hundreds of great lights that hung over the despairing multitude began to scatter toward the earth like fiery shooting stars. The Guardians, which were now in human form, were fast approaching, appearing as warmongering soldiers descending from the twilight sky. They charged with their elliptical shields in front; the Guardians brandished their double-edged swords and giant spears, all imbued with the power of their respective elements.

When the immortals saw the army of Guardians raining down from the heavens, they raised their hands high as a sign of abandoning their cause. The people continued to cry out to the Guardians, "Forgive us! We surrender!" But the Guardians showed no apparent evidence of desire to stop the war.

Windzer called out to the weeping mob, "Listen to me! They will not stop! You must fight or they will trample over your bodies mercilessly!"

But all of the immortals ignored Windzer's voice and continued to stretch out their hands, reaching for the sky. Everyone stuck together, forming one large conglomerate mass that waved thousands of open hands in the air. They wailed for mercy in unison and begged for their lives to be spared.

"These people will not listen to reason!" sputtered Windzer. "I don't understand. We can win this only if they stand to fight." He curled his lip. "Why won't they listen?"

"Maybe they're having a relapse," said Rendall. "Their fear of what happened nearly a hundred years ago remains in their hearts. There was nothing they could do then, so they must still be thinking that there is nothing they can do now."

The people moaned in their despondence. The salty tears would not stop flowing. While the Guardians above bellowed their war cries, the immortals below screamed out their cries for mercy. It was a sight that Windzer found repulsive.

Since the townspeople resigned themselves to simply wait and do nothing, Windzer finally decided to take matters into his own hands. He glared at the crowd of immortals and screamed, "Run and hide, you pathetic cowards! You may have given up all hope, but I have not! You undeserving nation, why won't you stand up and fight to save your own lives? I will fight your battle! Remember until the moment you perish that I fought for you!"

Windzer turned his glare to the Guardians that were prepared to storm the remnants of the land. He squeezed the scythe with his grip and twirled it around. Shades of purple swirled with intense energy and formed an aura around him. He then, with a mighty blow, struck the head of his scythe against the ground; the visible energy was shattered, dissipating into the earth.

Windzer told Rendall, "Protect me."

Rendall wasn't quite sure of what Windzer was doing, but he nodded back.

Windzer became enclosed in a radiating ray of violet. "Come forth my minions—all you creatures, beasts and monsters of the earth! To battle! Today you shall fight for my sake as I have fought for yours!"

The galling noises of screeching and cawing filled the air. The forests weaved and stirred. All of a sudden, a massive black cloud formed in the distance and soared toward the capital. The cloud was actually the combination of hundreds of monsters. They flew overhead as one flock, casting a massive shadow over the weeping immortals. All sorts of beasts were in the sky: bat-like monsters called Ruevens with six beady eyes and a neck that twisted like rubber; odd beasts known as Vaiers, which had long bodies shaped like the quill of a feather, long and flat; the reptilian Zortzels, which were capable of spewing acid through holes in their tongues; and many other strange things came to fight on Windzer's behalf. Together, these monsters formed a thick shield around the immortals, preparing to intercept the enemy.

Once the Guardians got closer, the swarm of flying beasts scattered and burst forth like pellets from a shotgun blast. Shrieking wildly, they attacked the Guardians with whatever they could, whether it was by clawing with powerful talons or gnashing down with serrated beaks and teeth. The Guardians tore through the monsters with their blades, spilling copious amounts of blood.

While the battle between the monsters and the Guardian spirits raged above them, Windzer kept still and silent within the beam of light. He appeared to be meditating with his eyes closed and his breathing regulated.

Rendall said, concerned, "What are you doing?"

"Don't speak—to me—unless important," said Windzer, his face strained. He spoke as though it was hard to form words. "I need—concentration—for control. Every creature—demands attention."

Suddenly, many helmets began popping up from the ocean. Guardians rose up and floated upon the surface of the water, as if they were buoys. Water dripped from their drenched armor as they headed for shore, walking calmly upon the waves. Once the whole army reached the beach, they fervently charged at the ruined capital together, dragging their swords across the sand.

Seemingly in tandem, many hands broke out from under the dirt at the outskirts of the capital. Covered in speckles of sand and rock, the Guardians pulled themselves out of the earth. They dusted off the grime from their faces and brandished their weapons so that they could join their comrades in war.

Rendall said, "Would you consider being surrounded on all sides as something important?"

Windzer briefly opened his eyes and glanced over the two smaller armies that traveled along the ground. "I'll handle—the south. You—head north. Take Hortmel—and any other—help you can—find."

Then Windzer broke his concentration for a second and shouted in a thunderous voice, "Come forth, Yvairedey! Crush the southern army!"

The monstrous earthworm violently broke out from the subterranean tunnels below and it emitted such a low, deafening cry that it sounded more like a deep oscillating roar to the onlookers below. The worm slammed its body in a rolling fashion over the army of Guardians, grinding them into the ground.

The Guardians ducked for cover from the relentless bashing that took place. Every powerful strike from the worm caused earthquakes that sent boulders sailing through the sky.

"It's coming again!" the warriors screamed. "What kind of monster is that?"

Meanwhile, Rendall accepted Windzer's instructions and proceeded to execute it swiftly. He ran to the throng of immortals, who still had their hands raised to the sky, and commanded them, "Heed my words—the words of an elder! Follow me! We'll make our stand against those beasts of war that destroyed our homes!"

But in spite of his supposed absolute authority, almost everyone there ignored him and continued on with their grieving. Only a few loyal men and women came up to him and, on bended knee, said, "We will continue to serve you. Please give us your orders."

Rendall took the few loyal soldiers, along with Hortmel, and they marched to the wrecked northern gates, where the Guardians were running to meet them in battle.

"Can we really win this?" said Rendall. "Taking on a hundred of those Guardians with only a few men? This is absurd! Hortmel, do you have any tricks up your sleeve for this?"

Hortmel grunted in reply. He took his club and smashed it on the ground. The wood chips flew off, revealing a short but stout sword that was hidden within the club. He drew out sturdy chains from his belt and linked it with the hilt of the sword, forming a chain blade. Taking the sword of the chain blade, he twirled it above his head like the beating of the rotor blades of a helicopter; he was spinning it so hard that it whirred and even gained lift off the ground. Hortmel slung his blade forward and it tore through the ranks of the Guardians.

One of the Guardians ran straight into Hortmel's chain blade and it sliced him perfectly in half. After the Guardian was severed, his body was reformed inside a green crystal.

Hortmel was like a skilled acrobat as he swung his chain blade around. He would thrust the chain blade forward and spin around with it, flailing it about while he performed flips and cartwheels. The result was a massive destructive torrent that left ruin and crystallized Guardians in its wake.

Rendall was quite amazed by Hortmel's incredible display of power. Now that Hortmel and Windzer were leading the battle, his spirit was lifted; the situation was much brighter.

"Windzer was right! They *are* much weaker now!" Rendall transformed into a lion and roared to the others with him, "Come on, men! Show them the might of the Immortal Alliance!"

Windzer stood in the same place for ten minutes. He wouldn't move. He had to remain perfectly still in order to maintain control over his monsters. If anything were to break his hold on the monsters, the result would be an embarrassingly quick end to the battle.

But at the moment, he wondered if it would make a difference because he was starting to have his doubts about whether they could make it out alive. In spite of his best efforts, his monsters would be unable to defeat the Guardians. Slowly but surely, the Guardians were gaining the upper hand in the tide of battle. The dead bodies of monsters continued to fall from the sky, pounding the battlefield with loud thuds. It was only a matter of time before the entire swarm of beasts was crushed.

Falling from the sky, a lucent ball of white fire came hurtling towards him. Windzer took notice of it and commanded several Zortzels to stop it. But the Zortzels, upon reaching it, flared up. The blood inside their veins boiled until their bodies literally exploded.

The ball of fire steadied its approach and gently landed in front of Windzer. The flames subsided, revealing Beld in full view before him. "I knew there was something strange going on here," said Beld. "You must have told them of our powers."

"What of it?" said Windzer. He did not particularly fear the Guardian, but there was a sense of powerlessness in this situation that held him in anxiety. He could not move from that spot, and since the others were too far away, there was no one to defend him either.

"Don't worry. I won't hold a grudge." Beld grinned with satisfaction. "Because it's finally checkmate."

CHAPTER 29
Deathmatch

"Back off, Azura," Sorren said. "Stop getting in my way."

"No," snapped Azura, "you back off. Darek hasn't done anything wrong!"

"You won't change your mind?" asked Sorren.

"No," answered Azura. "I'm not that pathetic."

Without warning, Sorren's shadow on the floor started to move on; it became a solid black form that lashed out from the ground beneath his feet. The attack was aimed for Darek, but Azura jumped to intercept. The impact of the shadow knocked her into the wall.

Azura got back up immediately, unfazed. "I guess we can't resolve this peacefully."

After closing her eyes for a split second, she disabled her nociceptors to avoid pain. A quick stretch of her arms and legs made her feel ready for anything. Sorren broke out a smile, but it was different from his usual calm smiles; his smile was now much more savage and beastly.

"I'll give you this warning: this fight won't end until someone dies." Sorren stretched out his hand and his hardened shadow began bombarding her with bludgeoning attacks.

Azura dodged the onslaught of his dark powers. The attacks he threw were fast, but she was able to evade them by sensing their movement in the air. She was used to this and was able to maneuver around it easily. Azura slipped past his dark arts and got close to him; once in close range, she hammered her fist against the pit of his stomach, causing him to buckle.

Sorren almost tipped over as he lost his breath. He recovered, straightening without so much as a wince. "You could have landed a few more blows."

Azura cracked her knuckles one by one. "I could've. But I'm still trying to figure out what you're doing here. You're acting really strange."

Sorren raised his sword vertically to cover half of his face, his lips mouthing words. Then, in the blink of an eye, his body vanished into a wisp. A loud ringing sound from his pulsating blade resounded throughout the chamber. Azura occasionally swung her head left and right, glancing about the room, her pupils bouncing rapidly. It was only by unwavering focus that she was able to catch glimpses of Sorren's afterimages as they were dispersed across the room.

Darek remembered this technique from his dreams. He wanted to utter words of advice, but his distraught state of mind left him unable to do anything but mouth words helplessly. His fears came true: the same Sorren, who had helped them out mere moments ago, was now seeking to take their lives. His blood thirst knew no bounds; his killing intent struck deep into Darek's mind, inducing terror. The feelings Darek had were similar to when he faced Sorren in his dreams. The only difference was that death would be real.

Azura heightened the speed of her eyes even further. Her eyes shifted from side to side, blurring her pupils. When she saw the fleeting image of the tip of his blade, she thrust her knuckles ahead. Her strong fist smashed into Sorren's grip on the hilt and the bones in his fingers cracked from the blow. Sorren reappeared, crouching on the ground. Wincing, Sorren clutched his hand. Several fingers were broken.

Azura sharply kneed Sorren in the face with such an impact that made him stand upright. He staggered back, but she did not relent. Azura let her fists fly; the might of her punches whistled through the air and struck him all over, nearly crushing the bones in his body.

As she tried to catch her breath, Sorren rotated his body and slipped off one of her punches. Having broken free from her assault, he rammed his shoulder against her. While his body was close to hers, he grabbed her arm and pushed up with the strength of his hips, initiating a body throw that tossed her across the room and out the window. She reflexively let her hand fling out and barely managed to cling onto the edge of the windowsill with her fingertips. But that was enough for her and, using only one hand, she pulled herself up.

Seeing as Sorren was right there waiting for her to jump back up, Azura spun her whole body, kicking to clear out a path. Sorren retreated and they returned to their initial positions, as if nothing ever happened.

"This could take a while," Azura grumbled.

They stood just a few feet of each other, closing the gap between them with small steps. Tension mounted as they exchanged glances, wondering whether to attack or to wait for a chance to counter. Azura struck first. Her punch just barely slipped off his cheek, but because she forced it through with the full strength of her body, she still managed to knock him off balance. Taking this chance in her favor, she floored him with a sweeping kick. The back of his head hit the ground first, sending him into a daze. Azura kept him pinned down. She pulled her arm back, maximizing her strength. Desperate to escape from her hold, Sorren clenched his fingers against her throat, but she ignored it and smashed him into the ground with a single punch. The floor crumbled away; everyone fell into the chamber below.

Sorren jumped out of a heap of rubble and dusted himself off. He felt a stinging sensation around his mouth and wiped his lip to discover drops of blood.

"It's good that you're serious," he said, grinning.

In the midst of her rage, Azura growled. She shifted her strength into her legs. The result was a powerful pounce. Then, as she reached her prey, she shifted her strength back into her arms and bashed Sorren back. Azura did not relent. With blistering speed, she continued to pummel Sorren from one side of the room to the other. With one last roundhouse kick, she sent him flying into the wall. Then she got down on one knee, breathless. Normally, she'd have enough energy to keep going, but she had already expended most of her strength fighting immortals in the Tower of Legai.

Sorren got back up. Though battered and bloody, he didn't seem to be in pain. A mist of darkness crept in through the cracks along the wall and floor. It gathered near his feet and he bent down to touch it. The thin wave of darkness lifted over him and wrapped tightly around his body like a cloak, turning him invisible.

Azura didn't know what to make of it. At first she thought it might be a simple trick similar to when he was moving too fast to see. Such a thing was easy for Azura to deal with. Her senses were far beyond a normal human's. Though he may hide the body from sight, he cannot hide movement or smell, things she can detect fairly well.

Azura was rooted in place. She whipped her head side to side, analyzing every inch of the room with extreme scrutiny. But she could not detect a single remaining trace of Sorren's presence. He had vanished, not only from sight, but hearing and smell as well. Could he have left the room without her knowing it?

There was a sudden draft by her fingers. She slipped her hand away as a cold blade tickled the hairs on the back of her hand.

"You're still here…" She could hardly believe it. Azura could not detect him at all, even though he was so close. It was now that she realized the truth. His anti-law only worked to hide his body. He had erased his presence by technique. His steps were absolutely silent; his movement avoided pushing air toward her; and he moved so swiftly that his scent was perfectly smeared across the room.

But she was not about to be outdone so easily. Even though she was exhausted, Azura still had several techniques up her sleeve. Scowling, she started to snarl and growl ferociously. Then, like a lion, she let out a thundering ROAR!

Sorren stopped moving, not by his own will, but rather by hers. His body had been paralyzed by fear. It was an instinctual fear, like a prey being frozen in submission in the face of a predator. Sorren couldn't help but be amazed at his helpless situation. He had learned to suppress fear through countless life and death battles, but now it was invoked by her stunning ferocity.

Since he was still, Azura took the time to accurately determine his position. She struck her fist forward, toward the air, where it looked as if nothing was there. The shadow veil was shattered like a broken mirror. The strike nearly crushed his Adam's apple and left him gagging and paralyzed.

Azura was not letting this opportunity escape her. She knew he would not be as vulnerable if they dragged out this fight; all she could tell was that he was holding back. If she wanted to end this fight, now was the time. She viciously struck his vital points repeatedly in succession. Sorren wasn't able to react because his brain was being jostled about.

However, perhaps out of mixed feelings, she missed her target once. Sorren could move again. He retaliated as fast as he could. There were no more tricks from this point forward. Azura knew that if he tried that invisibility anti-law once more, she might not survive. A head on fight was her forte and she was going to see this through to the end.

Azura unleashed her fists, landing several blows, while dodging Sorren's strikes, which she was not able to escape from completely. Their attacks were imprecise, stemming from the bewilderment as to why they were fighting each other in the first place. Blood sprinkled like a gentle fountain, staining the walls and the floors with dots of crimson. But no matter how much they were being cut and hurt, neither side was willing to give in.

Darek watched them tear each other apart in this escalating brawl. He could only watch in horror and fear as his two friends were at each other's throats, quite literally. However, while this fray prevailed on the outside, something was happening on the inside of his mind. Sealed memories of the past were being evoked piece by piece.

"This is just like that time," uttered Darek, thinking upon the past. "When everything was taken away..." As Darek's memories began to surface, his vision became fuzzy and warped. All he could see was flashing lights as the world before him faded away. Yes—he finally remembered the truth about that day, for it had been sealed through the passages of time.

The orphanage, which he had lived in, was never a normal orphanage. Those who knew its purpose also knew that it was nothing like an orphanage. The children who lived there were not necessarily orphans to begin with. In fact, even Darek wasn't an orphan.

"Mom!" Darek came running full speed through the front door. "I did it! I finally did it!"

His mother, Allys Wayker, scolded him, "You should know better. Someone could hear you. Call me Miss Kurt."

"I'm sorry," said Darek, looking abashed. "I forget when I'm excited."

"And please," Allys warned, "speak softly. No one must overhear our conversation."

Darek nodded glumly, bowing his head.

Allys shook her head for a moment and then broke into a smile; she couldn't stay angry with her son for long. "Now, what did you do?"

Though excited, he said softly, "I manifested my power."

"Really?" Her eyes widened. "Show me."

Darek gazed at his hands with complete concentration. After a few seconds, they were illuminated with a fiery glow. The strings of light coiled around his fingers and slowly materialized into black gloves.

Allys's eyes glittered when she saw his newfound power. She embraced her son tightly. "That's great! I'm so proud of you. You accomplished it just in time!" She examined his hands and said, "But what do they do? What kind of power is this?"

A little dejected, he shrugged and said, "I don't know. It doesn't do anything."

Allys could see the worry imprinted on his countenance. She smiled and said, "This is the first step. No one can use their powers fully when they first get them."

Darek frowned. "Slade and Elize have no problems with their powers."

Allys said, "I'm sorry, Darek. I wish I could help you, but I can't. I'm only a Vespar. I don't know anything about your powers. But tonight, when you meet with the others, they'll be able to teach you everything you need to know."

Rex barged into the room. "Oh, there you are, Darek! Did you finish your chores yet? I need you to help me look for something."

"Okay," said Darek, as he jammed his hands into his pocket nervously. "I'll be right there. Wait for me at the backyard."

Rex ran off. Darek was about to leave as well, but his mother clung onto his shirt. He turned back with a quizzical look on his face.

Allys said, "You mustn't let Rex see your power. He's a normal person."

Sounding annoyed, Darek said, "I know, I know. You've told me a million times! Do you really think I'd forget something that important?"

Allys said, "I'm more worried that you might accidentally trigger your power. You haven't had experience controlling it yet. If your power manifests, do your best to hide it."

On that day, three strange visitors wandered the streets of the small town of Marwood. These mysterious men wore brown trench coats. They strolled around town, careful to hide their faces.

"Khris," said one of the men, "according to our information, they should be here."

Khris nodded. "No doubt we'll encounter Vespar patrols."

"Vespar? Oh, is that the name for those—"

"Yes," replied Khris. "The Vespar—the independent division of Heroes who work for the Judges. They're trained warriors. It'll be dangerous to deal with them."

The man said, "Can you locate them?"

Khris said, "I can spot them easily. I've worked closely with them before. But it won't be easy to get rid of all of them. I estimate five or so patrolling the neighborhood and fifteen or more at the outskirts of town."

"It shouldn't be too hard for you to clear the town, right?" said the other man. "By nightfall, we can make our final move. The only question is if we can find the right house in time. We can't storm the houses carelessly or else the other guards will react."

While lying in bed, Darek looked out at the moons that clear night. He was filled with mixed feelings and couldn't sleep. A part of him was excited, bursting with joy and adrenaline. It was time for his life to change—time for him to move on. He was finally going to be a Judge with Slade and Elize. This is what he wanted to do, but there was another part of him that deeply regretted this. It was because they would no longer be complete. Out of this close group of four friends, there was one who didn't match. Rex was not one of them and, by the morning, Darek would never see Rex ever again.

Rex was truly an orphan. His parents died in the war when he was young. But there were no orphanages around and no one wanted to take care of him. Was it luck or destiny that brought him to their doorstep? Darek wasn't sure. But Darek did understand that Rex had become a firm part of their group. However, not everyone could become a Judge. Candidates for Judges were chosen at birth. Rex could never become a part of their secret world.

"Darek!" Slade was outside the house, peering through the window. "Get out here, now!"

Darek grunted, "What's going on?" He tied his shoes in a hurry.

"Rex isn't in his bed," Elize explained quietly. She grabbed her bag and motioned for Darek to follow her out.

"Did you double check?" said Darek, unconvinced. "Maybe he's hiding somewhere."

"We've checked everywhere," said Elize. "He has to be outside!"

"Then we should probably tell Mom," said Darek. "We shouldn't be going out tonight. She warned us it could be dangerous…"

"Are you kidding? She'd kick out Rex," said Slade. "He was never one of us. If she finds out he disobeyed the rules—"

"No," said Darek. "We'll all be in big trouble if she finds out we snuck out!"

Slade said in a strong whisper, "Hush! You'll wake her up! Who cares about that anyway? The Judge will be coming soon to take us. We won't be in trouble! Let's just go get Rex and come back!"

Darek conceded and followed them out, closing the door behind them gently; once they were outside, they darted through the streets.

"Rex must be looking for his paper airplane," said Slade. "He looked pretty bummed about losing it this afternoon. I told him we could call it off, but he still—"

Elize pointed down the road. Though it was dark and there were no lights, she could make out several silhouettes. "There are some people there, maybe they've seen him."

Rex was actually among the group of four people who were standing suspiciously in the streets. Darek overheard Rex say to the other men around him, "Who are you people? What do you want?"

"Just tell us where the orphanage is in this town," said one of the men. The three men were strangers in trench coats.

Rex growled, "No! I don't even know who you are!"

"Rex!" said Darek, running to meet him. "What's going on here?"

"There they are!" said one of the men. "Those are the children!"

One of the men grabbed Rex from behind, pulled a knife to his neck and then said to the children, "Stop where you are or your friend here will bleed."

Wary of the dangerous confrontation, Slade pulled Elize and Darek back. Slade knew that Rex wouldn't be able to defend himself in a scuffle. He wanted to avoid a conflict at all costs.

"Calm down," said Slade. "We only want to know what you want."

"You are what we want." A man stepped forward. "More precisely, we want you dead."

Darek rubbed his eyes and looked upon the man's visage once again. It was a tall thin bearded man that Darek knew.

"Dad?" said Darek. "Is that you?"

The man beamed at Darek. "Look at you," he said. "My, you've grown so fast."

The man was Khris Wayker, a Hero among Heroes and father of Darek.

"What are you doing here?" said Darek. "You shouldn't be here."

"I've come to take you home," Khris replied. "You don't have to be a Judge."

Darek snapped, "You of all people should know that this is my destiny!"

Khris said scornfully, "Destiny? You're just spewing the nonsense your mother has been feeding you! The life of a Judge is no laughing matter. You'll live your life in hiding, stalking through the shadows and seeking blood. After you've become a Judge there is no way to escape it except by death. Is that what you really want?" His lips curved into a smile. "Come with me. We can go home and you can live a normal life."

Darek knew what he wanted. He always wanted to be a Judge. There were many tales that his mother had read to him about the courageous deeds and the suffering they endured to make it possible for the hopes and dreams of others to thrive. He always wanted to change the universe for the better, even if it meant throwing his life away. Darek yelled, "Stop putting words in my mouth! I want to be a Judge and that's that!"

Darek's mother, Allys Wayker—who had taken on the alias of Jess Kurt to protect her son's identity—heard the outside commotion of barking dogs. Since it was the middle of night, she was still in her rose-patterned pajamas and her hair was a mess, but she was always cautious and decided to inspect the cause of commotion, regardless of her attire. Allys was concerned when she saw that the kids were not in their beds.

But Allys did not storm out the house; instead, she crept quietly above the tree branches, and when she saw everyone on the streets, she listened to their conversation from afar. Allys recognized her husband, a Hero who was sworn to secrecy about the Judges, and knew without a doubt that he was up to no good. But her highest priority was to rescue Rex, for he was but an innocent child.

Allys drew a thick needle from her side and licked the tip with her tongue. Her saliva was poisonous, but to refrain from killing, she normally used only trace amounts to paralyze opponents. With pinpoint accuracy, she flung the needle and it penetrated the shoulder of the man who held onto Rex. The man released his grip; his entire arm went numb and he flailed it about, appalled at his arm's condition. Rex tried to run, but the other man pulled out a gun and was prepared to open fire.

Allys landed near Rex and fired off several more needles, which she had hidden under her clothes. The man wanted to pull the trigger, but the needles had already slipped into the barrel of the gun and jammed it. She then finished him off quickly, impaling him with ten needles in a fraction of a second. The man convulsed a bit, then slumped to the ground as his limbs seemed to wither; only his eyes could move now and he did nothing but stare wide-eyed at the one who paralyzed him.

"Ah, Allys," said Khris, grinning. "Another person I wanted to see. Don't you want to run away with Darek and me? We can go somewhere nice. I've already quit being a Hero."

"What do you think you're doing?" snapped Allys. "Have you gone mad? Don't you understand how serious the situation is? Go back to Fallence this instant and maybe you can be pardoned by the Overlord for this crime."

"Mad?" barked Khris. "What's wrong with a man who wants to stay with his family? Why should some garbage of a destiny pry my wife and kids out of my hands? Who cares about the Heroes and the Judges? There are enough of them! We don't need to get involved. This is *our* life we're talking about. I'm not letting anyone else tell us what to do with it!"

Then he softened his voice and said tenderly, "It's been so long since I've last seen the two of you. It took me forever to find you. I even had to go to the underworld to seek help in locating you. At the very least, can't this whole Judges thing wait until Darek is older?"

"What's gotten into you?" said Allys. "This is the way it's always been throughout the generations. How can we step away from tradition for selfish reasons?"

"I see you're as stubborn as always," said Khris. "No matter. I'll take Darek with me. He's barely thirteen years old! He should have a real chance at life. If you want to come, great, but if not, then…this is goodbye." Khris approached Darek, but Slade and Elize tried to stop him.

Khris swung the flat of his blade against them, knocking them unconscious. He had a beautiful amber-colored sword. Its form was clean, perfect and stainless. Its cross-guard was crafted to look like the wings of an angel.

With a quick snap of her wrist, Allys hurled a wave of needles against Khris, but he deflected it skillfully with his sword. Allys continued to bombard Khris with wave after wave of needles, her hands and arms moved so fast that it gave off the illusion of having over ten arms. She kept drawing needles from all over her body; her clothes were packed with them, but how she kept hundreds of these needles from being even slightly visible was a mystery known only to her. However, her barrage had no effect, and so she engaged in a close-combat battle, thinking that all she needed was one clean hit to leave him disabled.

They were both overly cautious, without even a pinch of killing intent. Khris only wanted to be a family again, but Allys knew that they could not go against the way of things, out of fear of the consequences. Though they fought each other, they both knew in their hearts that they did not want to hurt each other.

But even so, Khris was stubborn. But did he have a right to be? When his son had turned five, the Vespar had told Khris that his son had been chosen to become a Judge. It was unfair. Khris would never see his son ever again—unless he disobeyed the Legion.

Ever since Darek had been taken away, Khris had communicated with everyone he could, even the most dubious of characters, on the subject. He had gone deep into the underworld, the place of chaos and villainy, to gain their trust and aid in the matter. He had also made agreements he wished he had never made. This was one of them. Khris had agreed to hand over the other children to the leaders of the underworld to confirm the existence of the Judges.

Bang! A loud shot echoed through the small village. The blood on her garments and the pained expression upon Allys's anguished face said it all: she had been shot. Her assailant was a sniper from the distance who was watching Khris' back. The fired shot alerted Vespar around the forests and they quickly detained the sniper and any others hidden with him.

Khris was as shocked as Allys was. He had never intended to hurt his wife, but the others had recruited snipers to ensure their success. In tears, he watched his wife bend down in agony. Khris wrapped his arms around her, embracing her and shielding her from any further attacks.

"Look...what you did..." said Allys in a feeble voice. She had been hit in a vital area and the bleeding wouldn't stop. "You fool..." Emotionless, she buried her face into his chest.

Khris's hands trembled uncontrollably as he held onto her lifeless body. Gently, he pressed his cheek against hers and sobbed; they remained on the ground, interlocked and motionless.

Interrupting this tranquil, sorrowful moment was a Judge; he had appeared out of the strange door that stood in the middle of the road. Upon seeing the scene before him, he deduced what had taken place.

The Judge drew forth his sword. With the tip of his blade he tapped on Khris's shoulder.

"You should know very well the penalty for meddling in these affairs, Hero."

Khris laid his wife's body on the dirt road and turned to the Judge. "I know," he replied, his voice trembling. "It is my fault. I will accept responsibility."

"No—wait!" Darek ran to stop the Judge, but it was too late. The Judge slashed him.

Placing his hand over the huge wound on his chest, Khris staggered to the cliff overlooking the valley below.

"Dad!" Darek cried out.

"Stay back." With an open palm, Khris gestured for Darek to stay where he was. "Darek, I'm so sorry...I didn't think it'd end this way...I only wanted..." Khris lost his footing and fell off the cliff, disappearing into the woods below.

"NO!" Darek crawled to the edge of the cliff and looked down, searching for the body of his father. "No...what is this...this isn't what I wanted..." Shaking his fist, he screamed to the heavens, "THIS ISN'T WHAT I WANTED! COME BACK!"

The Judge helped Elize and Slade up. "So you are the candidates. We must leave quickly before anything else should go wrong."

Elize looked over her shoulder and glanced at Darek. "Darek's one of us too."

Darek stormed up to the Judge and shouted, "You've already taken away my family...I have nothing left here! Take me with you!"

The Judge looked at Darek with sorrowful eyes and said, "I'm sorry, but it is no longer your time. I don't quite understand it, but destiny has changed."

"What do you mean?" stammered Darek.

"Show me your power," said the Judge. "Your power is your proof."

Darek held out his hands. In his grief, he tried to force out the gloves upon his hand. The gloves would not appear no matter how hard he tried. "What...this can't be...I don't understand. I could do it this morning!"

"I suppose it was the interference by the other boy," said the Judge. "I was the one who should have died tonight. Somehow, destiny was changed. You, Darek, were to be my replacement. I am taking Elize and Slade with me. With my life still intact, we have twelve."

"You can't be serious!" said Darek, frustrated. "You kill my father, you let my mother die, and you won't even respect my last wish?"

The Judge turned away. "This is the way it has become. I cannot do anything about it."

Darek said out of anger, "If I kill you, then will it be okay? Can I set things straight? Will I get my powers back? Will I—" Tears ran down his cheek. Vexed, his face was red in anger. Darek ran to the Judge, but his foot tripped over a rock. He fell on his face, weeping.

The Judge shook his head, disheartened by the way Darek was responding. "You do not have what it takes: an iron heart—a cold heart. Maybe this is why your destiny was changed. You are not yet fit to be a Judge. With that weak heart—you never will be a Judge." The Judge turned away again and told Elize and Slade, "Let us go. It is time."

"Elize! Slade!" said Darek, wiping away the tears. "Don't you guys dare leave me here!"

Elize picked Darek up and hugged him. "Be strong, Darek." Then she pushed Darek away and ran into the portal. Darek could hear her faint cries from the other side of the mystical door.

Slade simply acknowledged Darek by raising his fist while disappearing into the door. His voice echoed through, "I'm sorry. But I've got to do this. You understand, don't you?"

Darek kneeled on the ground before the portal. The Judge walked into it without so much as a goodbye. The door closed behind him and, shrinking away, it vanished without a trace. Darek was left behind. His dream of being a Judge would forever remain a dream. The last seven years of training had been in vain.

There was no point to remember those years wasted. There was no point in remembering his dreams of becoming a Judge. There was no point in remembering the death of his parents and the disappearance of his friends. There was no point to remember the truth. And so he conjured up a fictitious story, believing that his friends ran away and that his parents were never alive. He believed from that point forward, that he was alone and that he had no hope. On that day, Darek shriveled his memories into the cocoon of his mind, hoping never to remember.

CHAPTER 30
End of the World

"Darek," exclaimed Azura, "snap out of it!"

Darek shuddered. Just a moment before, he had been preoccupied about the past; what seemed to be the reliving of an unforgettable night, only took place in a matter of minutes. But now he was back inside the castle, once again observing the fight between Azura and Sorren.

However, the situation was not the same as before. Somehow, over the course of a few minutes, the stalemate that once existed between the two warriors had withered away into nothing. Azura's back was against the wall and she had suffered a number of painful injuries.

"Darek!" shouted Azura. "Why didn't you run?"

Sorren sheathed his sword and thrust his palm forward. A dark gooey liquid shot out of the floor and pinned Azura to the wall. She writhed about, attempting to break free from his grasp. The dark mass engulfed Azura and tightened around her, making it hard for her to breathe. She passed out. Then Sorren released his hold and her body sunk to the floor.

Darek stumbled as he retreated back. There was no place for him to hide or run. His only choice was to fight back. But if Azura couldn't win against Sorren, what chance did he have?

"Darek," said Sorren, "if you want to live, you know what to do."

Darek refused to speak to Sorren. Instead, he huddled in the corner of room, his face buried in his arms. After recalling his past, now he was afraid of Sorren for another reason: Sorren reminded him of his father. The resemblance had nothing to do with appearance, but rather his stubbornness and cruel betrayal.

"Sorren!" The door flung open. Windzer rushed into the room. "Are you in here—" A gasp came from his lips. He saw Azura stained in blood, lying unconscious on the ground. Then he noticed Darek in the far corner, frightened and in despair.

Windzer turned his eyes scornfully at Sorren. "What do you think you're doing?"

"None of your business," said Sorren.

"If you kill him," said Windzer, scowling, "you ruin everything!"

Sorren ignored Windzer's words and started to reach for the cowering Darek. But Windzer promptly slashed at Sorren.

"You wish to get in my way as well?" said Sorren.

"Get in your way? If I don't stop you, you'll regret it. I'm doing you a favor." Windzer stood in a defensive position, waiting for Sorren's next move.

Sorren smiled. "If you haven't noticed, it's dark out."

"I know," said Windzer.

"And you still wish to fight?"

"You know me. I never really cared about the odds."

Sorren raised his hands. The blackness of the extremely dark afternoon sky seemed to crawl into the room from the window. The mass of dark energies swirled upon his hands and was sucked into his palms, as if it were being drained; Sorren bared his teeth as the energy flooded into his bloodstream.

"Come forth now!" Windzer slammed the bottom of his scythe against the floor, sending a blue shockwave rippling across the floor. The walls of the chamber cracked and crumbled away, revealing the remains of the city below them.

Ear-piercing shrieks came from the outside. Clusters of Zortzels circled the castle and, upon Windzer's call, they dove into the chamber, thrusting their sharp beaks at Sorren.

As the flock of flying lizards came rushing towards him, Sorren flicked his hand up, prompting a wall of darkness to rise up and shield him. The lizards pounded against the dark mass. The weaker ones were repelled and sent back out of the castle. The stronger ones dropped to the ground like dead flies.

Windzer took the opportunity, now that Sorren was distracted, to sneak up behind him. Windzer slashed through the unsuspecting Sorren with his giant scythe—only to find that his body dissipated into the air. "A shadow…"

Sorren then reappeared next to Windzer and began his assault against him. His blade honed in on the weak points of the body and continued slashing, without any sign of losing momentum. Windzer defended himself well, making sure he would not even get cut. But he had been severely weakened by the heavy use of his powers beforehand and knew it would not be long before he would succumb to Sorren's blade. Every time their weapons clashed, Windzer thought his joints would snap apart like twigs. After being pushed back several times, Windzer felt a cold breeze. He glanced over his shoulder and was staring right outside, where the wall was gone. He was at the very edge of the floor. The gusts of wind started to make him waver and wane.

"Surrender," Sorren said. "You have nothing to do with this."

Windzer screamed at Sorren's face, "Hey, Vile, can you hear me?"

Darek wondered what was going on. It looked like Windzer was talking to someone else. But there was no one else in the room with them.

Windzer was cornered by Sorren's steady advance and could not see a way to escape. "Why won't you respond? Vile! Come here!"

Sorren stopped his attack, revealed a cruel smile, and then said in a dark tone, "It isn't my time to awaken. Why must you call me out?"

"Finally!" said Windzer with a sigh of relief. "Listen, Sorren is going to kill me if you don't do something. Take full control right now!"

Sorren shook his head. "He doesn't want me to and you know I don't want to disobey. Why should I care if he kills you anyway? You're already dead."

"He'll kill us all, even Darek! Regardless of what Darek might do in the future, you can't kill him for crimes he has yet to commit! Now, come on, I know you aren't heartless, and both you and I know that Sorren doesn't want to do this. Do as I say and take control. We have to get Darek out of here."

Sorren laughed wickedly. "You know *nothing*. I'll help you this once, but never again. In fact, if I ever see you again, I'll kill you. But since I owe you one, I guess one time won't hurt. But man, Sorren's going to be pretty mad when he wakes up." After Sorren said those words, the darkness encircled him.

Sorren cried intensely as a throbbing pain came over his mind. He held his head with his hands and threw himself to the ground, convulsing. It almost seemed like he was about to tear his hair out. His screams grew louder as he thrashed about, pounding his fist against the stone floor.

"What's going on?" Darek asked Windzer, concerned. "What's wrong with him?"

"He's…coming back to his senses," replied Windzer. "He'll be fine in a few seconds."

A wave of dead silence surfaced in the chamber. The screaming stopped and Sorren slowly rose again. He cracked a twitching smile that seemed nothing like his usual self. He was usually serious if not a bit dull, but now, he had changed into something else. To Darek, it looked as if Sorren was a different person.

"So," Windzer said to Sorren, "you have control?"

"Yeah," he replied once again in a deep voice. "Now what do you want me to do, master?" He said it sarcastically and laughed it off.

Windzer thought for a moment. "I don't know. I haven't thought that far ahead."

"Wait," interrupted Darek. "Before we do anything, I'd *really* like an explanation. One moment, Sorren is on our side, and then he turns on me without any hesitation. And now, after he had a painful seizure, he looks somewhat different. What's going on here?"

A loud rumbling overtook the castle. The rafters came tumbling down. The floors were splitting. The room was falling apart piece by piece. It almost seemed as if the whole building was swaying back and forth.

Windzer grunted, "No time to explain. Just leave it to your imagination."

The thick clouds began to fade away and the sun continued its trek across the sky; the pitch-black sky became smeared in a blend of orange, red and violet. The suffocating dust across the battlefield settled down. The stagnant stench of sweat and blood was blown away by a cleansing wind. Every sword and element was silenced. The battle was over.

A loud trumpet blast sounded the signal for retreat. Hundreds of Guardians used up the last of their energy to transform into orbs of light, taking to the skies in haste, leaving the desolate world.

The Guardians were gone and the immortals had won, but from the immortals came no cheer or dance of victory. The survivors looked wearily upon their once glorious domain and saw nothing but ashes. Even the castle, which had been constructed with the most ingenious plan of architecture that the greatest minds on the planet could conceive, was irreparable. The number of deceased totaled more than four thousand. The remaining immortals wasted no time to bury their dead.

"They sure left in a hurry," said Windzer, staring at the vanishing lights in the sky.

Sorren said enviously, "I don't blame them. The world won't last. If I could fly well, I'd be long gone too." His legs gave way. He knelt on the ground on his shaky knees trying to maintain his balance.

"What's wrong?" asked Windzer.

"This is your fault," growled Sorren. "Sorren is struggling to awaken. It's exhausting to keep him restrained against his will. I..." Without finishing another sentence, Sorren collapsed. After a period of inhaling and exhaling heavily, he lost consciousness.

"Don't blame me. Sorren started it." Windzer dragged Sorren under a tree where he could rest.

"It's not wise to leave him," said a deep voice from behind. "Best take him with us."

Windzer turned around and saw his friend. "Hortmel, you made it! I guess the Guardians couldn't keep you down, could they?"

"Of course not." Hortmel hummed, pleased with himself. "What about you? I didn't see you. Thought you were a goner."

"I thought so too," said Windzer as he recalled the event. "I came face to face with Beld. I was sure he was going to kill me."

"Then?"

"Some guys ambushed him from the back. Before I knew it, all the immortals were retaliating against the Guardians. Boy, was I in luck. I was totally exhausted. Wouldn't have been able to hold up the fort much longer."

"What do you think we should do now?"

Windzer considered their options. "Did you find our ship?"

"Everything in the basement was crushed," said Hortmel. "There's nothing left."

Windzer said, "Nothing at all?"

Doleful, Hortmel shook his head.

Windzer slammed his fist against the tree. "So we're really stuck here? Well, this is a fine way to die! Maybe I should have just let Sorren kill me. It would've been less stressful. Now we can count the seconds till we pass away. And Dionus gets his wish. We'll all perish here—including Darek."

Hortmel's eyes widened. "Dionus? Did you see him?"

"Sort of," said Windzer. "I saw him leave with some Heroes. It seems he has gained control of the Legion. I'm not entirely sure what he's planning, but he must be the reason why Sorren decided to attack Darek."

"Maybe he wants revenge."

"Maybe." Windzer nodded.

"So Dionus is alive and well," uttered Hortmel. Then Hortmel said jokingly, "It is a good time to die then. Wouldn't want to stay around for what happens next."

"Is that hysteria or joy?" said Windzer. "I haven't seen you laugh in a long time."

Darek came crawling out of the castle window with Azura sleeping comfortably on his back. He groaned and grunted every step of the way. His red face looked ready to burst. She was heavy and he was dreadfully tired. He never imagined she would be this heavy. After he settled her on the ground gently, he brushed off the sweat from his face.

Darek panted. "I can't believe you guys just left us back there." He glanced at Windzer. "It wasn't like you had anyone to carry. You could have at least waited or even helped me out."

"Sorry, sorry," apologized Windzer. "I forgot you guys were still in there."

"Forgot? You were talking to me!" Darek glared at Windzer with piercing eyes, but his eyes quickly softened as he caught sight of Sorren under the tree. "It doesn't make any sense…Why did Sorren—"

Windzer pursed his lips. "It's because you—"

"Wait," Hortmel interrupted him. "Should you really tell him?"

Windzer ignored Hortmel. "Darek, you are a Judge—you know that right?"

Darek shook his head. "I'm not really a Judge. I had the training but I never became—"

"You are a Judge," said Windzer strongly. "No human decides it. It is governed by destiny. The moment your powers awakened is the moment you have been elected. A Judge has been removed from his position."

"How do you know about my powers?" Darek was surprised by Windzer's knowledge.

Windzer pointed at Darek's hands. The gloves had formed again. "The gloves on your hand. I have high spiritual sensitivity and can tell that those gloves aren't real. Judges have the power to manifest their spirit into the physical realm."

Darek shrugged indifferently. "Okay, what does that have to do with anything? Even if I am a Judge, why does that matter?"

Windzer explained, "Sorren was born into an ancient assassination group known as the Black Raven Rogues, who were very dangerous. But the Judges exterminated the Black Raven Rogues long ago. He is the last survivor. Though his kind is now extinct, he would be considered a hunter of Judges—an avenger of sorts. Do you understand now? You are natural enemies, destined to fight each other."

"What?" Darek was stunned and could barely contain his bewilderment. "Can't he let it go? It was a long time ago, right? I guess he has a reason to be mad, but revenge is meaningless."

"He is a stubborn one," said Windzer.

Darek sighed. "I guess there's no helping it. That's a shame too. After all we've been through, I thought we could be friends. I probably shouldn't be here when he wakes up." Darek then turned his attention to the ruined city and pointed to it. "Is this the work of the Guardians? It looks like they meant business."

"Yeah," Windzer mumbled under his breath. "It wasn't pretty. I never expected it to be easy, but I never thought they'd go this far. Guardians are usually cautious beings. Because they no longer give birth and cannot repopulate, they keep their distance and retreat at the first sign of danger. But this time, they risked their lives completely, willing to die for the cause. It's almost as if they knew…" Windzer's voice trailed off, but Darek didn't seem to notice because he was preoccupied by many questions and thoughts.

Feelings of remorse swelled up inside Darek. He had never seen a real war, never saw the gloomy field of lifeless skin and bones, the testament of brutality on a large scale. He had always heard about them, but experiencing it firsthand was eye opening and even nauseating. Now that he caught a glimpse of it, it made him one step closer to understanding the atrocity of war.

"Have you seen Merdon around?" said Darek. Seeing the piles of corpses made him worried that someone he knew could've been buried under.

Windzer said, "I haven't. I left the battle early."

"I want to see for myself. Can you watch over Azura?" asked Darek.

"Sure," replied Windzer. "Do what you have to."

When Darek was gone, Hortmel said, "I don't mean to pry, but is there any reason you lied to him?"

Windzer chortled, "Because it's fun to see what happens next! If we make it out alive, things will be very interesting…"

Groaning, Sorren stirred in the grass. Windzer's annoying laughter woke him up. Recovering from a headache, Sorren said disdainfully, "What's so funny?"

"You've awakened," said Windzer. "Didn't think you'd be awake this early. Are you feeling all right?"

"As all right as I can be." He closed his eyes for a moment and groaned again. "What's the situation?"

Scratching his cheek, Windzer said, "World's going to end in an hour or two. No way to escape." He then noticed Sorren was walking away. "Where are you going?"

"There's something I must get," said Sorren.

"At a time like this?"

"There's no better time."

Darek wandered away from the castle ruins into the charred debris of the battlegrounds. Every step he took was carefully placed in order to avoid desecrating the bodies with the sole of his foot. Because he forced himself to look where he was walking, he couldn't help but see the faces of the dead looking back at him. Some of them had suffered severe burns that rendered them unrecognizable, while others had faces of anguish. It was ironic to him: they would die in fear, pain and agony; yet while their faces would be molded into that expression, their spirits may actually be at peace.

The whole planet began experiencing with violent tremors. The waves of the oceans popped and fizzled with hundreds of bursting bubbles that vaporized into steam. The grand trees of the forest were uprooted, toppling over. Swarms of animals and monsters took to the hills and open fields, scurrying in different directions, looking for a place to hide.

The planet split in half, as if it had been cut clean with a knife straight down the middle. The two hemispheres were lightly torn apart, but the gap was steadily widening.

"Wait! What? Is this it?" said Windzer. "It hasn't even been fifteen minutes!"

"Time's up," said Hortmel. "It's all over."

"There has to be some way!" Windzer grimaced at the thought of death.

Hortmel said, "All the optimism in the world doesn't change the fact that we've got, at most, a few minutes left."

"Give me some of your spirit," said Windzer suddenly.

"*What?*" Hortmel raised a brow.

"Just do it!" shouted Windzer. "There's no time!"

Hortmel's hand glowed green and with his hand, he smacked Windzer in the back. Windzer felt the slight boost of energy seep into his body. He slammed his scythe into the ground. "Get over here!"

The giant earthworm was resting its head upon a pillow comprised of tree branches, soft dirt and grass when it heard Windzer's call. It wriggled immediately across the landscape to find its master; as they met, it stood tall at attention and would have saluted too—if it had arms.

Windzer commanded it, "Swallow us up."

The worm nodded happily in reply.

"Will this really work?" said Hortmel, understanding what Windzer was trying to do.

Windzer snapped, "Right now, we don't have much of a choice, do we?"

Hortmel said, "But what about Sorren? Did you not want him to live for now?"

"It's his fault for running away at this time! There's nothing we can do about it."

They held onto Azura and waited patiently as the massive mouth of the worm came diving down on top of them, devouring them and the surrounding environment with one gulp.

Darek held firmly onto a nearby tree because it was hard for him to stay standing.

"Merdon, where are you?" he yelled with his hands around his mouth. "Is there anyone out there?"

The vibrations of the earth did not stop or pause, it had gone on for several minutes with no signs of slowing down and even started to increase in magnitude.

The land beneath his feet broke apart and he ran from the crumbling dirt that sank into the ground. A faint red glow seeped out of the cracks on the surface of the planet. This was not an isolated case, however, for all of the continents were breaking apart into millions of tiny islands that were now suspended over the expanding core.

Darek was now trapped and alone, kneeling on the floor. The fragmented pieces of land were actually being expelled a distance away from the core, such that it was practically floating high above and Darek was able to look down and see the core from a distance. The core had lost its luster and had changed so much that it was unrecognizable. It was now a giant unstable glob, covered by a dense, semi-transparent cloud.

A stray drop of magma was launched out of the core and splattered to the ground, just a few feet from where Darek was positioned. The tiny blob of lava squirmed around for a bit and then it shook about like a wet dog casting off excess water. Once the lava was whittled down, Darek saw that there was actually a little person inside.

Darek said, almost in tears, "Ios, you're alive! What a surprise!" While he was happy to see Ios, he was much more relieved to not be alone in his final hour.

"Ah, Darek," said Ios. "What luck! I've been sent to look for you!"

"Me?" said Darek, surprised. "Why are you looking for me?"

"My master told me to give you these instructions: touch the core."

Darek sputtered, "Touch the core? You're telling me I should just die?"

Ios shook her head. "No, I just want you to touch to core. I didn't tell you to die."

Darek scratched his head. "Let me get this straight. You want me to jump down several miles and touch the core."

Ios nodded.

Darek continued, "So in other words, I should die from either radiation poisoning, impact with the core, or getting completely burned up by the core. Now tell me, in what way will I even have the slightest chance of survival?"

"Stop fussing and get down there!" Ios opened her mouth and spewed balls of flames.

Darek was startled by the flames and stumbled off the floating rock, falling deep through the cloud of strange particles. Ios jumped in after him and clung to his back.

Ios said confidently, "I'll shield you from everything else. All you need to do is touch the core." As they descended, Ios exploded into a brilliant light that glittered and wrapped around Darek.

"So is this the last experience I'll ever have in my life, huh?" Darek spread out his arms like wings and embraced the warm air that caused him to float like a feather over the flames. "It's not a bad feeling. I might as well enjoy it!" Caught up in the moment, Darek screamed over the prevailing winds, "If anyone out there can hear me, this is goodbye!" His strong voice echoed through the floating islands.

As soon as they reached surface of the core, Darek quickly stuck out his hands and touched it, as instructed. His hands were still shielded by the gloves and when he touched the core, it didn't feel hot at all, only a little warm. Then, all of a sudden, Darek felt a rushing sensation flowing into the palm of his hands. The feeling stunned him at first, causing him to cry out in terror as he wondered what was happening. It was as if he was draining out the core, sucking it dry.

The color of the core faded away; the core became a dark gray matter, solid and crusty like charcoal. The scattered plots of land started to drop in altitude, falling towards the core with ever increasing acceleration. Darek could feel himself getting sucked in by a powerful vacuum.

"Ios! What's happening?" said Darek, sounding terribly frightened.

"I'm not quite sure myself," said Ios. "I just came to deliver instructions."

Soon, in the blink of an eye, the sum of the planet was sucked into a hole, a tear through the fabric of their dimension. All the land, people, trees and moving creatures were sucked in. Everything had vanished without a trace.

CHAPTER 31
Lacuna

A lone snowflake glided on the wind. It made its way into a warm meadow, where it rested gently atop Darek's nose and melted away. Several more snowflakes followed in the same fashion and soon the repetitious descent of cold droplets upon his face roused him.

Darek opened his eyes, blinking slowly. He stared straight up. At first he thought he was dreaming because whatever he was seeing made no sense. Far above him was another world. It was like he was looking down at the surface of another planet. However, he found it peculiar because, as he looked to his side, he realized he was lying in grass and dirt.

"Where am I? Is this heaven?" Darek pinched himself. "Ouch. I guess I must be dead." He sighed. Using his sleeve, Darek wiped off the moisture from his face. He yawned as he stretched. Standing up, he brushed off the dirt from his clothes.

Everything was strange. The small meadow that he stood in was both warm and lively. To his left he saw a snowstorm raging in the tundra a few hundred yards away. To his right he saw a massive rainforest, its canopies towering high above. He had been to different planets over the course of his lifetime, but all of them had relatively stable climates. But here in this place, it was as though all the different seasons were woven together in a quilt. Each of the environments had different sizes as well. The tundra stretched for miles and he could not see the end of the rainforest. But the meadow was so small that he could see the full extent of it by spinning around.

Another thing that boggled his mind was the warm light that filled the meadow. There was no sun. Where did the light come from? He guessed it was beyond the rainforest.

Seeing as the tundra was much too dangerous to traverse, Darek headed into the rainforest. Following along the path, he cut down the thick vegetation with his daggers.

The forest was much more vibrant than Darek expected. Thousands of ants marched up and down the tree trunks. Chirps, tweets, and screeches from all sorts of birds resounded through the higher branches. Occasionally, he would see a small rodent dash away as he made his approach.

When Darek was deep into the forest, he heard the sound of rushing water. Anxious for a drink to cool his parched throat and dampen his cracked lips, he ran in the general direction of the noise. After running through some thick foliage, he reached a steep slope. He tried to slow down but ended up skidding down the hill. He completely lost his balance and tumbled over. Desperate to save himself from falling, he reached out his hand and grabbed hold of a vine.

Dangling from the vine, Darek turned his attention below. The sound of the water was not a river as he had hoped, but rather, it was the sound of the ocean's waves battering the beach. The thought of drinking the salt-infested water made him cringe. He had never done it before, but he was sure it wasn't going to be pleasant. Since he did not find what he was looking for, he attempted to climb back up.

The vine thinned and snapped. Darek groped along the side of the cliff, but he couldn't find anything to hold onto. He quickly assumed a diving position, hitting the water with a big splash.

While treading the waters, he found shore not far from him. He swam toward the beach. As he reached the shoreline, the bottom of his shoe got caught in the rocks below. Darek shook his leg vigorously to break free. The harder he pulled, the more he was dragged back until he was completely submerged. Holding his breath, Darek looked down at his feet. It appeared that he had his foot snagged on a sharp rock. It took a moment for him to understand that it was a giant pincer clamped onto his shoe. He had been stepping on the back of a giant crab.

Luckily for him, the large pincer became greedy and, after releasing Darek's shoe, now aimed for his pants. Darek panicked as several more giant pincers moved toward him. With his dagger, he frantically cut off the edge of his pants and tore off as much as he could in a hurry, so he could free himself. Then he stuffed the dagger in his satchel and swam for shore. Within moments, he scrambled onto the beach. Breathing heavily, he lay on his back to rest. He lifted his head and stared at the ocean's surface. Three giant crabs stormed the beach. They would not settle until Darek was firm within their grasp. The pincers came clawing their way through the sand—until they were right on top of him. Darek let out a fearful yelp.

A female voice snapped, "Stop playing with our dinner!"

At that very second, the crabs shrank back, retreating into the waters.

Darek looked over his shoulder to see who was there.

"Darek? Is that you?" said the female voice. "What are you doing here?"

After recognizing her, Darek jumped to his feet. In a bout of excitement, he ran to her and embraced her. "Elize! I never thought I'd ever see you again! Is Slade here too?"

Slightly embarrassed, Elize replied, "Yes, he is with the others right now. I'm just here to watch over the food because—well, you never know when others will try to steal it." Elize paused. "But what are you doing here?"

"What am I doing here?" said Darek. "What are you doing here? Are you dead too?"

"What? What kind of silly question is that?" barked Elize. "Of course I'm not dead! I haven't seen you for so long and this how you greet me?"

"Good! You're alive!" Looking bewildered, Darek asked, "Then where exactly are we?"

"You don't know? This is Lacuna."

"Lacuna? Is that a name of a planet? Never heard of it."

Elize shook her head. "No, it's not a planet. Lacuna is the gap between the two dimensions that exist in our universe. This is a limitless flat plane that stretches as far as the universe spans. Most of the land you see here isn't native to Lacuna. It usually comes from being sucked into a black hole."

"Ah," said Darek. "So that explains it. The planet I was on was collapsing. Next thing I know, I'm here. I guess I got sucked into a black hole."

"Really?" Elize sounded surprised. "Is that possible?"

"What do you mean? I thought you just said that things get sucked in here."

"Yes," said Elize. "Having stuff get sucked into this void is normal. But I never really expected a living being to survive a black hole. The only way I know for a human to enter Lacuna without dying is through a portal, which isn't a normal occurrence."

"Then how come everything here is intact?" said Darek. "Wouldn't everything get messed up in a black hole?"

Elize shrugged. "That's something I don't know. To be honest, I don't know much of this place. We only use it as our hideout. I assume most of the stuff here already existed."

Darek sat back down. He was so caught up in the excitement of seeing Elize again that he forgot how exhausted he was from propelling himself through the waves. He took deep breaths, enjoying the smells of the beach. "You got any water? I'm really thirsty."

Elize handed him the flask that was around her neck. "It's good to see you, Darek."

"Yeah," Darek chortled. "It's good to finally be here. This is the place, right? The place I've always wanted to go."

"Yes," said Elize. "Are you ready?"

"You mean—am I ready to join the Judges?"

Elize nodded.

Darek's eyes sparkled. "Can I really join or are you just kidding around?"

"Would I kid about something like this?" Elize laughed and helped him stand. "There's room for one more. It's time. If you pass the test, you'll be in. I'm sure Slade will be pleased. We'll run it by everyone else and I think they'll be fine with it too."

"Speaking of which, where is everyone?"

"They're out working on some cases. They'll be back by nightfall."

"Nightfall?" Darek looked up to the sky and still didn't see the source of the daylight. "How can there be day and night?"

"Again, something I don't know," said Elize, shrugging. "But enough of that, how about you help me catch some dinner for tonight?"

"What do you want me to do?"

"Go back into the water and lure a crab out," said Elize. "Simple enough?"

Darek laughed. "Making me play as bait? You remind me of someone else I know."

"Do I? Well, you can tell me all about that later."

A flickering campfire lit up a small clearing in a dim forest. A boiling pot simmered gently over the flames. Windzer rested upon a broken log, stirring up the pot and taking a few sips with the ladle for good measure. Though the forest was almost void of light, it was filled with the sounds of the living. Among other things, crickets chirped and owls hooted, forming an orchestral piece of the night. Windzer took a moment to stop and listen to the music of the forest.

Rubbing the back of her head, Azura groaned. She woke up with a rough headache and the pain throbbed all the way down to her neck. Her body was no longer in critical condition, thanks to her regenerative abilities, but she was left drained and dehydrated.

"You don't look so good." Windzer passed her some water in a pouch.

"You're not one of good looks either." Azura ripped the pouch from his hand and chugged down a few gulps. "How long have I been asleep?"

"We've been waiting for you to wake up for two days now," replied Windzer.

Azura watched the campfire. As her senses began to awaken, she was startled by the other presence with them. "What is he doing here?"

"He? What are you talking about?"

"The dirty, no-good, lying, conniving traitor." Azura tried to stand up but was pretty shaky. Having not used her legs for two days, they quivered as she leaned against a tree. With a disdainful look, she pointed at Sorren. "What is this *villain* doing here?"

Windzer laughed. "You already made your point before you pointed the finger."

"It's not funny," Azura barked. "This psycho almost killed me!"

Windzer handed her a bowl of soup. "He didn't kill you and he's not trying to kill you now. Why don't we drop the angry tone and sit down comfortably for a nice hot meal?"

Azura slapped the bowl out of his hands and it fell into the fire. "If he's staying, I might as well be going." When Azura pushed off the tree, she stumbled again. Windzer kept her from falling. She bowed her head as a gesture of thanks and started to walk toward the forest.

Windzer called out to her, "Are you sure? You're in no condition to go anywhere. You don't even know where we are. I'm telling you right now, this place is *very* dangerous."

"I refuse to stay within five feet of him." Then Azura left them.

"Are you just going to let her leave like this?" Windzer asked Sorren.

"Didn't you hear her? She specifically doesn't want me around," replied Sorren.

"Wrong answer," grunted Windzer, unsatisfied by his response. "You're plotting something...I know you are. That whole scene with Darek, you could have killed her but you didn't. And now I bet you're worried about her condition, aren't you?" Windzer took a quick sip of his hot broth. "Now, I don't care if she hates you, you have to go after her. But don't let her see you. Follow her from a distance and keep her out of trouble."

"Since when do I take orders from you?" Sorren stood up.

Windzer smirked. "You say that, but you're still going."

"I might as well," said Sorren, sighing. "But I'm not doing it because you told me to. Our temporary alliance is now over." Sorren started to follow after her.

Windzer waved goodbye. "Until next time then."

As he was leaving, Sorren said over his shoulder, "Before I go, I do have a question." He paused. "What are you up to?"

Windzer put down his bowl. "You think I'm up to something?"

Sorren nodded.

Windzer laughed. "I'll tell you what I'm up to if you tell me what you're up to. If you tell me why you wanted Darek dead, I'll tell you why I went to that desolate world."

Sorren shrugged. "Forget I said anything."

Azura limped through the dense underbrush. She had never felt this tired in her before. Yet her overly exhausted state was not entirely a product of her regeneration. She was emotionally torn, her body felt sapped of any remaining strength. She was depressed, distraught by the betrayal of trust. With every step she took, she wobbled and clung onto a nearby tree. Every fiber in her body ached, causing her to let out sharp howls every now and then. After taking ten excruciating steps, she paused from her short trek to take a much-needed rest.

A large stick fell from the heights of the forest trees. It plopped right in front of her. She studied it and found it to be the perfect walking stick: it was stripped clean of any splinters and protruding branches, and it was the right size for her height. Azura ignored the stick and went on her way, trudging through the branches and foliage.

After another short painstaking journey, she came across a small river. Tiny fish joyfully leaped up from the crisp waters. Though the river was small, the rushing flow could still sweep her away. While she pondered on her next course of action, she heard a loud crack. A tree on the other side broke down and landed right in front of her, conveniently giving her a bridge to safely cross over. Azura stared at the makeshift bridge. Then she crept into the cool waters, opting to wade through the stream instead.

Drenched, cold and shivering, Azura climbed to shore. She uncontrollably gasped for air and lay on the ground motionlessly; her body was now far exceeding the normal limits. Yet, in spite of all the pain, she didn't want to stop for a moment.

Azura became increasingly worn out and cold as the night went on. The temperature began dropping; every breath that was huffed out of her mouth left a wispy trail. After three hours had passed, she had not seen a single settlement or hint of civilization; Azura became concerned. What if there was no one else around for miles? She had always imagined her last hour to be a glorious act of fighting villainy—not a restless bout with hypothermia.

No matter how hard Azura struggled to keep walking, her movement finally slowed to a halt. Her body succumbed to the exhaustion. She sat on the ground, unsure if she could go on. Walking gave her hope—the hope that, as she kept on walking, she may eventually find someone who could help her. But now that she couldn't walk, no one would ever find her. For all she knew, they could be on a deserted world. And if that were the case, why bother going forward?

The night seemed to never end and the air only got colder. Her body quaked and the skin on her face started to go numb. She looked up and gawked in awe of the night sky. There was no moon with its guiding light, nor were there stars to lead the way. The sky was just nearly pitch black like she had been sealed up in a dark box. A vague glimmer of light did catch her eye, but it was distant and she knew not what it was or where it came from.

Then she heard sounds of laughter a short distance away. She saw the glow of fire breaking through the wall of trees before her. She scrambled across the forest floor on hands and knees. Azura desperately crawled as fast as her arms could pull her.

The sounds of laughter came from several dancing shadows and silhouettes around a large bonfire. However, once she reached the fire, she did not see a single soul. The shadows were from small trees swaying in the wind in the presence of the blazing fire. She had been tricked. But this was not a trick of nature, but of a man. Drained from her last spurt of energy, Azura passed out beside the warmth of the flame.

When she awoke a few hours later into the morning, she felt the heat of the flames tingling her face. She had not noticed it at night, but in the morning light, Azura could see that she was now within a clearing in the forest. With the bright rays shining down on her and the fire radiating before her, her clothes were much dryer. She was more comfortable than before. The spot she was in was tidied up; there was even a soft bed of leaves covered by a thick blanket for her to rest upon. Roasting over the open fire was a succulent piece of meat. A large bowl of water was prepared for her to drink. She looked at everything and sighed, wondering how to respond to this. She knew Sorren was still around, but his presence was too far away for her to sense.

Azura screamed aimlessly at the top of her lungs, "DON'T EVEN THINK FOR A SECOND THAT THIS EVENS ANYTHING OUT! YOU HEAR ME? YOU ROTTEN…"

She broke off, bursting into tears. Still bitter, Azura took the piece of meat and devoured it. After she was full, she had the urge to get up and continue the journey, but a fever was coming on and made it difficult for her to see straight; whenever she stood, she would get a dizzy spell and would fall to the grass. Azura gave in and remained quietly in that place to rest.

The next morning, Azura became sick. She coughed, sniffled and wheezed the entire day. She slept as much as possible, and whenever she awoke, she would find plenty of broth, food and water prepared, all ready for consumption. Each day was like this; she could not do much but rest and recuperate. During that time, the skies were overcast. The clouds relented from pouring down its harvest of rain, but remained persistent in darkening the land with its gloomy presence. It only helped to solidify Azura's depression.

It did not last, however. After a week, the illness had passed and Azura felt better. She was still a little sick, but there was drastic improvement in her condition. On that day, even the clouds began to break away, leaving the sky only partly cloudy. Such a wonderful change in both health and weather warranted a stroll.

Slowly, she got up from her bed and stretched out; she took a deep breath and her mood was lifted. Her legs were shaky; having not moved much in a while, she felt like her body was getting too weak. A little exercise was tempting, but she was worried she might strain something. It was then that Azura took notice of the perfect walking stick, which was right there beside her. It wasn't there yesterday, and it was almost as if Sorren knew she would be strong enough to start walking again. Seeing that she had already eaten his food and slept in the bed he provided, she figured she might as well use the stick.

With both hands firmly on the stick, she leaned on it; as expected, it was strong enough to support her weight. Azura took a few steps and was happy with how the stick made it much easier to walk. But she did not crack even the slightest smile. She was not about to give him any sort of satisfaction for his deed.

"I'm not going to thank you for anything," mumbled Azura.

Using the stick as a crutch, Azura staggered around the forest, staying close to the clearing. She was from a tribe that respected nature, and by staying so close to it, she was able to regain a peace of mind, as if nature carried a piece of home to her heart. A cute little bird perched itself on a tree branch overhead. It chirped out a beautiful song. Azura beamed at it. Swelling up with warm feelings, Azura limped over to where the bird was and reached up to pet its back.

A loud growl from the forest startled the bird. It took off in a fright. Azura shuddered as the low growling pierced through the thicket. She stumbled back and fell off her crutch. A large beast hopped out of the trees, roaring at her. It stood nearly ten feet tall and had the form of a large silver gorilla, except with tusks protruding from its lips and devilish quills lining its back.

Azura had no idea what to do, for she could barely stand. She was paralyzed in fear and winced at the beast's terrifying glare. It then howled in agony and fell prostrate before her.

"Sorry. There were a few of them. One managed to slip by me." Sorren stepped out from the shadows and asked, "Are you okay?"

"No," snapped Azura, scowling. "What are you doing here? Why not leave me to die?"

Sorren sighed and started to leave, afraid to get into a quarrel.

"Wait! Are you just going to walk away?" said Azura, reproachful.

"Well, what do you want me to do?"

Azura jumped to her feet and wrestled him to the ground. Leaning over his face, she slapped him and shouted, "What's wrong with you? Don't you have feelings or remorse? You think you can just run away from me? I'm so confused right now that I don't know what to think anymore! One moment you try to kill me and next you're tending to my needs! How am I supposed to continue to hate you if you don't give me a reason to? Stop helping me so I can go back to HATING YOUR ROTTEN GUTS!"

Sorren grimaced. Her loud voice almost deafened his hearing. "I can see you're angry."

"Is that all you have to say?" she asked, calming down.

Sorren didn't respond, but he looked away, unwilling to face her. Azura exhaled. The week of rest had dulled her temper and, gazing upon his current state, she felt awkward being angry when he was this calm. She released him and fell back onto the grass, still feeling a bit sore. She said, "Why'd you want to kill Darek? Is there a reason to your stupid insanity?"

Sorren sat up and said, "I'll tell you—but first, let's get you back to the camp."

Azura's face was flushed as Sorren picked her up by the shoulder and brought her back to the small campsite.

As soon as Azura was in a comfortable position, Sorren said, "This is kind of hard to explain. The simple reason is because there is a prophecy concerning Darek. It is said that he will be the beginning of the end. He will bring terror and destruction to our universe, unrivaled in the past, present and future." He paused. "I have a duty to fulfill. I must prevent the disaster."

"I've never heard of such a prophecy," said Azura. "What if it's not real?"

"The one who told it was a dear friend—I trusted him with my life," said Sorren. "More importantly, Darek's existence proves that it is true in a way."

"It says his name?"

Sorren shook his head. "It doesn't say his name, but it tells of his power. His power is…special. Let me explain. The Judges all have the power of the spirit. Through their channeled spiritual energy, they can manifest things in the real world. They are not doing anything to the real world other than creating something real for themselves. For Darek, what he manifests is a set of gloves. However, his gloves actually have the power to literally change the world—transmutation—if you will. Do you understand? For such a thing to exist is dangerous."

"But if Darek uses it for good, what harm can there be?" said Azura.

"We never fully know the consequences of our actions. Even if he intends good, the result may be otherwise. With a power of such catastrophic size, a mistake cannot be afforded."

Azura said, "Sure, he makes mistakes, but we all do. But he won't do anything that he knows would cause harm to others. I don't think he's the one you are referring to."

"Believing or not, does not change the fact that he—"

Azura interrupted him. "You still don't know whether those are facts! Isn't it wrong to make assumptions? What if it isn't him all along? Then you pay dearly for your mistake! You may have wasted your time and effort in all the wrong places!"

Sorren considered her ideas and said humbly, "You could be right. I'll admit that I am not one hundred percent sure. But at that time, I was afraid to let that chance escape."

"Promise me this," said Azura. "You will not kill Darek unless you are certain—without the *slightest* doubt in your mind—that he is the one. And if you uphold this promise, then I promise you that I will help you become a Hero. That is what you wanted, isn't it?"

"So you're saying that if I kill Darek, you won't let me be a Hero?"

Azura smiled. "Exactly."

Sorren glanced at a single blade of grass, looking deep in thought. After a drawn out silence, he said, "Being a Hero is *very* important to me. I will uphold this promise."

Azura said, "Although I can't trust you fully, I hope you can keep your word this time."

Sorren straightened up. "I will do my best to regain your trust."

The next morning was beautiful and cheery. The sky opened up, revealing the other world above them. There was not a single cloud in the space between the two worlds. The clearing was filled with radiant light and it made the woods look so gorgeous with its glistening drops of rain and dew that Azura almost thought she was still dreaming when she awoke.

Sorren was waiting for her by the side of the fire. "Are you good to go now?"

"Yup." Azura nodded contently. "I feel great today!"

"Then I'll be going," said Sorren, pulling out the Currie from his robe. "I believe this is yours." The Currie, upon seeing Azura, jumped ecstatically into her arms.

"Currie!" Azura lifted it up, rubbing its fur against her cheeks. "Where'd you find it?"

"It was hiding in one of the underground shelters," said Sorren. "I grabbed it before the world collapsed."

"Does this mean you're not coming with me?" asked Azura, surprised. "I thought you said you wanted to be a Hero."

"I didn't mean now," said Sorren. "I have some *things* I must take care of first. And I need some time to think things over, especially things concerning Darek."

Azura folded her arms. "Then at least tell me where I am and where I should go."

"Oh right, I almost forgot," said Sorren. "This may be hard for you to believe, but believe it anyway. We are now in another dimension from our own, but it's more of a gap between dimensions. You'll see that it won't truly follow the laws of our dimension. The weather may change erratically and even gravity and atmosphere may change from place to place. There are several ways out of here, but I'll tell you the easiest way." Sorren motioned for her to follow.

Sorren leapt high into the tree branches. Azura followed after him. By jumping swiftly from branch to branch, they were able to quickly ascend the trees. When they were at the highest point in the forest and could see beyond the vast number of trees, Sorren showed her a distant mountain.

"Behind that mountain is the home of the Judges, the Court of Verras. Since you're a Hero, they'll help you out," said Sorren. "Darek might even be there now. Send him my regards—and my apologies." Sorren turned to her and said, "Any more questions?"

"No, that'll be all," replied Azura softly. "I guess this is goodbye then."

"For now," said Sorren. "We'll meet again. I'm not giving up on being a Hero."

"Thanks for everything," said Azura.

With no more words, the two of them went their separate ways. Azura headed for the mountain that Sorren told her about. Sorren, however, disappeared into the forest.

"Darek is the one without a doubt," he said to himself. "The end draws near. Darek, by not showing hatred against me, you have passed my test. You are worthy of being the key to destruction. Be on your guard, Darek. Everyone will hate you. Everyone will want to kill you. I will do my best to protect you until you fulfill your destiny. I swear on my life, Darek—I will die before you."

CHAPTER 32
Peace at Last

Under the night sky, the loud clangs of silver cups and plates could be heard. A group of nine sat merrily around a fire. Small torches were planted around them in a circular fashion to ward away pesky bugs. The beach would've been peaceful, had it not been for the jolly festivities of the Judges.

"To Darek!" Everyone shouted in acclamation.

They feasted on huge chunks of crabmeat and chugged down sweet, cool beverages. Every morsel and sip did not have to be savored; it just had to fill them up sweetly. Darek eyed the meat before digging in. After his tongue tasted its rich flavor, he chomped away. It was so good that he would smack and lick his lips after every single bite.

Darek had never eaten so much crab in his life; it was almost sickening. Even the giant pincer was enough to be considered three meals for the average person, yet for this small group of Judges, one crab was barely enough for the night.

"Enjoy this," said Slade, beaming. "We don't eat it much. But today, we have a reason to celebrate!"

"Thanks," said Darek, feeling pleased to be so welcomed and accepted. "I didn't think you guys would take me in so easily."

"What are you saying?" said Elize. "We've been waiting for this day for such a long time. We knew you'd return. It was just a matter of when."

"Yeah," said Slade. "No offense, but even though you're a good friend, we wouldn't have saved you from the Federation otherwise. We only stick our neck out for one of our own."

"I didn't need to know that," said Darek. The memory of almost being executed was firmly burned in his mind.

"Hey," said Slade, "it all worked out in the end."

Darek looked around, as though he were looking to find something or someone.

"I'm curious. I thought there were twelve Judges. Where are the others?"

Slade explained, "The three others always hide within our headquarters. They don't fight like we do; they only make decisions and monitor the situation in the real universe. They are called the Conclave. I'll explain later. We'll begin training you tomorrow."

"Great," said Darek with a broad smile.

"We even have a job lined up for you when you're done. We'll need your help to hunt down the traitor that left our ranks. He's been making it hard on us, but once we have our full team, we'll be able to work more efficiently."

Darek said nothing, staring at his own reflection in his cup of water.

Slade said, "Is something wrong?"

Darek licked his lips clean of any bits of crab. Emotionless, he said, "No, no. Everything is perfect. I just find it hard to believe that I'm actually sitting here right now with you guys. It's almost like a dream." He glanced over at Slade and Elize to find them looking concerned. He chuckled. "I don't know how to really explain what I'm feeling right now. It's like a void has been filled. All this time I've been searching for my home, and now that I've found it, it's unbelievable." He held up his cup and shouted, "To make the universe a better place!"

"YEAH!" Everyone around the fire agreed and they drank in unison.

After the feast had ended, everyone dozed off in the sand. Though they were the hope of the universe and though they fought day in and day out, back in their home, they were laid back and took the time to rest, without a care in the world.

It was during this night that Darek was lying in the cool sand, gazing above. The world above was shrouded in darkness, impossible to be seen. There were a few specks of light that abruptly sprang up in the sky. Seeing that stars would be impossible in Lacuna, he guessed that, somewhere in the other world above, people were lighting up fires or switching on the lights in their homes.

He lay there in silence, still finding it hard to come to grips with what had happened. Up until a few days ago, he would have never considered the existence of another place separate from their universe. Yet there he was, now inside the Lacuna, a place that seemed so mysterious and mystical. Darek was still feeling a bit incredulous about the whole concept. How does this patchwork of varying lands exist? If there is no sun, then how can there be different seasons and how can there be night and day? The existence of this place was utterly impossible and ludicrous. Yet it did exist and he was able to see, feel, and hear everything about it.

But that wasn't the only thing on his mind. It seemed ironic. Just a few weeks ago, he was sitting on the roof, looking at the sky, and thinking about what Slade and Elize were doing. However, it was different now. Slade and Elize were right beside him. But he couldn't help but wonder if Azura and Sorren were okay. For some reason, whenever he gains friends, he loses some and that thought made him feel a bit melancholic. Why couldn't everyone be together?

He was also afraid to meet Sorren again. If what Windzer said was true, then Sorren would never get along with the Judges. If they were to meet again by chance, it would be as enemies. Darek decided that should the day ever come, he would show no mercy to Sorren, just as Sorren did not show mercy to him.

But is that the right way to think? Surely, you could give him a second chance.

"I don't know," said Darek. "I would like to think otherwise, but it's just hard, you know? He just doesn't seem like the type to listen to reason." Darek turned around, thinking someone was talking to him. He saw no one. "Hello? Uh—Is someone there?"

No one in particular, said the strange voice.

"All right," said Darek nervously. "You're freaking me out. Show yourself!"

I would, but that's something you must help me with.

"What?"

Touch the campfire. Go on.

"Not this again." Darek said mockingly, "Go on and touch the exploding core. Go on and drink the water of death. Go on and wander into enemy territory alone. Go on and put your hand in a roaring flame! Can't I ever get a break with this nonsense?"

Darek reluctantly walked over to the fire. He figured he might as well get this over with. Too afraid to look, he shut his eyes as put his hand inside the flame. Gloves mysteriously reappeared on his hand and all the flames flared higher as if it was sprayed with oil.

A man suddenly emerged from the flames and stood before Darek. "Hello." The man was literally clothed with the fire, though it did not look like he was actually being burnt. His facial features were smooth, his brows were long and fuzzy, and his plump nose was short and crooked.

Darek had never seen this man before, yet his face was familiar. "Do I know you?"

The man said, "We've spoken momentarily before. But I did not have time to properly introduce myself. My name is Chrovel. You've met my servant, Ios."

"What? Then you're—"

"Yes," Chrovel replied. "I am the core—or rather, I was the core, until you freed me."

"Ah," said Darek, "so it's you. No wonder you looked familiar. Why are you here?"

Chrovel said, smirking, "It's not like I have much of a choice. You absorbed me, after all. I am now a part of you."

"You're—a part of me?" Darek looked thoroughly perplexed. "What? What are you anyway? Are you really a core of a planet?"

"What am I? You've met my kind, I'm sure. I am a Guardian, one spirit of many."

"What was a Guardian doing inside the core of a planet?" asked Darek.

"It's a long story," said Chrovel, not seeming pleased to have to recount it, "but I'll try to keep it short for you. In the beginning of time there was a great war. Some of the Guardians believed that humans needed to be erased for the problems they caused, and these wayward Guardians became known as the Coranites. The Coranites were defeated by an alliance between man and Guardian. All of the Guardians and Coranites that were 'killed' during the war were thrown into the Great Core, the place of no return, or so we thought. After being tossed in, I thought I would never be seen again, but for some unknown reason, I had become imprisoned inside a planet, locked away for two thousand years."

"Do all cores of planets have spirits within them?"

"No," replied Chrovel. "I'd estimate that there are only about several hundred thousand planets with Guardians and Coranites locked within their cores."

Darek fell back into the sand and stared at the dark sky above with its starry lights. "Wow, that's still quite a lot. They must be pretty bored, having to stay in one place for so long."

Chrovel laughed at Darek's comment. "Yeah, I was bored out of my mind!"

"I wonder if they're waiting for me to free them," said Darek. "I was imprisoned for a short time and hated it. I can't imagine being imprisoned for hundreds or thousands of years."

"A word of advice," said Chrovel gravely. "Never consider freeing another core."

"What? But I freed you, didn't I?"

"And I'm grateful for that. But I only accepted that because your life was in danger. Had you been able to escape on your own, I would have never told you to absorb me. We were imprisoned for a reason. We should not be freed so recklessly."

"But why?"

Chrovel replied, "Many defeated Coranites also reside within cores. They may have once been Guardians, but now they are full of hatred and jealousy. They are dangerous and should never be allowed to set foot in the universe."

"Not that," said Darek. "I meant to ask, why does my life matter so much? You want to save me while others, like Dionus, want to kill me. What's this all about?"

Chrovel explained, "There are differing prophecies about you. Some say you will save the universe while others say you will destroy it. Though it borders on both ends of the extremes, your existence is necessary because the universe, as it is, is in trouble. I, and others like me, will not allow you to die until your purpose is complete. Maybe the fate of the universe is in your hands, but it may also be your decision about which way it goes. At least for me, I think you will make the right choices."

Darek smiled. "I don't even know you, but I'm already starting to like you." Darek paused for a moment. "So you won't go back to the Guardians? You're going to stay with me?"

"Even if I wanted to leave, it's not that easy, so I'll stay with you for now. But I will try to be helpful. You can borrow my spirit energy, though the amount you borrow will be dependant on how well you can control it. You've already borrowed it once. I am a Guardian of fire so my abilities will grant you the power of flame." Chrovel turned around and stepped back into the fire. "I'll be around, waiting inside your mind. Call me if you need me."

"Wait!"

Chrovel stopped. "What is it?"

Darek said, "Is Ios all right? Is she okay?"

"She is fine. She is a part of me, just as I am a part of you."

Darek scratched his head with a clueless look upon his face. "What does that mean?" But before he could say anything else, he blacked out. He was completely unaware of it, but bringing out Chrovel's form wasted away his strength. It felt like he had fainted for only a second. But when he awakened it was bright as day and everyone else was already up and about; most of the Judges had already left, leaving only Slade and Elize sitting on the sand, looking into the ocean.

Elize saw that Darek was awake. "Oh, you're finally up. I was starting to get worried."

Darek let out a long yawn. "Where'd everyone go?"

Elize folded her arms. "You've been asleep for more than a day! No one's going to wait around for you. If you're going to be lazy, do it in a safer place."

Darek blinked in amazement. "A day? I guess I shouldn't be doing it that often."

"Doing what?"

"Oh...I um..." Darek's voice trailed off as he decided on the spot to keep Chrovel's existence within him a secret. Elize would probably think it was creepy; there was no point in scaring her. "It's nothing. I was just saying that the party was pretty tiring."

"Speak for yourself. Only you were out like a brick."

"Enough about that," said Slade, standing behind Elize. "We'll be starting in a bit. Freshen up and get changed." He handed Darek his new attire.

"Why? What are we doing?" said Darek.

"The training," answered Slade.

"Oh yeah, the training...how long does it take?"

Slade shrugged. "Depends on the trainee. Anywhere from three months to a year."

"That long?" said Darek, surprised.

Slade nodded. "That's why you should hurry up!"

Darek walked to the ocean and splashed the cool water on his face. He looked far past the ocean and saw many strange and wondrous lands before him. Darek wanted to explore as far as he could see because he had been feeling more adventurous ever since his long journey began. But that would have to wait. He had finally made it to where he was longing for: a real home.

As he looked across the vast dimension, he knew that Sorren, Azura, Merdon, Rathos and Thedes were all out there, somewhere. He didn't know how he knew, but that didn't matter. What mattered was that everyone else was safe and alive, possibly starting new lives like he would.

There were many things he still wondered about, but for now, he cast aside all worry and embraced the peace—at last.